CARTOON NETWORK

REGULAR SHOW™

COMIC CONNED

ROSS RICHIE CEO & Founder • JOY HUFFMAN CFO • MATT GAGNON Editor-in-Chief • FILIP SABLIK President, Publishing & Marketing • STEPHEN CHRISTY President, Development • LANCE KREITER Vice President, Licensing & Merchandising • PHIL BARBARO Vice President, Finance & Human Resources • ARUNE SINGH Vice President, Marketing • BRYCE CARLSON Vice President, Editorial & Creative Strategy • SCOTT NEWMAN Manager, Production Design • KATE HENNING Manager, Operations • SPENCER SIMPSON Manager, Sales • SIERRA HAHN Executive Editor • JEANINE SCHAEFER Executive Editor • DAFNA PLEBAN Senior Editor • SHANNON WATTERS Senior Editor • ERIC HARBURN Senior Editor • WHITNEY LEOPARD Editor • CAMERON CHITTOCK Editor • CHRIS ROSA Editor • MATTHEW LEVINE Editor • SOPHIE PHILIPS-ROBERTS Assistant Editor • GAVIN GRONENTHAL Assistant Editor • MICHAEL MOCCIO Assistant Editor • AMANDA LaFRANCO Executive Assistant • JILLIAN CRAB Design Coordinator • MICHELLE ANKLEY Design Coordinator • KARA LEOPARD Production Designer • MARIE KRUPINA Production Designer • GRACE PARK Production Design Assistant • CHELSEA ROBERTS Production Design Assistant • ELIZABETH LOUGHRIDGE Accounting Coordinator • STEPHANIE HOCUTT Social Media Coordinator • JOSÉ MEZA Event Coordinator • HOLLY AITCHISON Operations Coordinator • MEGAN CHRISTOPHER Operations Assistant • RODRIGO HERNANDEZ Mailroom Assistant • MORGAN PERRY Direct Market Representative • CAT O'GRADY Marketing Assistant • BREANNA SARPY Executive Assistant

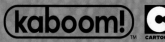

CARTOON NETWORK
REGULAR SHOW

COMIC CONNED

CREATED BY JG QUINTEL

WRITTEN BY
NICOLE ANDELFINGER

ILLUSTRATED BY
MATTIA DI MEO

COLORS BY
CRISTINA ROSE CHUA

LETTERS BY
MIKE FIORENTINO

COVER BY
MATTIA DI MEO

DESIGNER
KARA LEOPARD

ASSISTANT EDITOR
MICHAEL MOCCIO

EDITOR
WHITNEY LEOPARD

WITH SPECIAL THANKS TO MARISA MARIONAKIS, JANET NO, CURTIS LELASH, CONRAD MONTGOMERY, KELLY CREWS, RYAN SLATER AND THE WONDERFUL FOLKS AT CARTOON NETWORK.

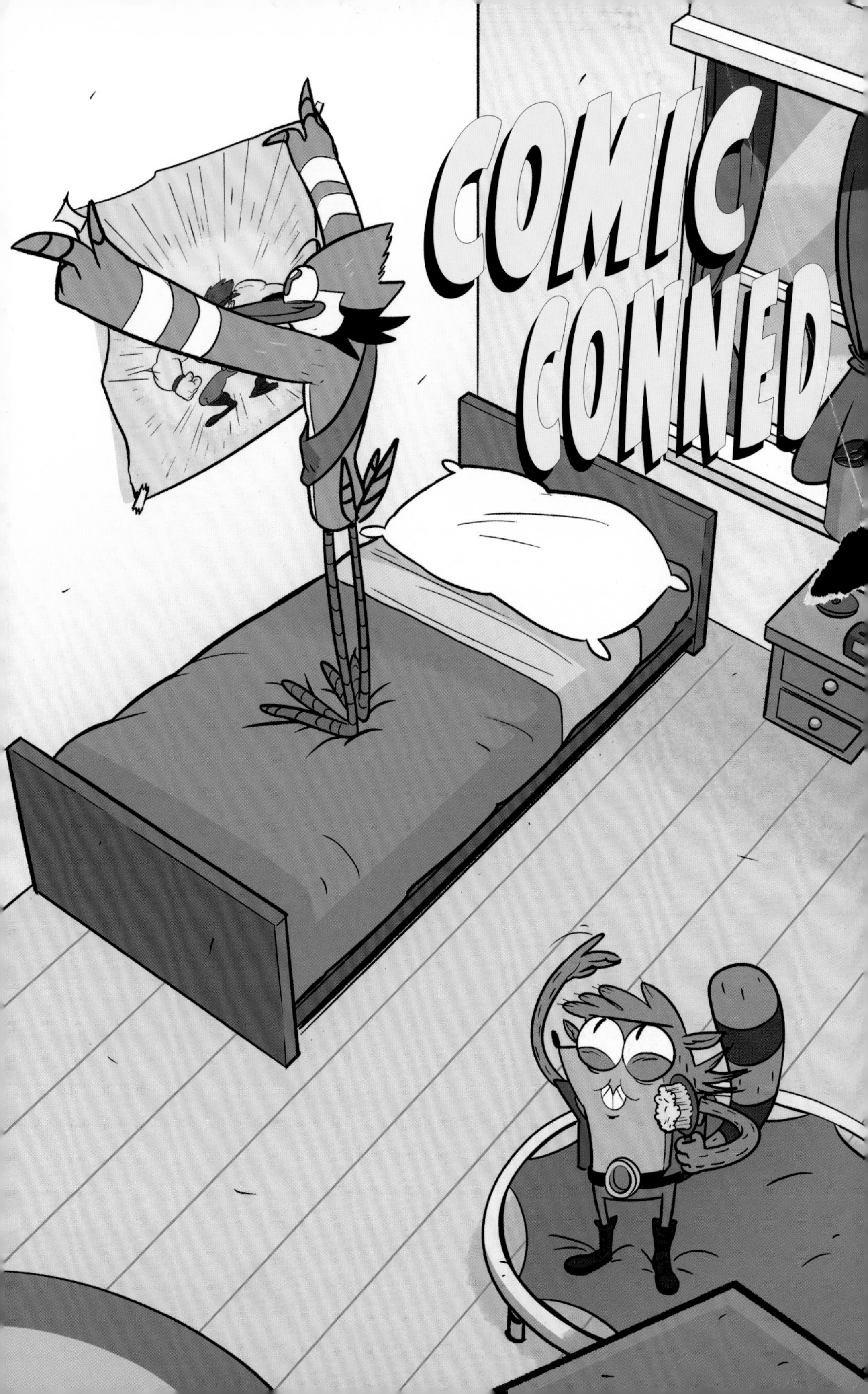
COMIC CONNED

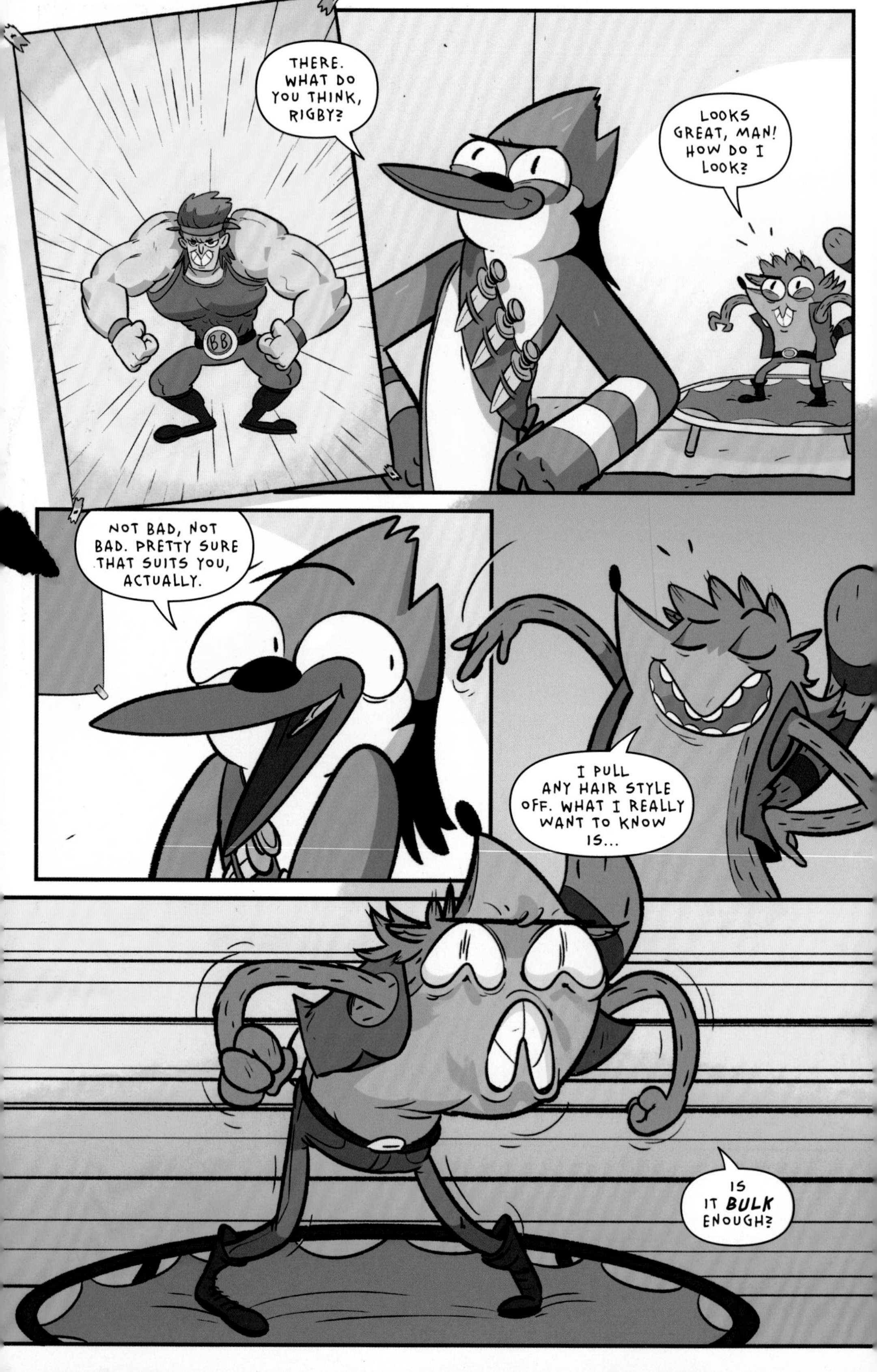
THERE. WHAT DO YOU THINK, RIGBY?
LOOKS GREAT, MAN! HOW DO I LOOK?
BB
NOT BAD, NOT BAD. PRETTY SURE THAT SUITS YOU, ACTUALLY.
I PULL ANY HAIR STYLE OFF. WHAT I REALLY WANT TO KNOW IS...
IS IT **BULK** ENOUGH?

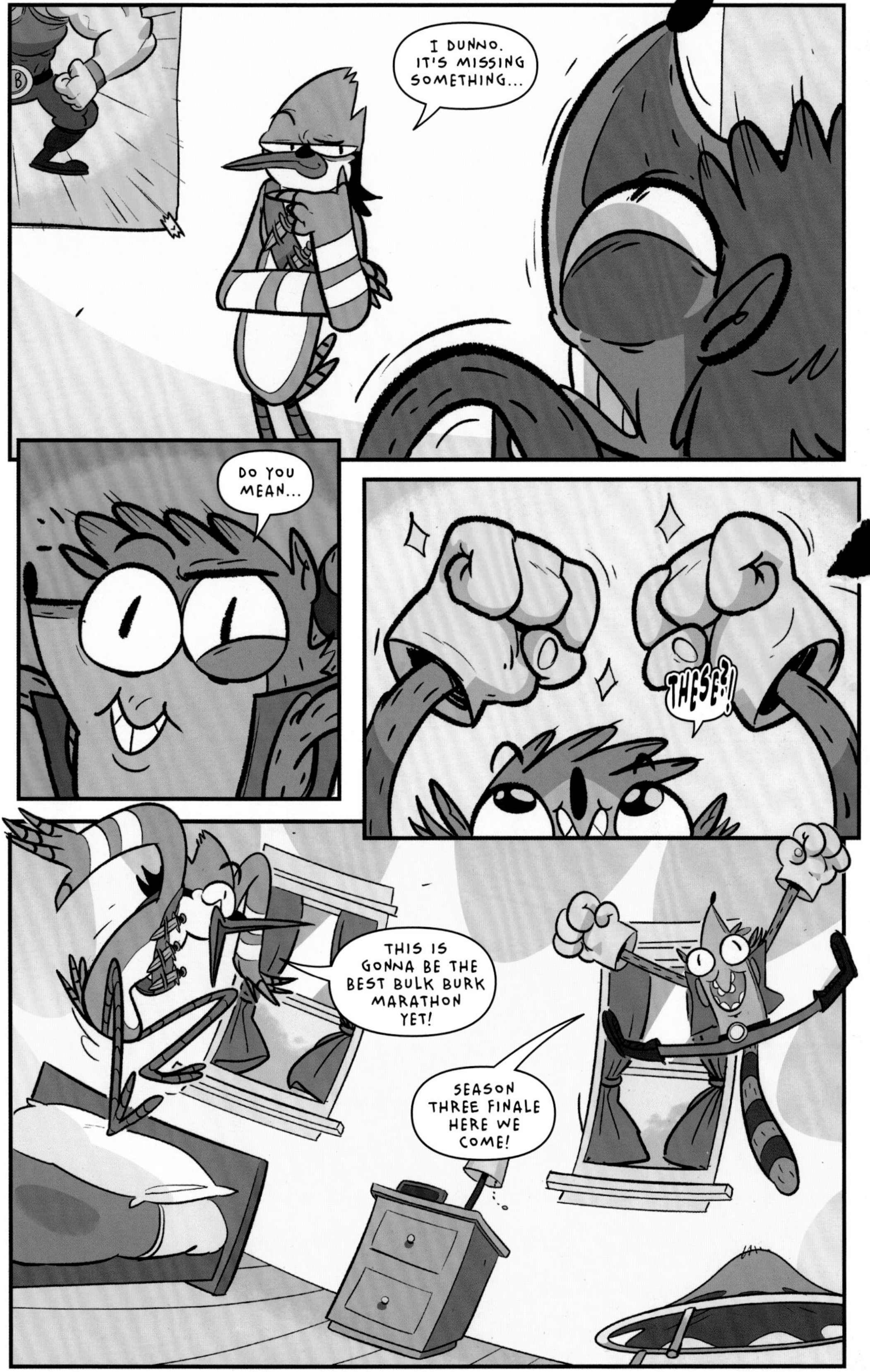
I DUNNO. IT'S MISSING SOMETHING...
DO YOU MEAN...
THESE?!
THIS IS GONNA BE THE BEST BULK BURK MARATHON YET!
SEASON THREE FINALE HERE WE COME!

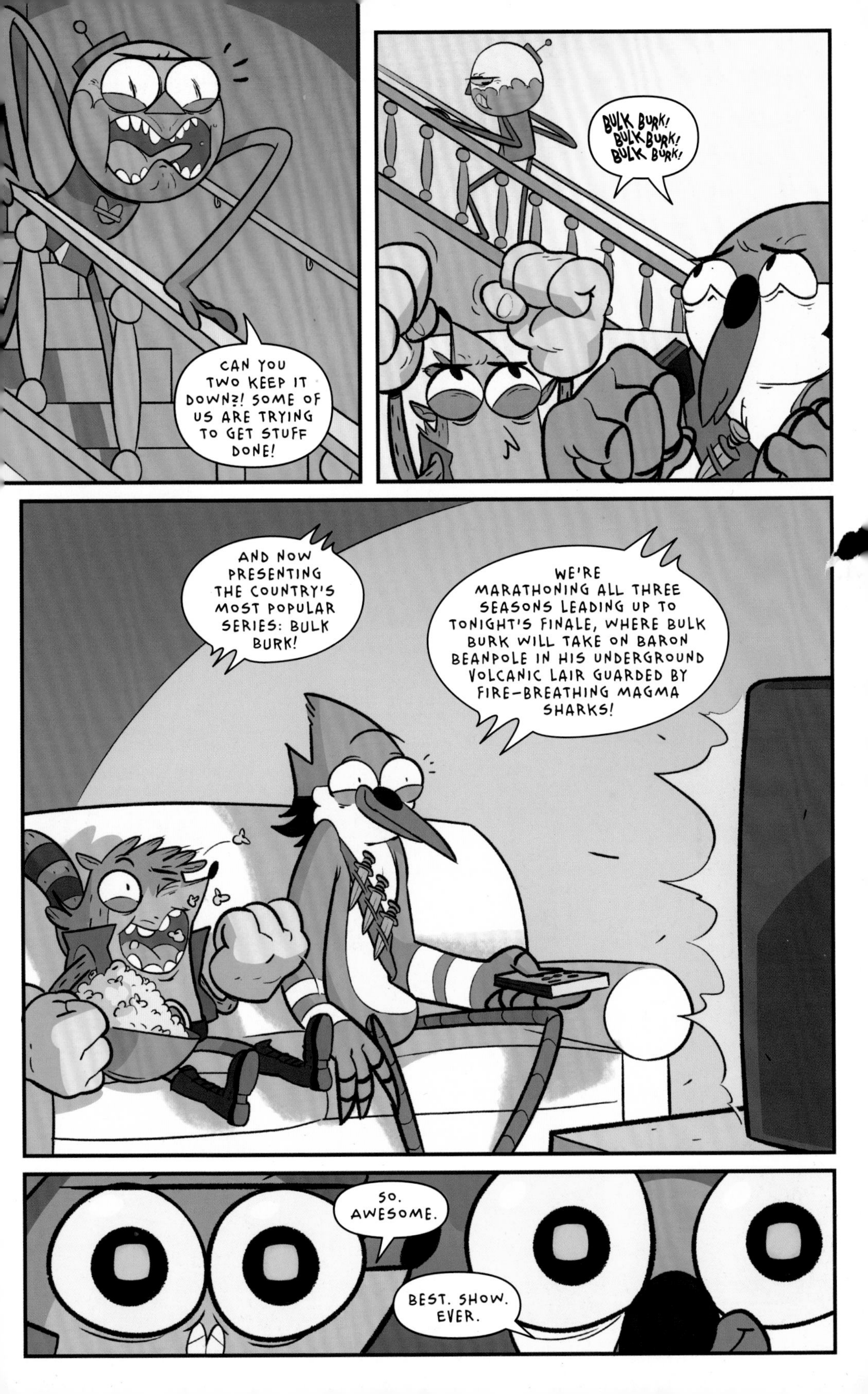
CAN YOU TWO KEEP IT DOWN?! SOME OF US ARE TRYING TO GET STUFF DONE!
BULK BURK! BULK BURK! BULK BURK!
AND NOW PRESENTING THE COUNTRY'S MOST POPULAR SERIES: BULK BURK!
WE'RE MARATHONING ALL THREE SEASONS LEADING UP TO TONIGHT'S FINALE, WHERE BULK BURK WILL TAKE ON BARON BEANPOLE IN HIS UNDERGROUND VOLCANIC LAIR GUARDED BY FIRE-BREATHING MAGMA SHARKS!
SO. AWESOME.
BEST. SHOW. EVER.

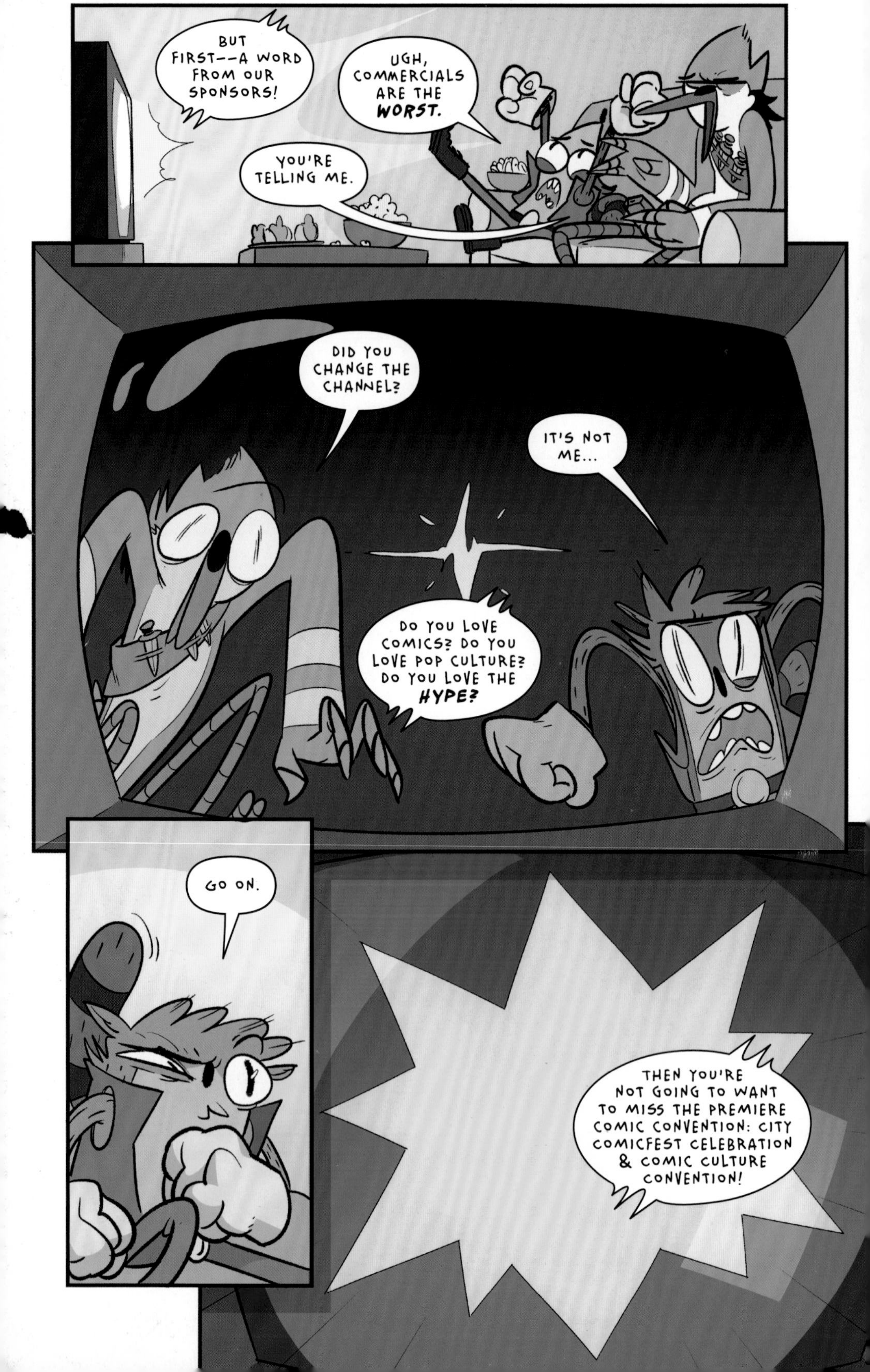
BUT FIRST--A WORD FROM OUR SPONSORS!
UGH, COMMERCIALS ARE THE **WORST.**
YOU'RE TELLING ME.
DID YOU CHANGE THE CHANNEL?
IT'S NOT ME...
DO YOU LOVE COMICS? DO YOU LOVE POP CULTURE? DO YOU LOVE THE ***HYPE?***
GO ON.
THEN YOU'RE NOT GOING TO WANT TO MISS THE PREMIERE COMIC CONVENTION: CITY COMICFEST CELEBRATION & COMIC CULTURE CONVENTION!

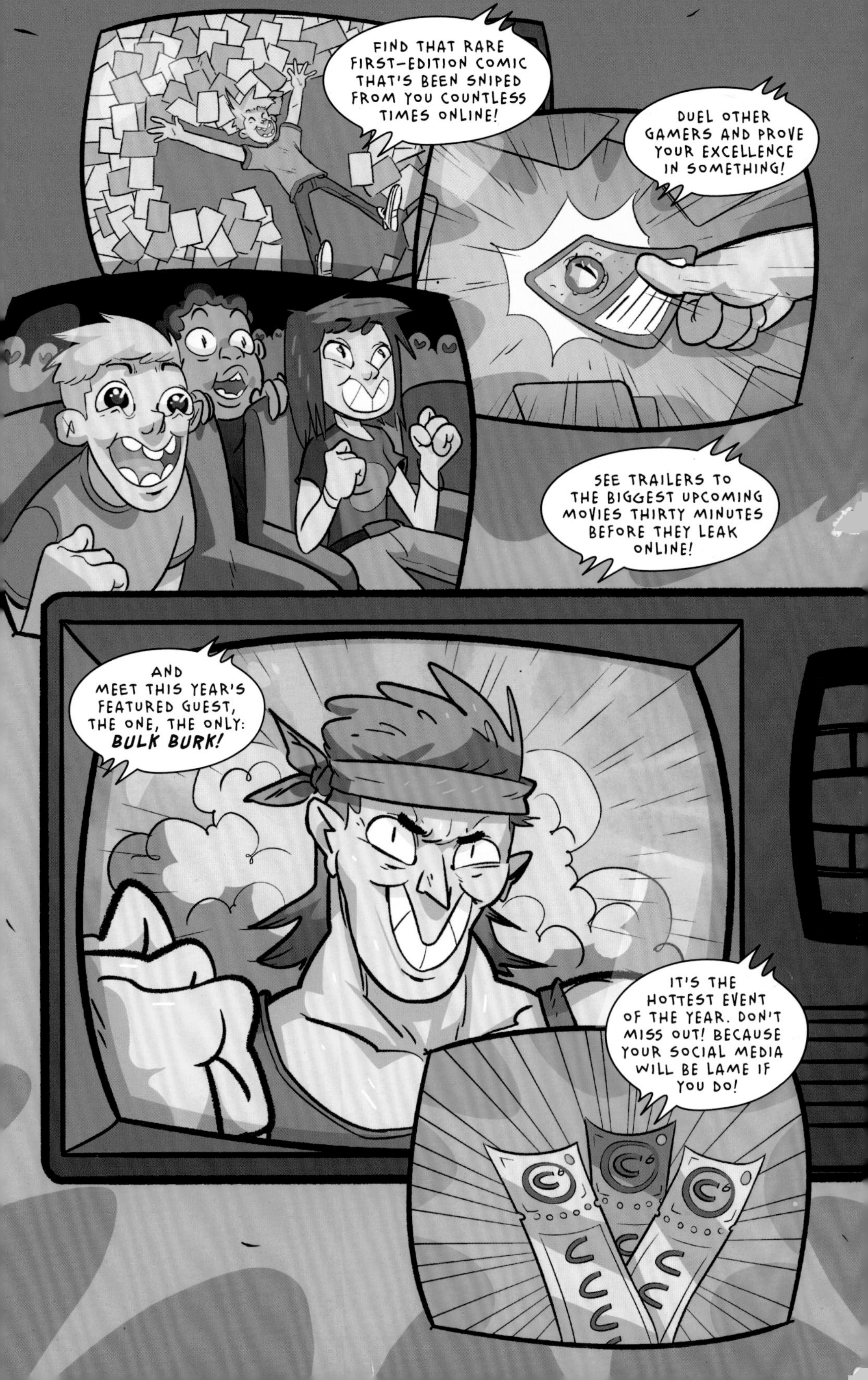
FIND THAT RARE FIRST-EDITION COMIC THAT'S BEEN SNIPED FROM YOU COUNTLESS TIMES ONLINE!
DUEL OTHER GAMERS AND PROVE YOUR EXCELLENCE IN SOMETHING!
SEE TRAILERS TO THE BIGGEST UPCOMING MOVIES THIRTY MINUTES BEFORE THEY LEAK ONLINE!
AND MEET THIS YEAR'S FEATURED GUEST, THE ONE, THE ONLY: BULK BURK!
IT'S THE HOTTEST EVENT OF THE YEAR. DON'T MISS OUT! BECAUSE YOUR SOCIAL MEDIA WILL BE LAME IF YOU DO!

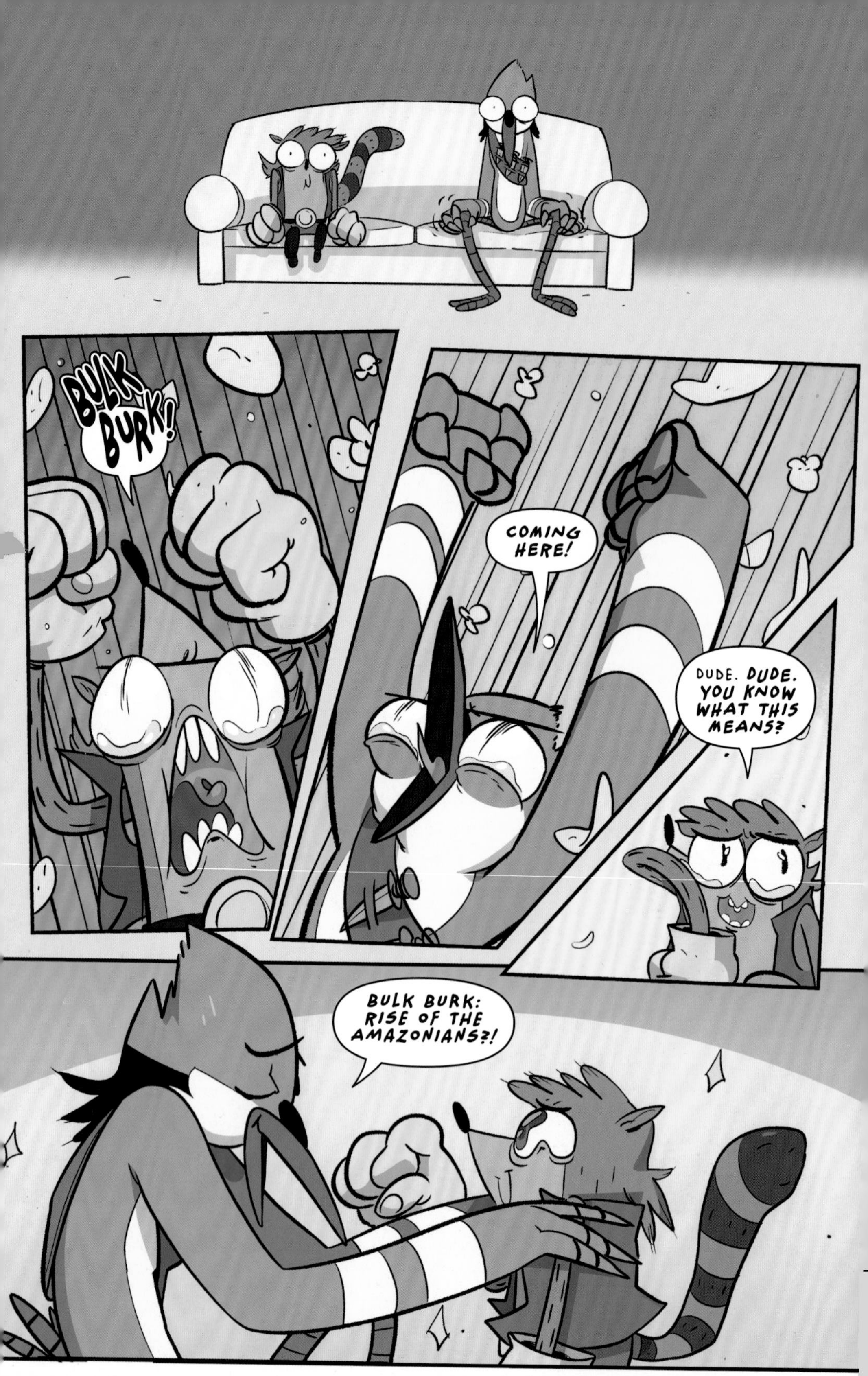
BULK BURK!
COMING HERE!
DUDE. DUDE. YOU KNOW WHAT THIS MEANS?
BULK BURK: RISE OF THE AMAZONIANS?!

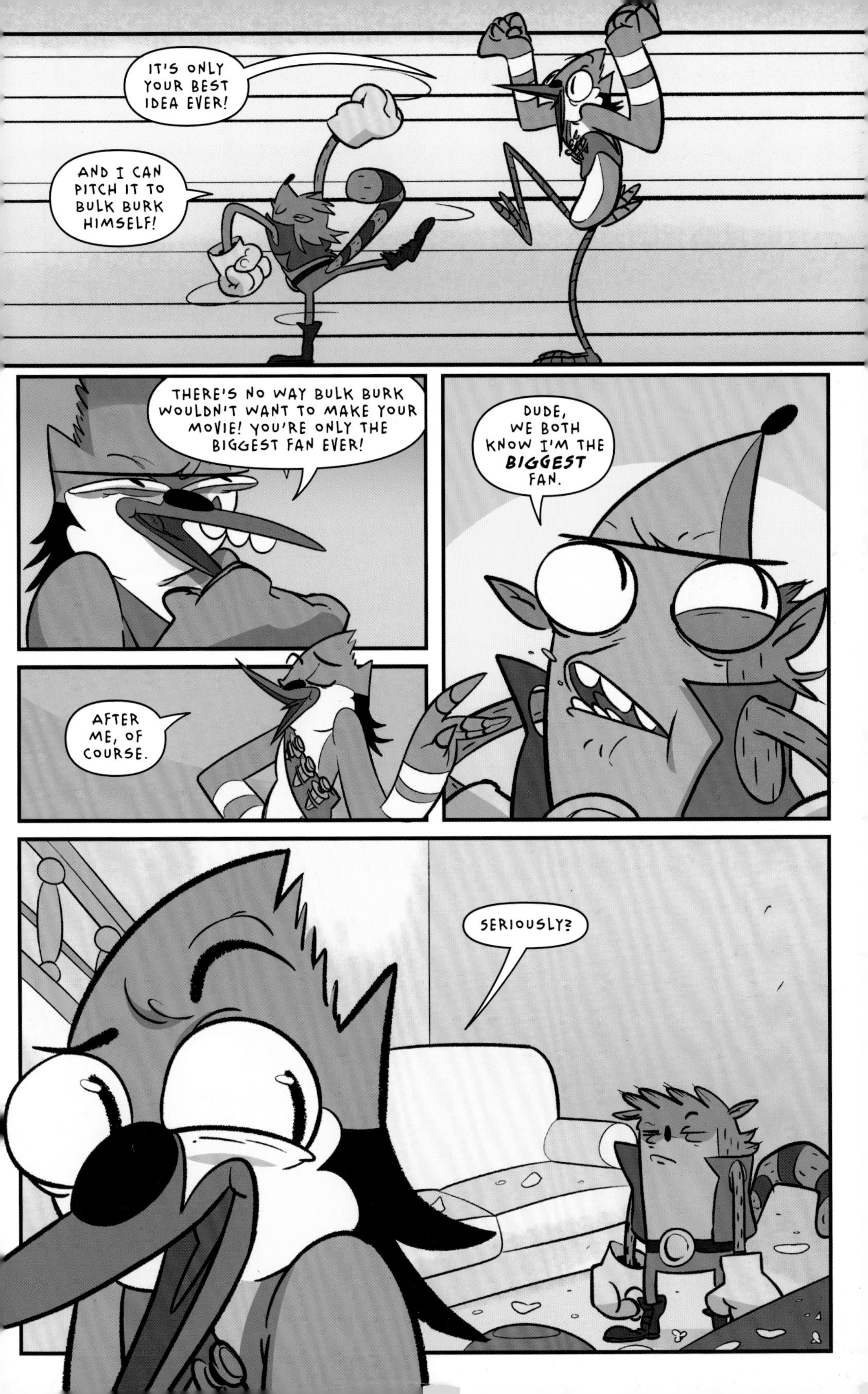
IT'S ONLY YOUR BEST IDEA EVER!
AND I CAN PITCH IT TO BULK BURK HIMSELF!
THERE'S NO WAY BULK BURK WOULDN'T WANT TO MAKE YOUR MOVIE! YOU'RE ONLY THE BIGGEST FAN EVER!
DUDE, WE BOTH KNOW I'M THE **BIGGEST** FAN.
AFTER ME, OF COURSE.
SERIOUSLY?

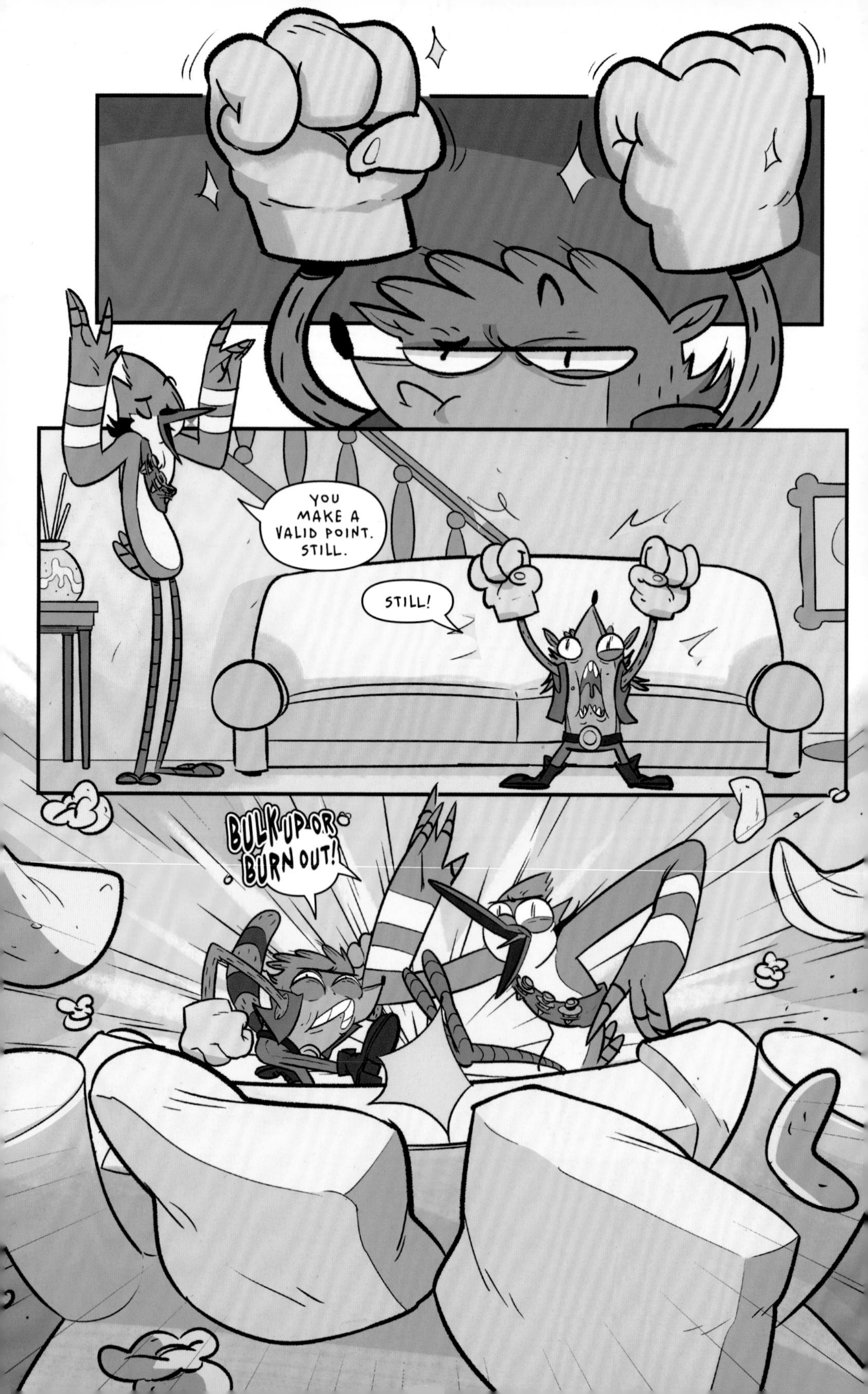
YOU MAKE A VALID POINT. STILL.
STILL!
BULK UP OR BURN OUT!

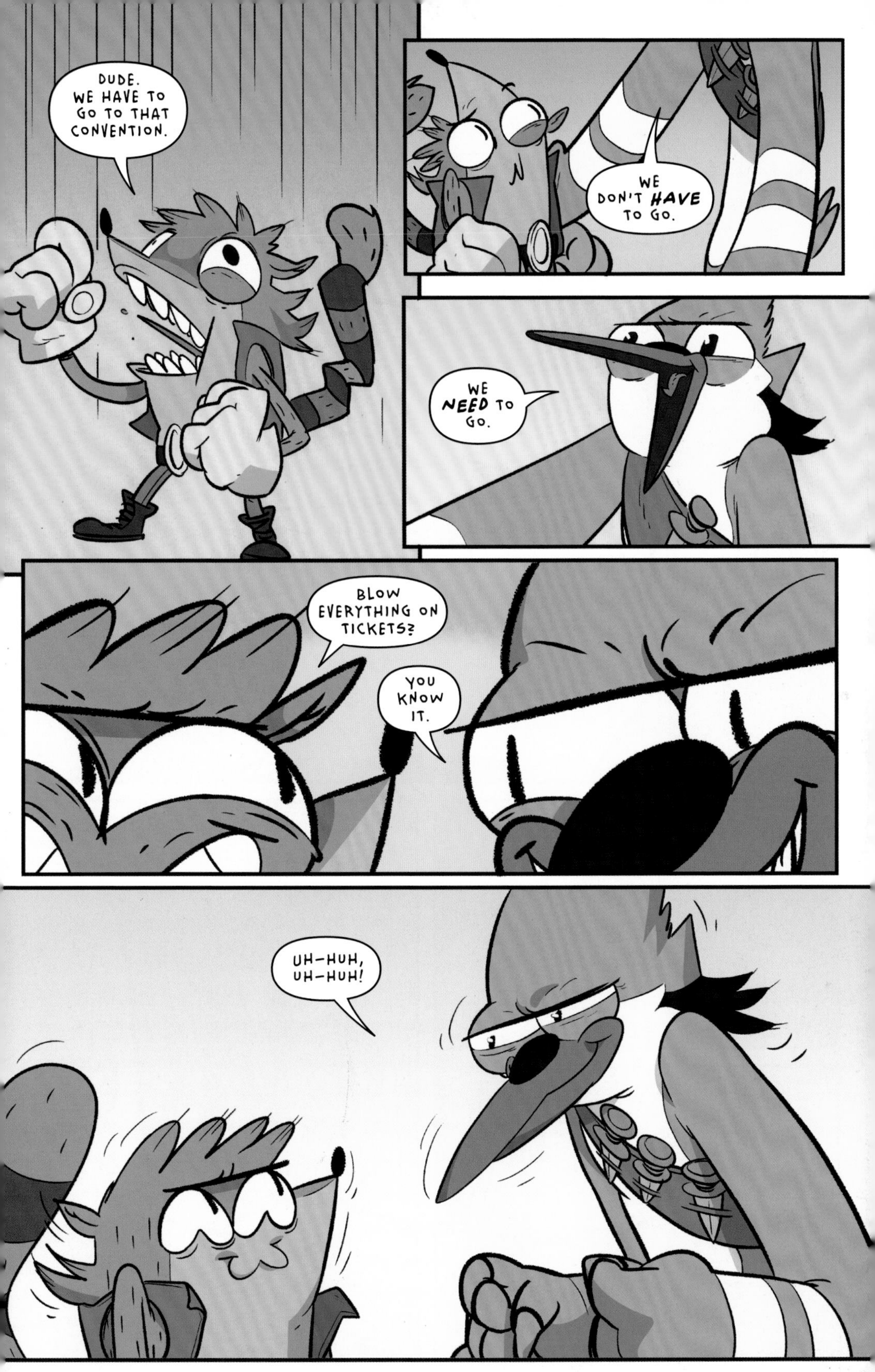
DUDE. WE HAVE TO GO TO THAT CONVENTION.
WE DON'T HAVE TO GO.
WE NEED TO GO.
BLOW EVERYTHING ON TICKETS?
YOU KNOW IT.
UH-HUH, UH-HUH!

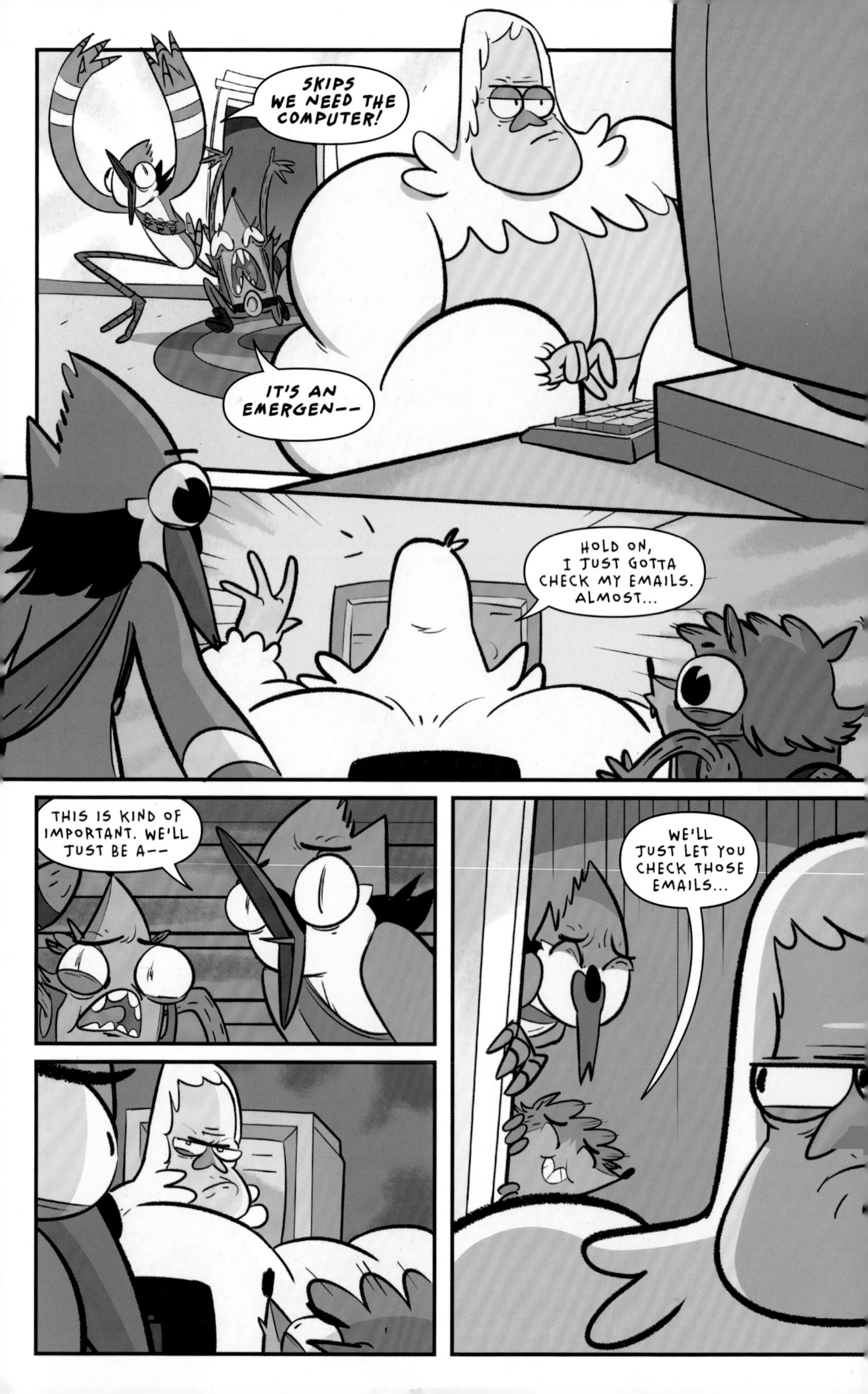
SKIPS WE NEED THE COMPUTER!
IT'S AN EMERGEN--
HOLD ON, I JUST GOTTA CHECK MY EMAILS. ALMOST...
THIS IS KIND OF IMPORTANT. WE'LL JUST BE A--
WE'LL JUST LET YOU CHECK THOSE EMAILS...

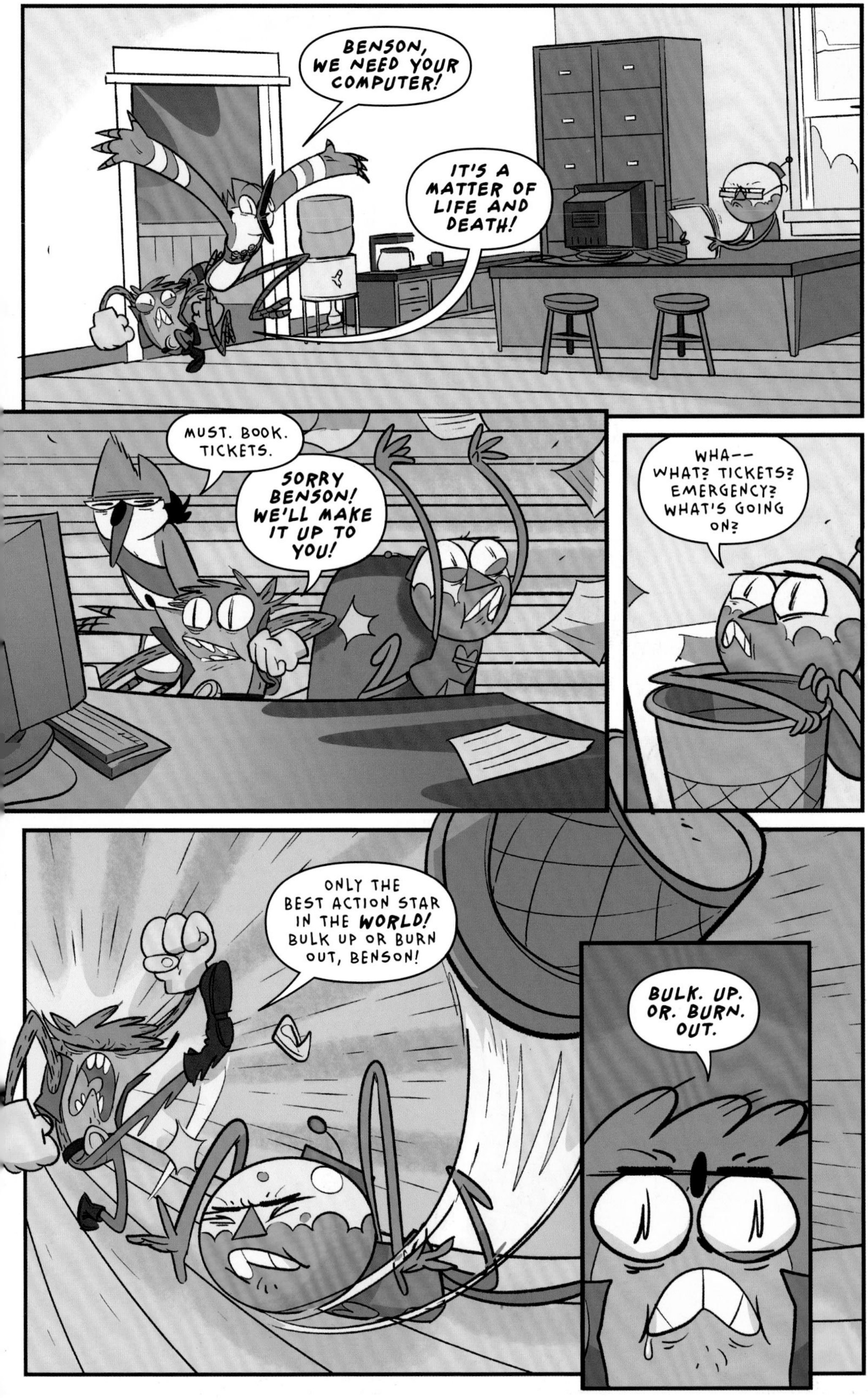
BENSON, WE NEED YOUR COMPUTER!
IT'S A MATTER OF LIFE AND DEATH!
MUST. BOOK. TICKETS.
SORRY BENSON! WE'LL MAKE IT UP TO YOU!
WHA-- WHAT? TICKETS? EMERGENCY? WHAT'S GOING ON?
ONLY THE BEST ACTION STAR IN THE WORLD! BULK UP OR BURN OUT, BENSON!
BULK. UP. OR. BURN. OUT.

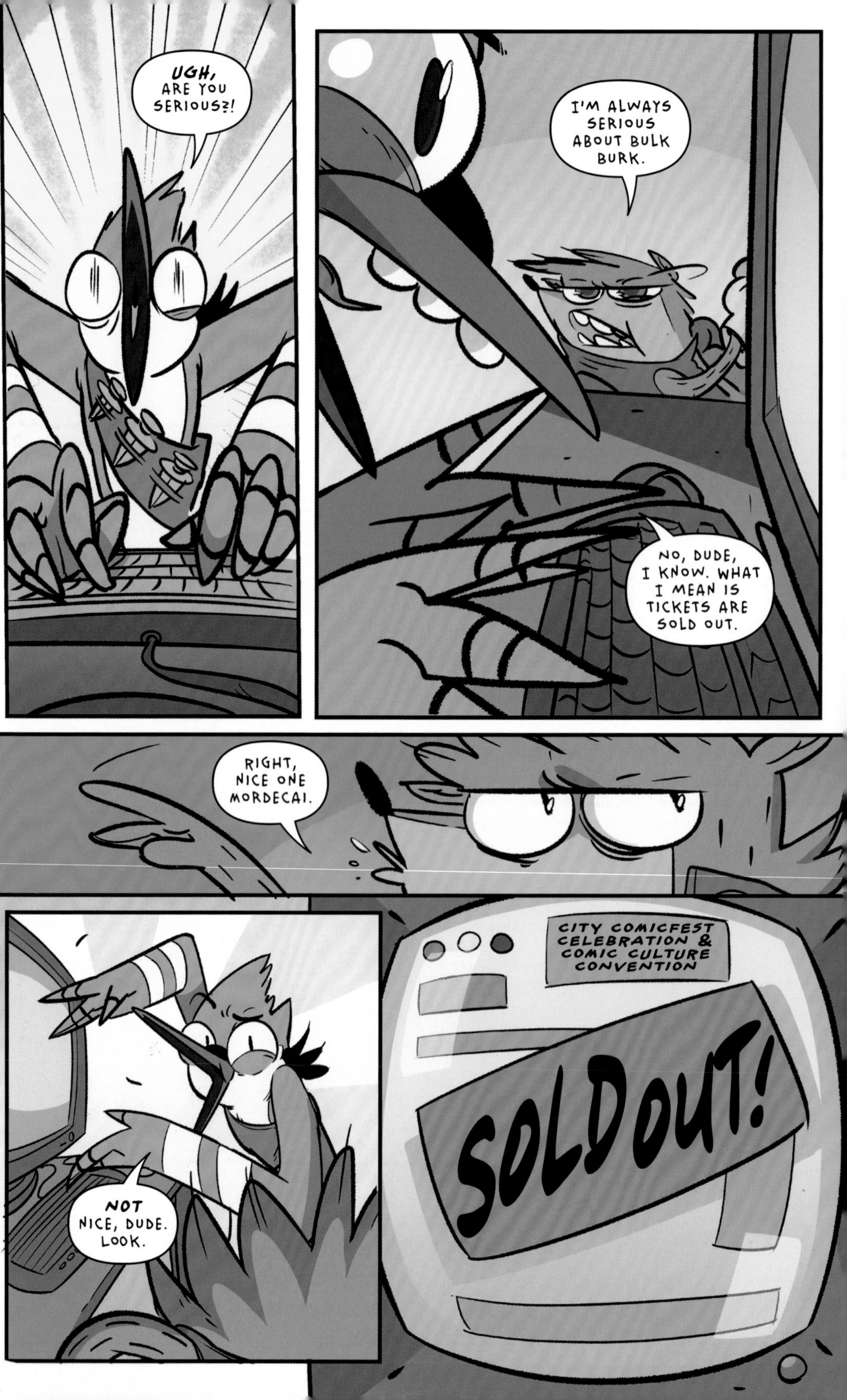
UGH, ARE YOU SERIOUS?!
I'M ALWAYS SERIOUS ABOUT BULK BURK.
NO, DUDE, I KNOW. WHAT I MEAN IS TICKETS ARE SOLD OUT.
RIGHT, NICE ONE MORDECAI.
NOT NICE, DUDE. LOOK.
CITY COMICFEST CELEBRATION & COMIC CULTURE CONVENTION
SOLD OUT!

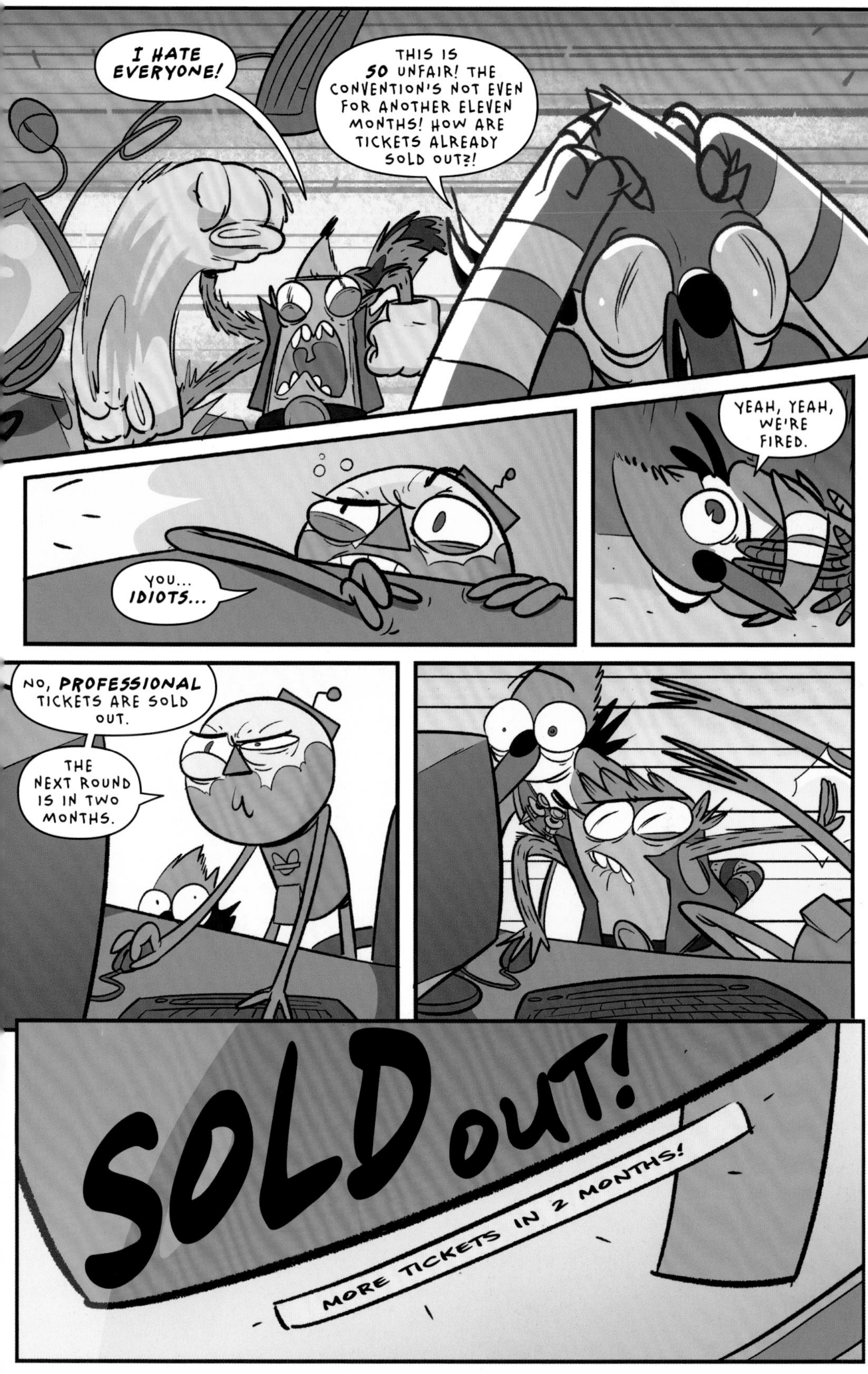

I HATE EVERYONE!
THIS IS SO UNFAIR! THE CONVENTION'S NOT EVEN FOR ANOTHER ELEVEN MONTHS! HOW ARE TICKETS ALREADY SOLD OUT?!
YOU... IDIOTS...
YEAH, YEAH, WE'RE FIRED.
NO, PROFESSIONAL TICKETS ARE SOLD OUT.
THE NEXT ROUND IS IN TWO MONTHS.
SOLD OUT!
MORE TICKETS IN 2 MONTHS!

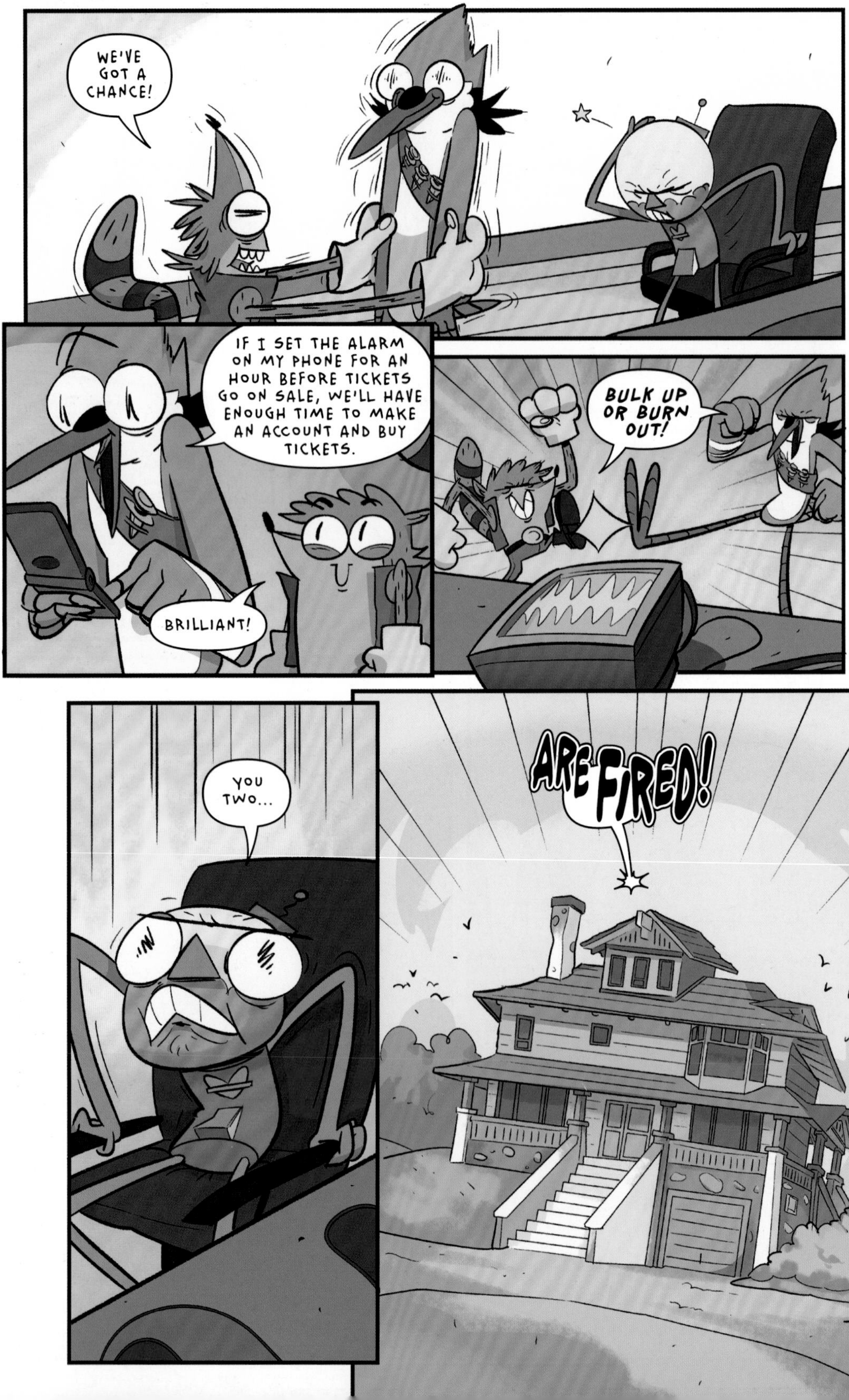
WE'VE GOT A CHANCE!
IF I SET THE ALARM ON MY PHONE FOR AN HOUR BEFORE TICKETS GO ON SALE, WE'LL HAVE ENOUGH TIME TO MAKE AN ACCOUNT AND BUY TICKETS.
BRILLIANT!
BULK UP OR BURN OUT!
YOU TWO...
ARE FIRED!

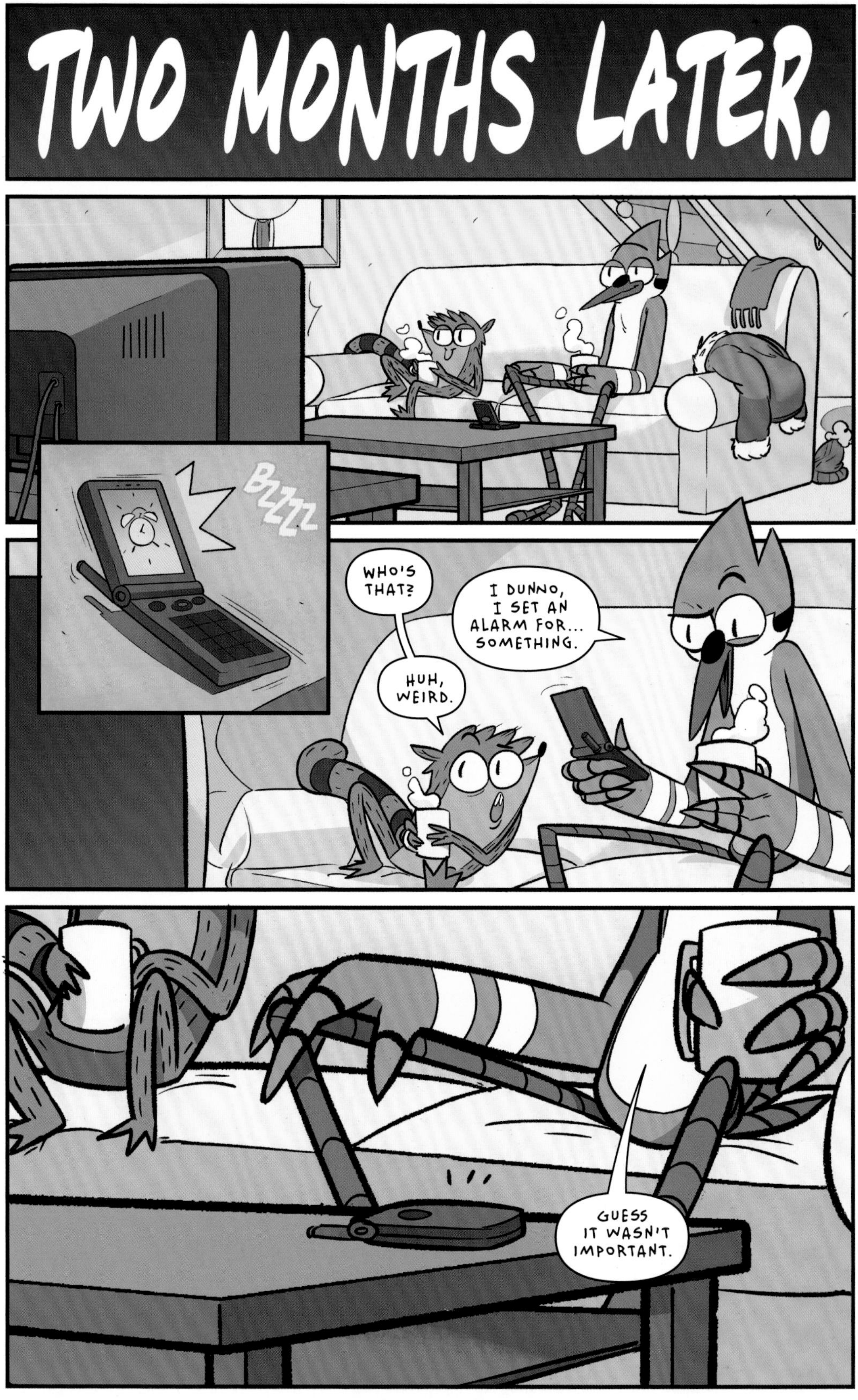
TWO MONTHS LATER.
BZZZZ
WHO'S THAT?
I DUNNO, I SET AN ALARM FOR... SOMETHING.
HUH, WEIRD.
GUESS IT WASN'T IMPORTANT.

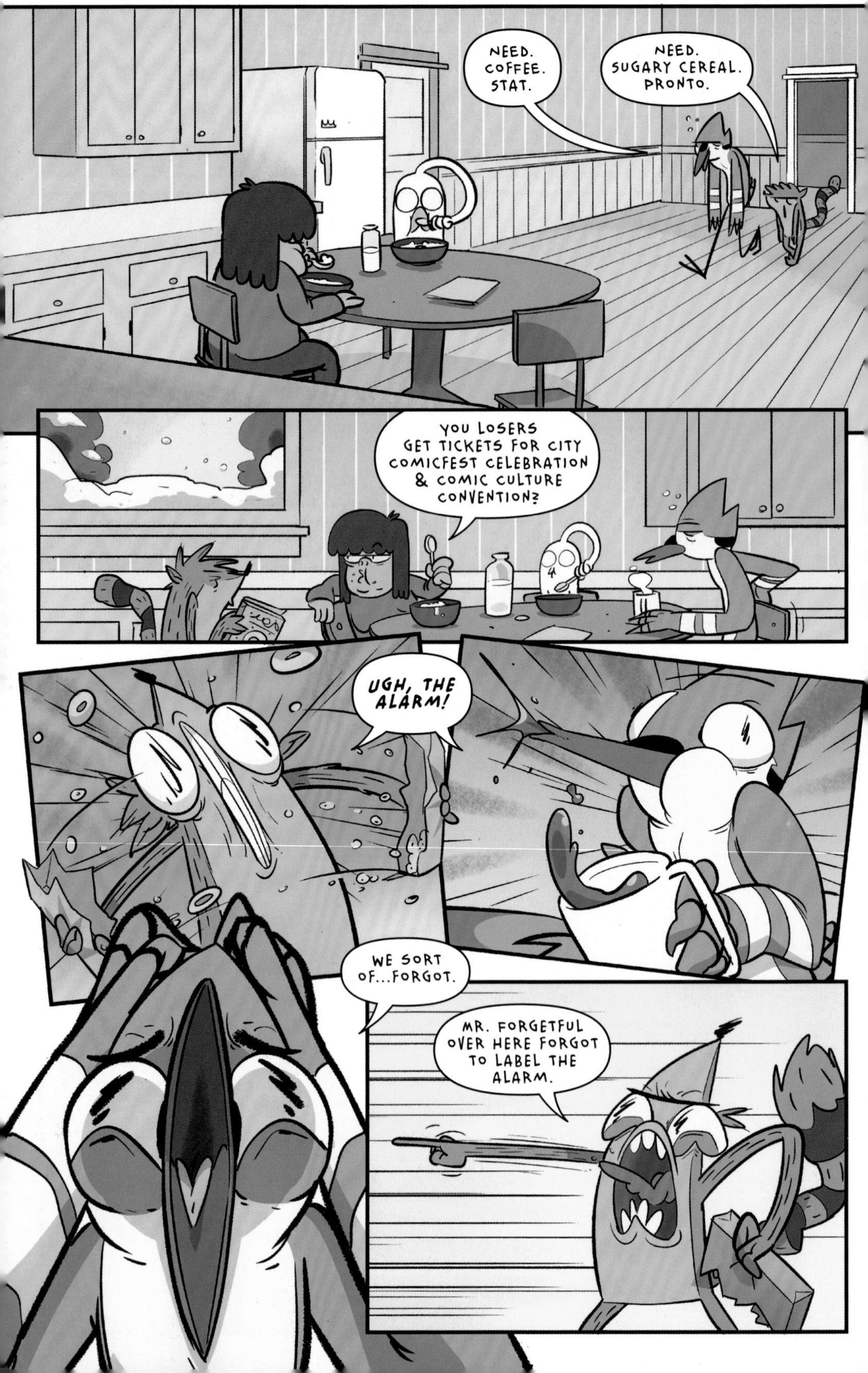
NEED. COFFEE. STAT.
NEED. SUGARY CEREAL. PRONTO.
YOU LOSERS GET TICKETS FOR CITY COMICFEST CELEBRATION & COMIC CULTURE CONVENTION?
UGH, THE ALARM!
WE SORT OF...FORGOT.
MR. FORGETFUL OVER HERE FORGOT TO LABEL THE ALARM.

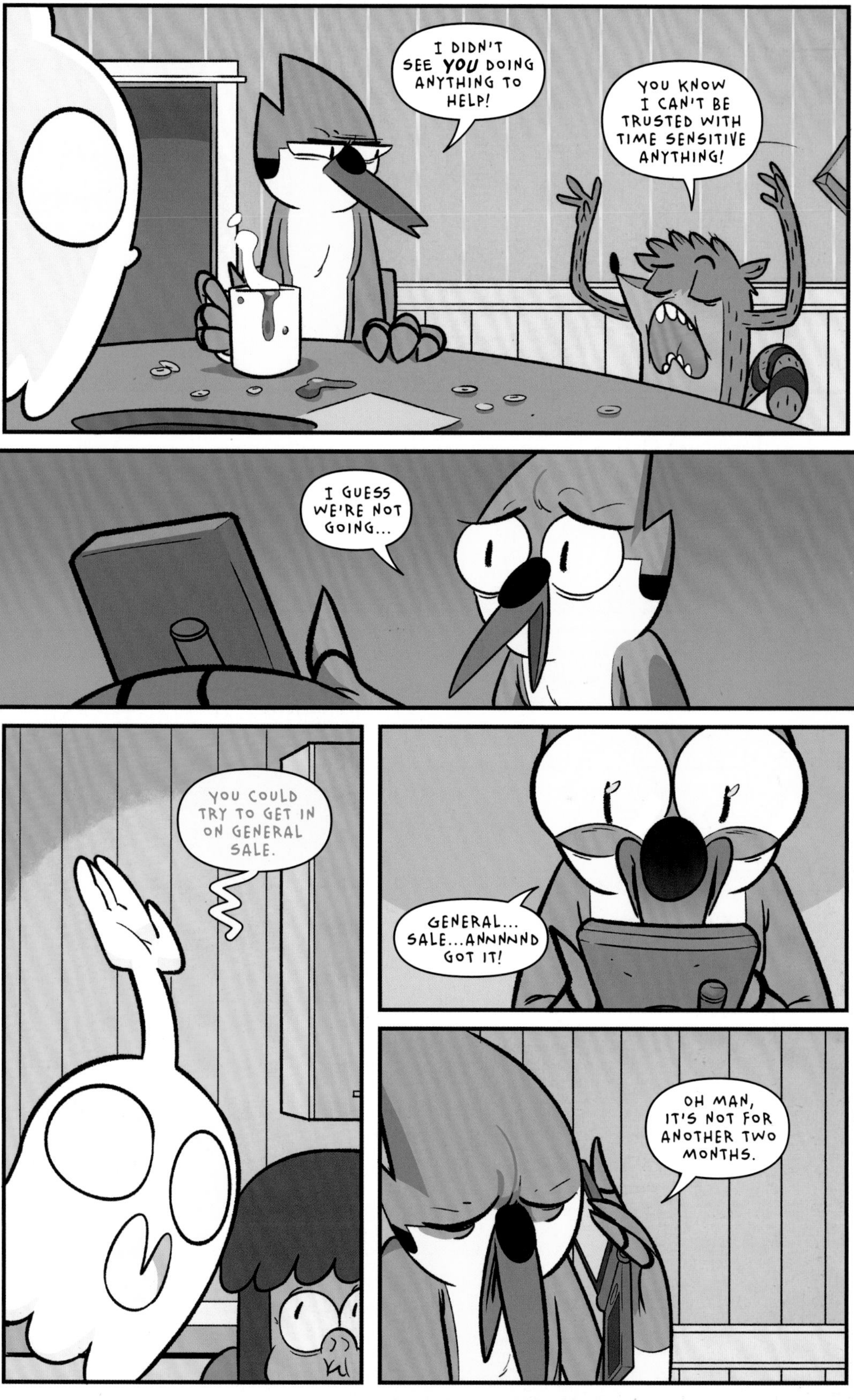
I DIDN'T SEE YOU DOING ANYTHING TO HELP!
YOU KNOW I CAN'T BE TRUSTED WITH TIME SENSITIVE ANYTHING!
I GUESS WE'RE NOT GOING...
YOU COULD TRY TO GET IN ON GENERAL SALE.
GENERAL... SALE...ANNNNND GOT IT!
OH MAN, IT'S NOT FOR ANOTHER TWO MONTHS.

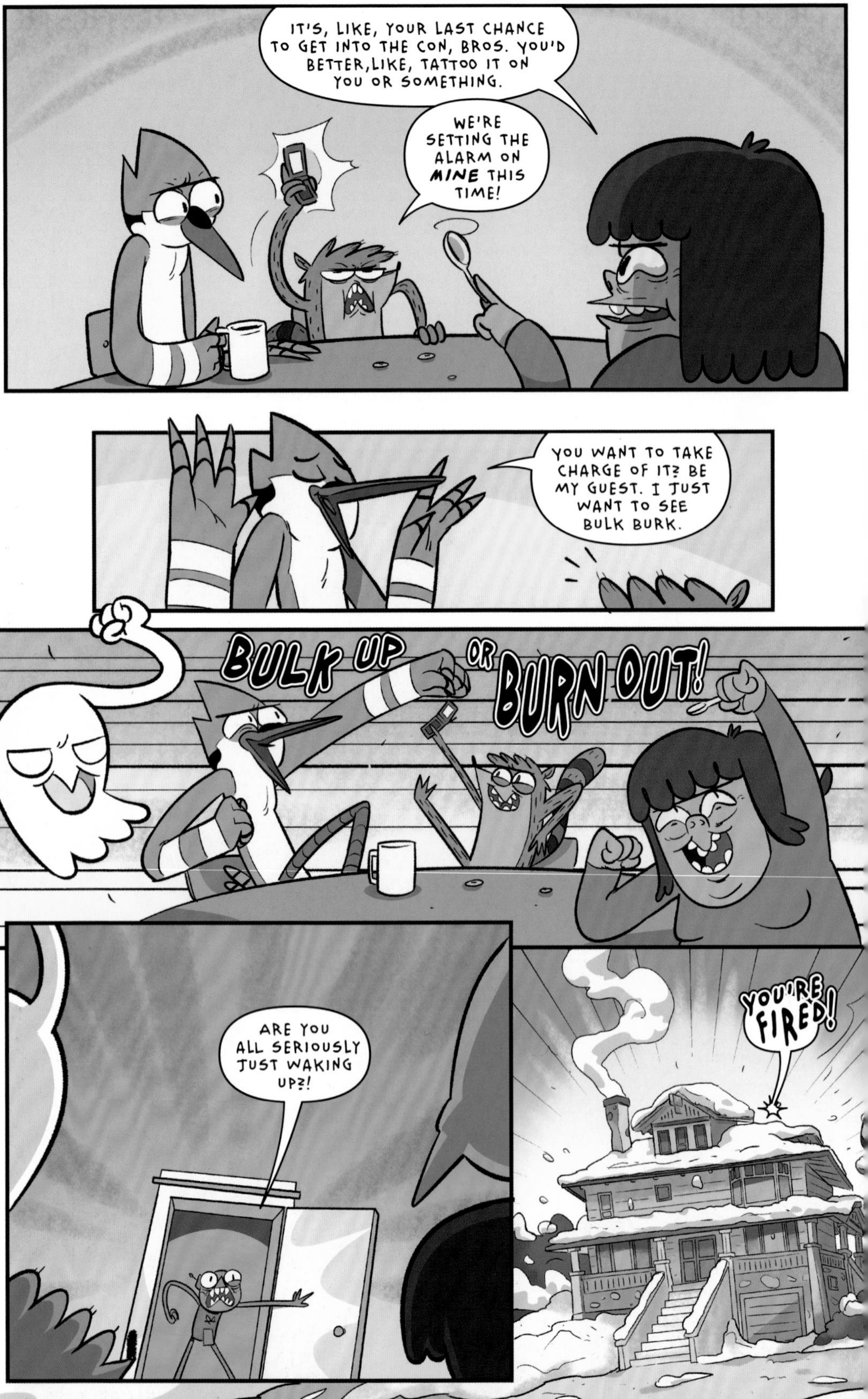
IT'S, LIKE, YOUR LAST CHANCE TO GET INTO THE CON, BROS. YOU'D BETTER,LIKE, TATTOO IT ON YOU OR SOMETHING.
WE'RE SETTING THE ALARM ON MINE THIS TIME!
YOU WANT TO TAKE CHARGE OF IT? BE MY GUEST. I JUST WANT TO SEE BULK BURK.
BULK UP OR BURN OUT!
ARE YOU ALL SERIOUSLY JUST WAKING UP?!
YOU'RE FIRED!

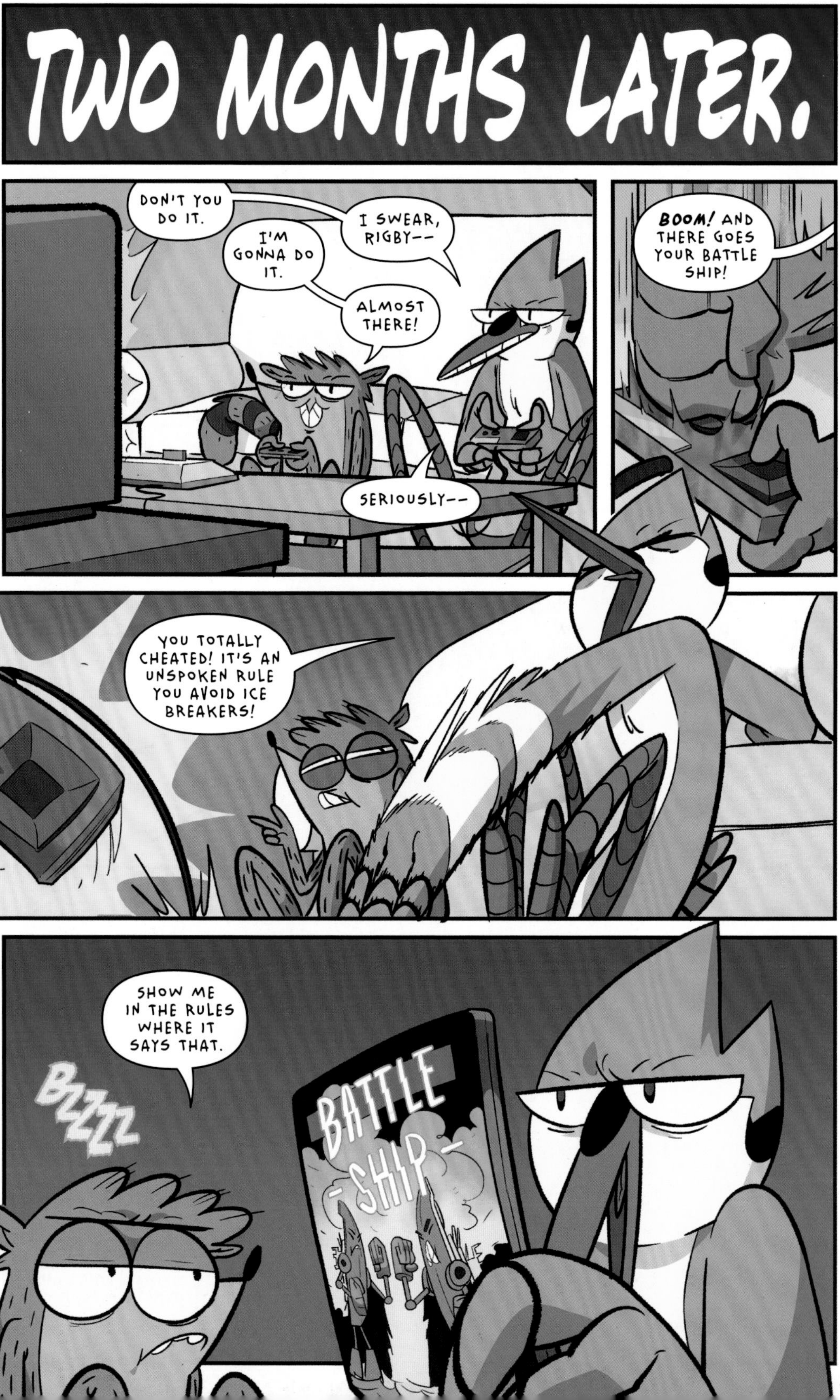
TWO MONTHS LATER.
DON'T YOU DO IT.
I'M GONNA DO IT.
I SWEAR, RIGBY--
ALMOST THERE!
SERIOUSLY--
BOOM! AND THERE GOES YOUR BATTLE SHIP!
YOU TOTALLY CHEATED! IT'S AN UNSPOKEN RULE YOU AVOID ICE BREAKERS!
SHOW ME IN THE RULES WHERE IT SAYS THAT.
BZZZZ
BATTLE -SHIP-

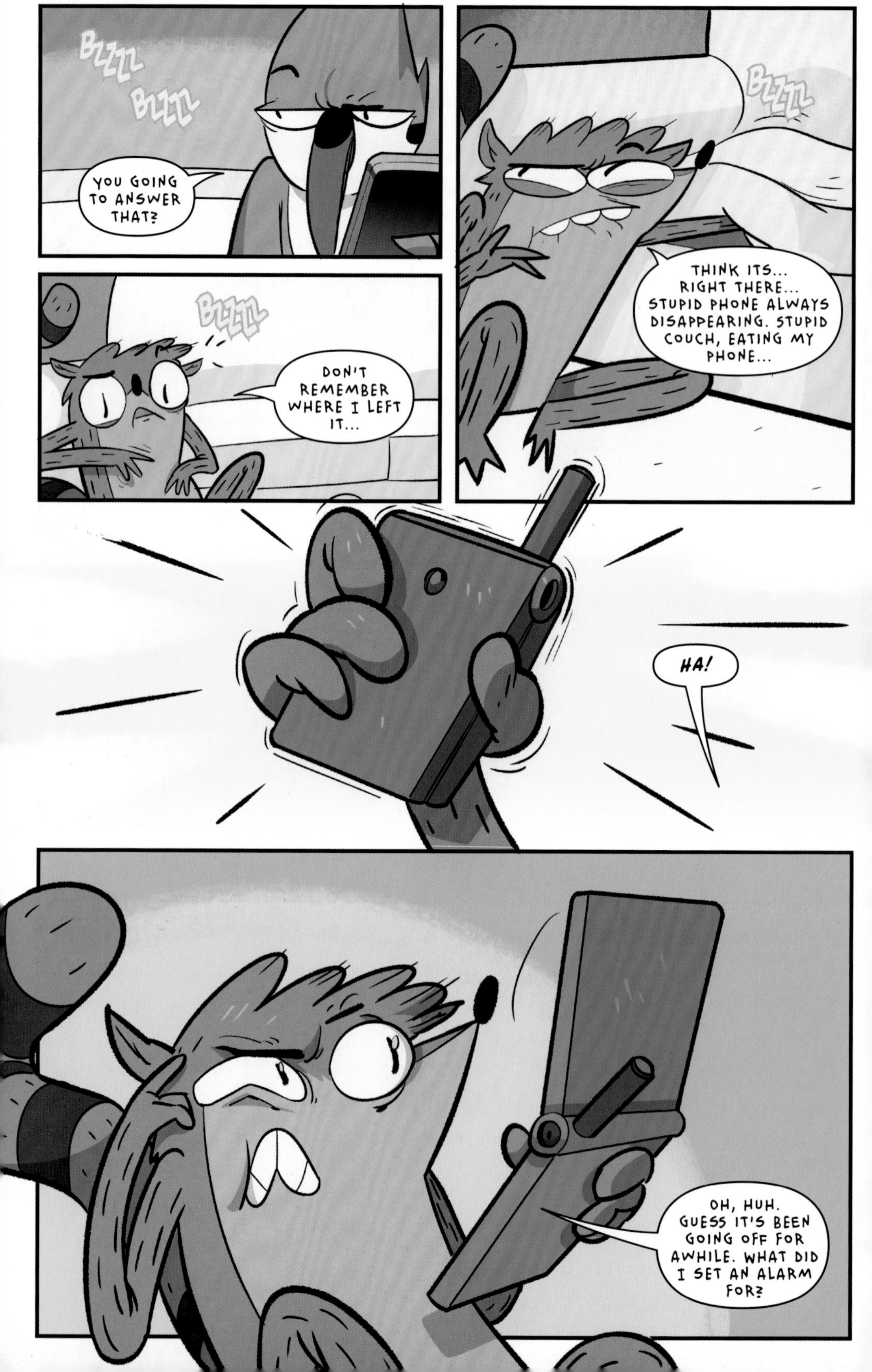
BZZZZ
BZZZZ
YOU GOING TO ANSWER THAT?
BZZZZ
THINK ITS... RIGHT THERE... STUPID PHONE ALWAYS DISAPPEARING. STUPID COUCH, EATING MY PHONE...
BZZZZ
DON'T REMEMBER WHERE I LEFT IT...
HA!
OH, HUH. GUESS IT'S BEEN GOING OFF FOR AWHILE. WHAT DID I SET AN ALARM FOR?

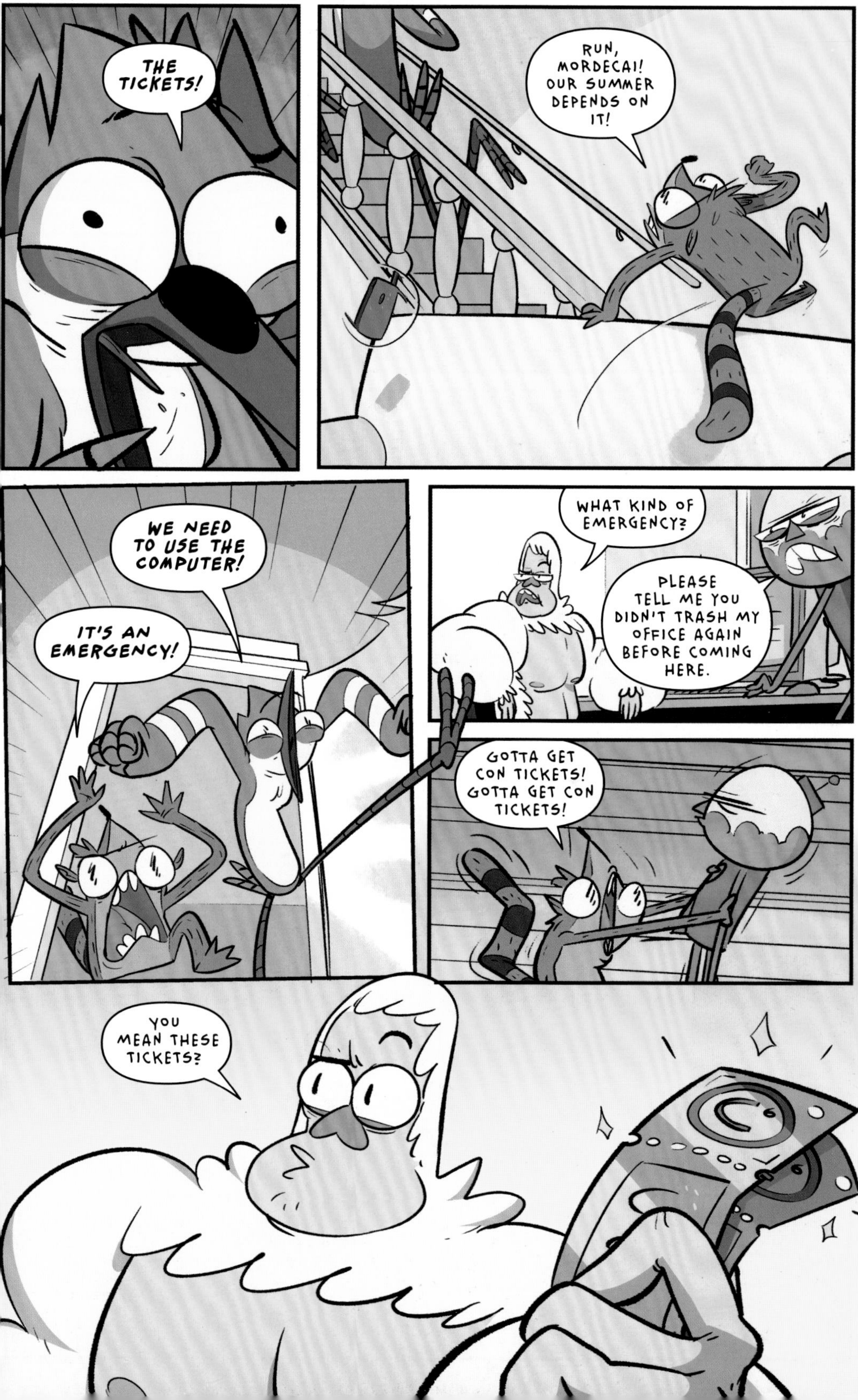
THE TICKETS!
RUN, MORDECAI! OUR SUMMER DEPENDS ON IT!
WE NEED TO USE THE COMPUTER!
IT'S AN EMERGENCY!
WHAT KIND OF EMERGENCY?
PLEASE TELL ME YOU DIDN'T TRASH MY OFFICE AGAIN BEFORE COMING HERE.
GOTTA GET CON TICKETS! GOTTA GET CON TICKETS!
YOU MEAN THESE TICKETS?

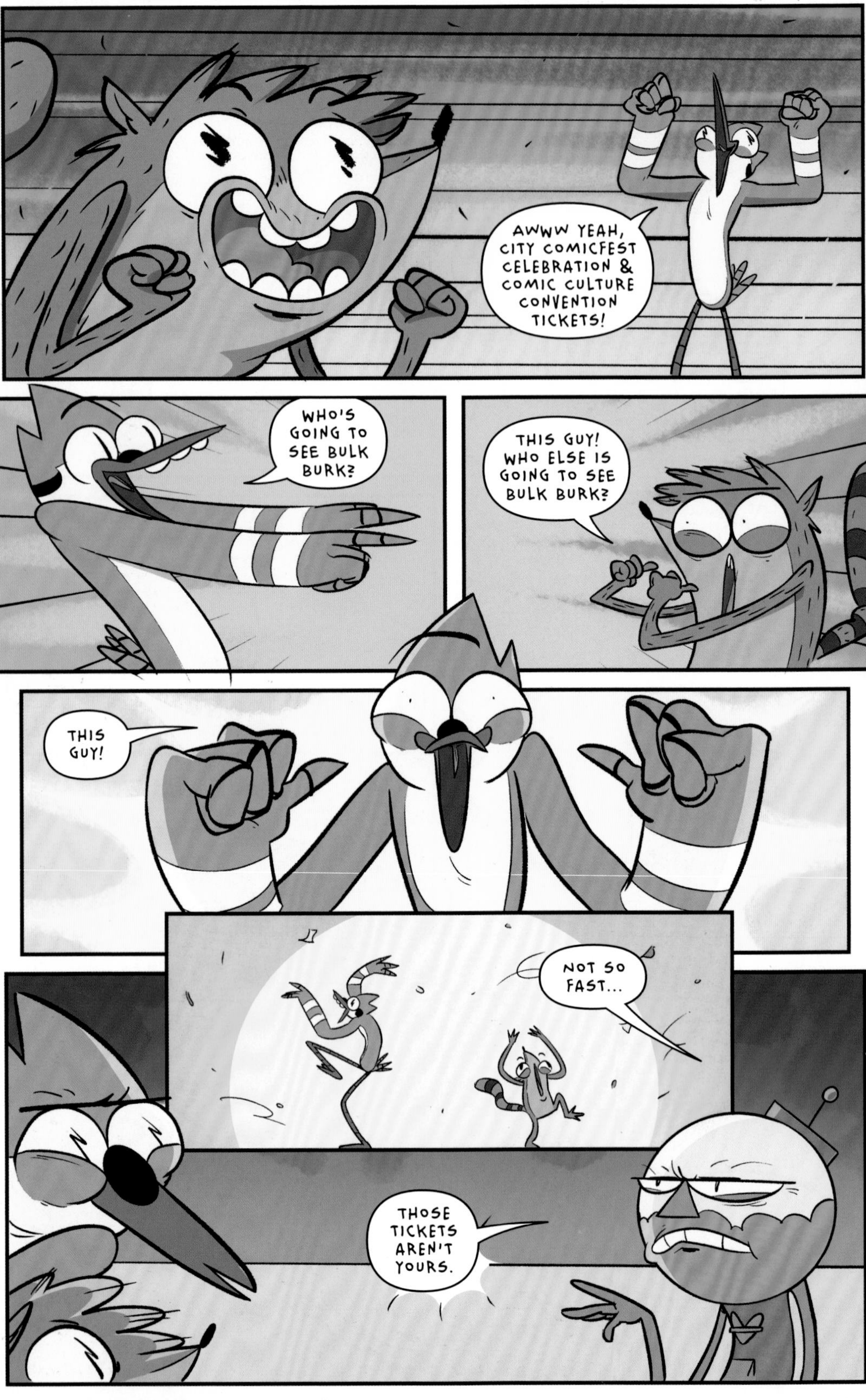
AWWW YEAH, CITY COMICFEST CELEBRATION & COMIC CULTURE CONVENTION TICKETS!
WHO'S GOING TO SEE BULK BURK?
THIS GUY! WHO ELSE IS GOING TO SEE BULK BURK?
THIS GUY!
NOT SO FAST...
THOSE TICKETS AREN'T YOURS.

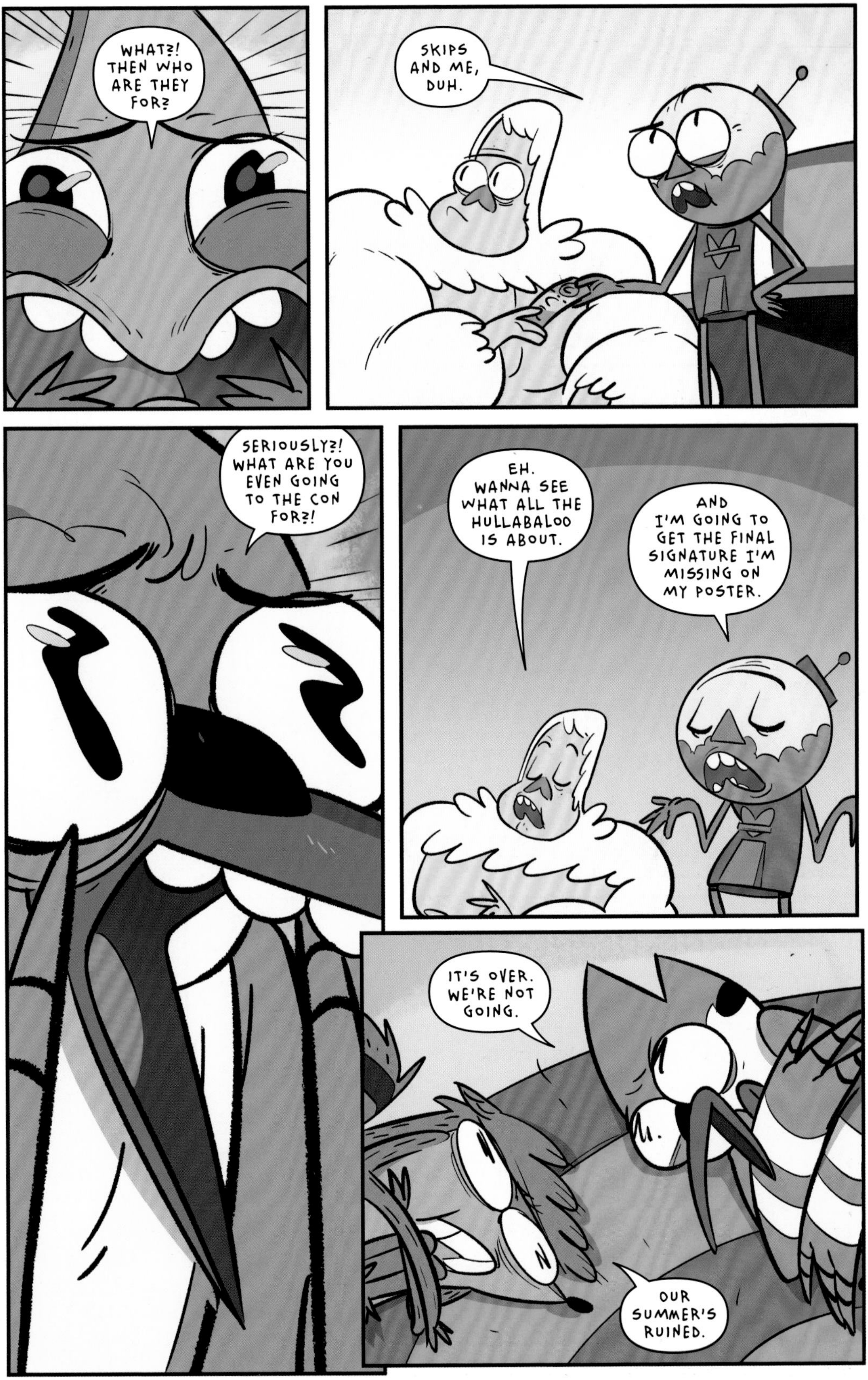
WHAT?! THEN WHO ARE THEY FOR?
SKIPS AND ME, DUH.
SERIOUSLY?! WHAT ARE YOU EVEN GOING TO THE CON FOR?!
EH. WANNA SEE WHAT ALL THE HULLABALOO IS ABOUT.
AND I'M GOING TO GET THE FINAL SIGNATURE I'M MISSING ON MY POSTER.
IT'S OVER. WE'RE NOT GOING.
OUR SUMMER'S RUINED.

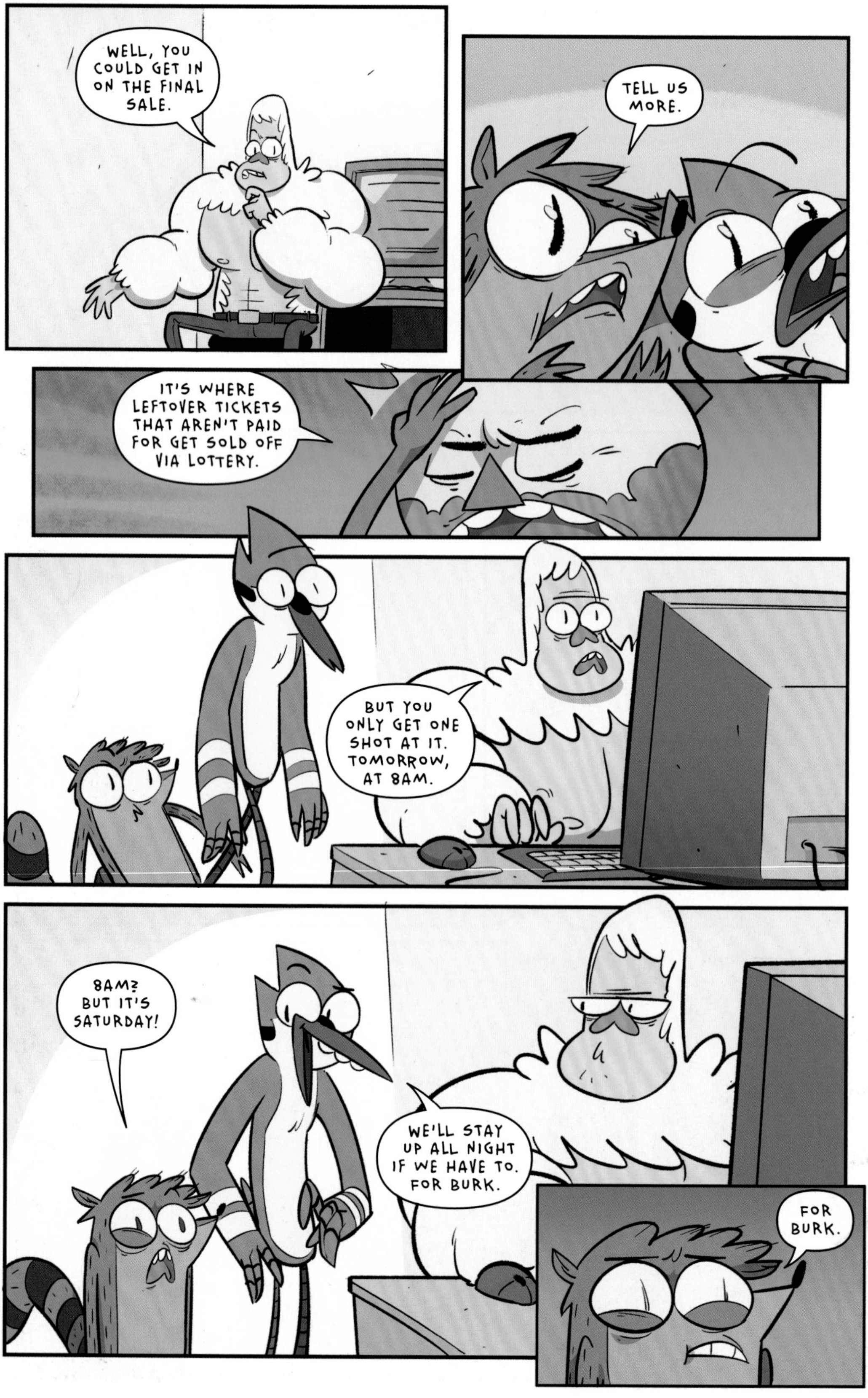
WELL, YOU COULD GET IN ON THE FINAL SALE.
TELL US MORE.
IT'S WHERE LEFTOVER TICKETS THAT AREN'T PAID FOR GET SOLD OFF VIA LOTTERY.
BUT YOU ONLY GET ONE SHOT AT IT. TOMORROW, AT 8AM.
8AM? BUT IT'S SATURDAY!
WE'LL STAY UP ALL NIGHT IF WE HAVE TO. FOR BURK.
FOR BURK.

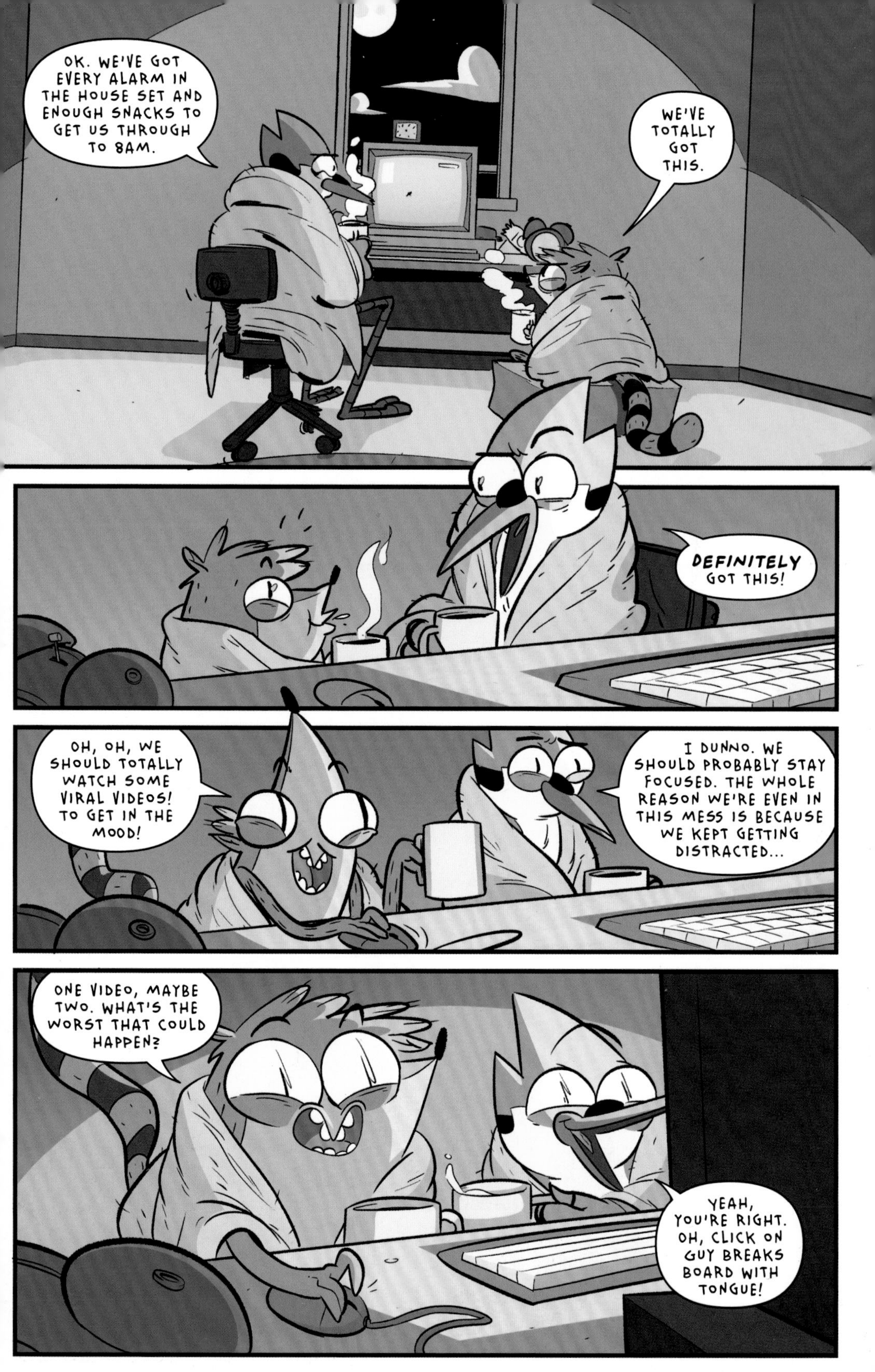
OK. WE'VE GOT EVERY ALARM IN THE HOUSE SET AND ENOUGH SNACKS TO GET US THROUGH TO 8AM.
WE'VE TOTALLY GOT THIS.
DEFINITELY GOT THIS!
OH, OH, WE SHOULD TOTALLY WATCH SOME VIRAL VIDEOS! TO GET IN THE MOOD!
I DUNNO. WE SHOULD PROBABLY STAY FOCUSED. THE WHOLE REASON WE'RE EVEN IN THIS MESS IS BECAUSE WE KEPT GETTING DISTRACTED...
ONE VIDEO, MAYBE TWO. WHAT'S THE WORST THAT COULD HAPPEN?
YEAH, YOU'RE RIGHT. OH, CLICK ON GUY BREAKS BOARD WITH TONGUE!

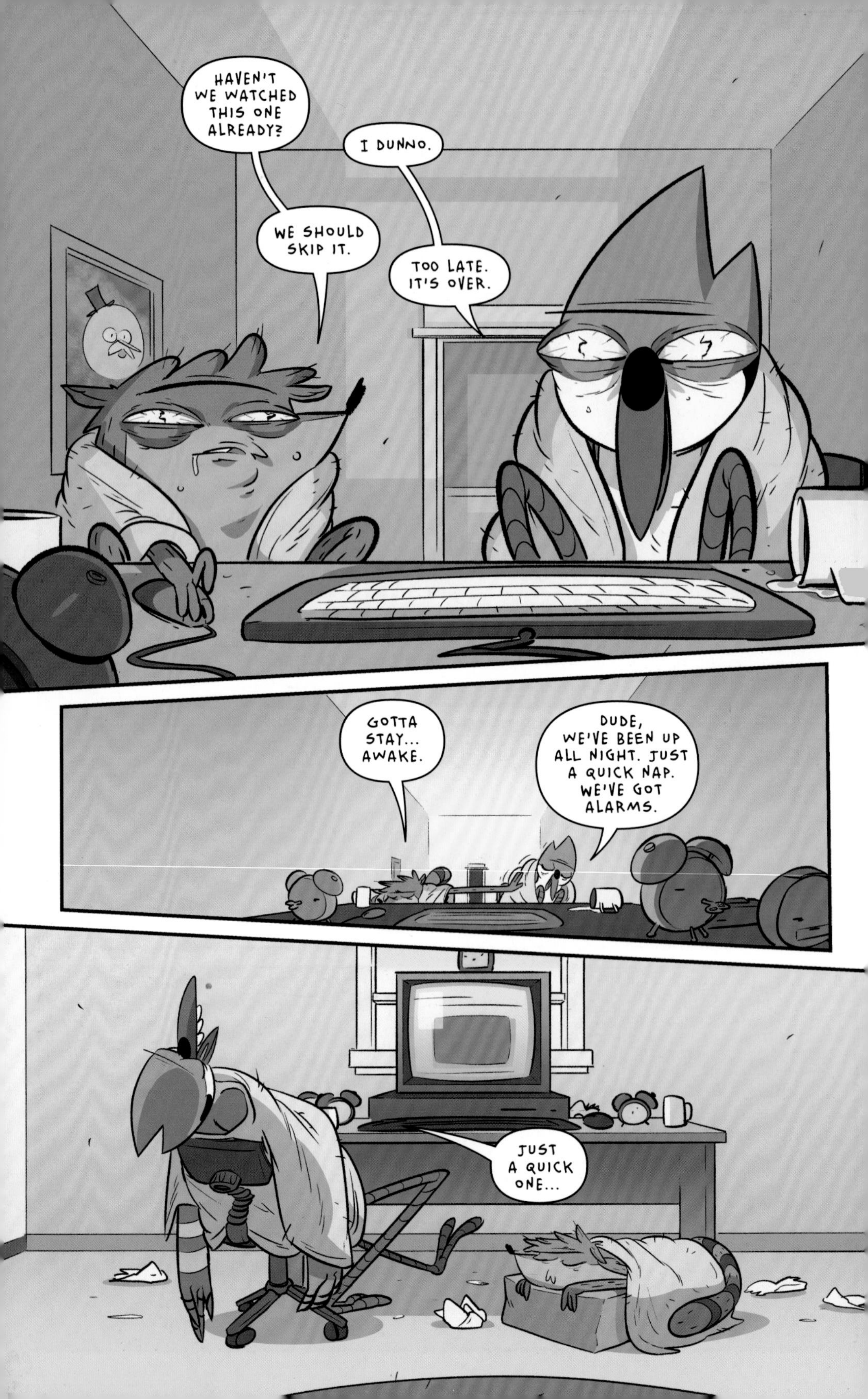
HAVEN'T WE WATCHED THIS ONE ALREADY?
I DUNNO.
WE SHOULD SKIP IT.
TOO LATE. IT'S OVER.
GOTTA STAY... AWAKE.
DUDE, WE'VE BEEN UP ALL NIGHT. JUST A QUICK NAP. WE'VE GOT ALARMS.
JUST A QUICK ONE...

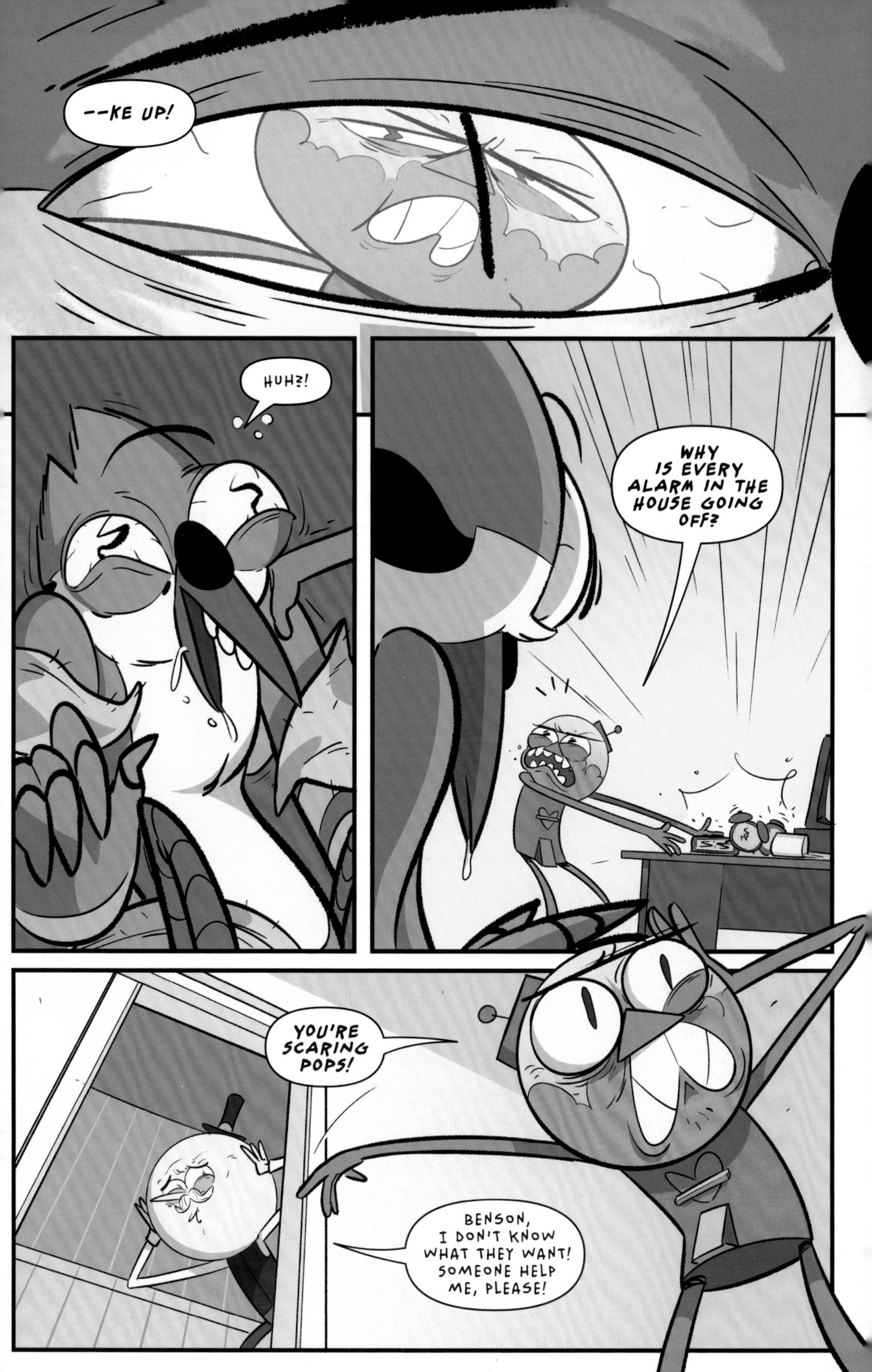
--KE UP!
HUH?!
WHY IS EVERY ALARM IN THE HOUSE GOING OFF?
YOU'RE SCARING POPS!
BENSON, I DON'T KNOW WHAT THEY WANT! SOMEONE HELP ME, PLEASE!

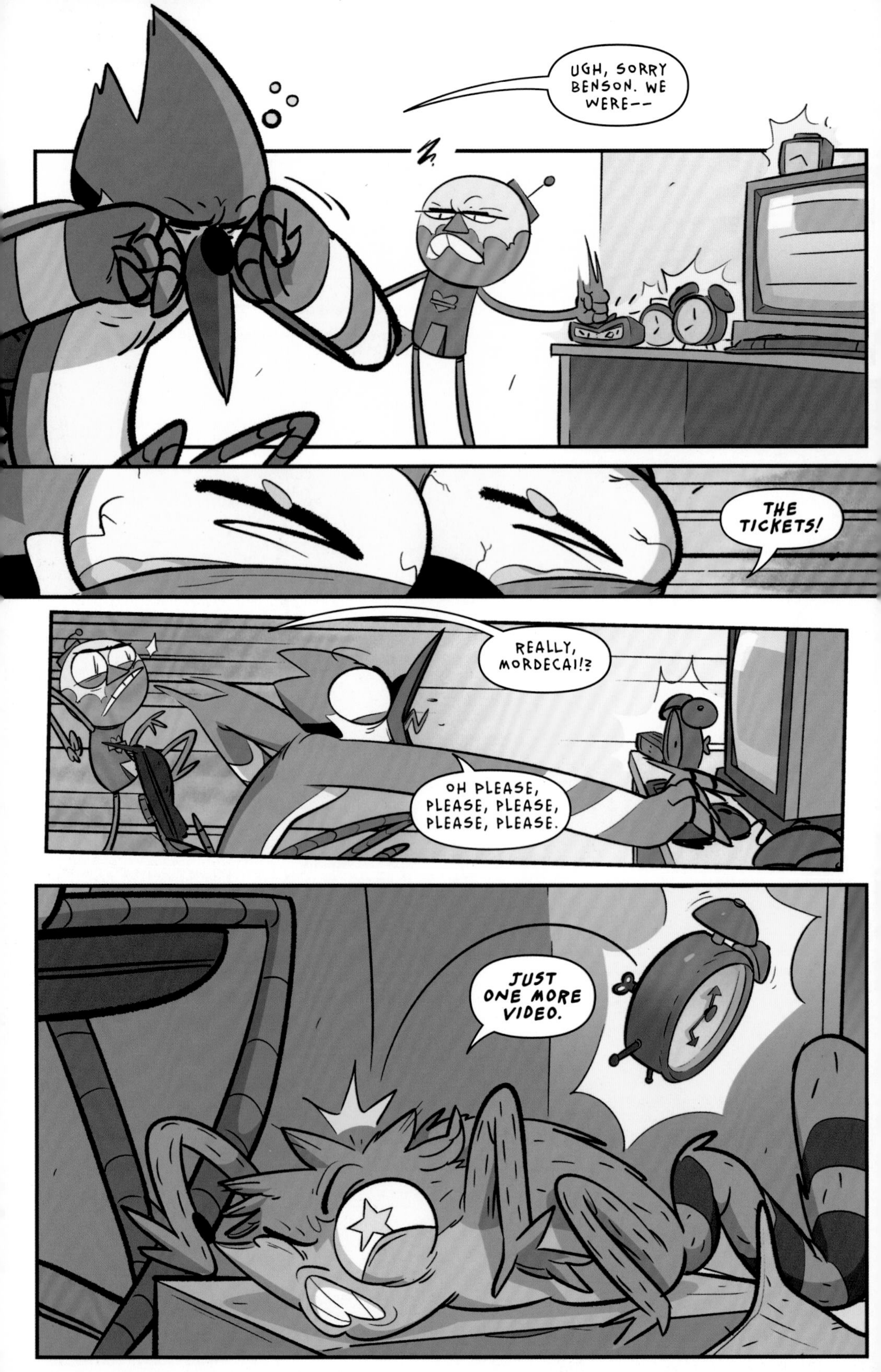
UGH, SORRY BENSON. WE WERE--
THE TICKETS!
REALLY, MORDECAI!?
OH PLEASE, PLEASE, PLEASE, PLEASE, PLEASE.
JUST ONE MORE VIDEO.

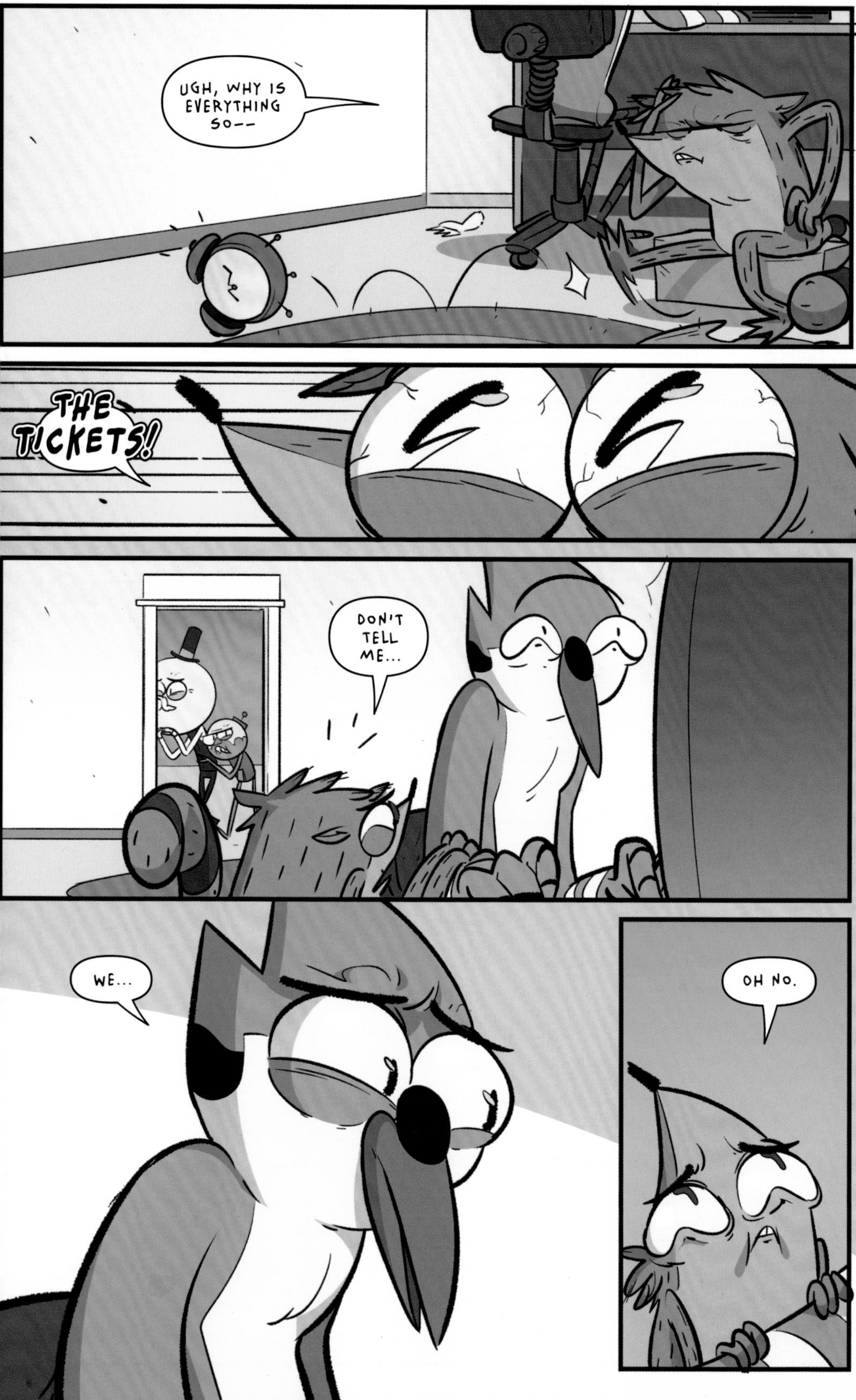
UGH, WHY IS EVERYTHING SO--
THE TICKETS!
DON'T TELL ME...
WE...
OH NO.

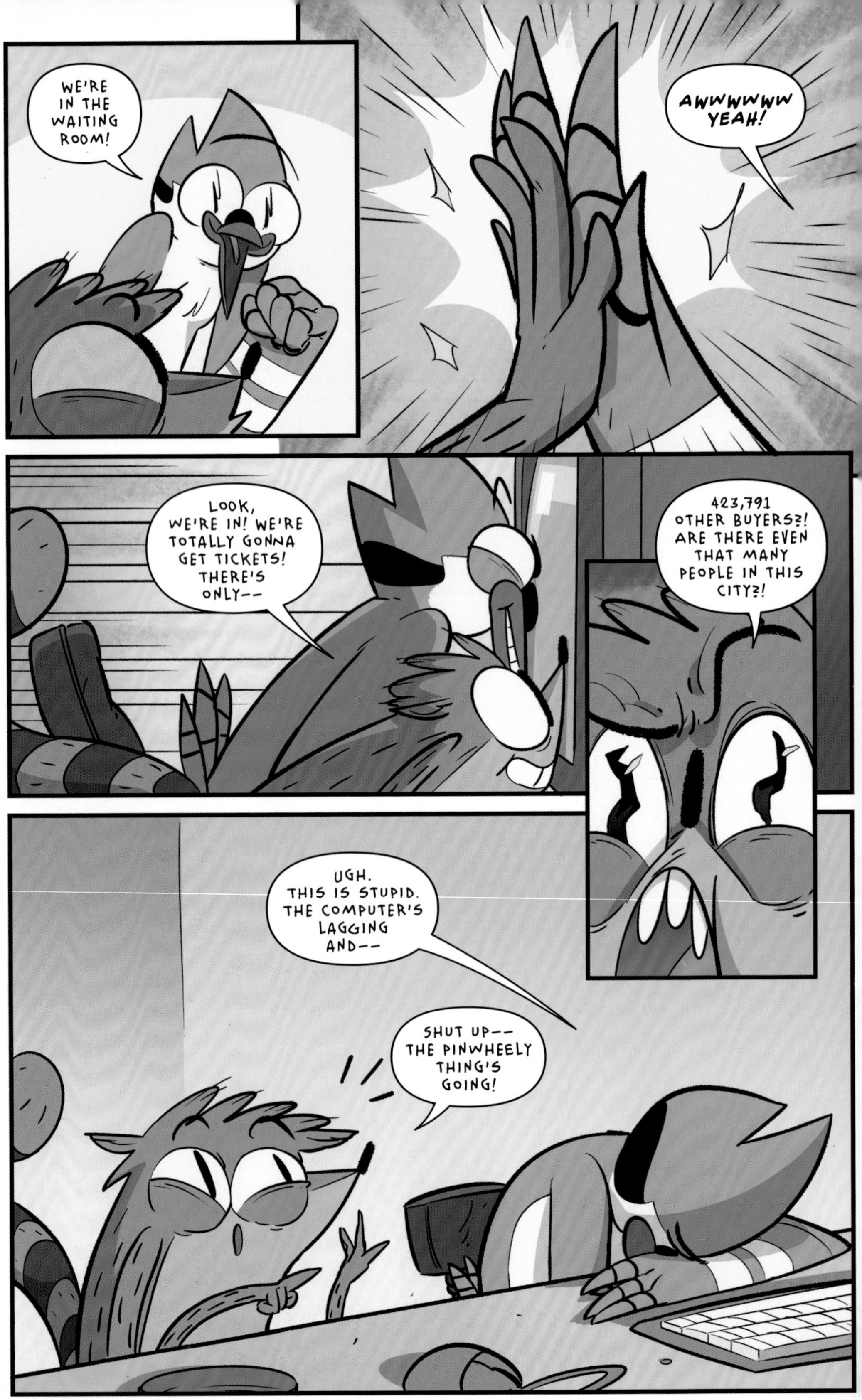
WE'RE IN THE WAITING ROOM!
AWWWWWW YEAH!
LOOK, WE'RE IN! WE'RE TOTALLY GONNA GET TICKETS! THERE'S ONLY--
423,791 OTHER BUYERS?! ARE THERE EVEN THAT MANY PEOPLE IN THIS CITY?!
UGH. THIS IS STUPID. THE COMPUTER'S LAGGING AND--
SHUT UP-- THE PINWHEELY THING'S GOING!

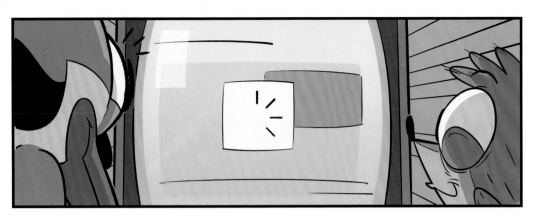

I CAN'T TAKE IT ANYMORE!

NO! YOU'LL LOSE OUR SPOT IN LINE!

IS THERE EVEN A LINE, MORDECAI?! **IS THERE?!**

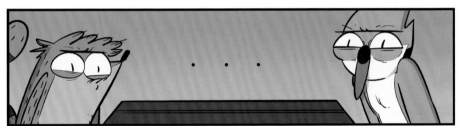

WHAT IF THIS WHOLE THING IS A LIE, AND WE'VE WASTED PRECIOUS HOURS ON HOPE AND DREAMS WE NEVER PHYSICALLY HAD A CHANCE OF REALIZING?

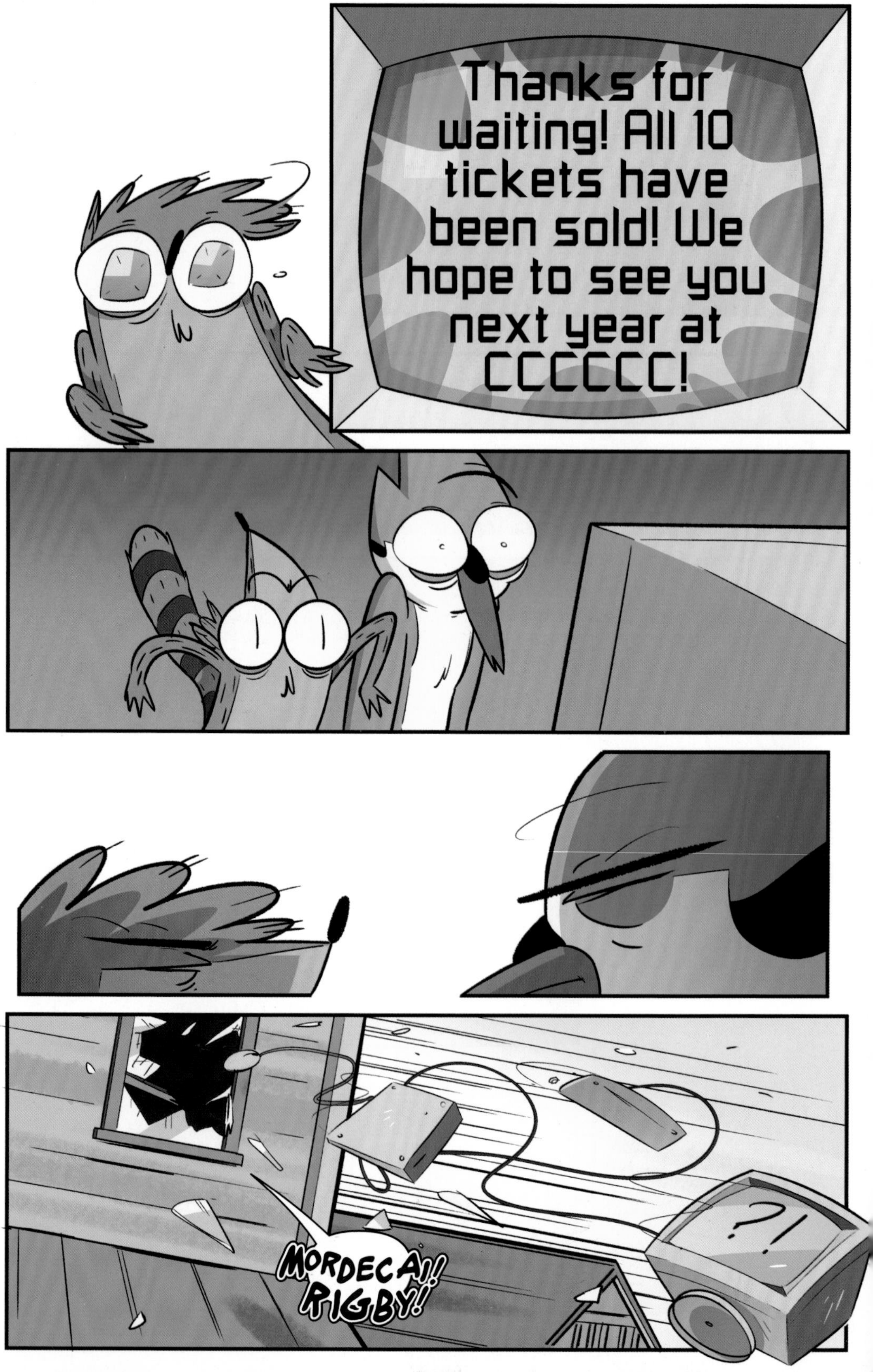
Thanks for waiting! All 10 tickets have been sold! We hope to see you next year at CCCCCC!
?!
MORDECAI!! RIGBY!

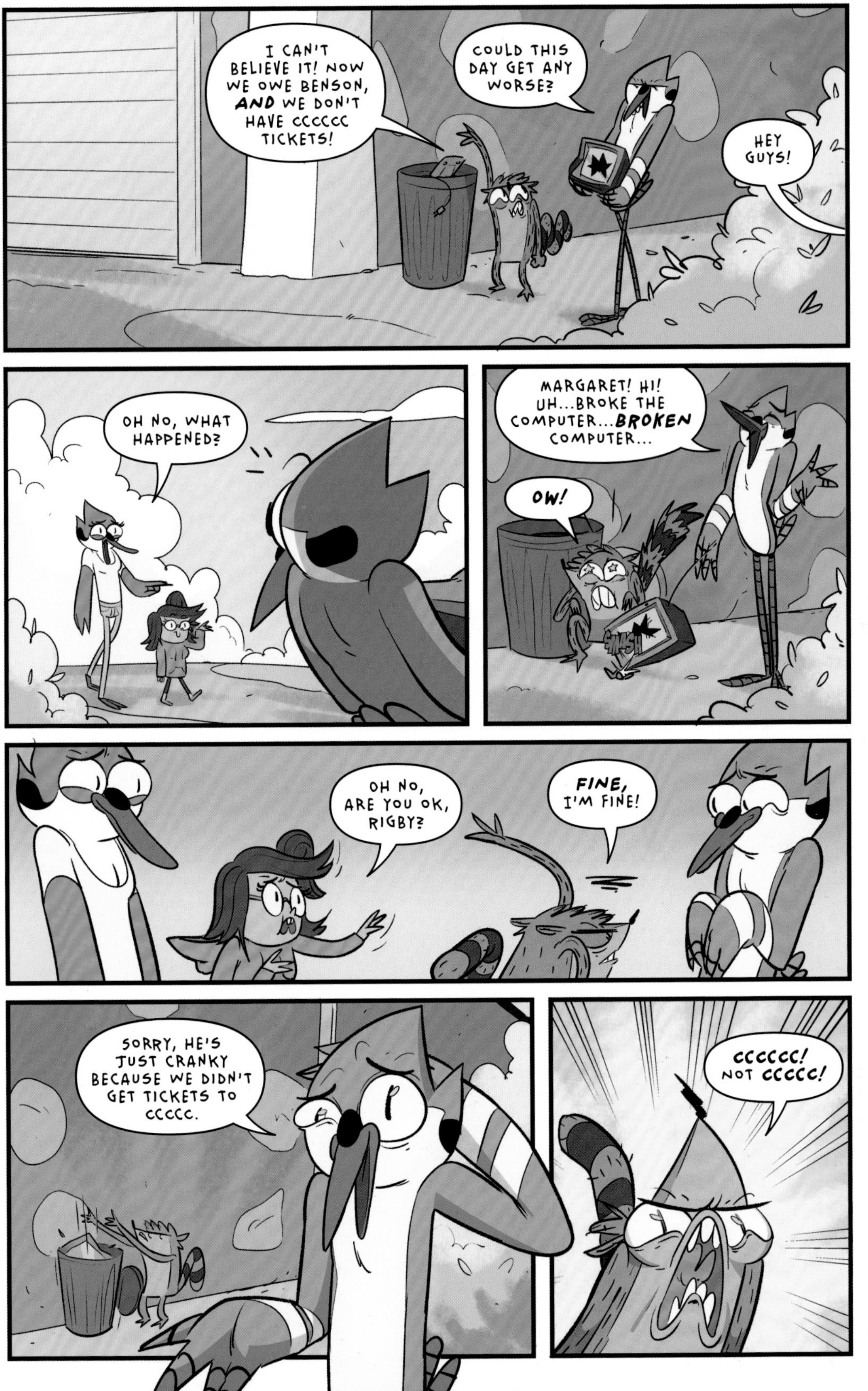
I CAN'T BELIEVE IT! NOW WE OWE BENSON, AND WE DON'T HAVE CCCCCC TICKETS!
COULD THIS DAY GET ANY WORSE?
HEY GUYS!
OH NO, WHAT HAPPENED?
MARGARET! HI! UH...BROKE THE COMPUTER...BROKEN COMPUTER...
OW!
SMASH
OH NO, ARE YOU OK, RIGBY?
FINE, I'M FINE!
SORRY, HE'S JUST CRANKY BECAUSE WE DIDN'T GET TICKETS TO CCCCC.
CCCCCC! NOT CCCCC!

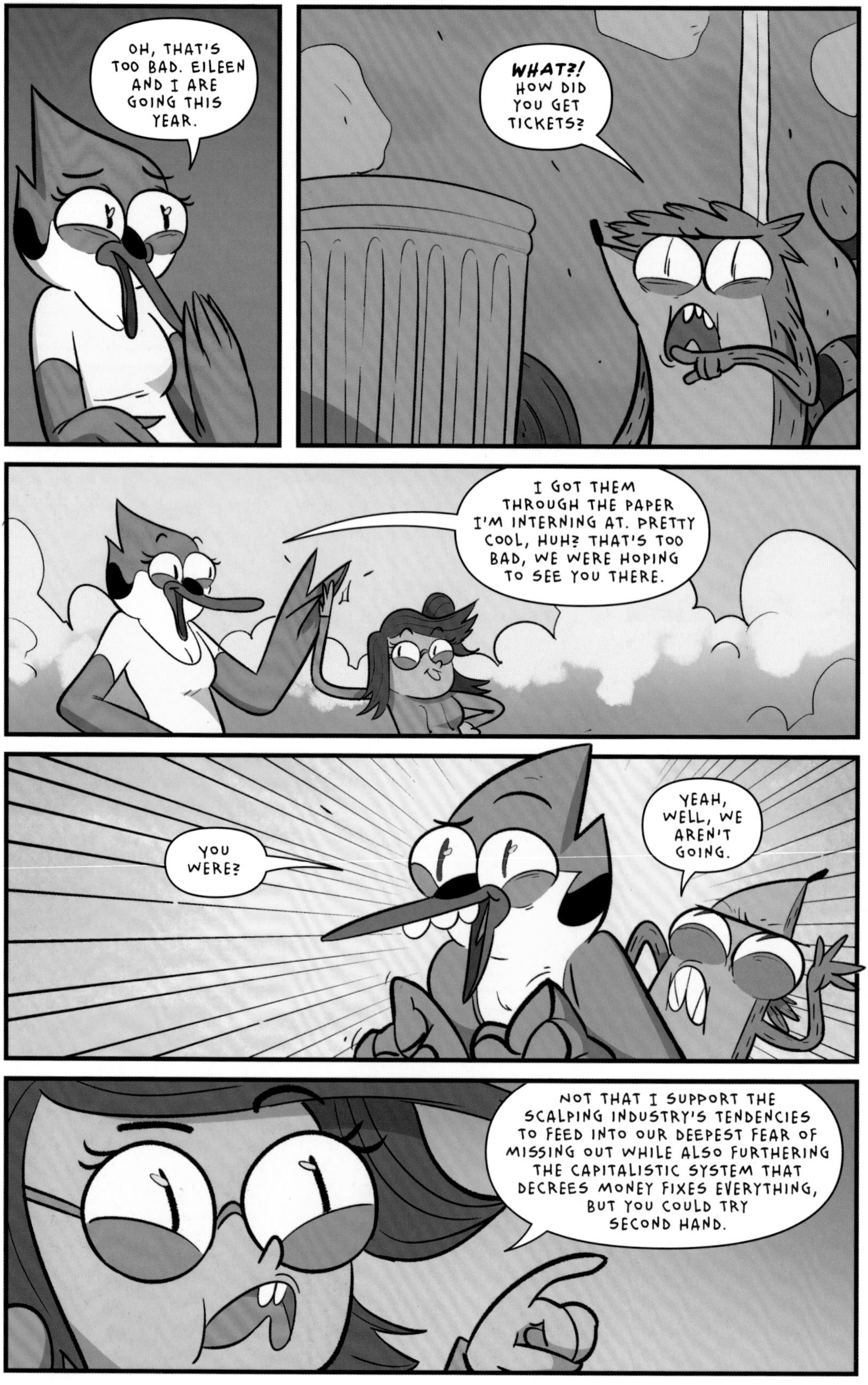
OH, THAT'S TOO BAD. EILEEN AND I ARE GOING THIS YEAR.
WHAT?! HOW DID YOU GET TICKETS?
I GOT THEM THROUGH THE PAPER I'M INTERNING AT. PRETTY COOL, HUH? THAT'S TOO BAD, WE WERE HOPING TO SEE YOU THERE.
YOU WERE?
YEAH, WELL, WE AREN'T GOING.
NOT THAT I SUPPORT THE SCALPING INDUSTRY'S TENDENCIES TO FEED INTO OUR DEEPEST FEAR OF MISSING OUT WHILE ALSO FURTHERING THE CAPITALISTIC SYSTEM THAT DECREES MONEY FIXES EVERYTHING, BUT YOU COULD TRY SECOND HAND.

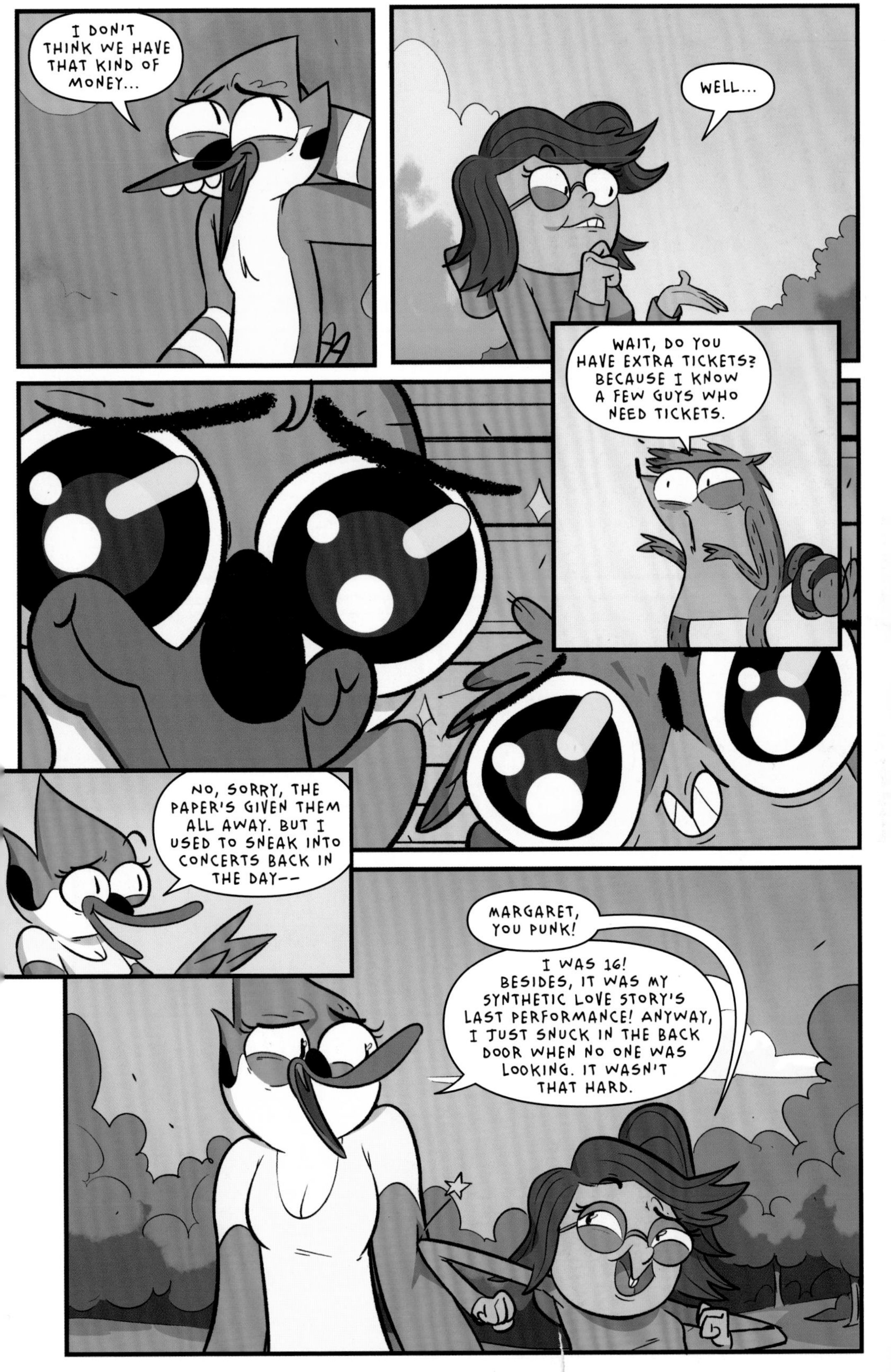
I DON'T THINK WE HAVE THAT KIND OF MONEY...
WELL...
WAIT, DO YOU HAVE EXTRA TICKETS? BECAUSE I KNOW A FEW GUYS WHO NEED TICKETS.
NO, SORRY, THE PAPER'S GIVEN THEM ALL AWAY. BUT I USED TO SNEAK INTO CONCERTS BACK IN THE DAY--
MARGARET, YOU PUNK!
I WAS 16! BESIDES, IT WAS MY SYNTHETIC LOVE STORY'S LAST PERFORMANCE! ANYWAY, I JUST SNUCK IN THE BACK DOOR WHEN NO ONE WAS LOOKING. IT WASN'T THAT HARD.

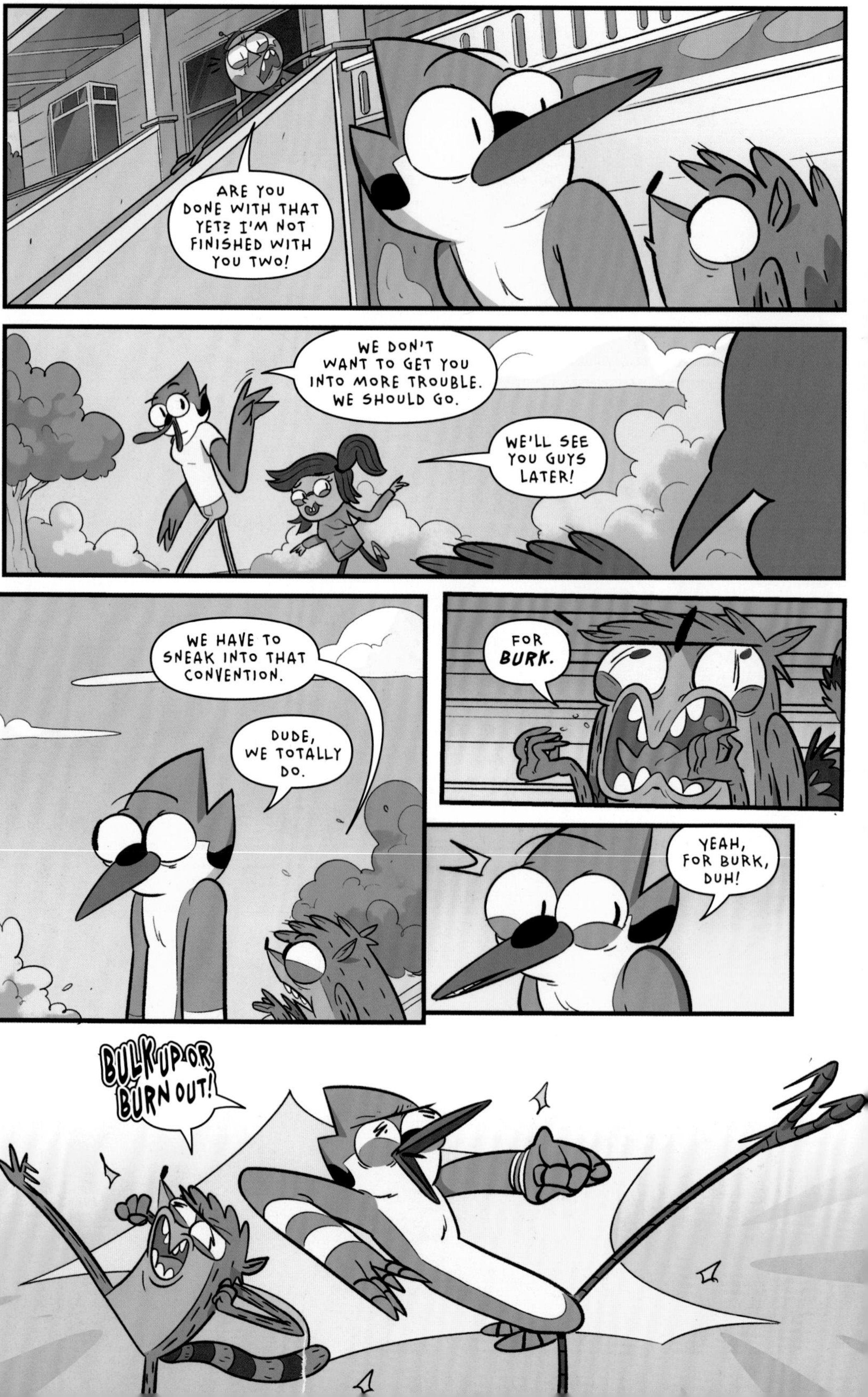
ARE YOU DONE WITH THAT YET? I'M NOT FINISHED WITH YOU TWO!
WE DON'T WANT TO GET YOU INTO MORE TROUBLE. WE SHOULD GO.
WE'LL SEE YOU GUYS LATER!
WE HAVE TO SNEAK INTO THAT CONVENTION.
DUDE, WE TOTALLY DO.
FOR *BURK.*
YEAH, FOR BURK, DUH!
BULK UP OR BURN OUT!

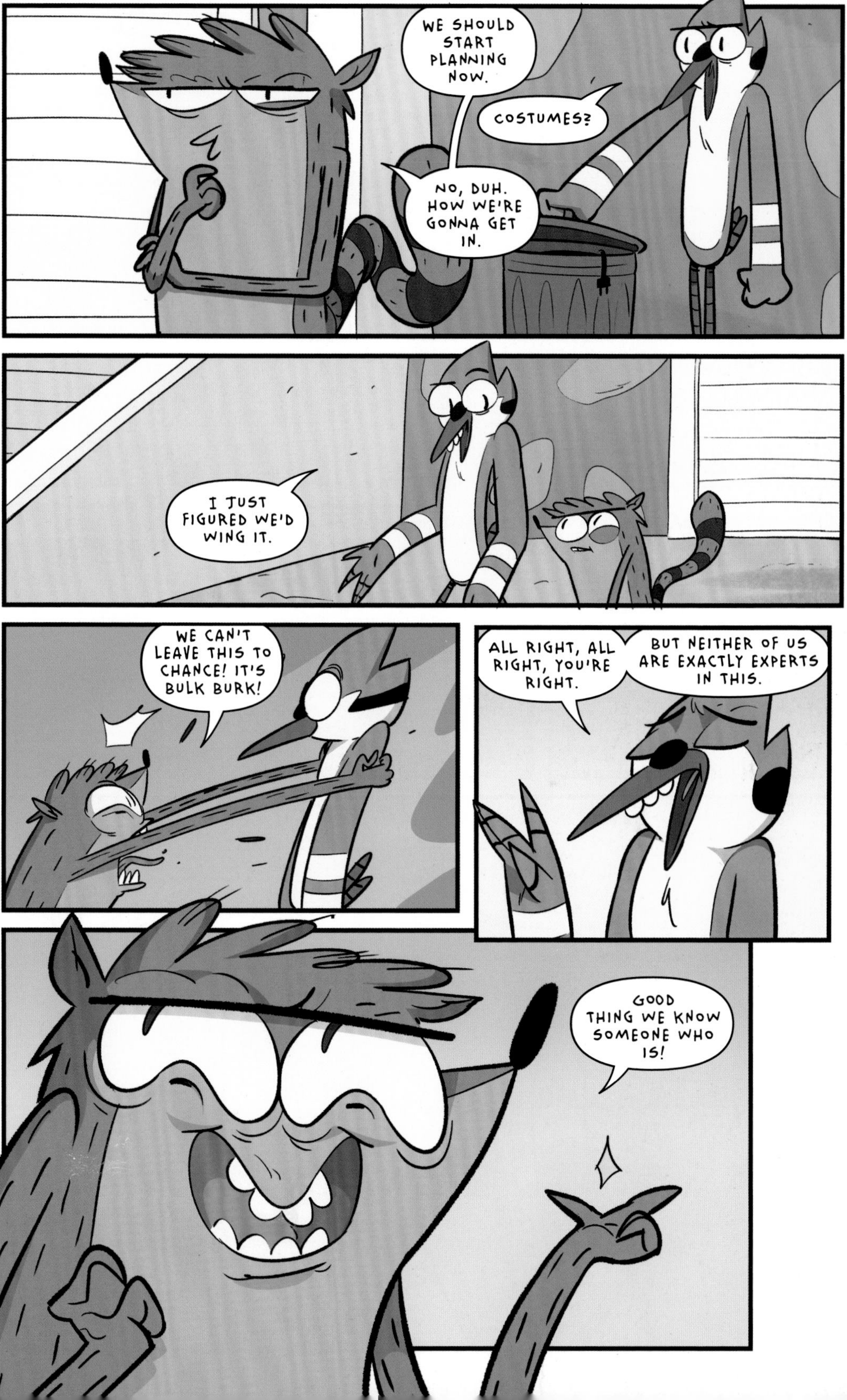
WE SHOULD START PLANNING NOW.
COSTUMES?
NO, DUH. HOW WE'RE GONNA GET IN.
I JUST FIGURED WE'D WING IT.
WE CAN'T LEAVE THIS TO CHANCE! IT'S BULK BURK!
ALL RIGHT, ALL RIGHT, YOU'RE RIGHT.
BUT NEITHER OF US ARE EXACTLY EXPERTS IN THIS.
GOOD THING WE KNOW SOMEONE WHO IS!

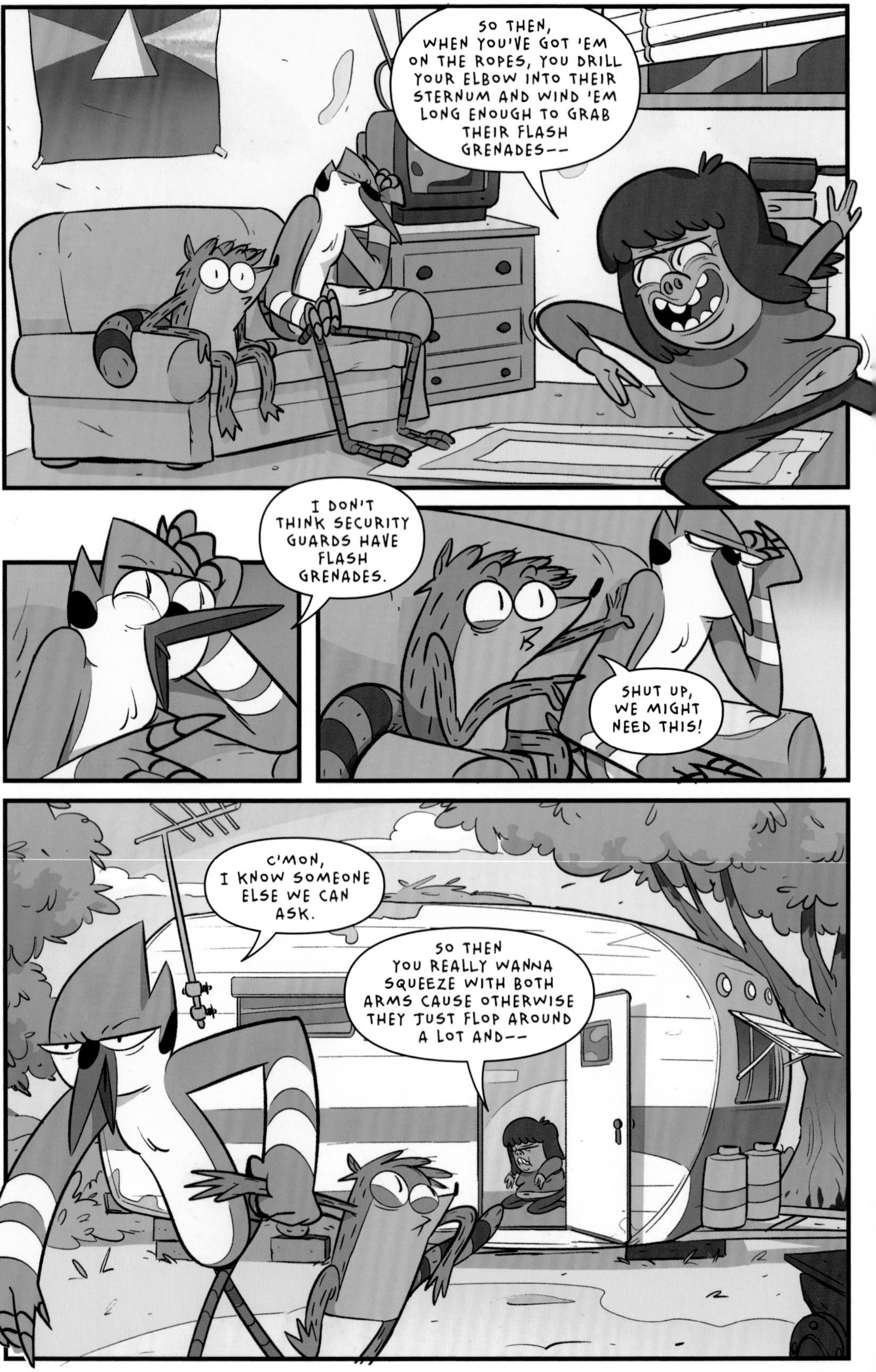
SO THEN, WHEN YOU'VE GOT 'EM ON THE ROPES, YOU DRILL YOUR ELBOW INTO THEIR STERNUM AND WIND 'EM LONG ENOUGH TO GRAB THEIR FLASH GRENADES--
I DON'T THINK SECURITY GUARDS HAVE FLASH GRENADES.
SHUT UP, WE MIGHT NEED THIS!
C'MON, I KNOW SOMEONE ELSE WE CAN ASK.
SO THEN YOU REALLY WANNA SQUEEZE WITH BOTH ARMS CAUSE OTHERWISE THEY JUST FLOP AROUND A LOT AND--

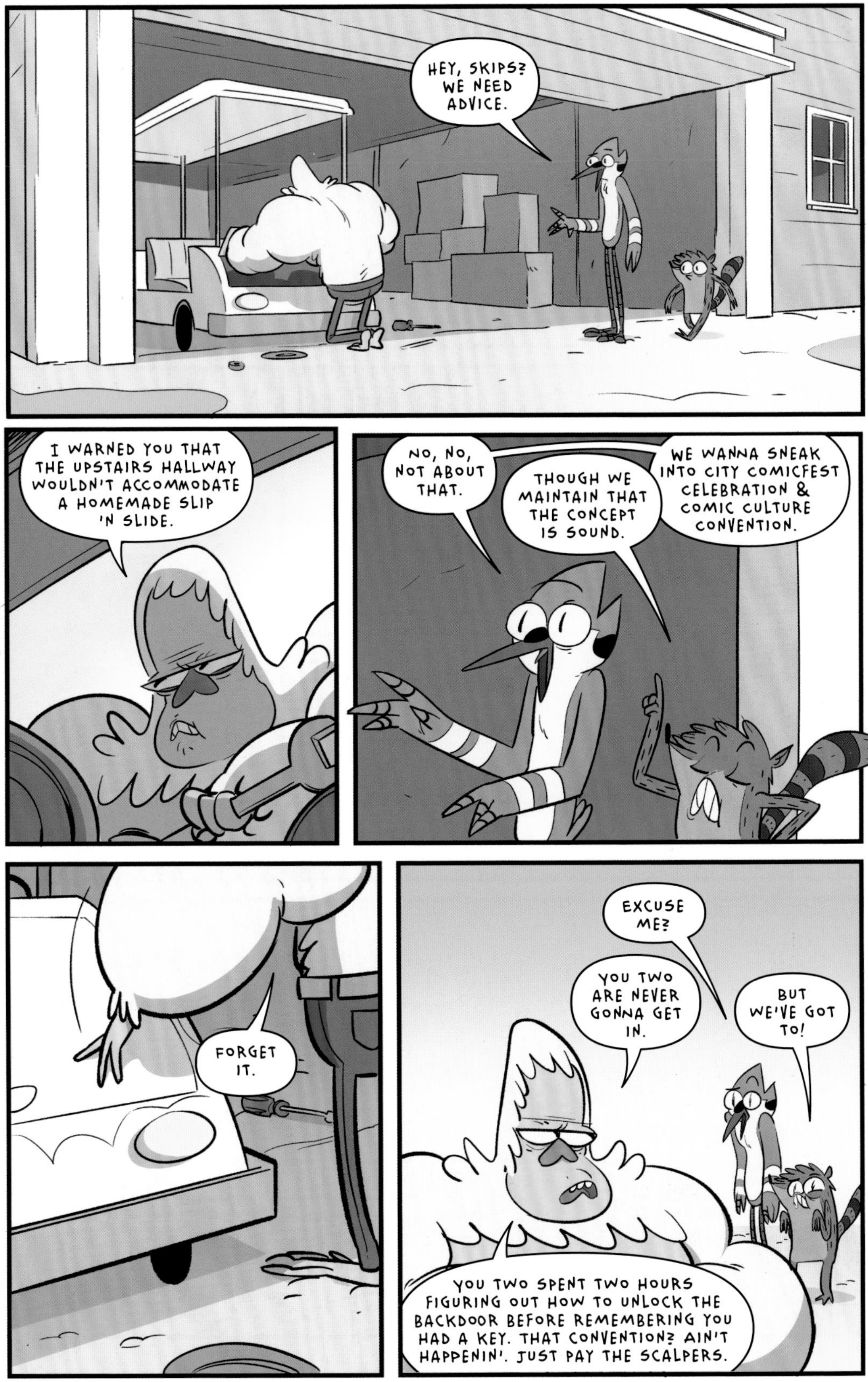

HEY, SKIPS? WE NEED ADVICE.
I WARNED YOU THAT THE UPSTAIRS HALLWAY WOULDN'T ACCOMMODATE A HOMEMADE SLIP 'N SLIDE.
NO, NO, NOT ABOUT THAT.
THOUGH WE MAINTAIN THAT THE CONCEPT IS SOUND.
WE WANNA SNEAK INTO CITY COMICFEST CELEBRATION & COMIC CULTURE CONVENTION.
FORGET IT.
EXCUSE ME?
BUT WE'VE GOT TO!
YOU TWO ARE NEVER GONNA GET IN.
YOU TWO SPENT TWO HOURS FIGURING OUT HOW TO UNLOCK THE BACKDOOR BEFORE REMEMBERING YOU HAD A KEY. THAT CONVENTION? AIN'T HAPPENIN'. JUST PAY THE SCALPERS.

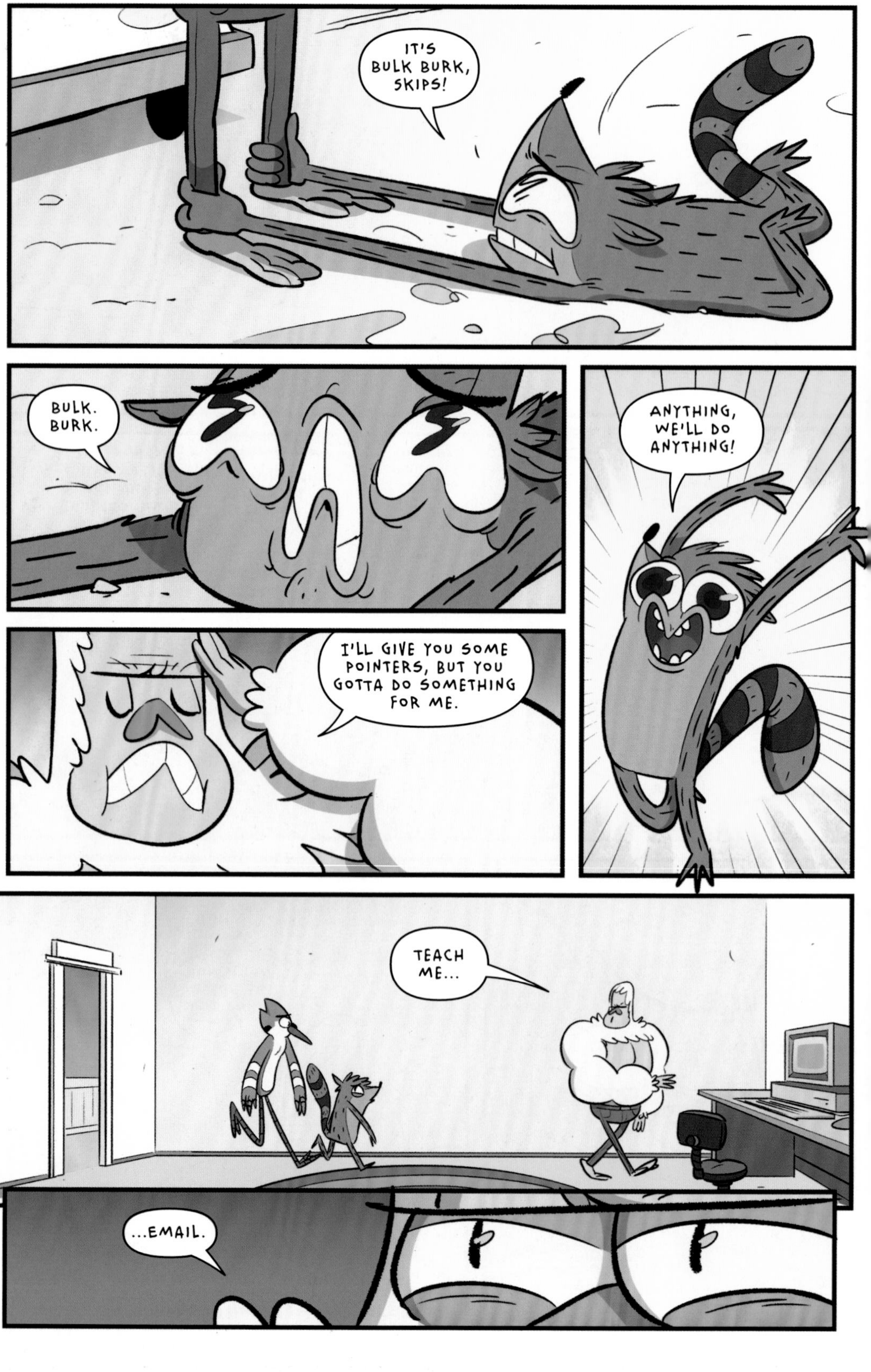
IT'S BULK BURK, SKIPS!
BULK. BURK.
ANYTHING, WE'LL DO ANYTHING!
I'LL GIVE YOU SOME POINTERS, BUT YOU GOTTA DO SOMETHING FOR ME.
TEACH ME...
...EMAIL.

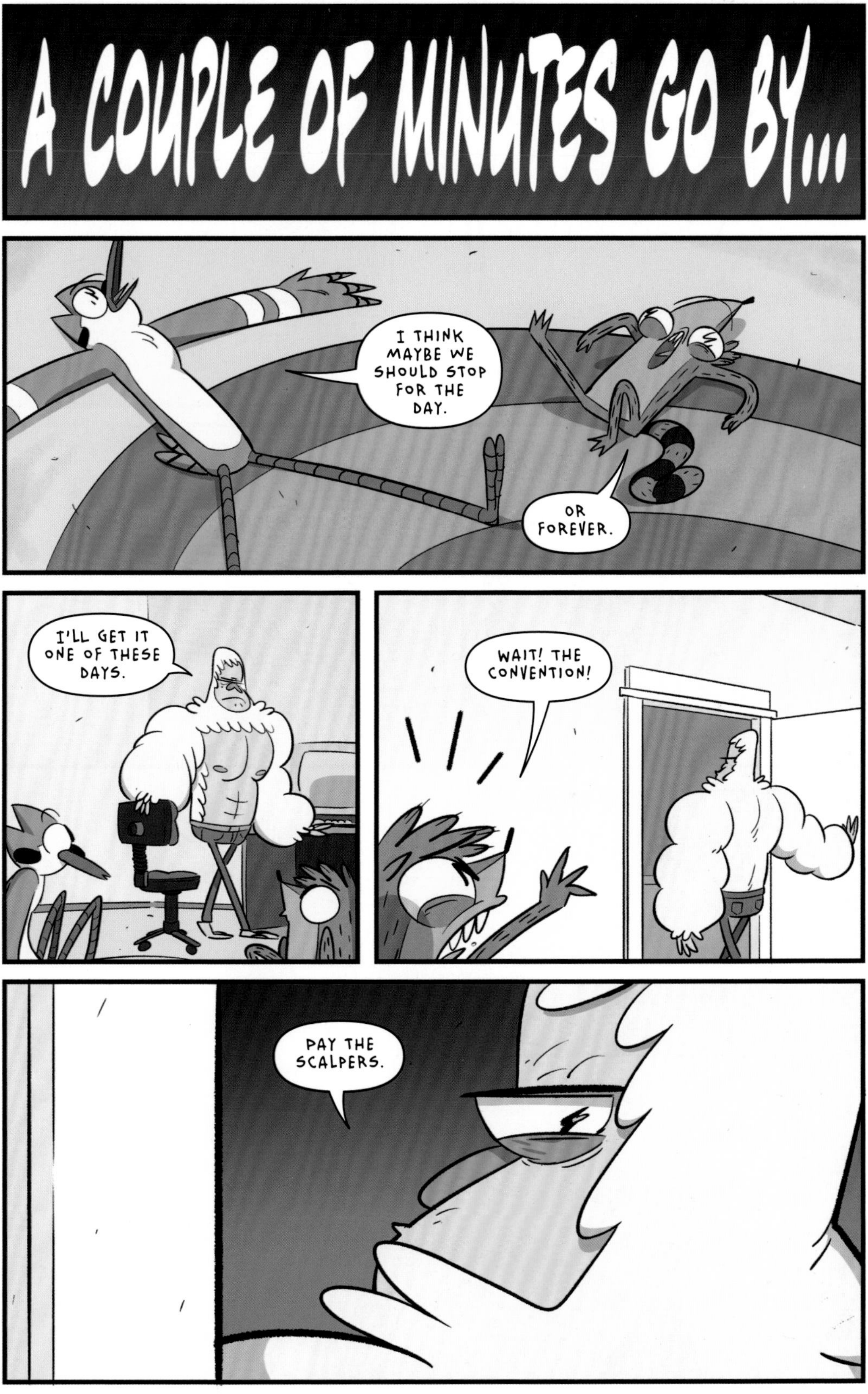
A COUPLE OF MINUTES GO BY...
I THINK MAYBE WE SHOULD STOP FOR THE DAY.
OR FOREVER.
I'LL GET IT ONE OF THESE DAYS.
WAIT! THE CONVENTION!
PAY THE SCALPERS.

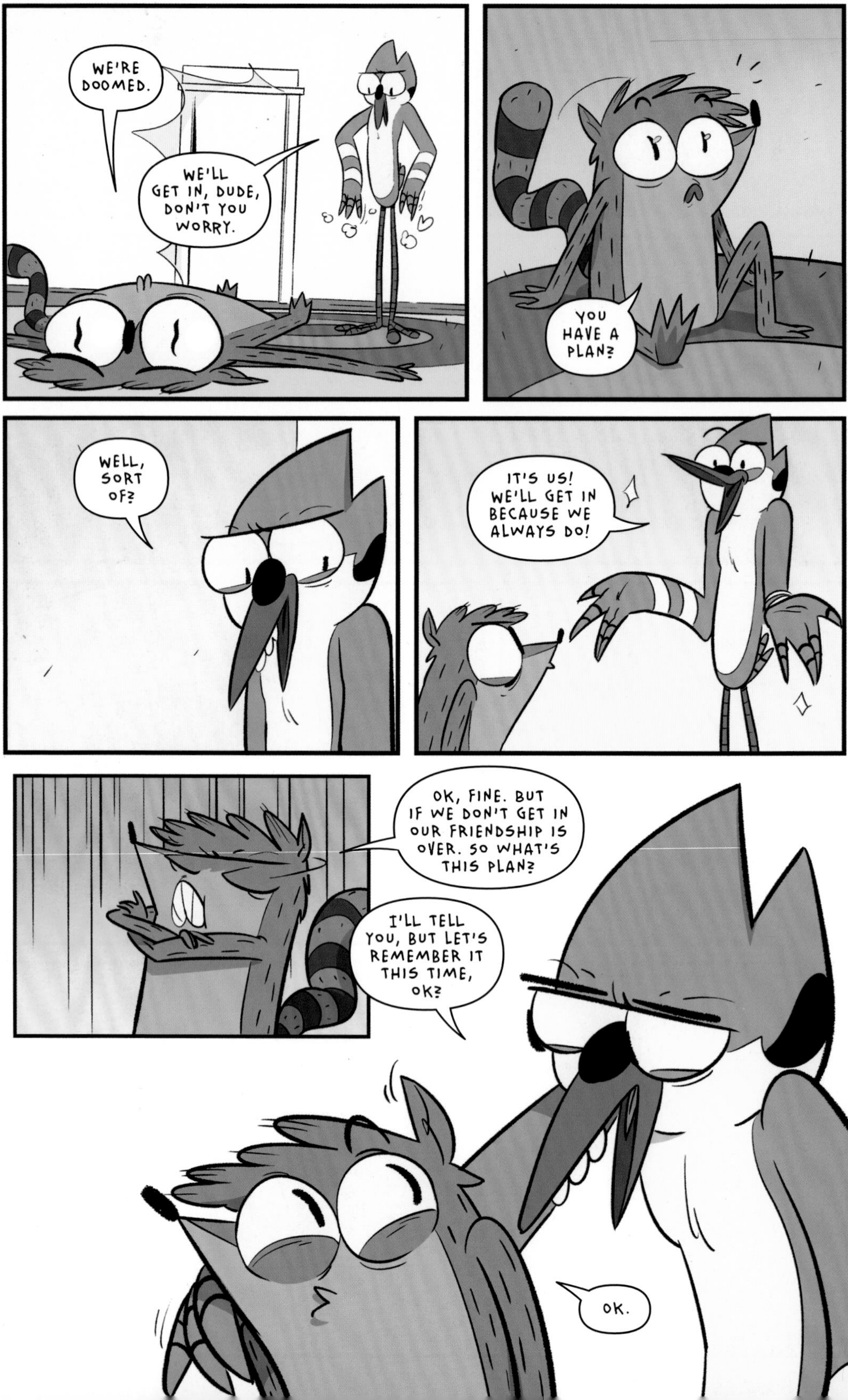
WE'RE DOOMED.
WE'LL GET IN, DUDE, DON'T YOU WORRY.
YOU HAVE A PLAN?
WELL, SORT OF?
IT'S US! WE'LL GET IN BECAUSE WE ALWAYS DO!
OK, FINE. BUT IF WE DON'T GET IN OUR FRIENDSHIP IS OVER. SO WHAT'S THIS PLAN?
I'LL TELL YOU, BUT LET'S REMEMBER IT THIS TIME, OK?
OK.

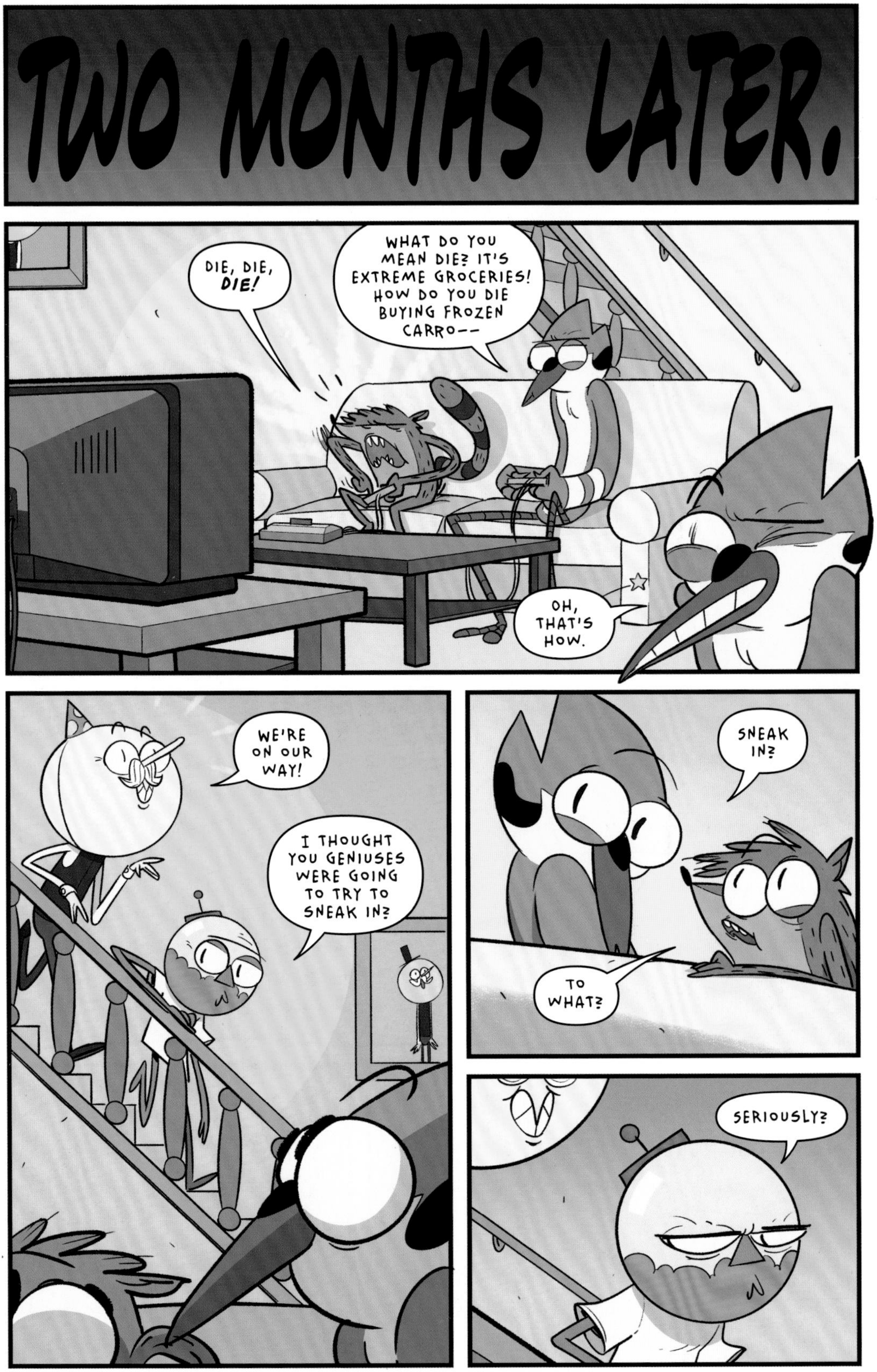
TWO MONTHS LATER.
DIE, DIE, DIE!
WHAT DO YOU MEAN DIE? IT'S EXTREME GROCERIES! HOW DO YOU DIE BUYING FROZEN CARRO--
OH, THAT'S HOW.
WE'RE ON OUR WAY!
I THOUGHT YOU GENIUSES WERE GOING TO TRY TO SNEAK IN?
SNEAK IN?
TO WHAT?
SERIOUSLY?

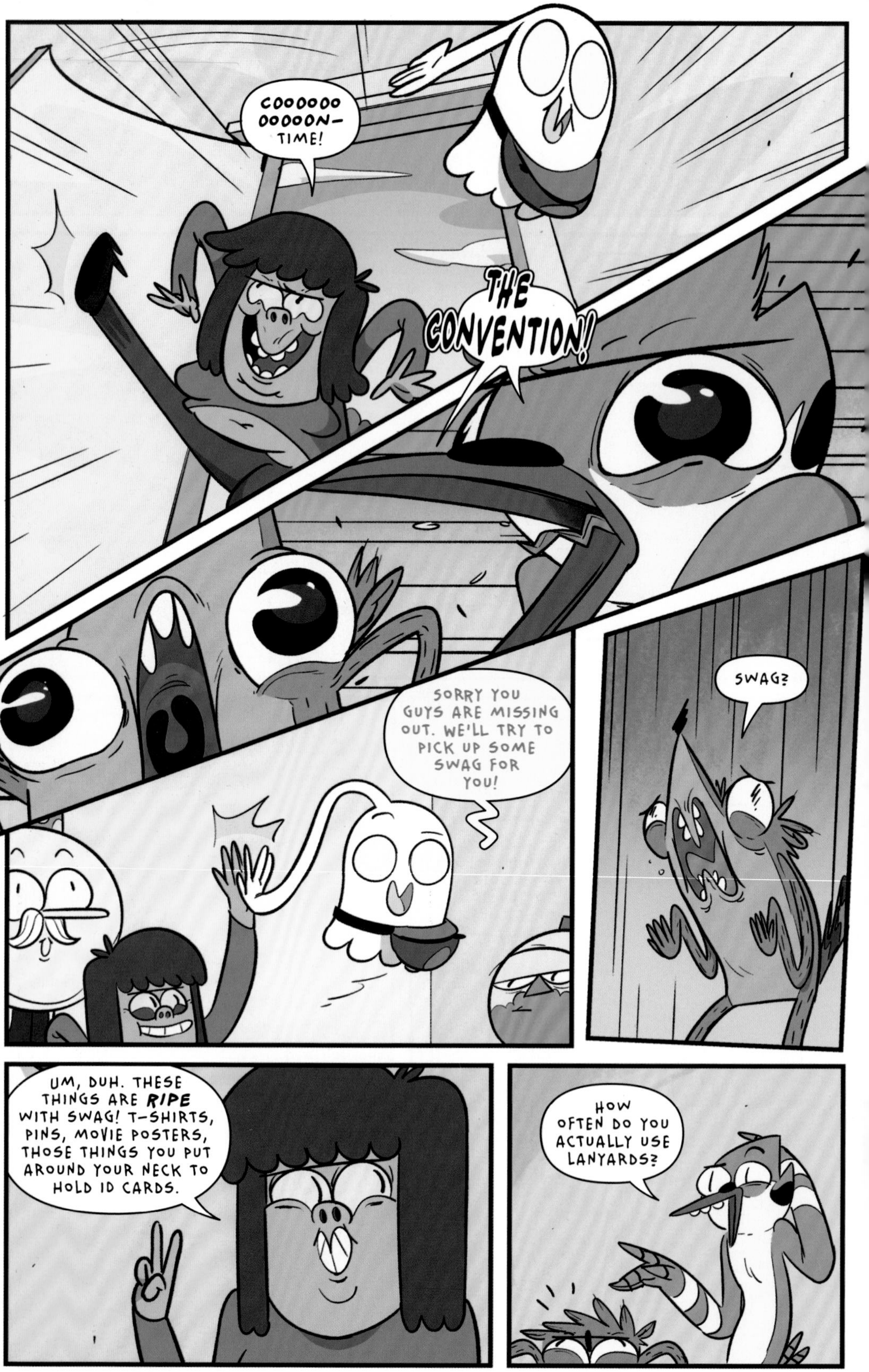
COOOOOO OOOOON-TIME!
THE CONVENTION!
SORRY YOU GUYS ARE MISSING OUT. WE'LL TRY TO PICK UP SOME SWAG FOR YOU!
SWAG?
UM, DUH. THESE THINGS ARE RIPE WITH SWAG! T-SHIRTS, PINS, MOVIE POSTERS, THOSE THINGS YOU PUT AROUND YOUR NECK TO HOLD ID CARDS.
HOW OFTEN DO YOU ACTUALLY USE LANYARDS?

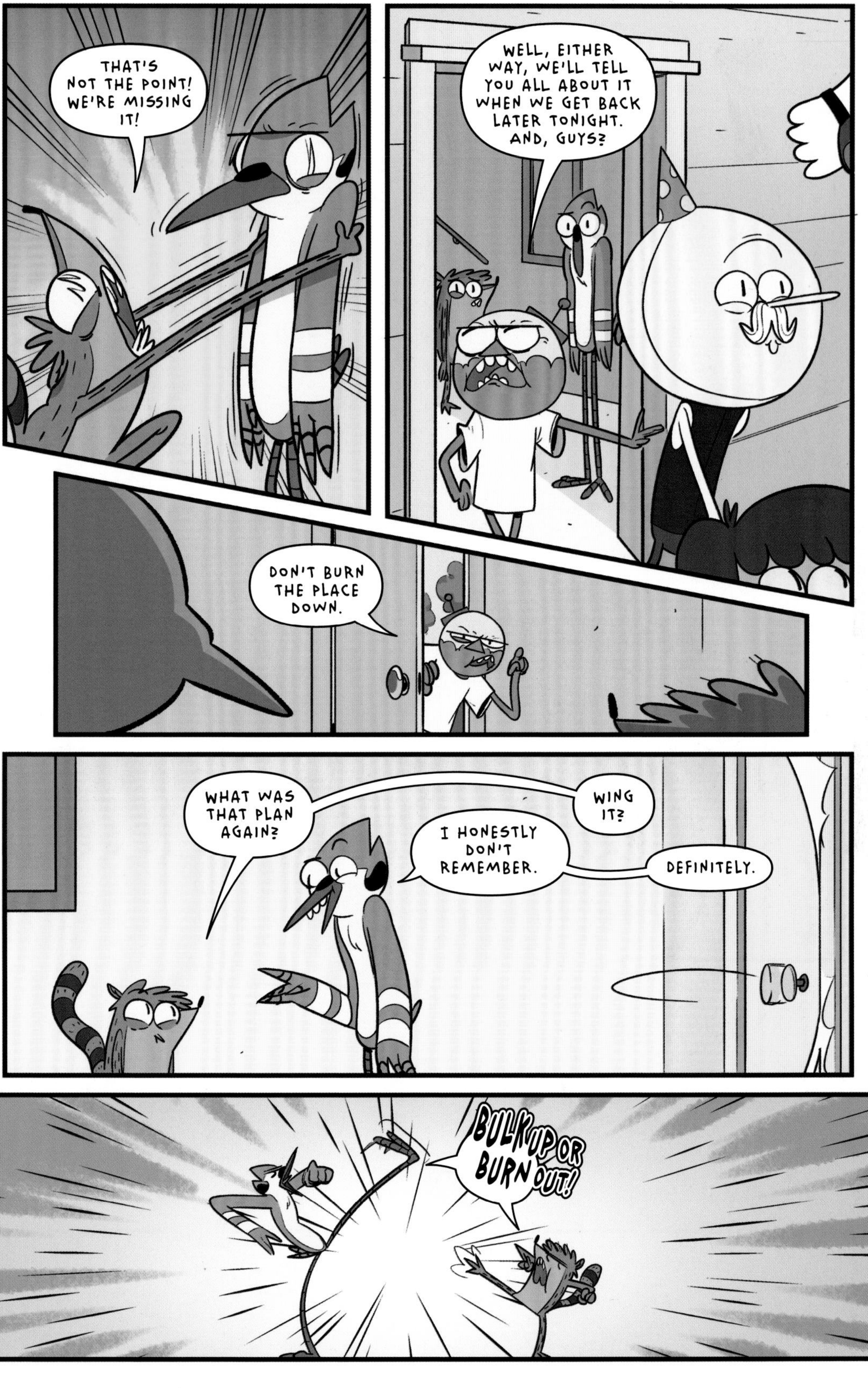
THAT'S NOT THE POINT! WE'RE MISSING IT!
WELL, EITHER WAY, WE'LL TELL YOU ALL ABOUT IT WHEN WE GET BACK LATER TONIGHT. AND, GUYS?
DON'T BURN THE PLACE DOWN.
WHAT WAS THAT PLAN AGAIN?
WING IT?
I HONESTLY DON'T REMEMBER.
DEFINITELY.
BULK UP OR BURN OUT!

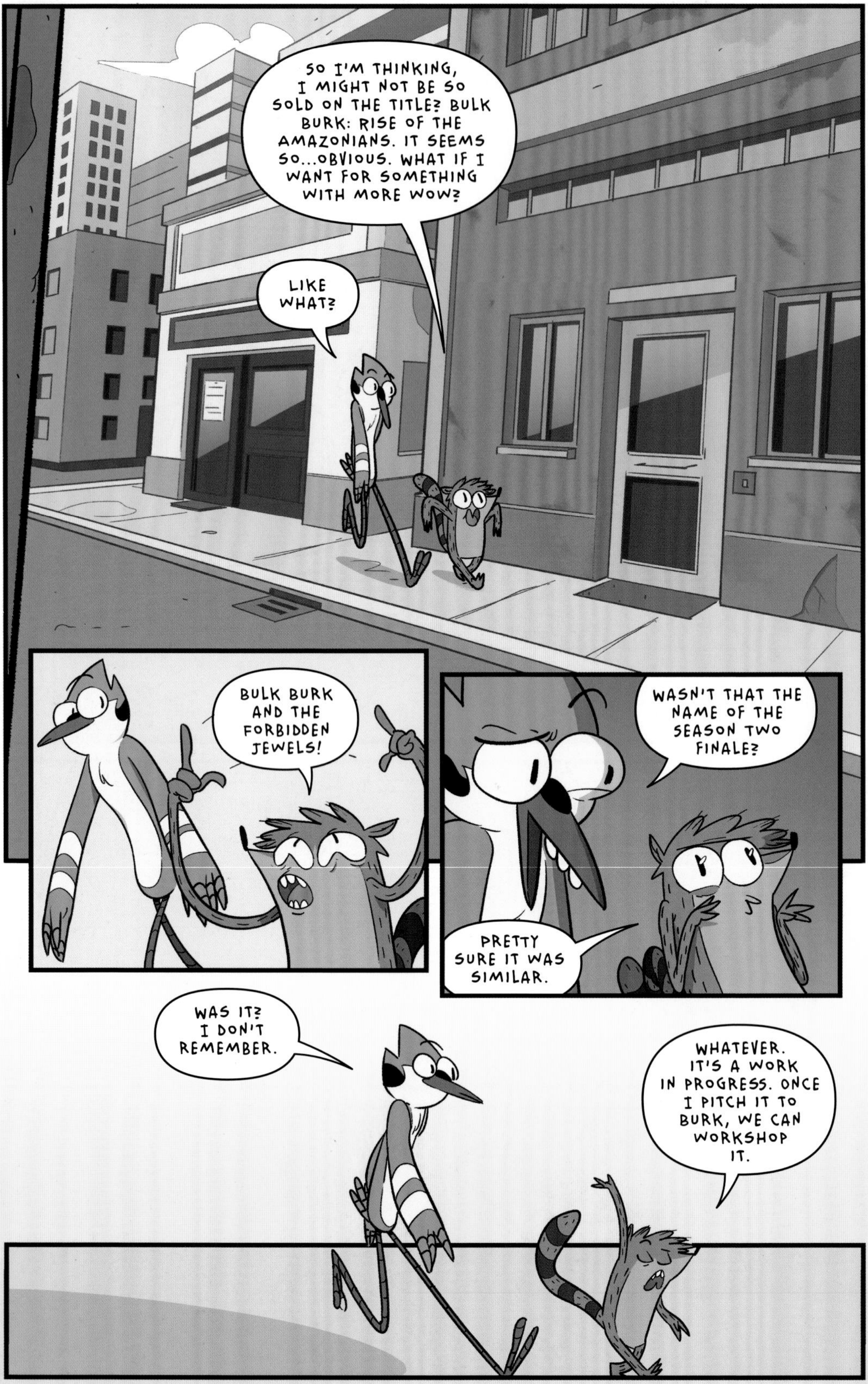

SO I'M THINKING, I MIGHT NOT BE SO SOLD ON THE TITLE? BULK BURK: RISE OF THE AMAZONIANS. IT SEEMS SO...OBVIOUS. WHAT IF I WANT FOR SOMETHING WITH MORE WOW?
LIKE WHAT?
BULK BURK AND THE FORBIDDEN JEWELS!
WASN'T THAT THE NAME OF THE SEASON TWO FINALE?
PRETTY SURE IT WAS SIMILAR.
WAS IT? I DON'T REMEMBER.
WHATEVER. IT'S A WORK IN PROGRESS. ONCE I PITCH IT TO BURK, WE CAN WORKSHOP IT.

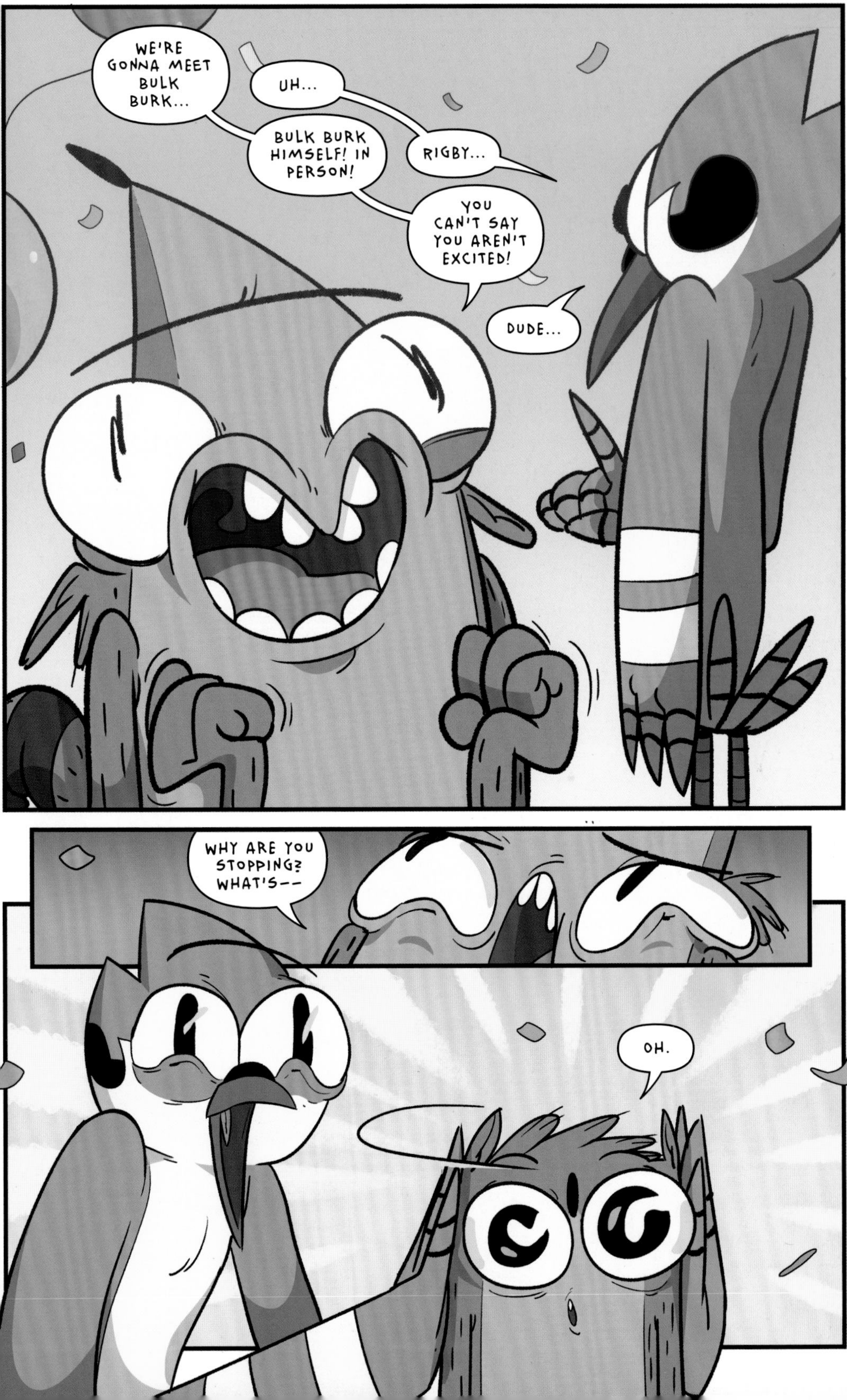
WE'RE GONNA MEET BULK BURK...
UH...
BULK BURK HIMSELF! IN PERSON!
RIGBY...
YOU CAN'T SAY YOU AREN'T EXCITED!
DUDE...
WHY ARE YOU STOPPING? WHAT'S--
OH.

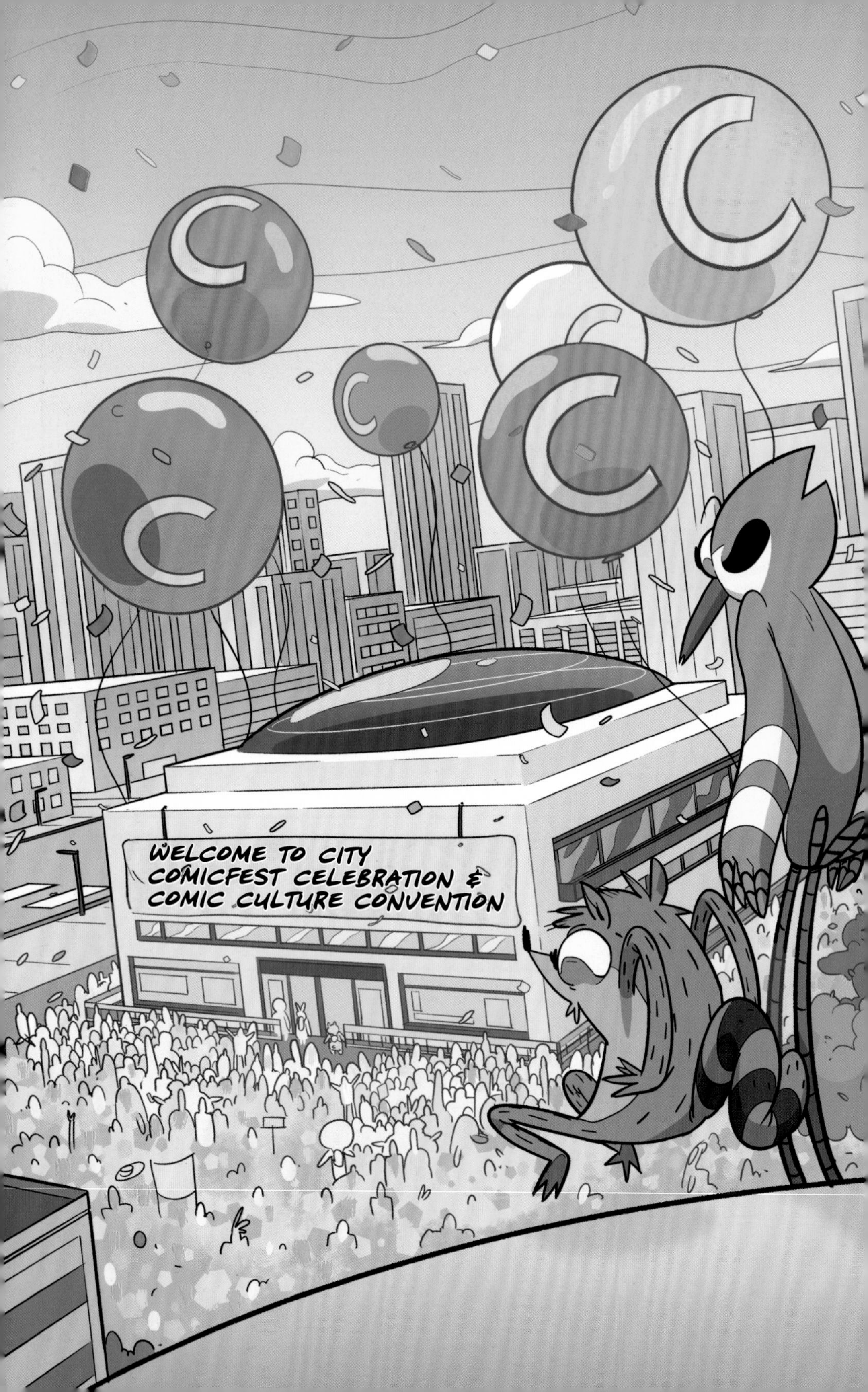
WELCOME TO CITY
COMICFEST CELEBRATION &
COMIC CULTURE CONVENTION

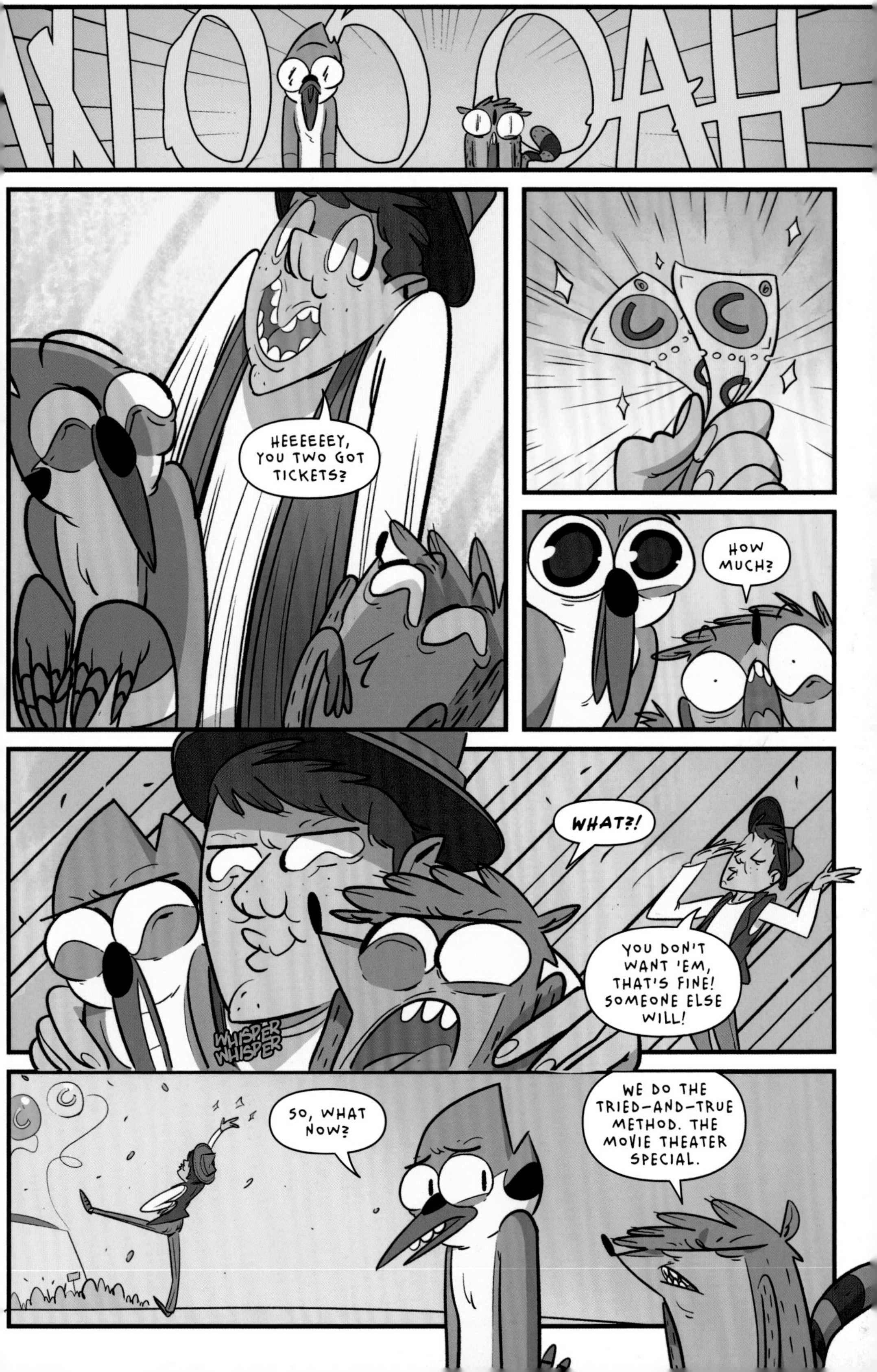
WHOOOAH!
HEEEEEEY, YOU TWO GOT TICKETS?
HOW MUCH?
WHAT?!
YOU DON'T WANT 'EM, THAT'S FINE! SOMEONE ELSE WILL!
WHISPER WHISPER
SO, WHAT NOW?
WE DO THE TRIED-AND-TRUE METHOD. THE MOVIE THEATER SPECIAL.

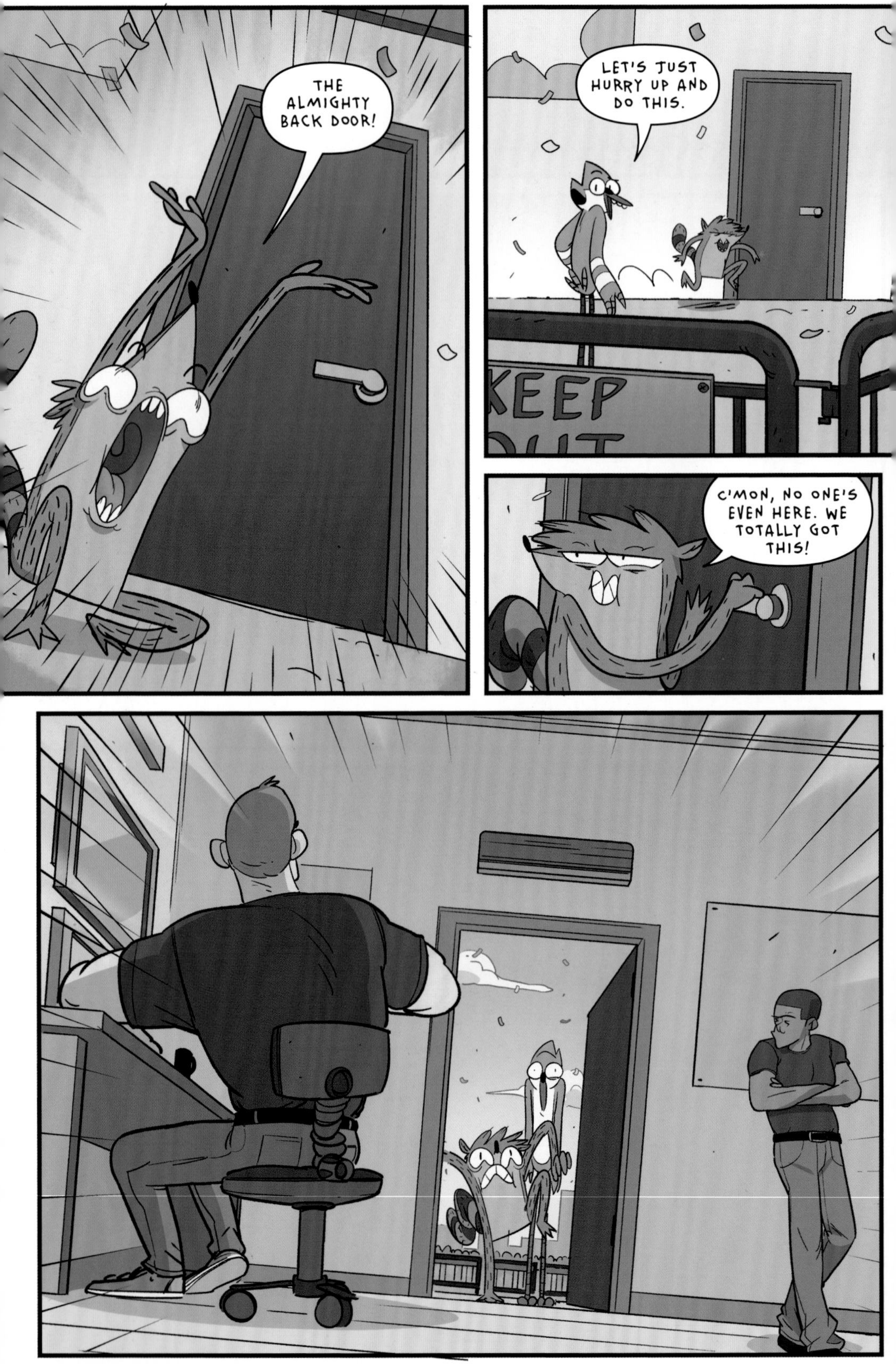
THE ALMIGHTY BACK DOOR!
LET'S JUST HURRY UP AND DO THIS.
KEEP
C'MON, NO ONE'S EVEN HERE. WE TOTALLY GOT THIS!

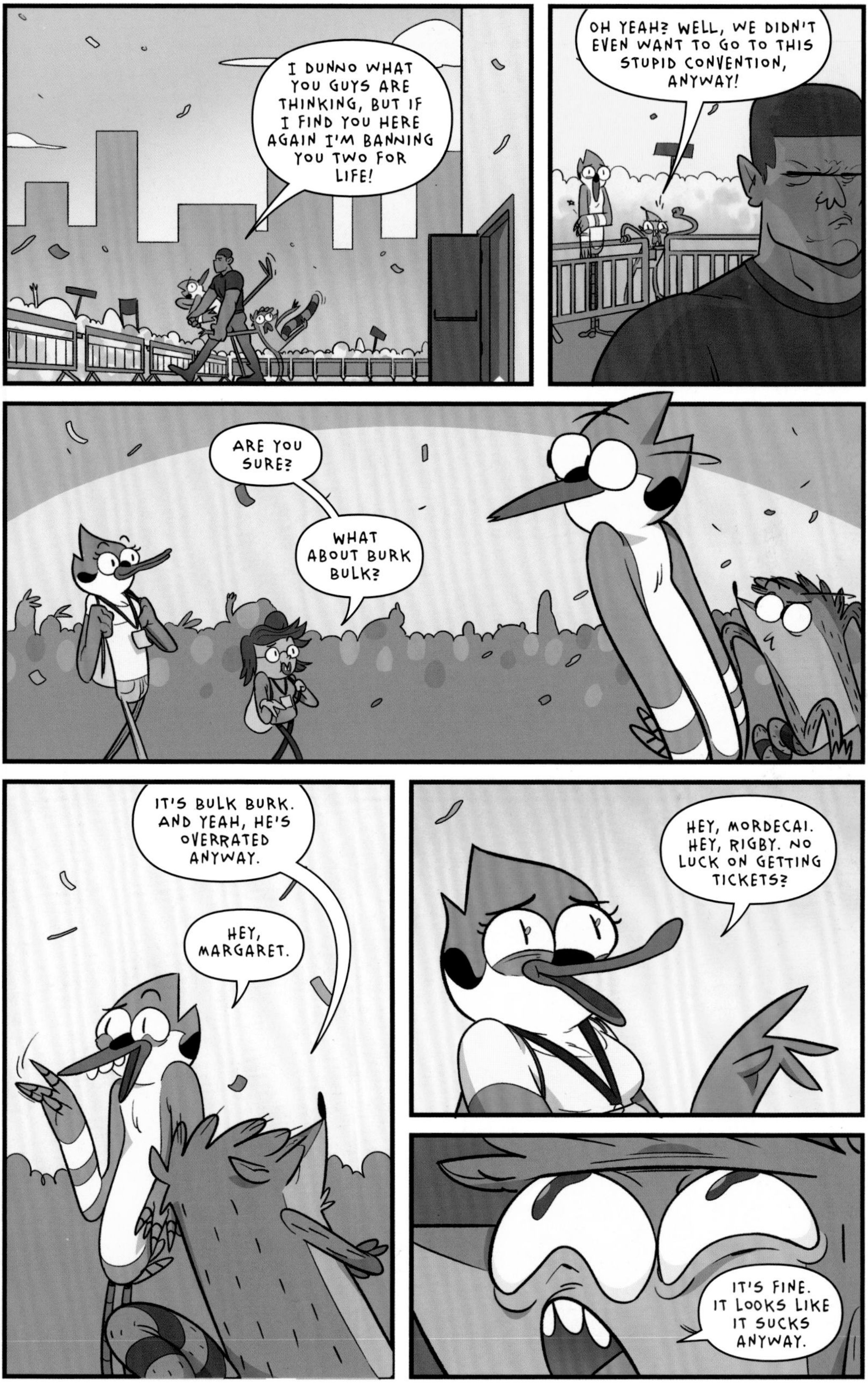
I DUNNO WHAT YOU GUYS ARE THINKING, BUT IF I FIND YOU HERE AGAIN I'M BANNING YOU TWO FOR LIFE!
OH YEAH? WELL, WE DIDN'T EVEN WANT TO GO TO THIS STUPID CONVENTION, ANYWAY!
ARE YOU SURE?
WHAT ABOUT BURK BULK?
IT'S BULK BURK. AND YEAH, HE'S OVERRATED ANYWAY.
HEY, MARGARET.
HEY, MORDECAI. HEY, RIGBY. NO LUCK ON GETTING TICKETS?
IT'S FINE. IT LOOKS LIKE IT SUCKS ANYWAY.

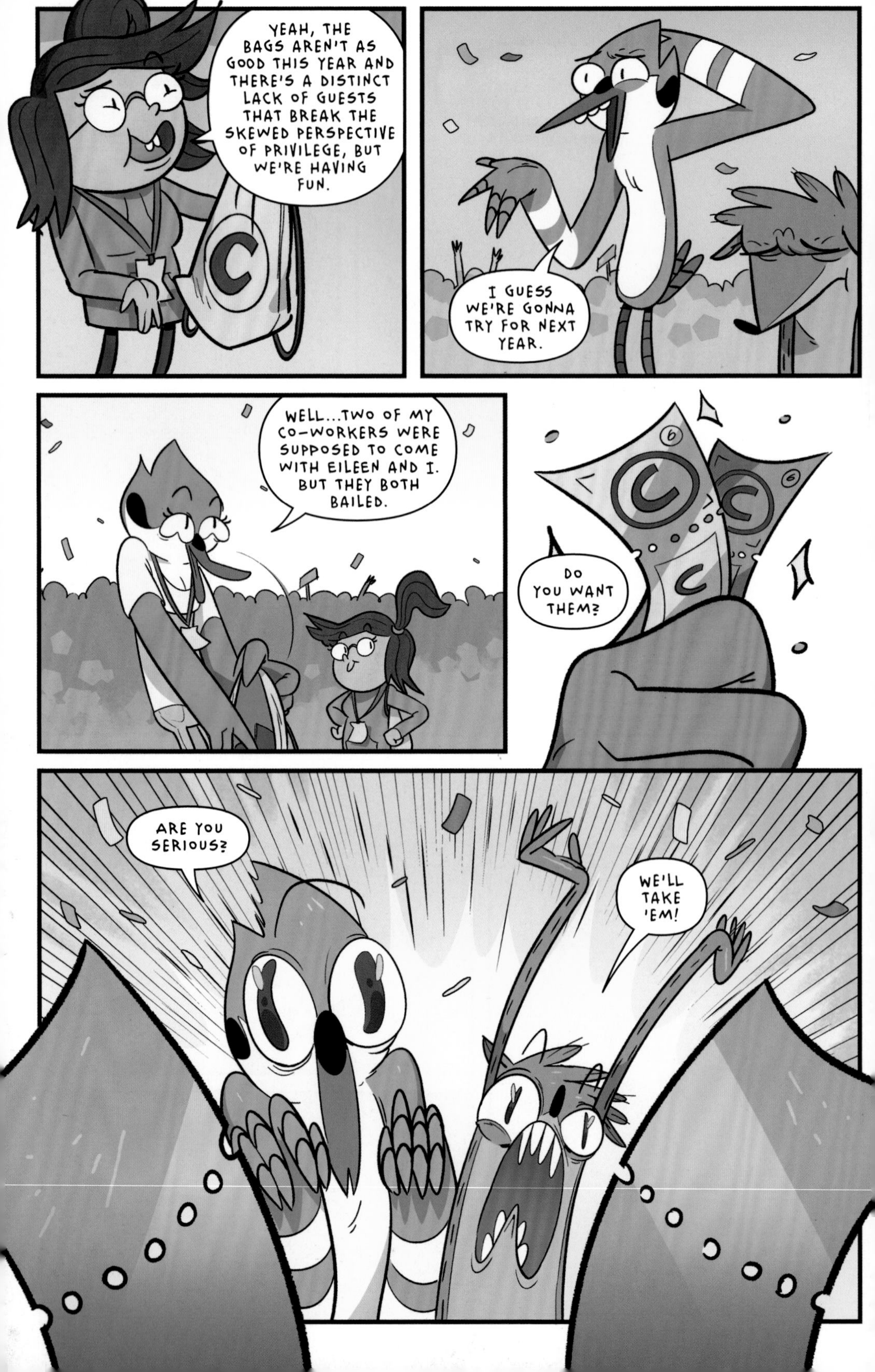
YEAH, THE BAGS AREN'T AS GOOD THIS YEAR AND THERE'S A DISTINCT LACK OF GUESTS THAT BREAK THE SKEWED PERSPECTIVE OF PRIVILEGE, BUT WE'RE HAVING FUN.
I GUESS WE'RE GONNA TRY FOR NEXT YEAR.
WELL...TWO OF MY CO-WORKERS WERE SUPPOSED TO COME WITH EILEEN AND I. BUT THEY BOTH BAILED.
DO YOU WANT THEM?
ARE YOU SERIOUS?
WE'LL TAKE 'EM!

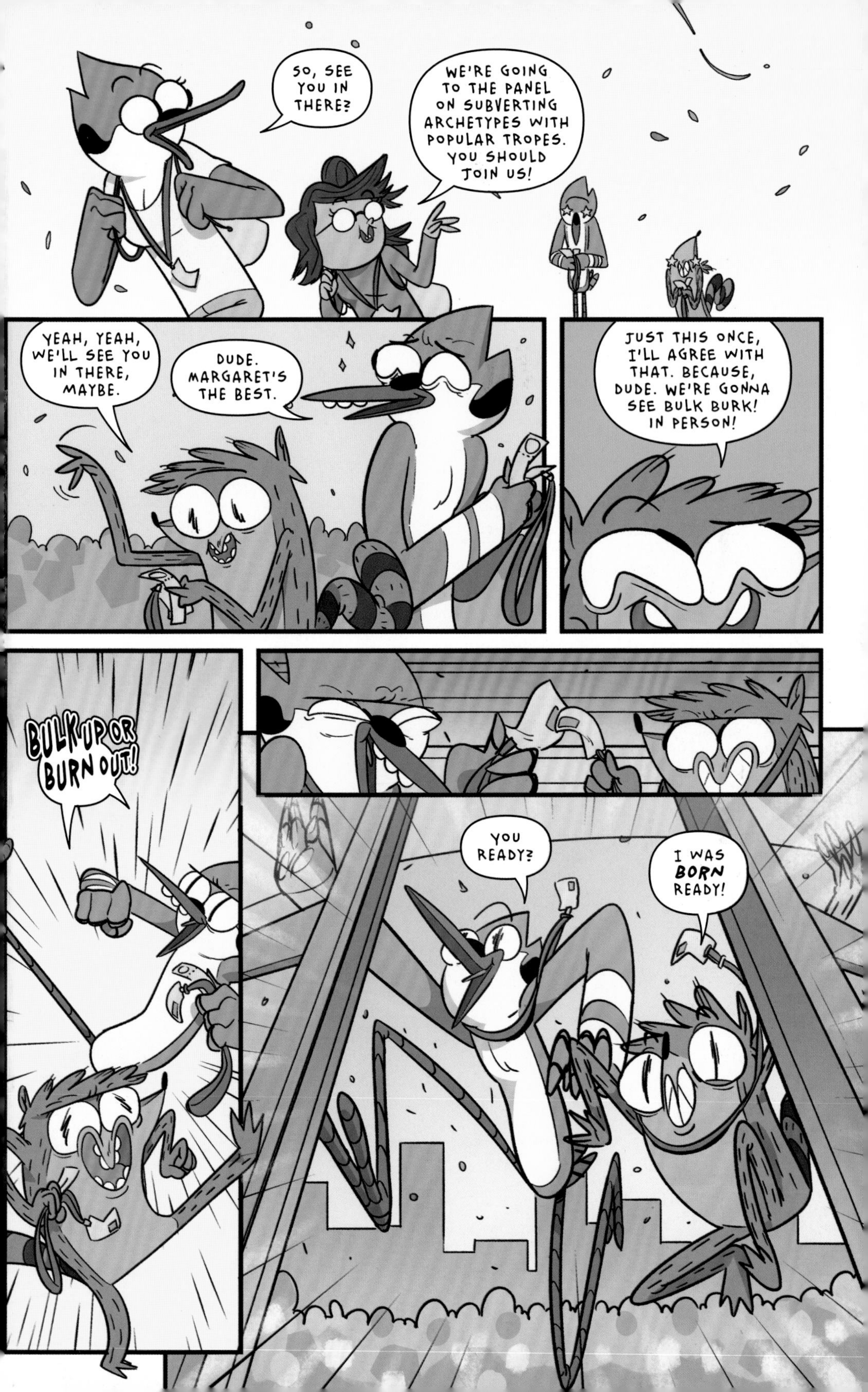
SO, SEE YOU IN THERE?
WE'RE GOING TO THE PANEL ON SUBVERTING ARCHETYPES WITH POPULAR TROPES. YOU SHOULD JOIN US!
YEAH, YEAH, WE'LL SEE YOU IN THERE, MAYBE.
DUDE. MARGARET'S THE BEST.
JUST THIS ONCE, I'LL AGREE WITH THAT. BECAUSE, DUDE. WE'RE GONNA SEE BULK BURK! IN PERSON!
BULK UP OR BURN OUT!
YOU READY?
I WAS BORN READY!

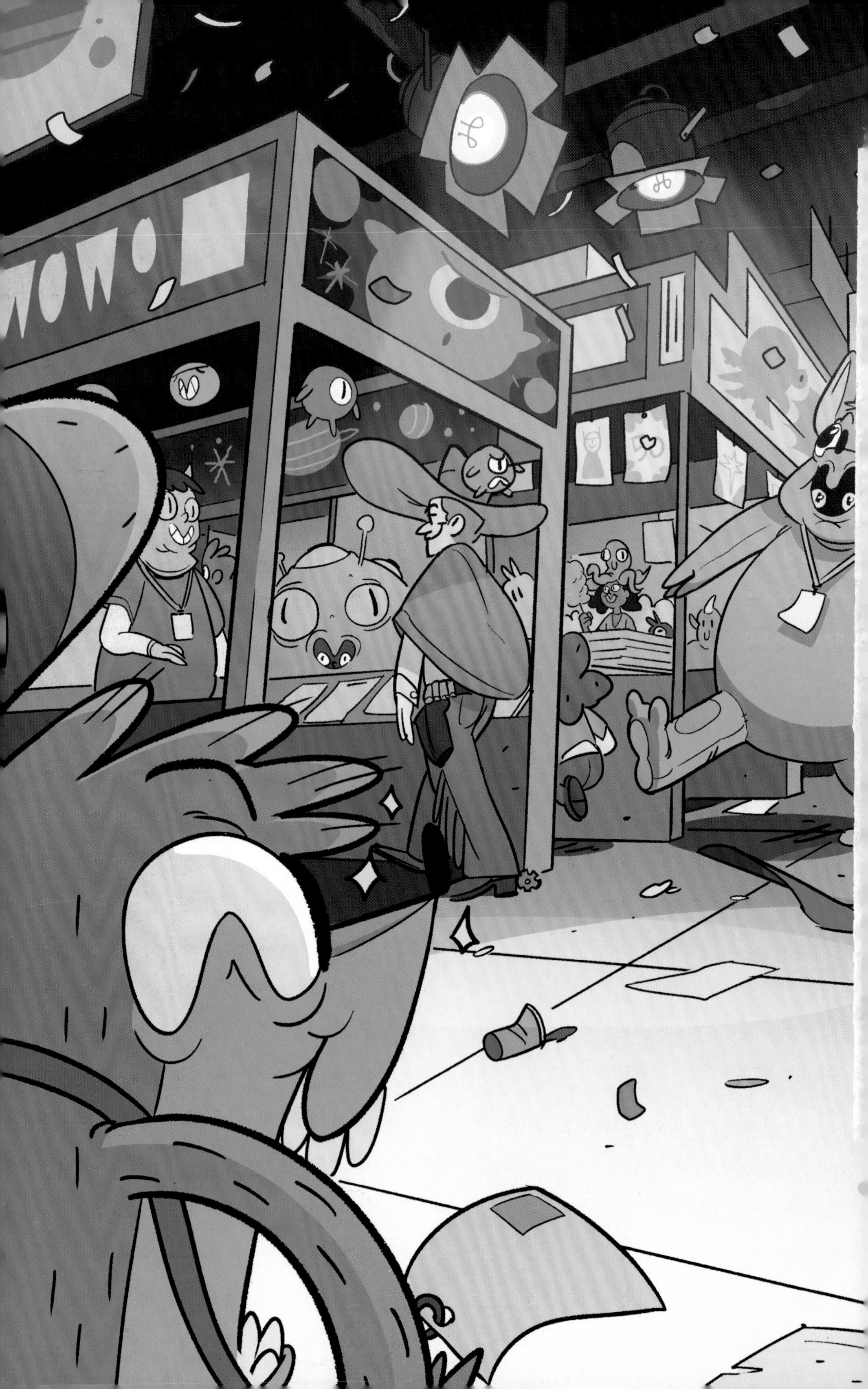
WOW

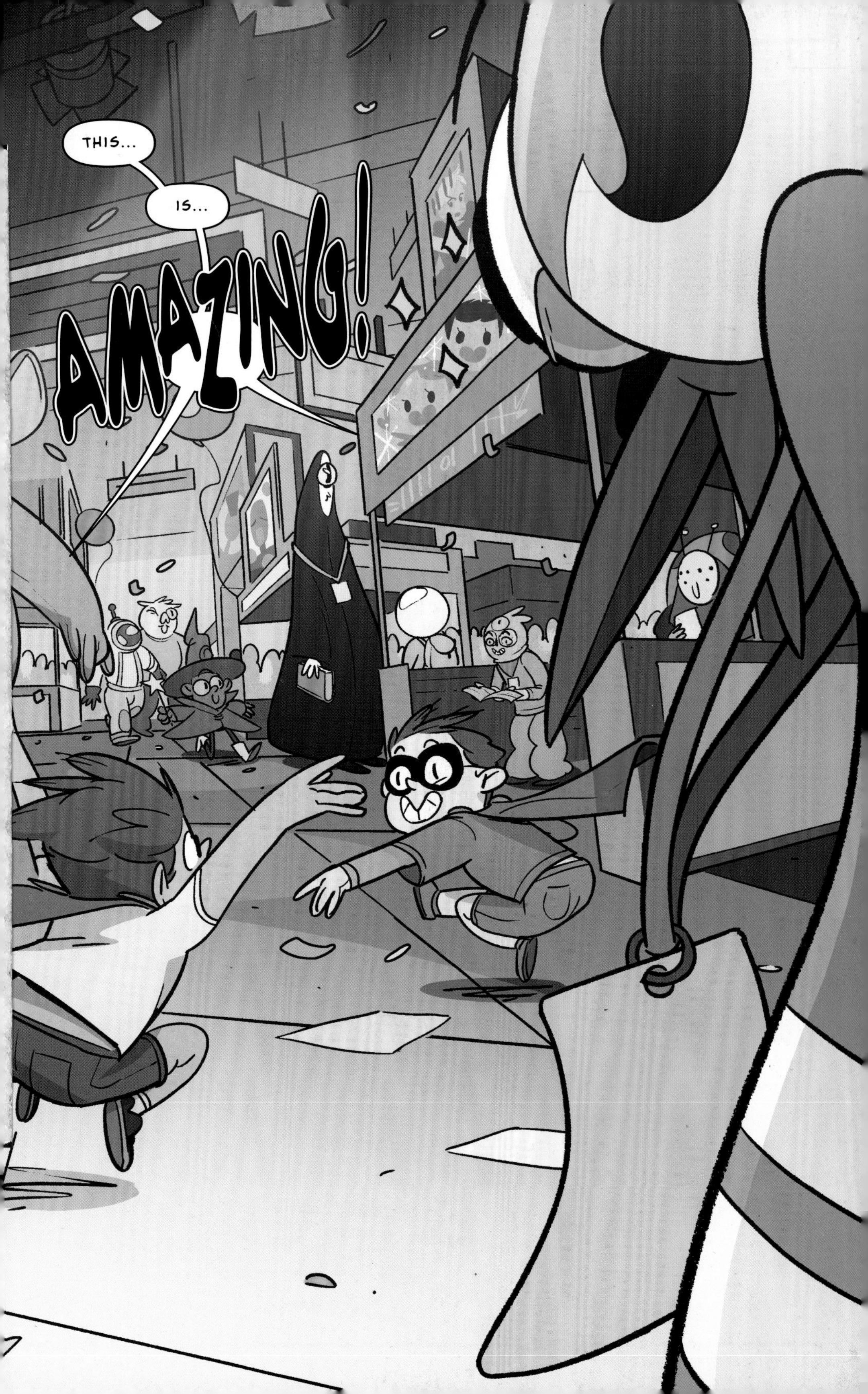
THIS...
IS...
AMAZING!

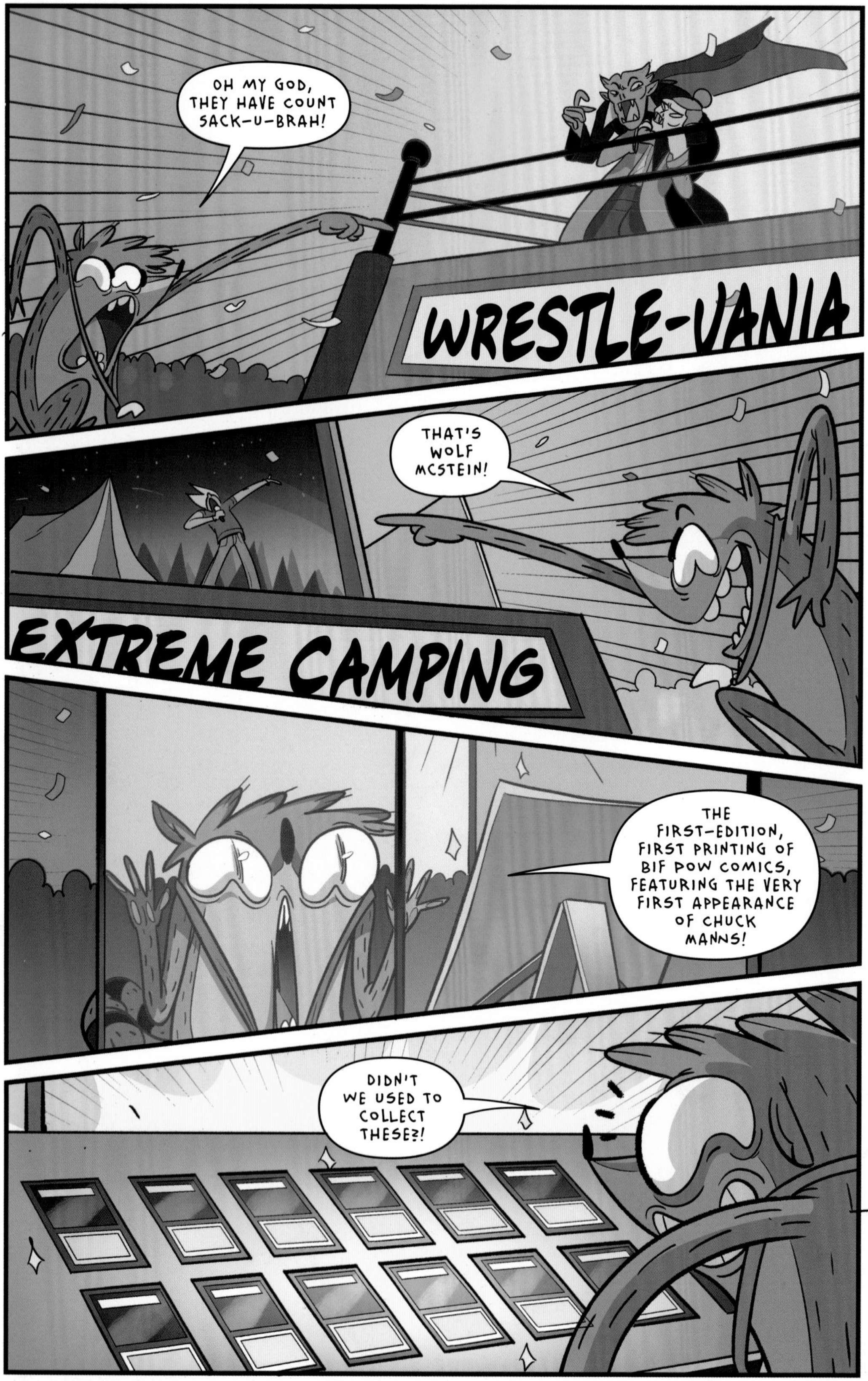
OH MY GOD, THEY HAVE COUNT SACK-U-BRAH!
WRESTLE-VANIA
THAT'S WOLF MCSTEIN!
EXTREME CAMPING
THE FIRST-EDITION, FIRST PRINTING OF BIF POW COMICS, FEATURING THE VERY FIRST APPEARANCE OF CHUCK MANNS!
DIDN'T WE USED TO COLLECT THESE?!

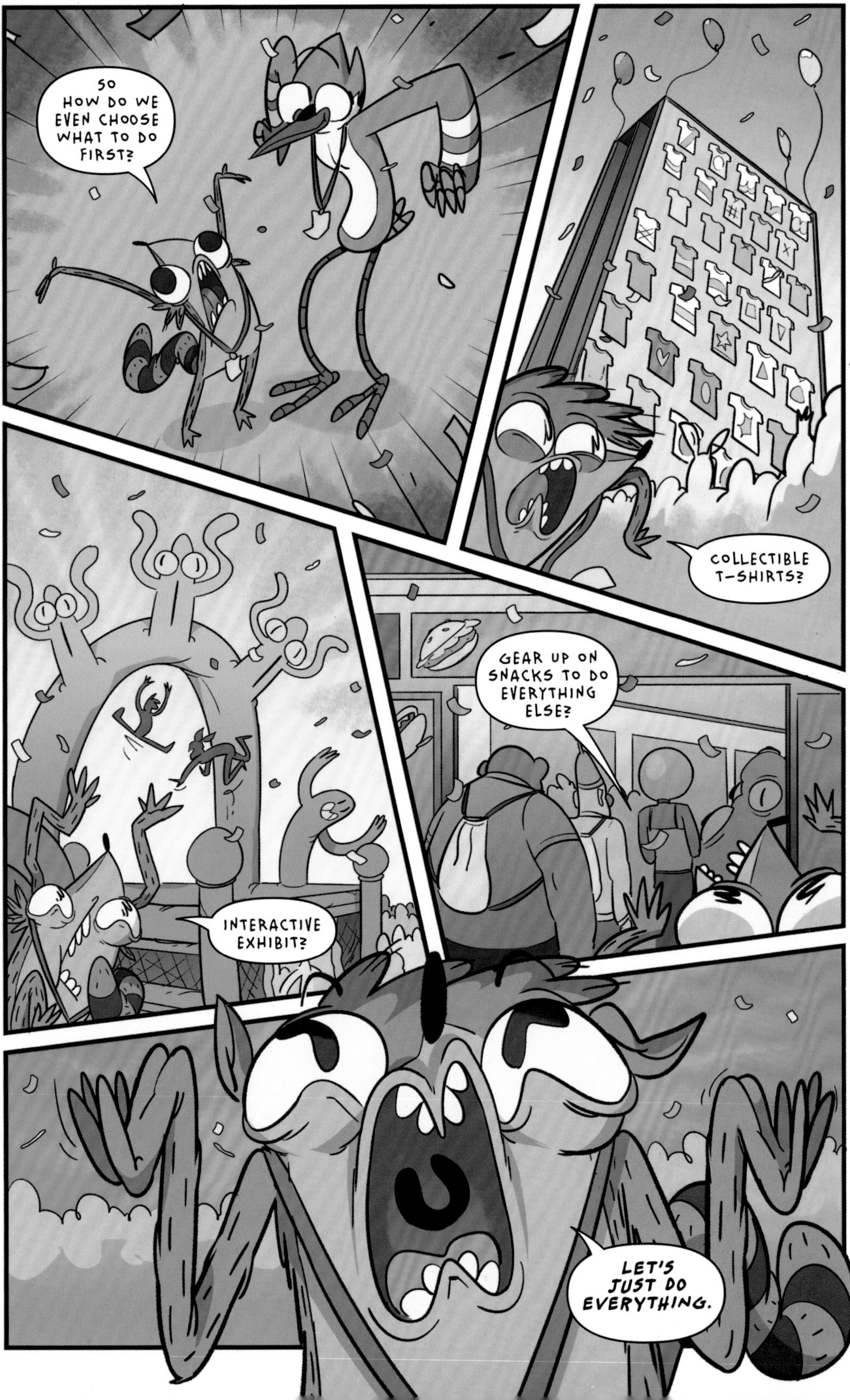
SO HOW DO WE EVEN CHOOSE WHAT TO DO FIRST?
COLLECTIBLE T-SHIRTS?
INTERACTIVE EXHIBIT?
GEAR UP ON SNACKS TO DO EVERYTHING ELSE?
LET'S JUST DO EVERYTHING.

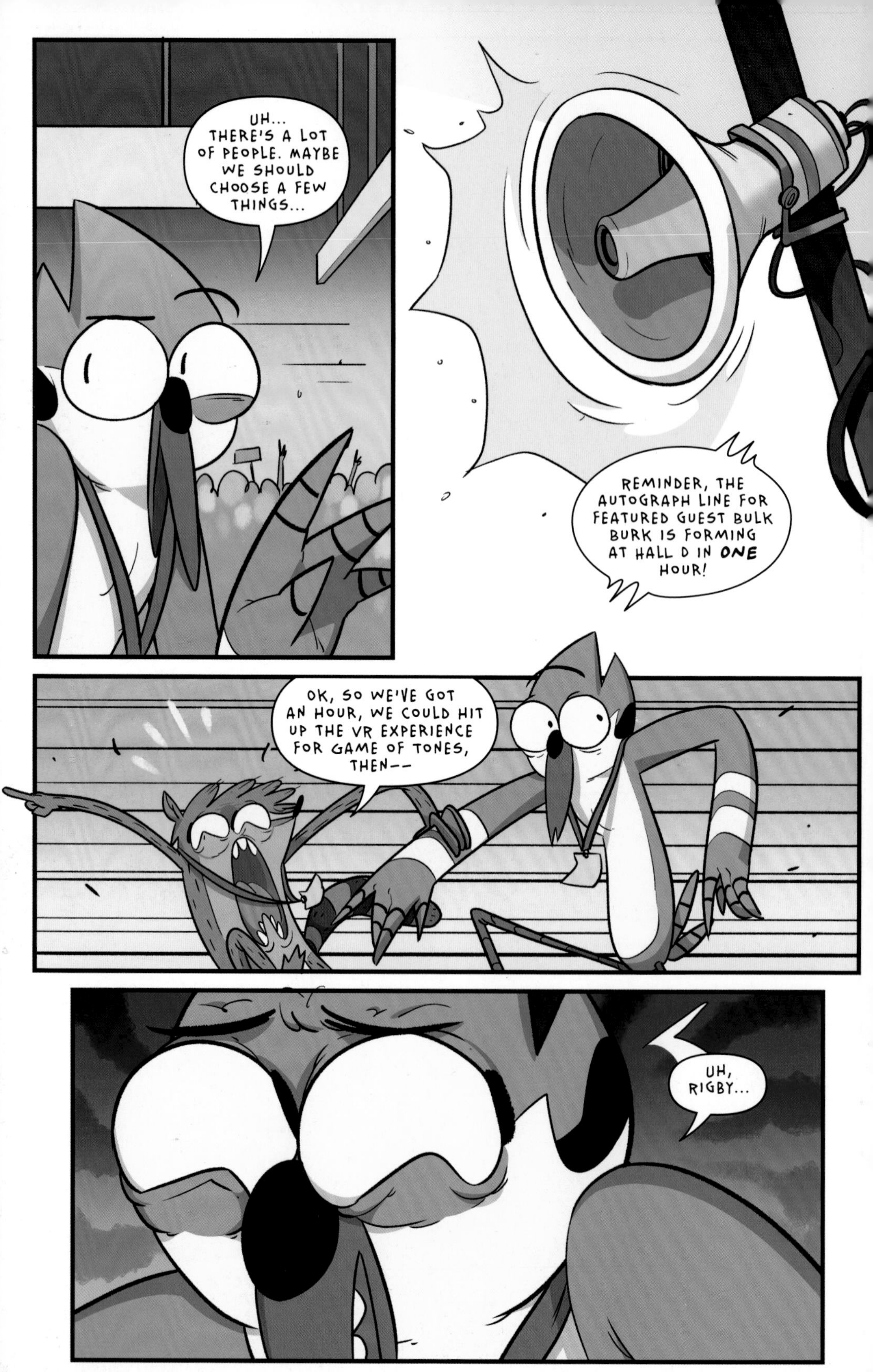
UH... THERE'S A LOT OF PEOPLE. MAYBE WE SHOULD CHOOSE A FEW THINGS...
REMINDER, THE AUTOGRAPH LINE FOR FEATURED GUEST BULK BURK IS FORMING AT HALL D IN ONE HOUR!
OK, SO WE'VE GOT AN HOUR, WE COULD HIT UP THE VR EXPERIENCE FOR GAME OF TONES, THEN--
UH, RIGBY...

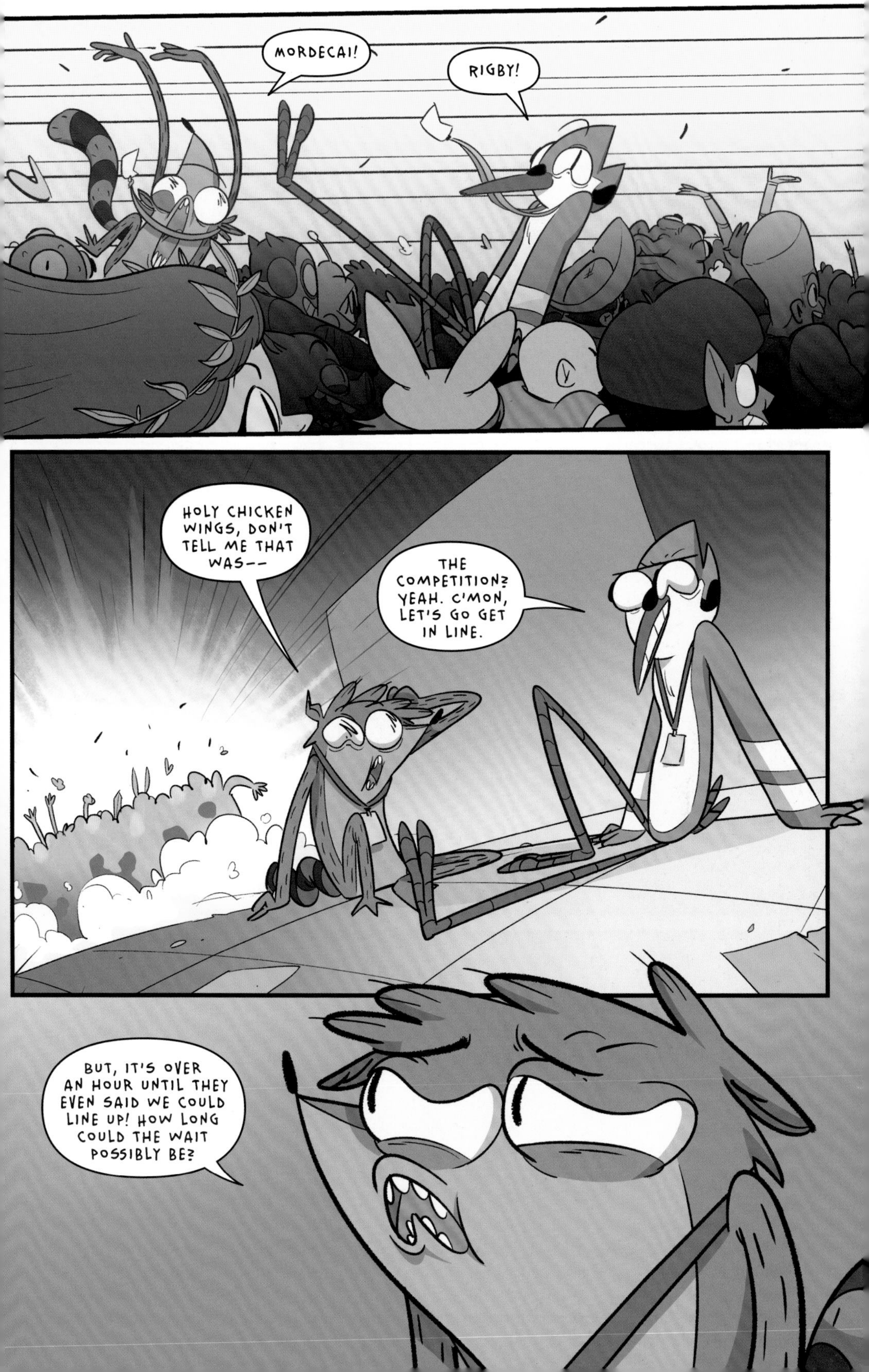
MORDECAI!
RIGBY!
HOLY CHICKEN WINGS, DON'T TELL ME THAT WAS--
THE COMPETITION? YEAH. C'MON, LET'S GO GET IN LINE.
BUT, IT'S OVER AN HOUR UNTIL THEY EVEN SAID WE COULD LINE UP! HOW LONG COULD THE WAIT POSSIBLY BE?

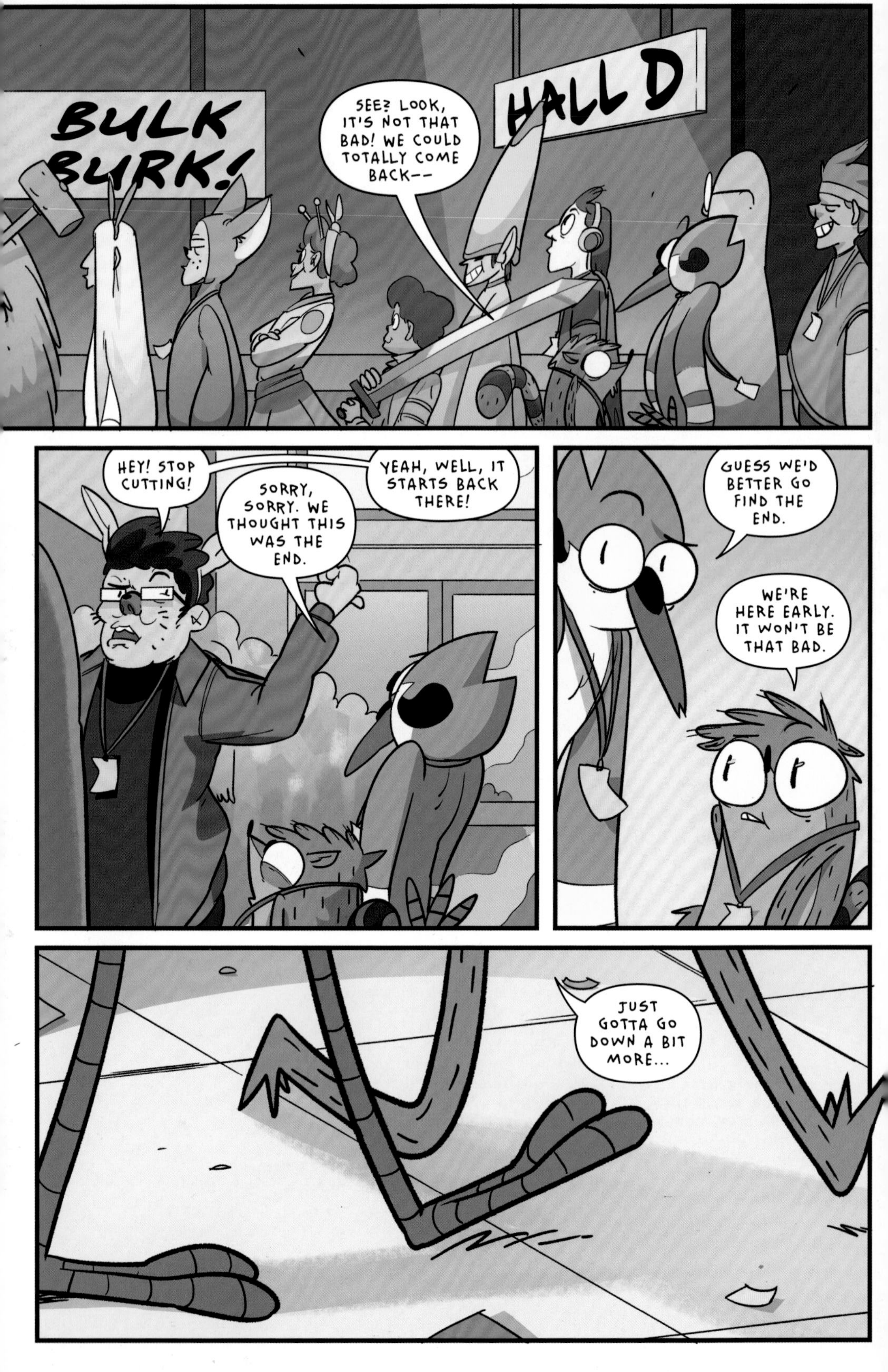
BULK BURK!
HALL D
SEE? LOOK, IT'S NOT THAT BAD! WE COULD TOTALLY COME BACK--
HEY! STOP CUTTING!
SORRY, SORRY. WE THOUGHT THIS WAS THE END.
YEAH, WELL, IT STARTS BACK THERE!
GUESS WE'D BETTER GO FIND THE END.
WE'RE HERE EARLY. IT WON'T BE THAT BAD.
JUST GOTTA GO DOWN A BIT MORE...

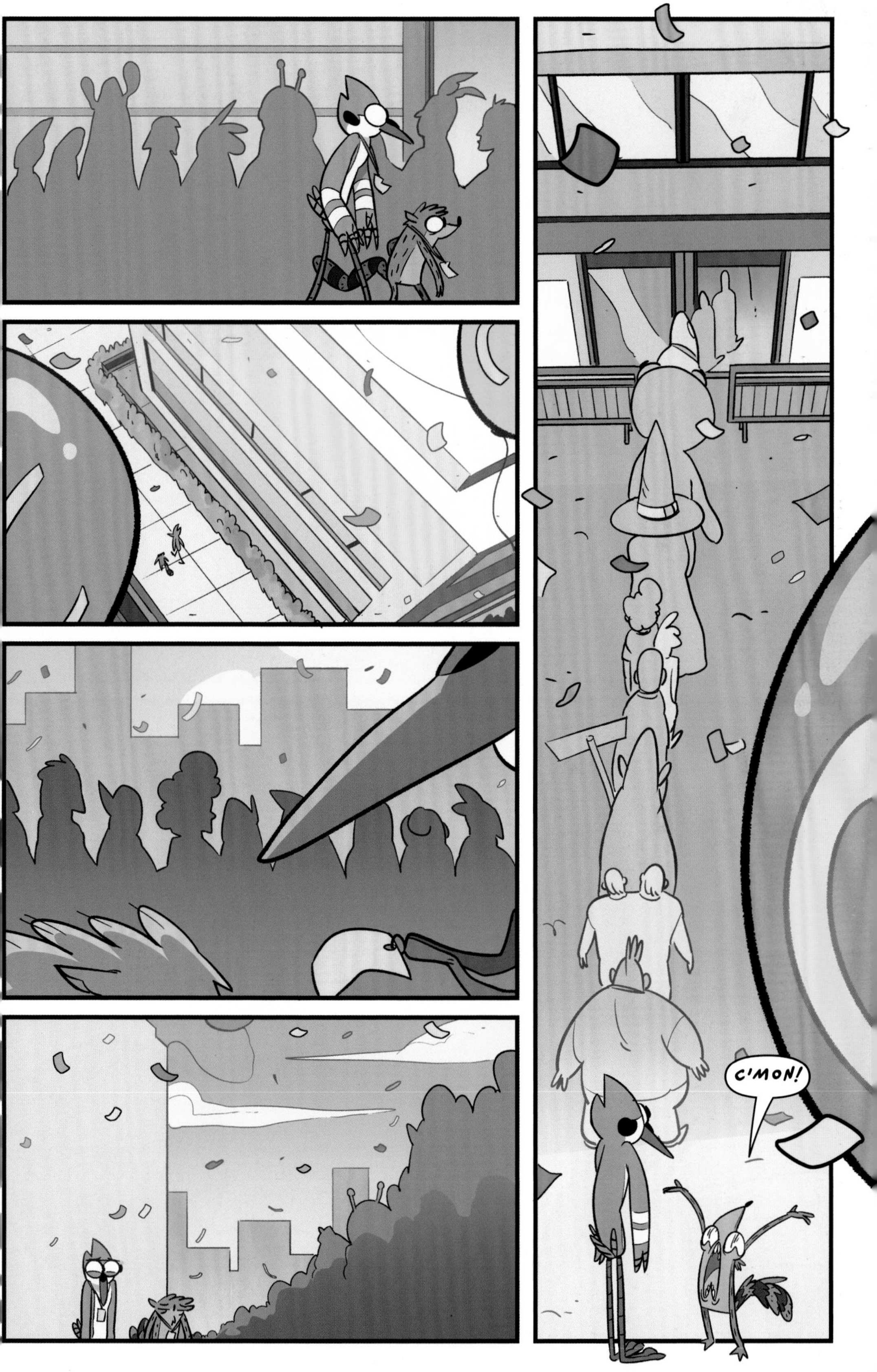
C'MON!

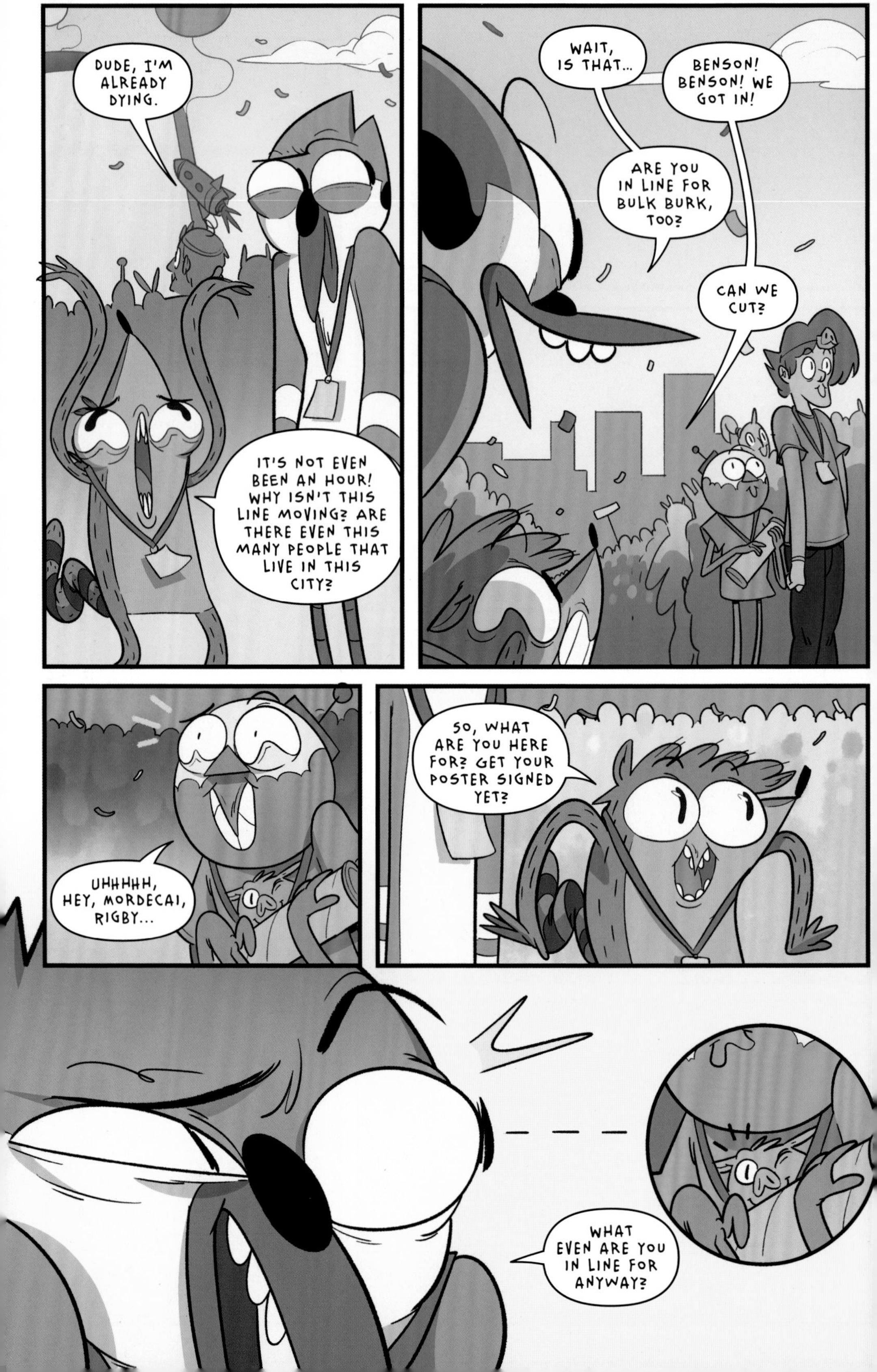
DUDE, I'M ALREADY DYING.
IT'S NOT EVEN BEEN AN HOUR! WHY ISN'T THIS LINE MOVING? ARE THERE EVEN THIS MANY PEOPLE THAT LIVE IN THIS CITY?
WAIT, IS THAT...
ARE YOU IN LINE FOR BULK BURK, TOO?
BENSON! BENSON! WE GOT IN!
CAN WE CUT?
UHHHHH, HEY, MORDECAI, RIGBY...
SO, WHAT ARE YOU HERE FOR? GET YOUR POSTER SIGNED YET?
WHAT EVEN ARE YOU IN LINE FOR ANYWAY?

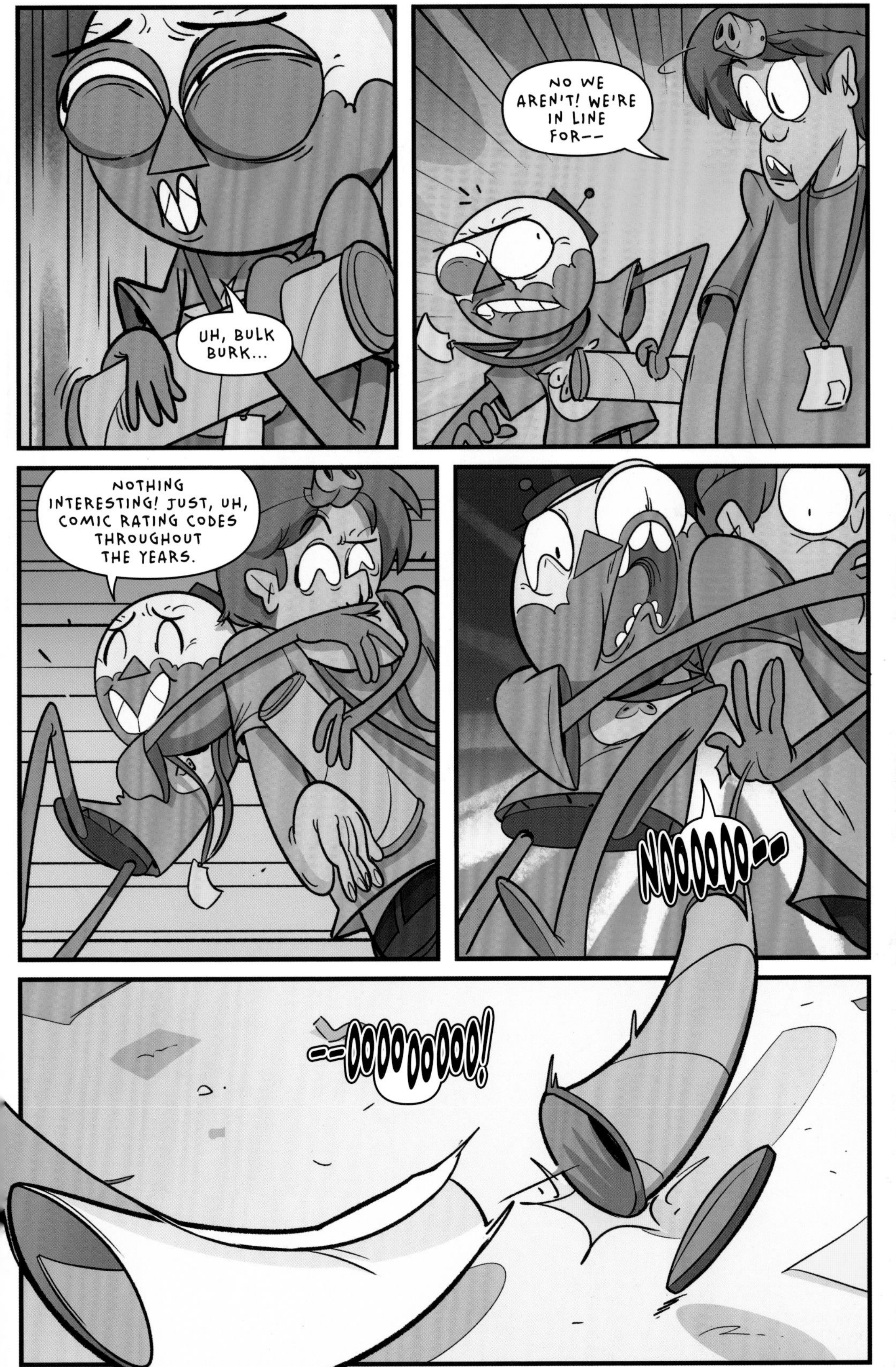
UH, BULK BURK...
NO WE AREN'T! WE'RE IN LINE FOR--
NOTHING INTERESTING! JUST, UH, COMIC RATING CODES THROUGHOUT THE YEARS.
NOOOOO--
--OOOOOOOO!

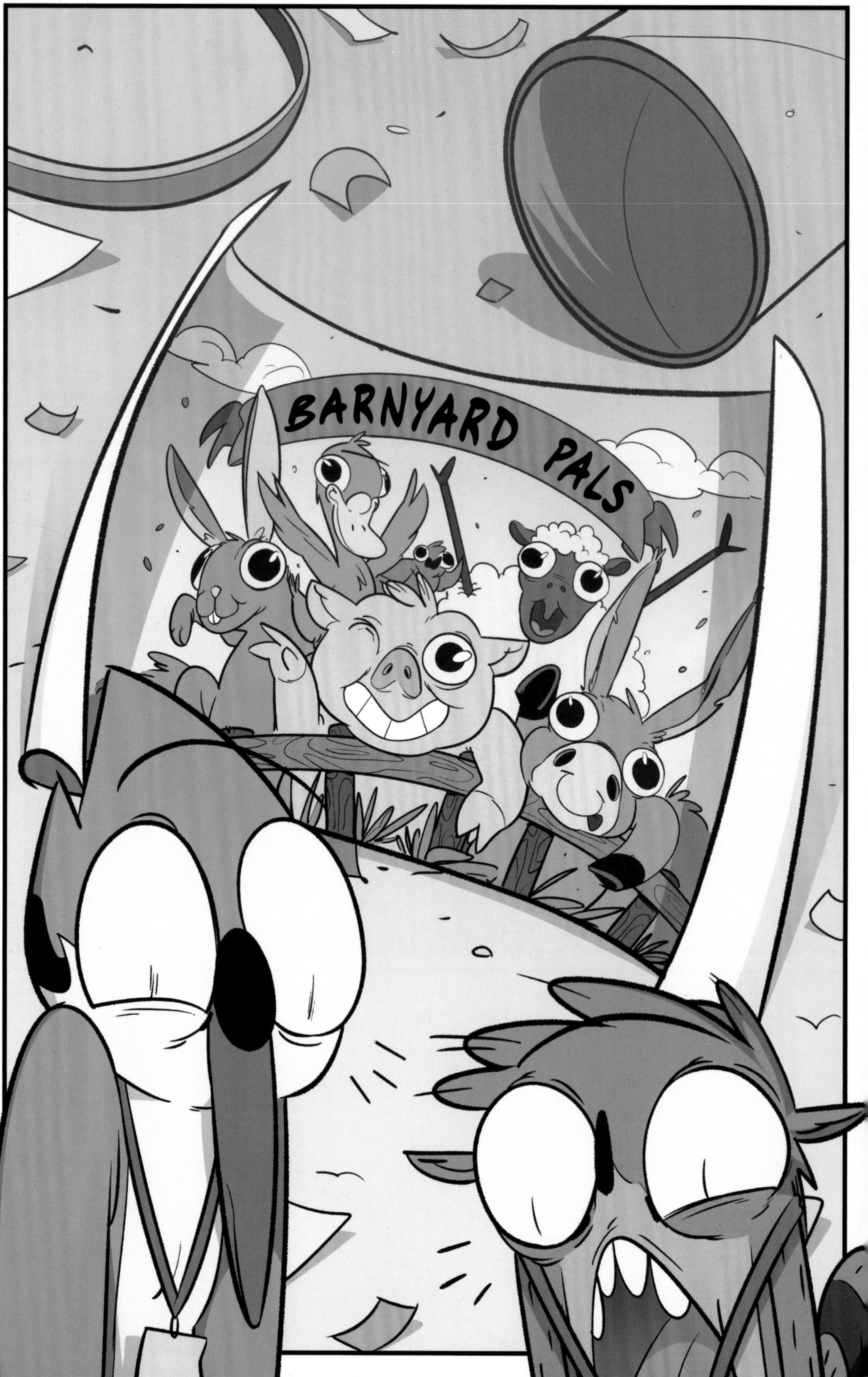
BARNYARD PALS

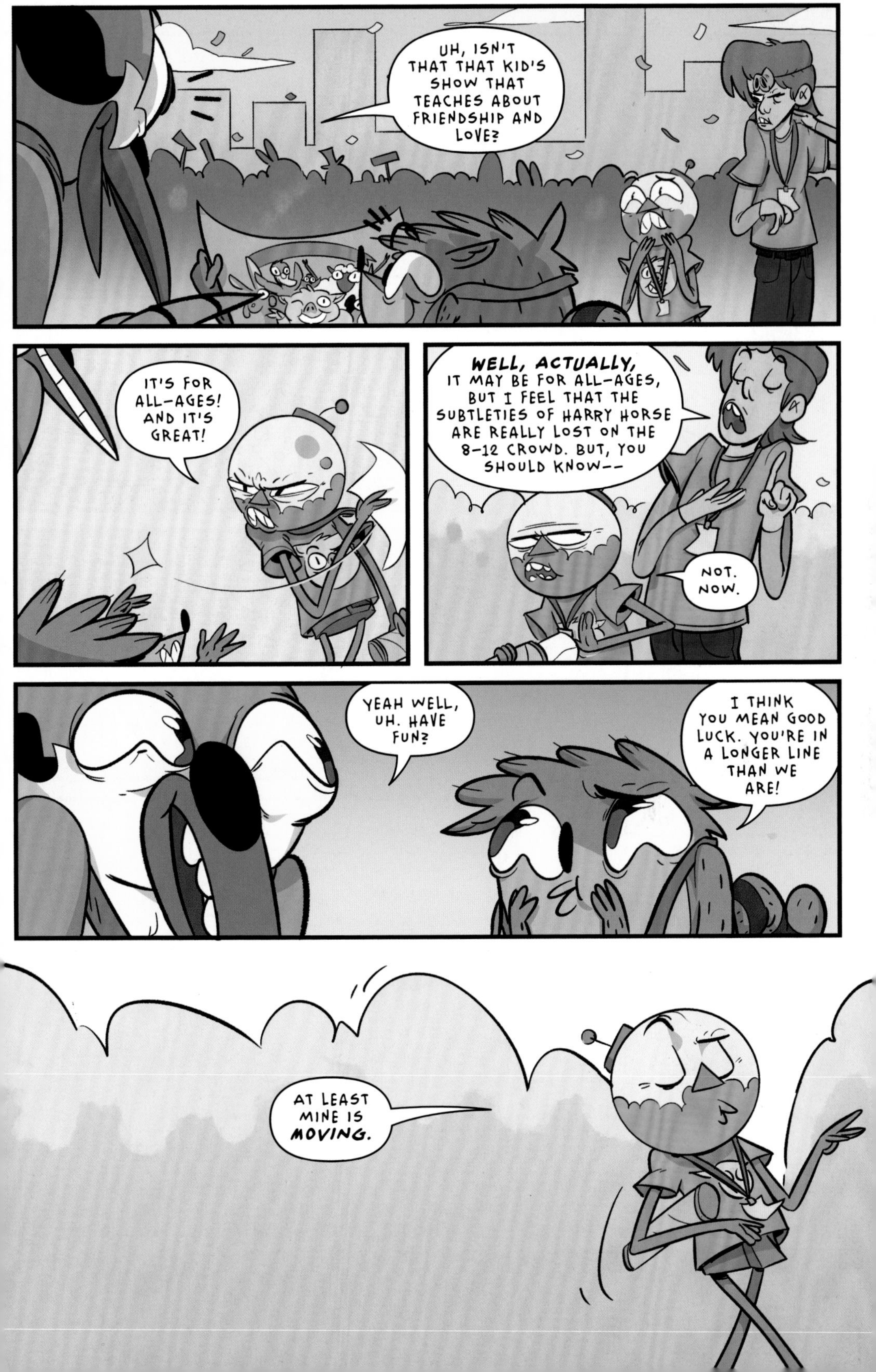
UH, ISN'T THAT THAT KID'S SHOW THAT TEACHES ABOUT FRIENDSHIP AND LOVE?
IT'S FOR ALL-AGES! AND IT'S GREAT!
WELL, ACTUALLY, IT MAY BE FOR ALL-AGES, BUT I FEEL THAT THE SUBTLETIES OF HARRY HORSE ARE REALLY LOST ON THE 8-12 CROWD. BUT, YOU SHOULD KNOW--
NOT. NOW.
YEAH WELL, UH. HAVE FUN?
I THINK YOU MEAN GOOD LUCK. YOU'RE IN A LONGER LINE THAN WE ARE!
AT LEAST MINE IS MOVING.

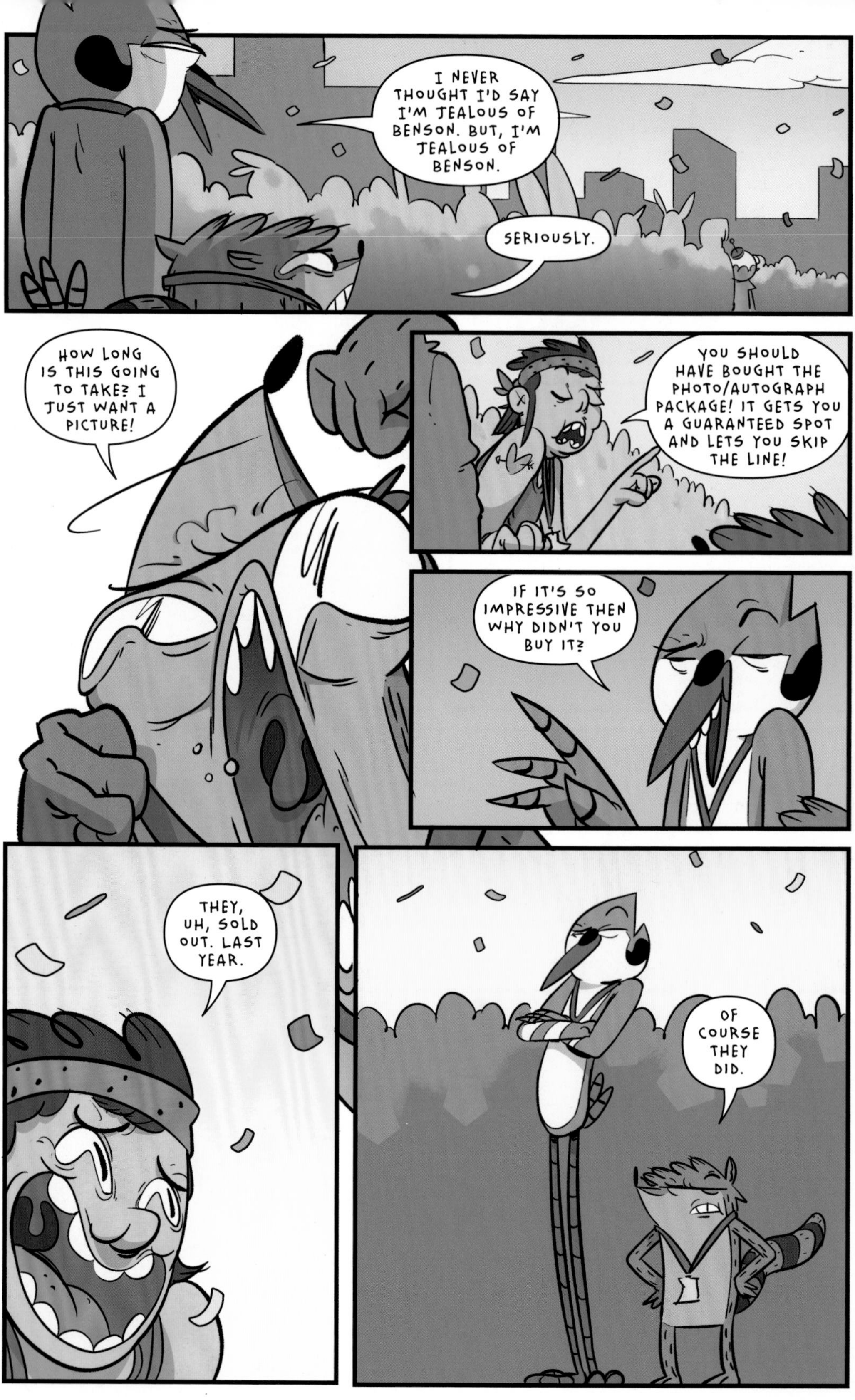
I NEVER THOUGHT I'D SAY I'M JEALOUS OF BENSON. BUT, I'M JEALOUS OF BENSON.
SERIOUSLY.
HOW LONG IS THIS GOING TO TAKE? I JUST WANT A PICTURE!
YOU SHOULD HAVE BOUGHT THE PHOTO/AUTOGRAPH PACKAGE! IT GETS YOU A GUARANTEED SPOT AND LETS YOU SKIP THE LINE!
IF IT'S SO IMPRESSIVE THEN WHY DIDN'T YOU BUY IT?
THEY, UH, SOLD OUT. LAST YEAR.
OF COURSE THEY DID.

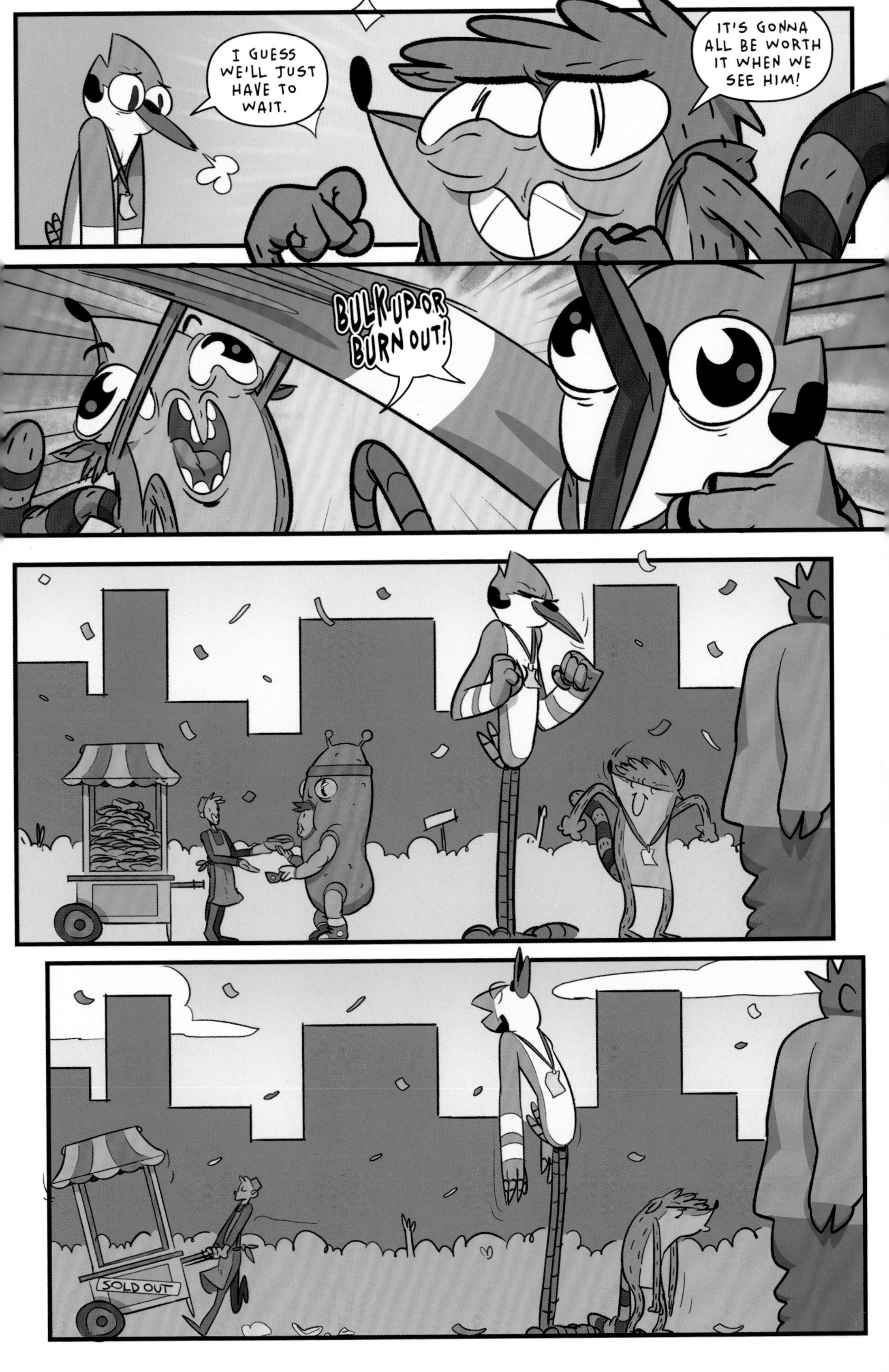
I GUESS WE'LL JUST HAVE TO WAIT.
IT'S GONNA ALL BE WORTH IT WHEN WE SEE HIM!
BULK UP OR BURN OUT!
SOLD OUT

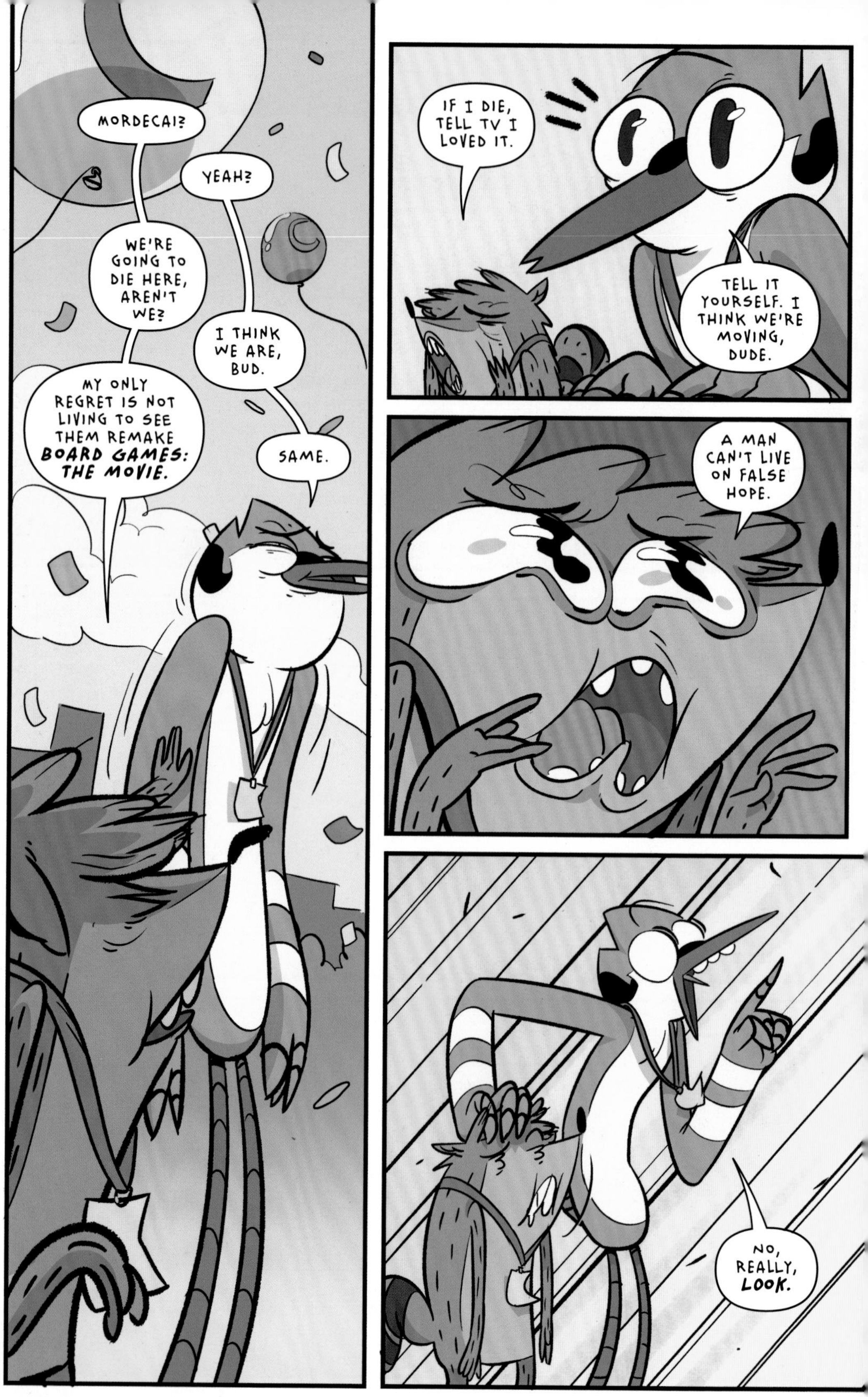
MORDECAI?
YEAH?
WE'RE GOING TO DIE HERE, AREN'T WE?
I THINK WE ARE, BUD.
MY ONLY REGRET IS NOT LIVING TO SEE THEM REMAKE ***BOARD GAMES: THE MOVIE.***
SAME.
IF I DIE, TELL TV I LOVED IT.
TELL IT YOURSELF. I THINK WE'RE MOVING, DUDE.
A MAN CAN'T LIVE ON FALSE HOPE.
NO, REALLY, ***LOOK.***

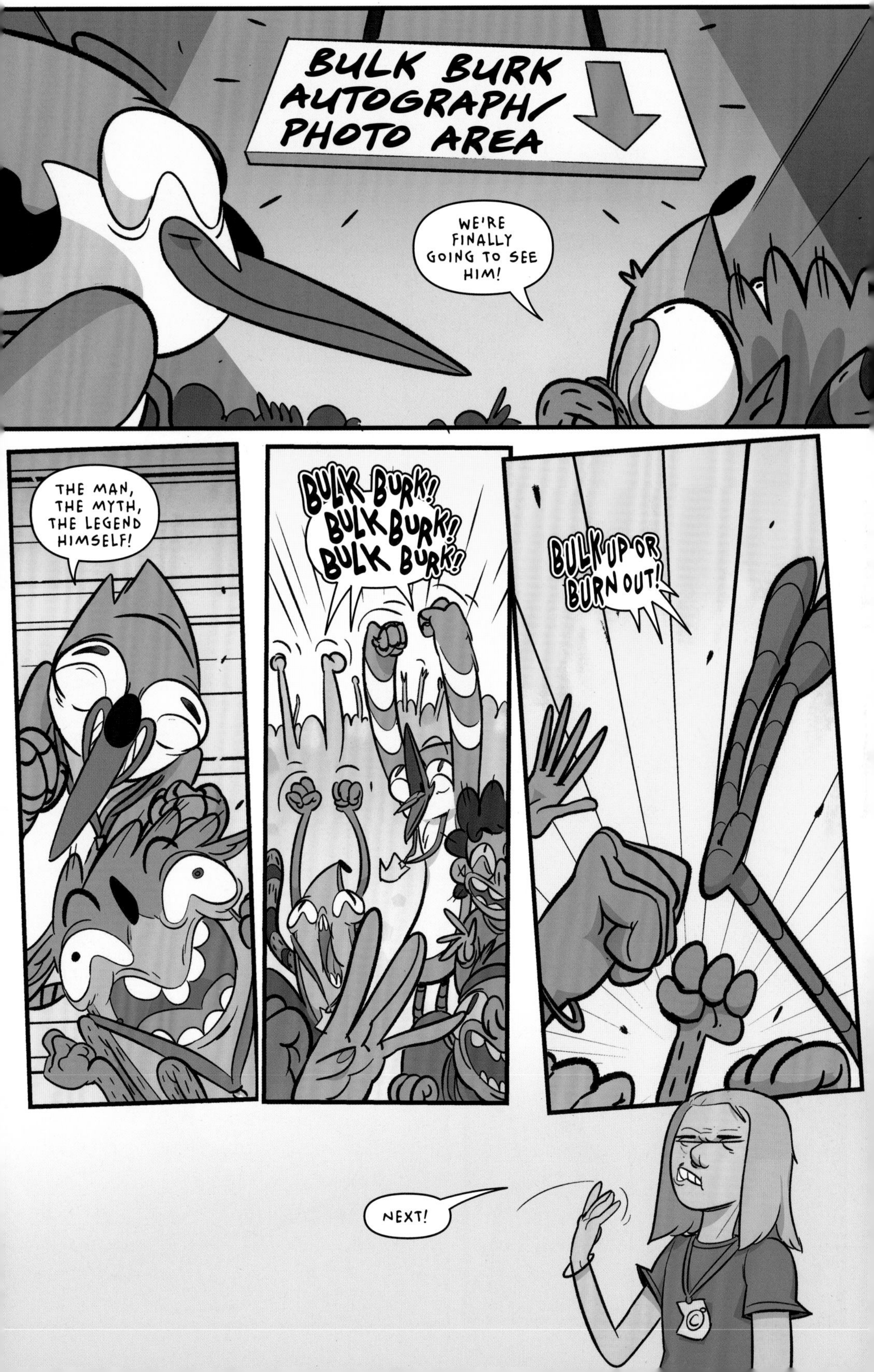
BULK BURK AUTOGRAPH/ PHOTO AREA
WE'RE FINALLY GOING TO SEE HIM!
THE MAN, THE MYTH, THE LEGEND HIMSELF!
BULK BURK! BULK BURK! BULK BURK!
BULK UP OR BURN OUT!
NEXT!

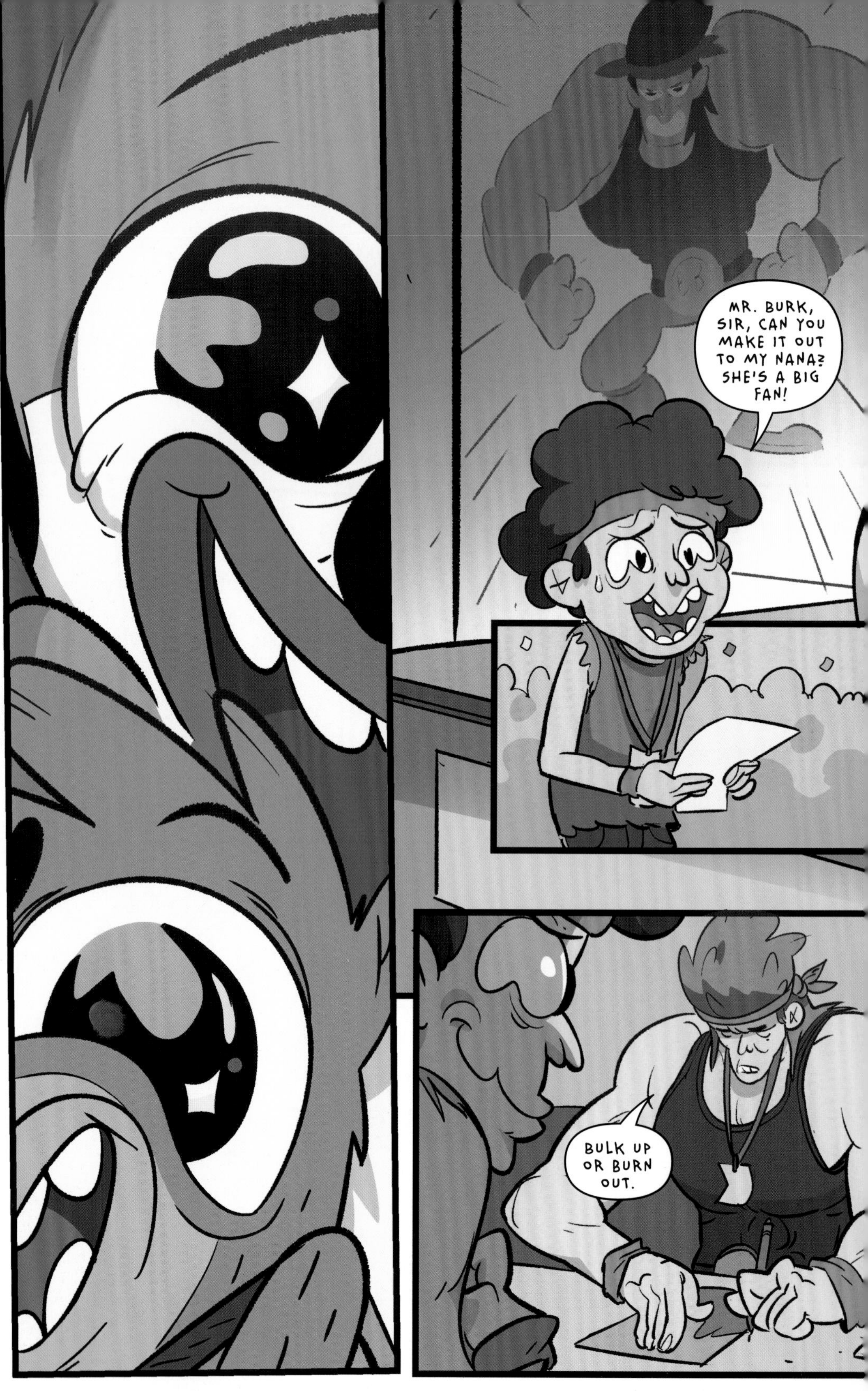
MR. BURK, SIR, CAN YOU MAKE IT OUT TO MY NANA? SHE'S A BIG FAN!
BULK UP OR BURN OUT.

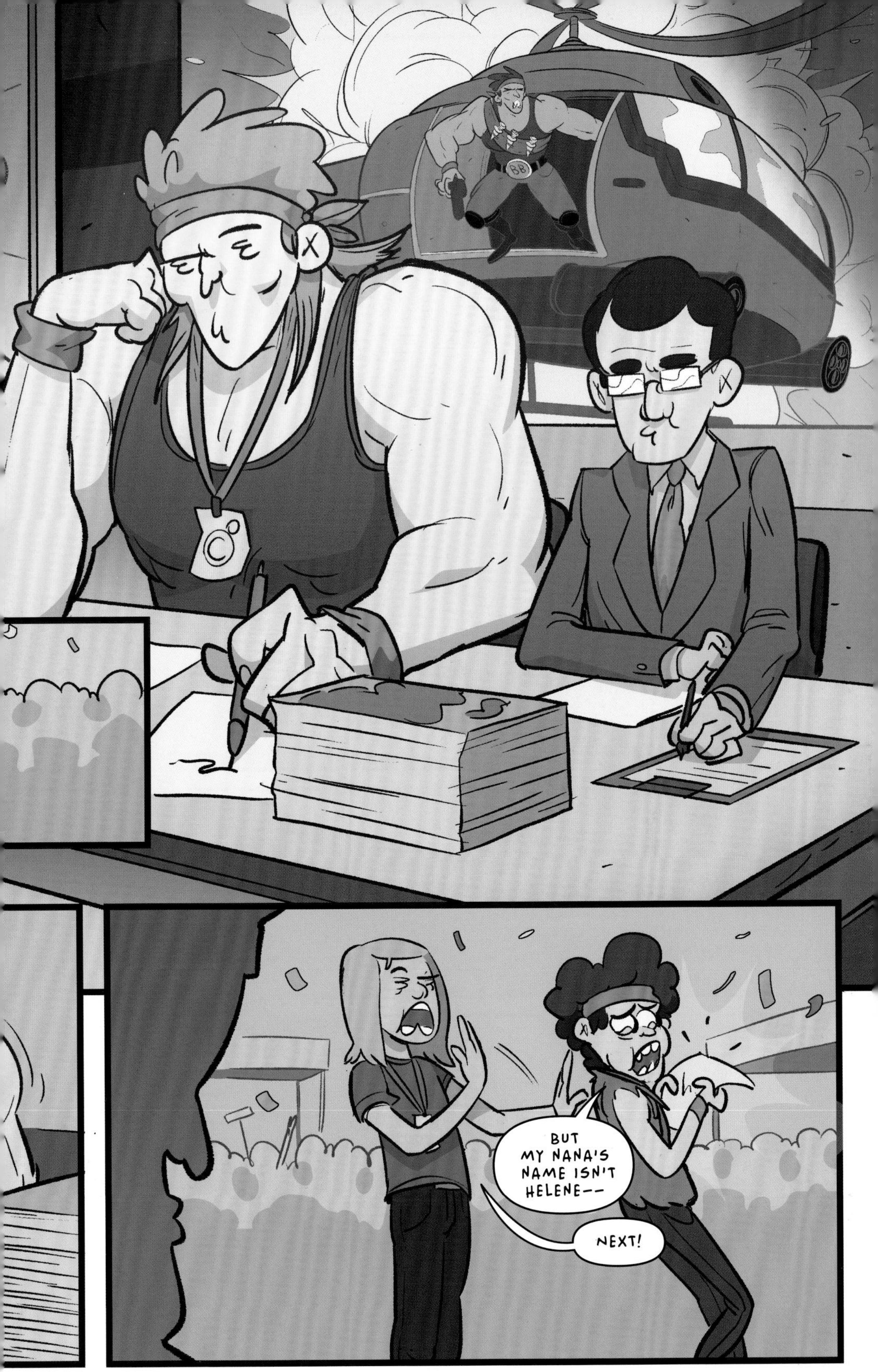
BUT MY NANA'S NAME ISN'T HELENE--
NEXT!

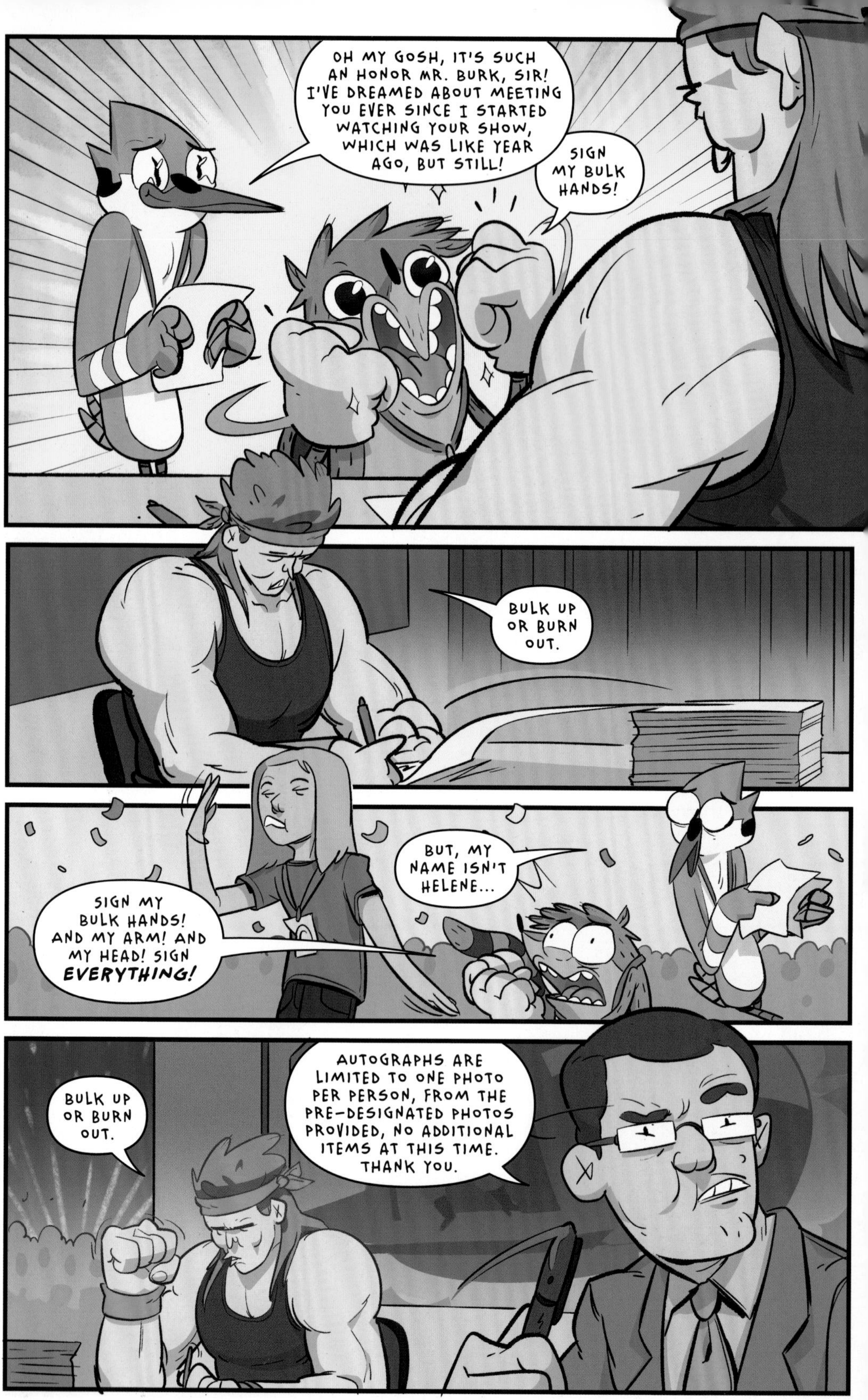
OH MY GOSH, IT'S SUCH AN HONOR MR. BURK, SIR! I'VE DREAMED ABOUT MEETING YOU EVER SINCE I STARTED WATCHING YOUR SHOW, WHICH WAS LIKE YEAR AGO, BUT STILL!
SIGN MY BULK HANDS!
BULK UP OR BURN OUT.
BUT, MY NAME ISN'T HELENE...
SIGN MY BULK HANDS! AND MY ARM! AND MY HEAD! SIGN EVERYTHING!
BULK UP OR BURN OUT.
AUTOGRAPHS ARE LIMITED TO ONE PHOTO PER PERSON, FROM THE PRE-DESIGNATED PHOTOS PROVIDED, NO ADDITIONAL ITEMS AT THIS TIME. THANK YOU.

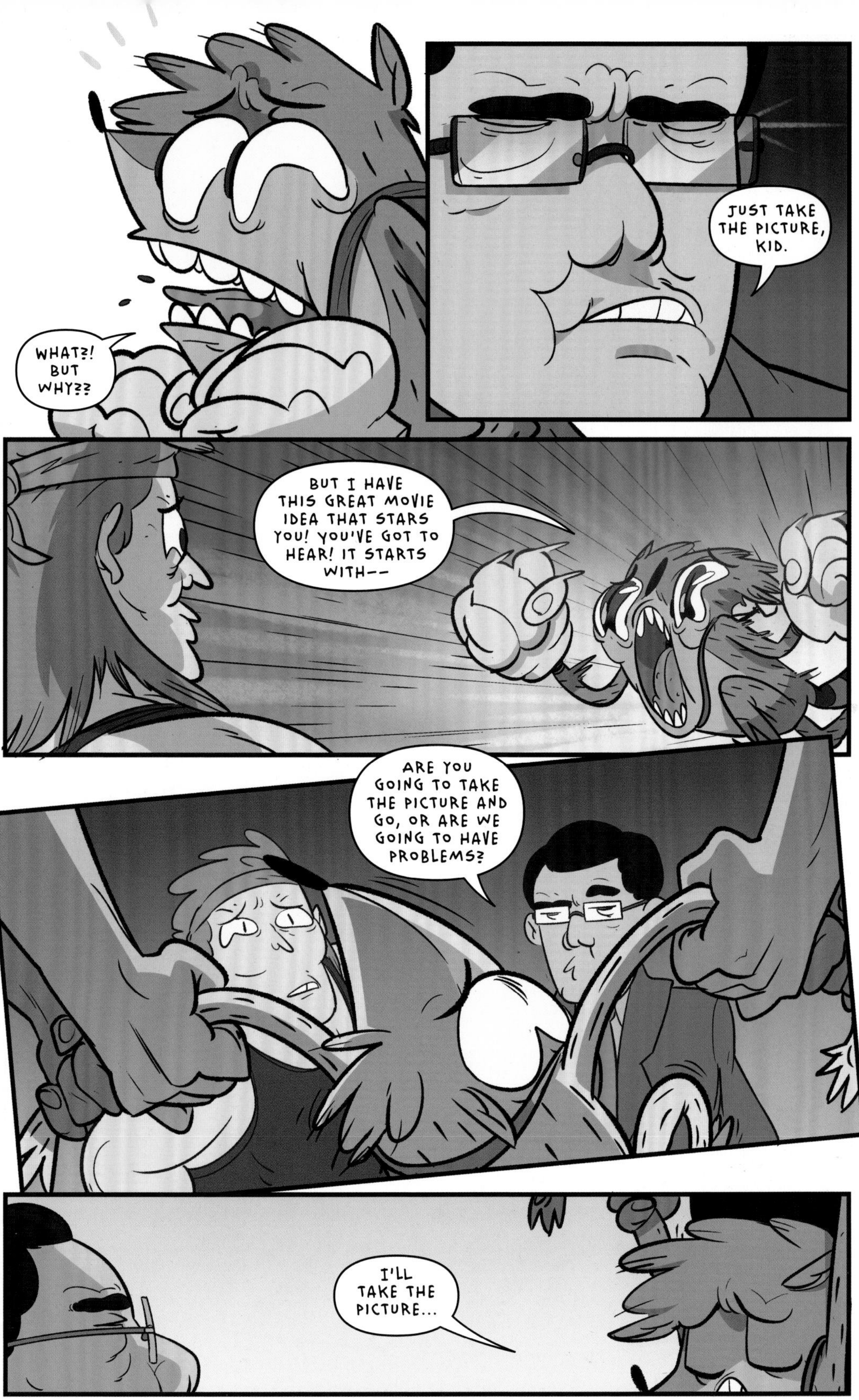
JUST TAKE THE PICTURE, KID.
WHAT?! BUT WHY??
BUT I HAVE THIS GREAT MOVIE IDEA THAT STARS YOU! YOU'VE GOT TO HEAR! IT STARTS WITH--
ARE YOU GOING TO TAKE THE PICTURE AND GO, OR ARE WE GOING TO HAVE PROBLEMS?
I'LL TAKE THE PICTURE...

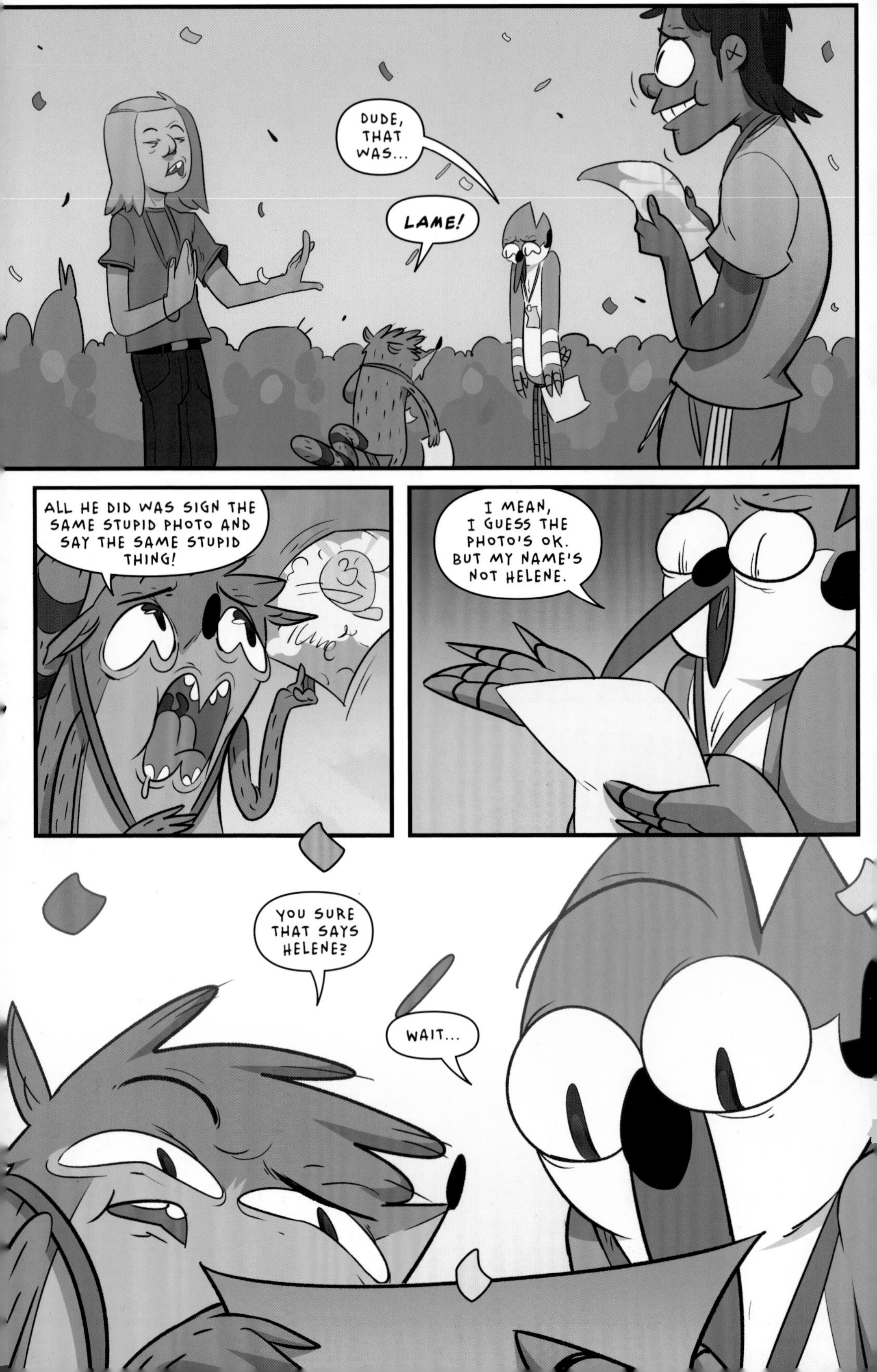
DUDE, THAT WAS...
LAME!
ALL HE DID WAS SIGN THE SAME STUPID PHOTO AND SAY THE SAME STUPID THING!
I MEAN, I GUESS THE PHOTO'S OK. BUT MY NAME'S NOT HELENE.
YOU SURE THAT SAYS HELENE?
WAIT...

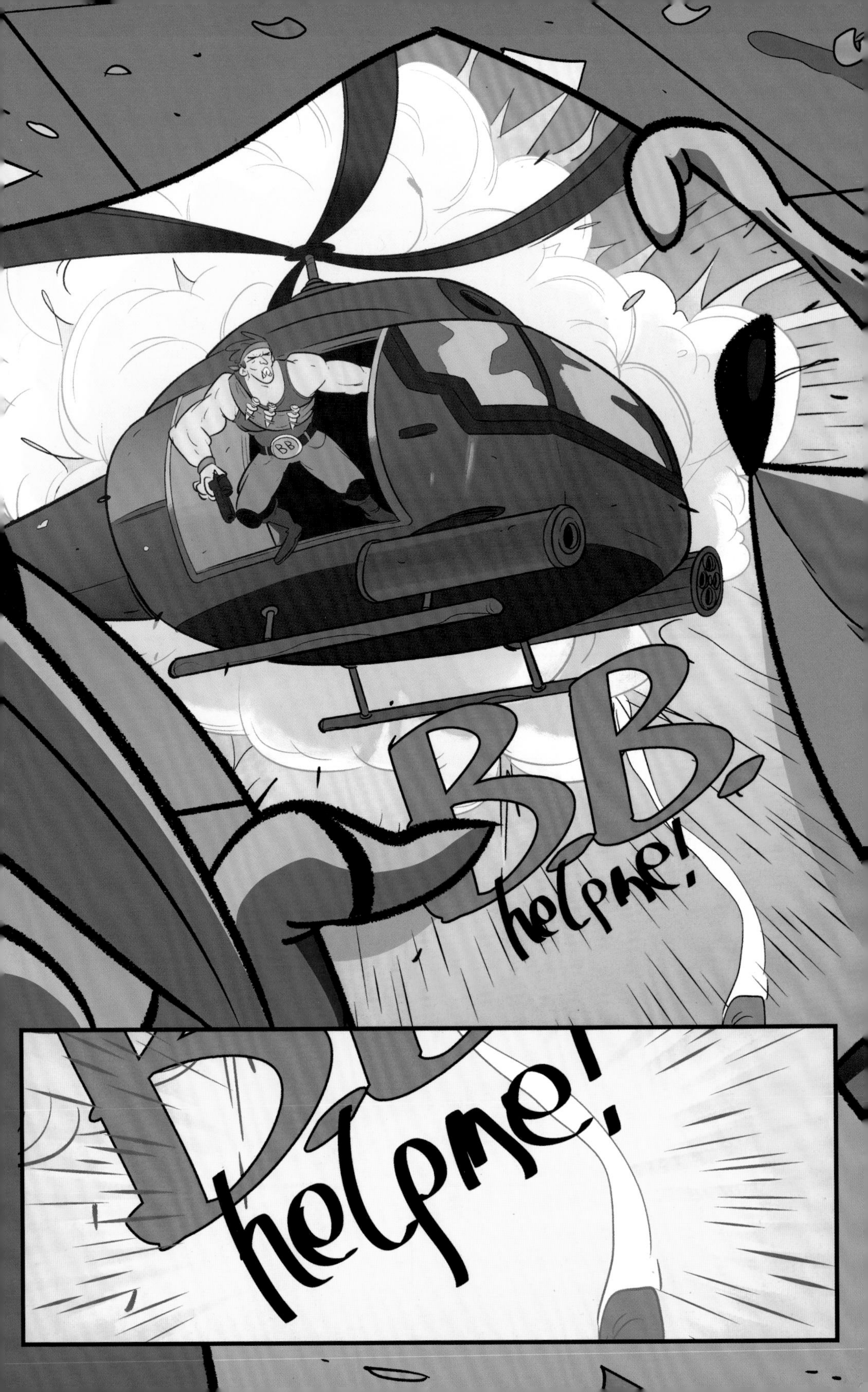
B.B.
help me!
help me!

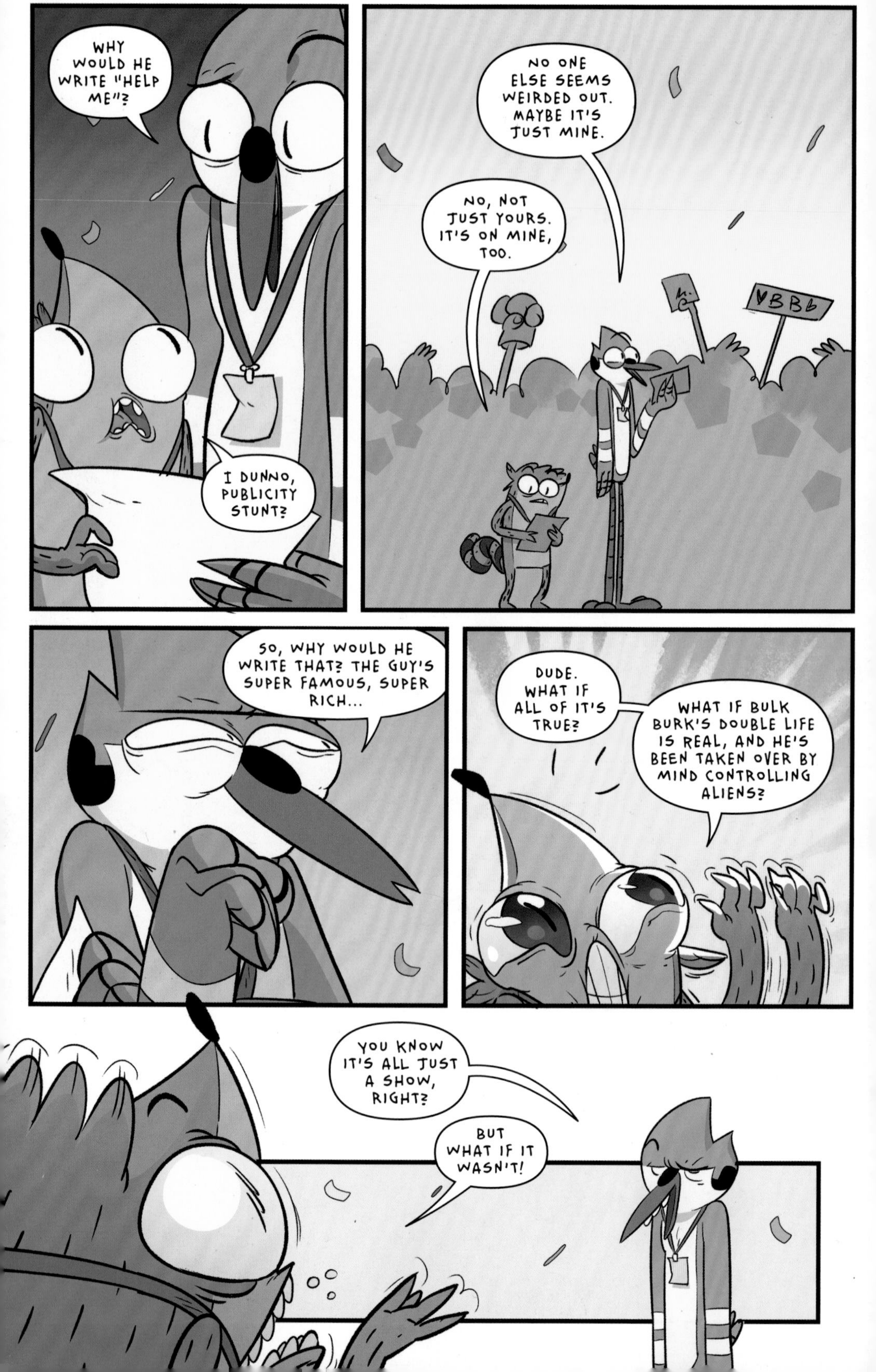

WHY WOULD HE WRITE "HELP ME"?
I DUNNO, PUBLICITY STUNT?
NO ONE ELSE SEEMS WEIRDED OUT. MAYBE IT'S JUST MINE.
NO, NOT JUST YOURS. IT'S ON MINE, TOO.
VBBB
SO, WHY WOULD HE WRITE THAT? THE GUY'S SUPER FAMOUS, SUPER RICH...
DUDE. WHAT IF ALL OF IT'S TRUE?
WHAT IF BULK BURK'S DOUBLE LIFE IS REAL, AND HE'S BEEN TAKEN OVER BY MIND CONTROLLING ALIENS?
YOU KNOW IT'S ALL JUST A SHOW, RIGHT?
BUT WHAT IF IT WASN'T!

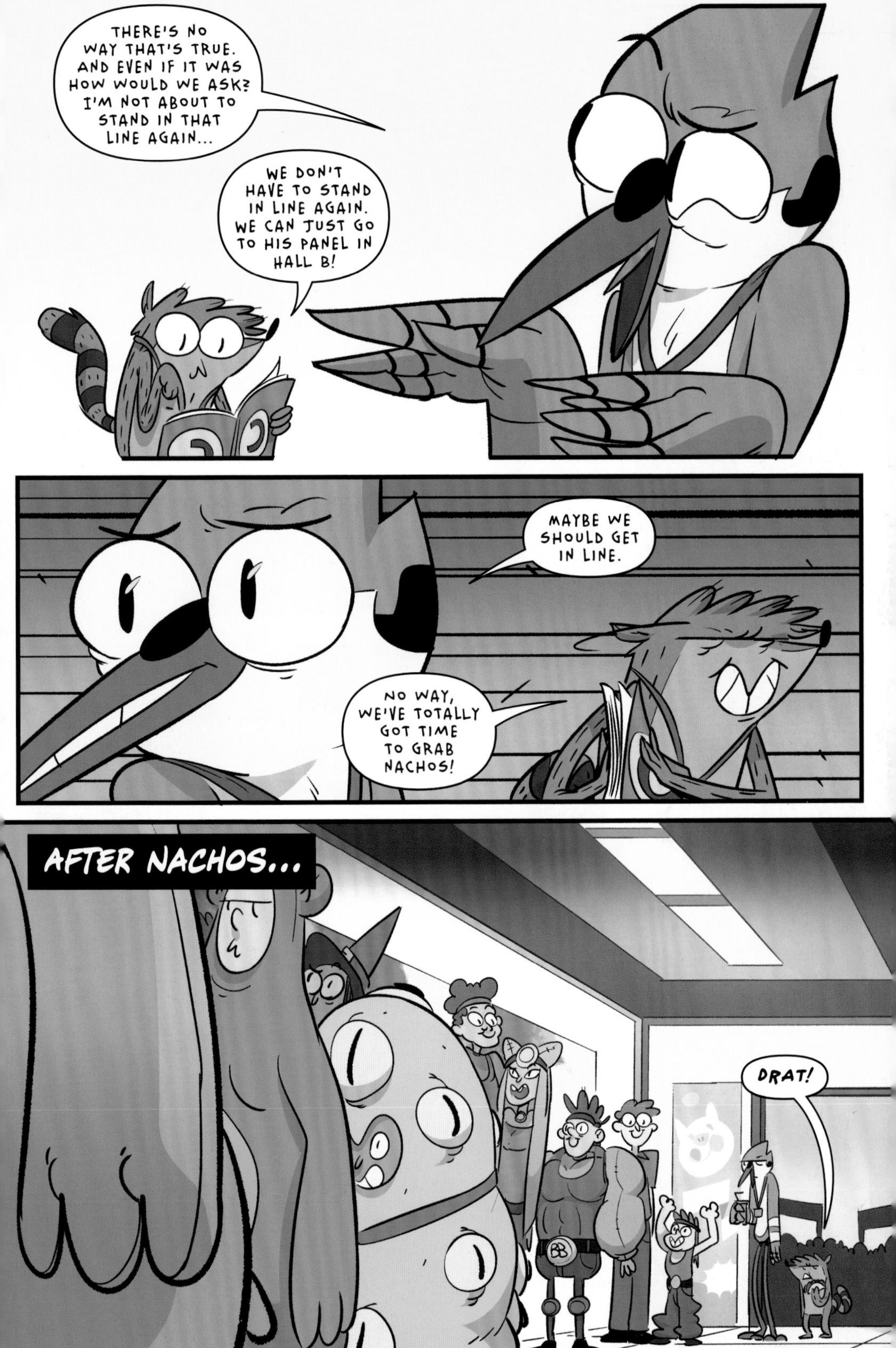
THERE'S NO WAY THAT'S TRUE. AND EVEN IF IT WAS HOW WOULD WE ASK? I'M NOT ABOUT TO STAND IN THAT LINE AGAIN...
WE DON'T HAVE TO STAND IN LINE AGAIN. WE CAN JUST GO TO HIS PANEL IN HALL B!
MAYBE WE SHOULD GET IN LINE.
NO WAY, WE'VE TOTALLY GOT TIME TO GRAB NACHOS!
AFTER NACHOS...
DRAT!

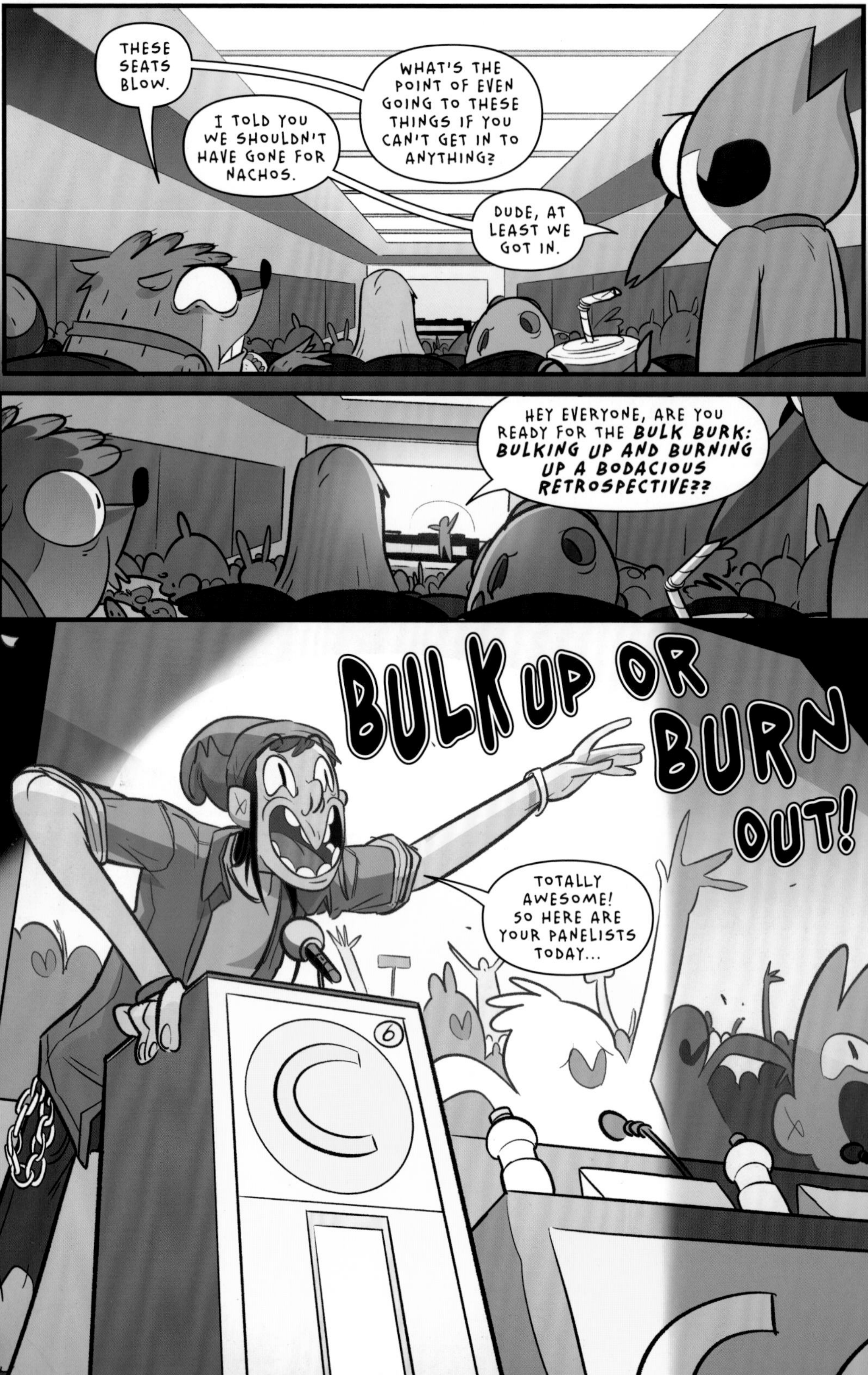
THESE SEATS BLOW.
WHAT'S THE POINT OF EVEN GOING TO THESE THINGS IF YOU CAN'T GET IN TO ANYTHING?
I TOLD YOU WE SHOULDN'T HAVE GONE FOR NACHOS.
DUDE, AT LEAST WE GOT IN.
HEY EVERYONE, ARE YOU READY FOR THE BULK BURK: BULKING UP AND BURNING UP A BODACIOUS RETROSPECTIVE??
BULK UP OR BURN OUT!
TOTALLY AWESOME! SO HERE ARE YOUR PANELISTS TODAY...

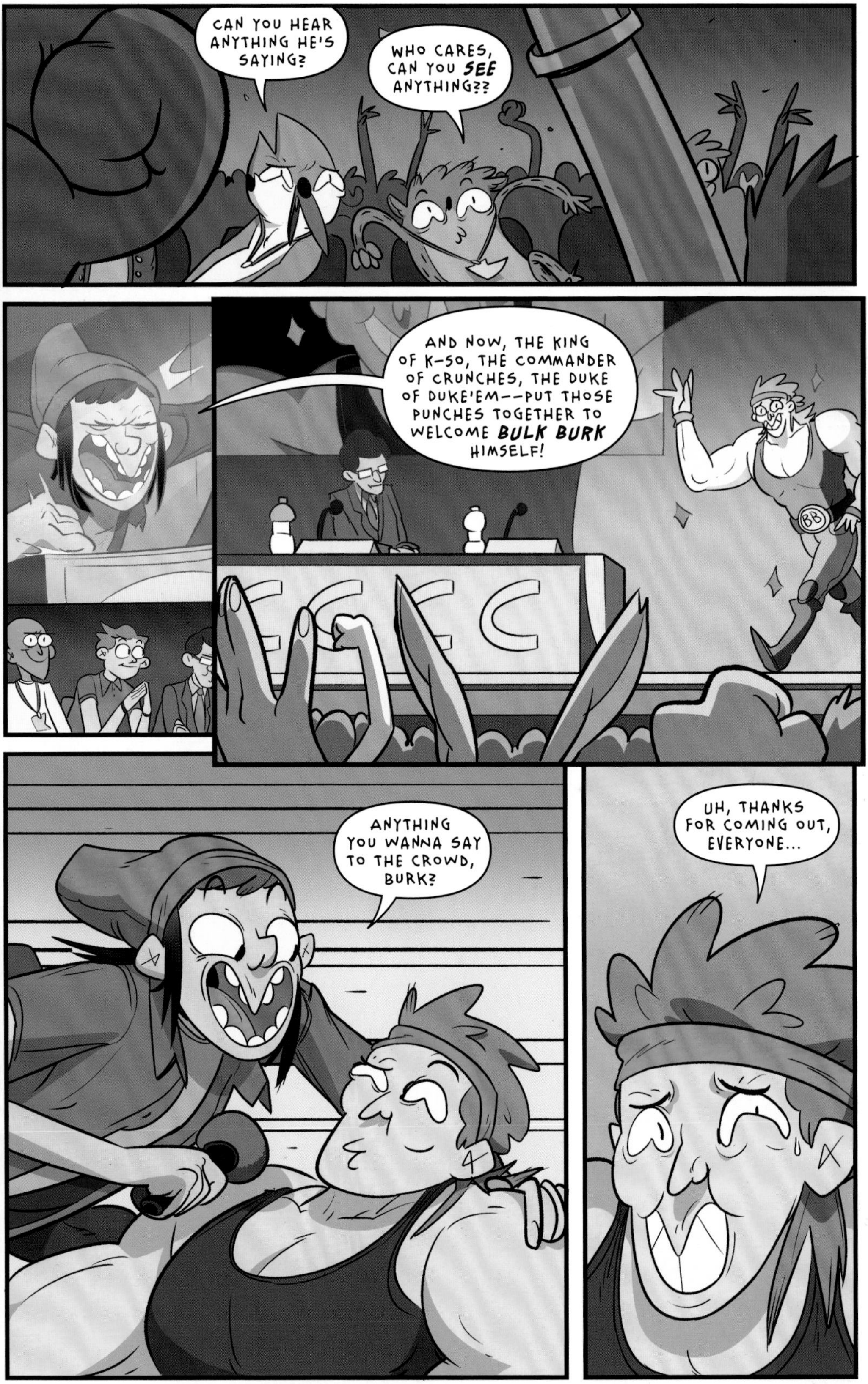
CAN YOU HEAR ANYTHING HE'S SAYING?
WHO CARES, CAN YOU *SEE* ANYTHING??
AND NOW, THE KING OF K-50, THE COMMANDER OF CRUNCHES, THE DUKE OF DUKE'EM--PUT THOSE PUNCHES TOGETHER TO WELCOME ***BULK BURK*** HIMSELF!
BB
ANYTHING YOU WANNA SAY TO THE CROWD, BURK?
UH, THANKS FOR COMING OUT, EVERYONE...

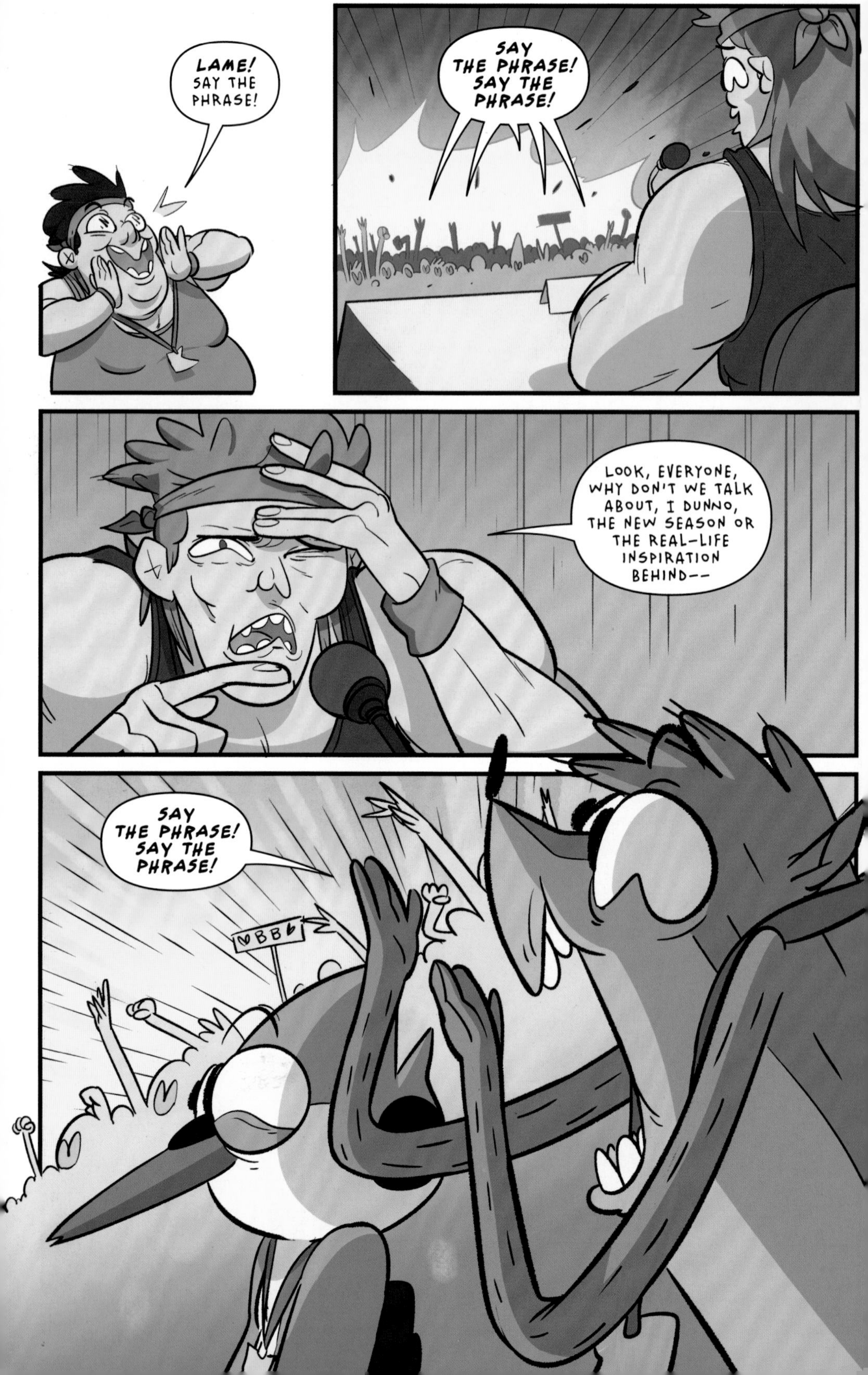
LAME! SAY THE PHRASE!
SAY THE PHRASE! SAY THE PHRASE!
LOOK, EVERYONE, WHY DON'T WE TALK ABOUT, I DUNNO, THE NEW SEASON OR THE REAL-LIFE INSPIRATION BEHIND--
SAY THE PHRASE! SAY THE PHRASE!

WELL, YOU HEARD THE FANS...

I CAN'T DO THIS!!!

THAT WAS WEIRD, RIGHT?

UH, YEAH.

SHOULD WE FOLLOW HIM?

DUH.

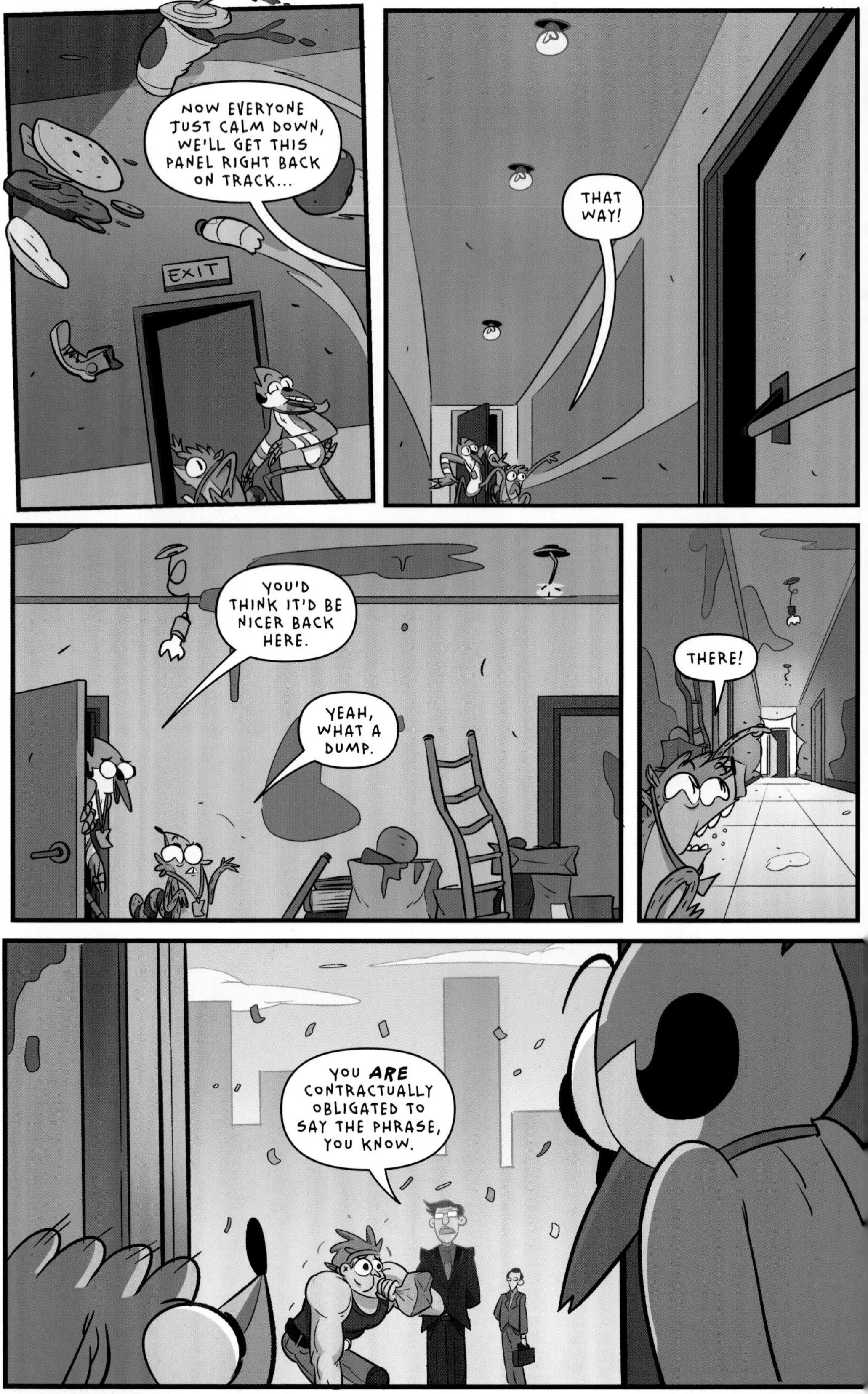
NOW EVERYONE JUST CALM DOWN, WE'LL GET THIS PANEL RIGHT BACK ON TRACK...
EXIT
THAT WAY!
YOU'D THINK IT'D BE NICER BACK HERE.
YEAH, WHAT A DUMP.
THERE!
YOU **ARE** CONTRACTUALLY OBLIGATED TO SAY THE PHRASE, YOU KNOW.

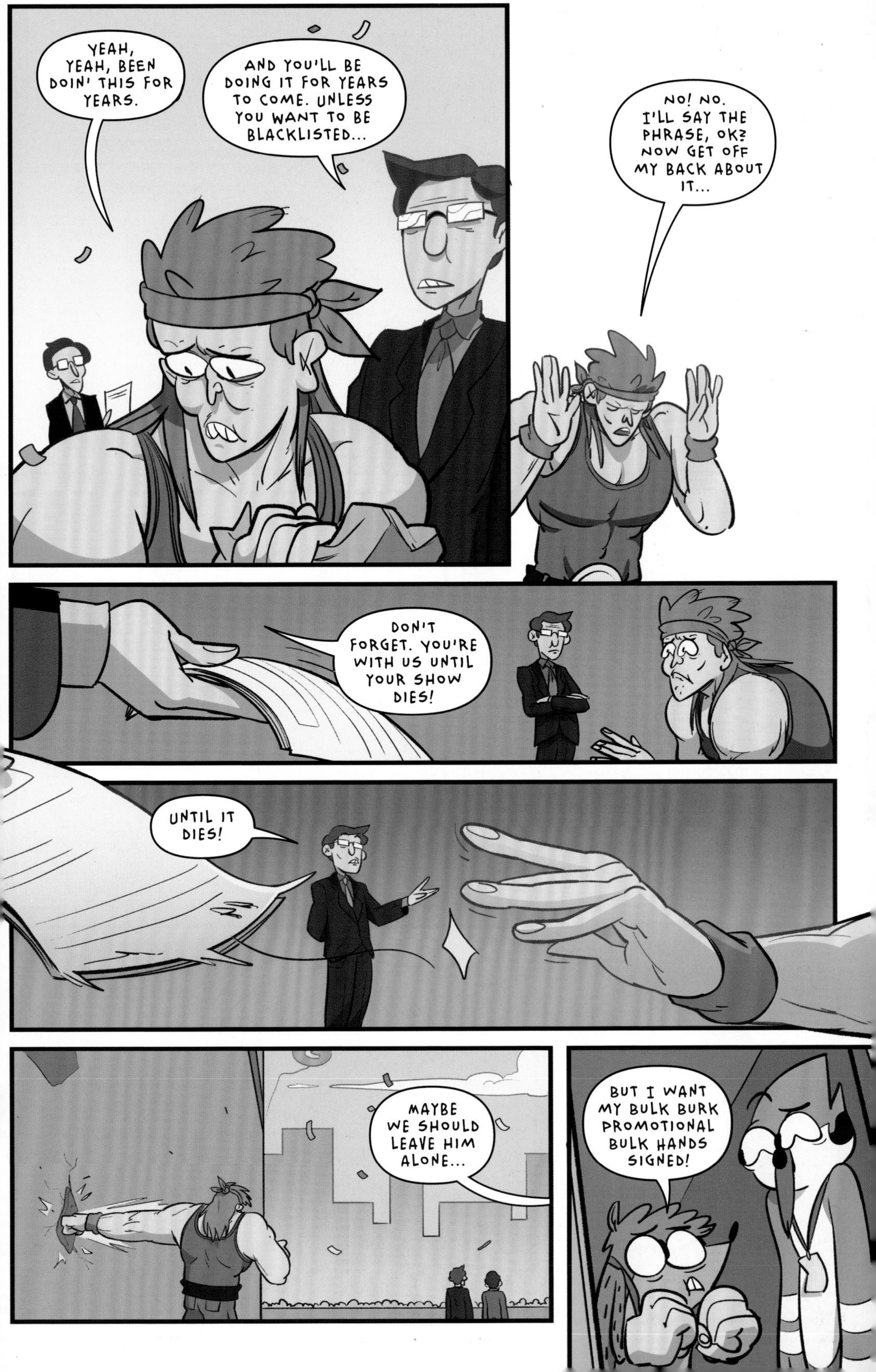
YEAH, YEAH, BEEN DOIN' THIS FOR YEARS.
AND YOU'LL BE DOING IT FOR YEARS TO COME. UNLESS YOU WANT TO BE BLACKLISTED...
NO! NO. I'LL SAY THE PHRASE, OK? NOW GET OFF MY BACK ABOUT IT...
DON'T FORGET. YOU'RE WITH US UNTIL YOUR SHOW DIES!
UNTIL IT DIES!
MAYBE WE SHOULD LEAVE HIM ALONE...
BUT I WANT MY BULK BURK PROMOTIONAL BULK HANDS SIGNED!

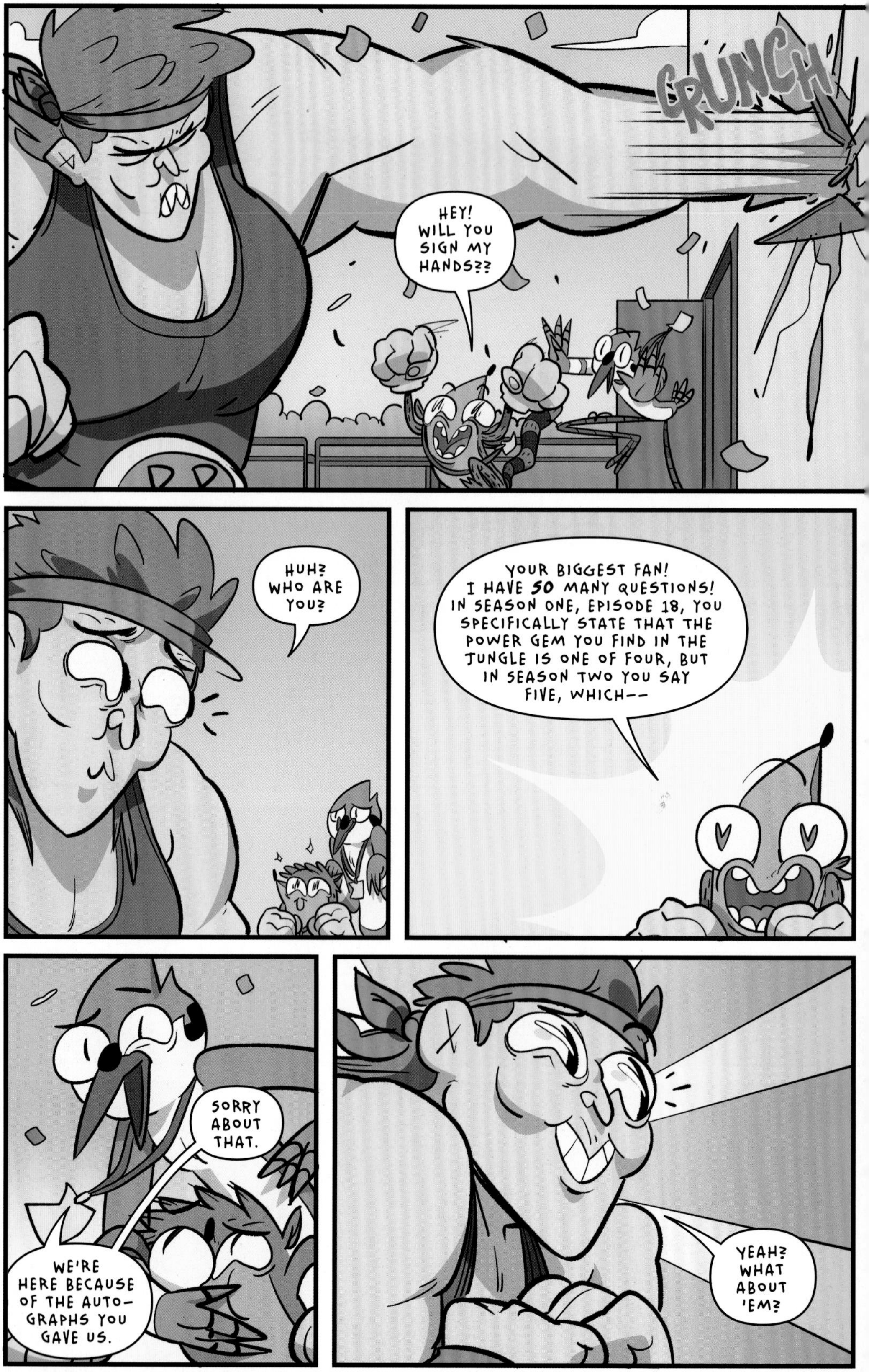
CRUNCH
HEY! WILL YOU SIGN MY HANDS??
HUH? WHO ARE YOU?
YOUR BIGGEST FAN! I HAVE SO MANY QUESTIONS! IN SEASON ONE, EPISODE 18, YOU SPECIFICALLY STATE THAT THE POWER GEM YOU FIND IN THE JUNGLE IS ONE OF FOUR, BUT IN SEASON TWO YOU SAY FIVE, WHICH--
SORRY ABOUT THAT.
WE'RE HERE BECAUSE OF THE AUTO-GRAPHS YOU GAVE US.
YEAH? WHAT ABOUT 'EM?

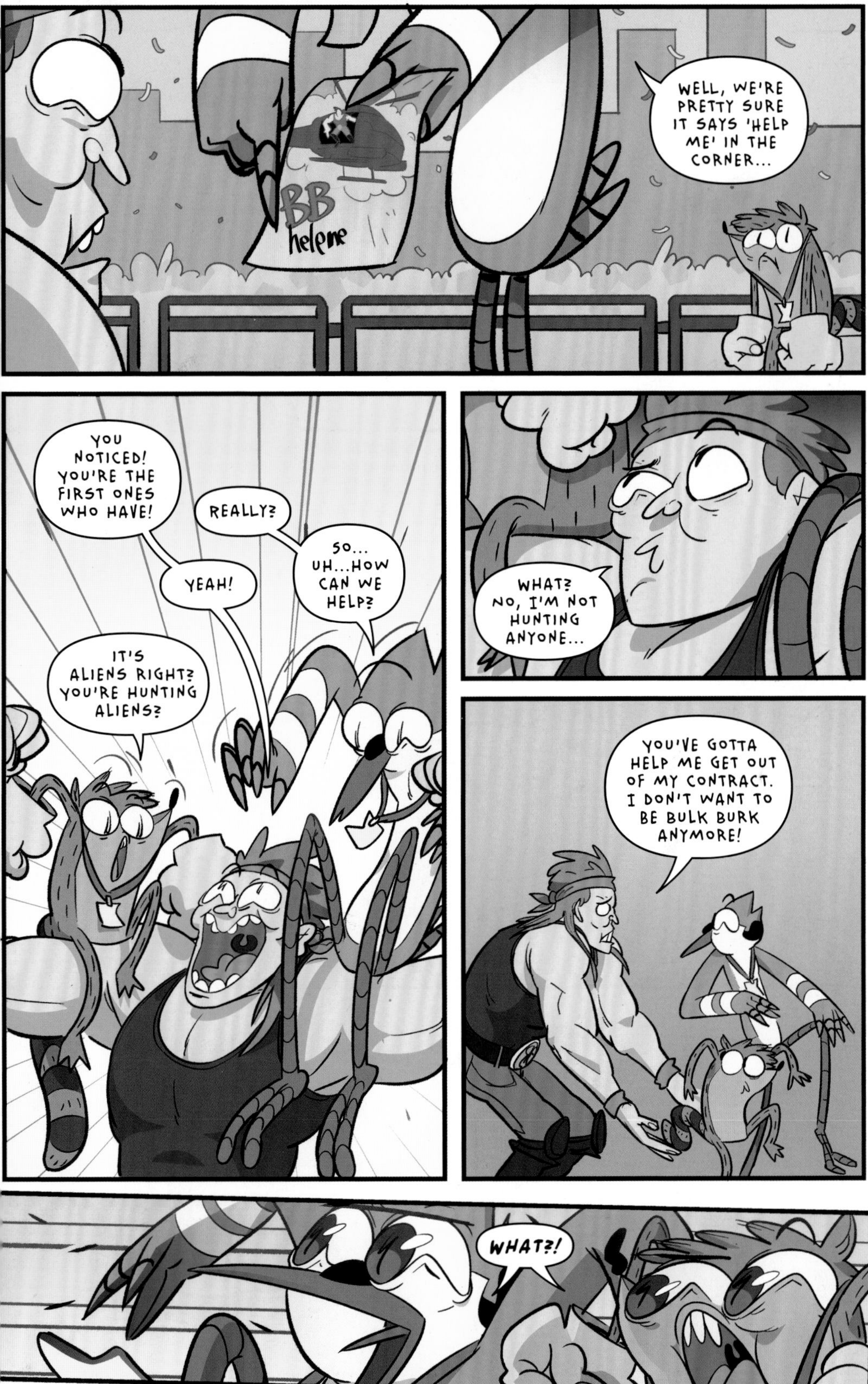
BB
helene
WELL, WE'RE PRETTY SURE IT SAYS 'HELP ME' IN THE CORNER...
YOU NOTICED! YOU'RE THE FIRST ONES WHO HAVE!
REALLY?
YEAH!
SO... UH...HOW CAN WE HELP?
IT'S ALIENS RIGHT? YOU'RE HUNTING ALIENS?
WHAT? NO, I'M NOT HUNTING ANYONE...
YOU'VE GOTTA HELP ME GET OUT OF MY CONTRACT. I DON'T WANT TO BE BULK BURK ANYMORE!
WHAT?!

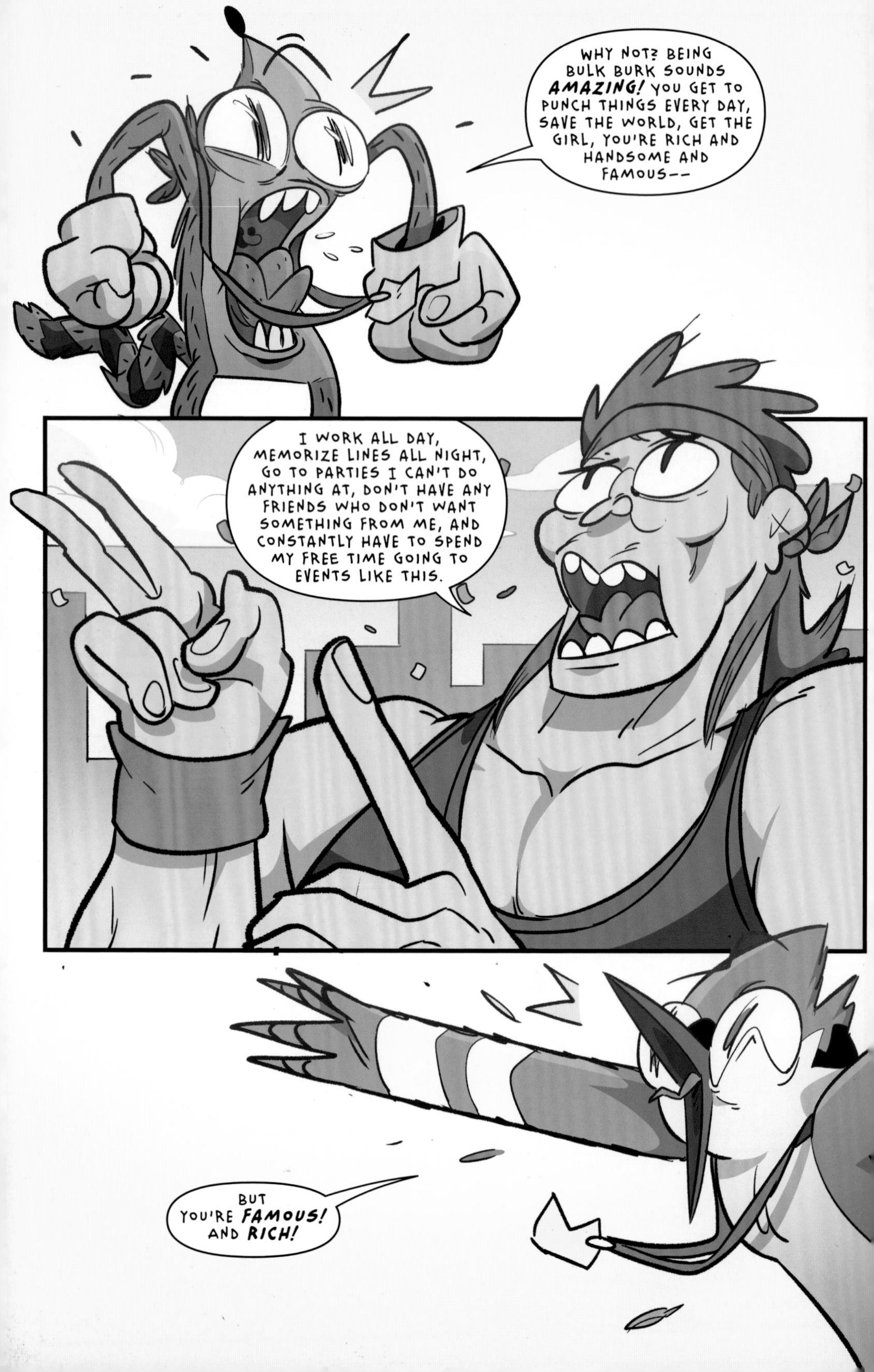
WHY NOT? BEING BULK BURK SOUNDS AMAZING! YOU GET TO PUNCH THINGS EVERY DAY, SAVE THE WORLD, GET THE GIRL, YOU'RE RICH AND HANDSOME AND FAMOUS--
I WORK ALL DAY, MEMORIZE LINES ALL NIGHT, GO TO PARTIES I CAN'T DO ANYTHING AT, DON'T HAVE ANY FRIENDS WHO DON'T WANT SOMETHING FROM ME, AND CONSTANTLY HAVE TO SPEND MY FREE TIME GOING TO EVENTS LIKE THIS.
BUT YOU'RE FAMOUS! AND RICH!

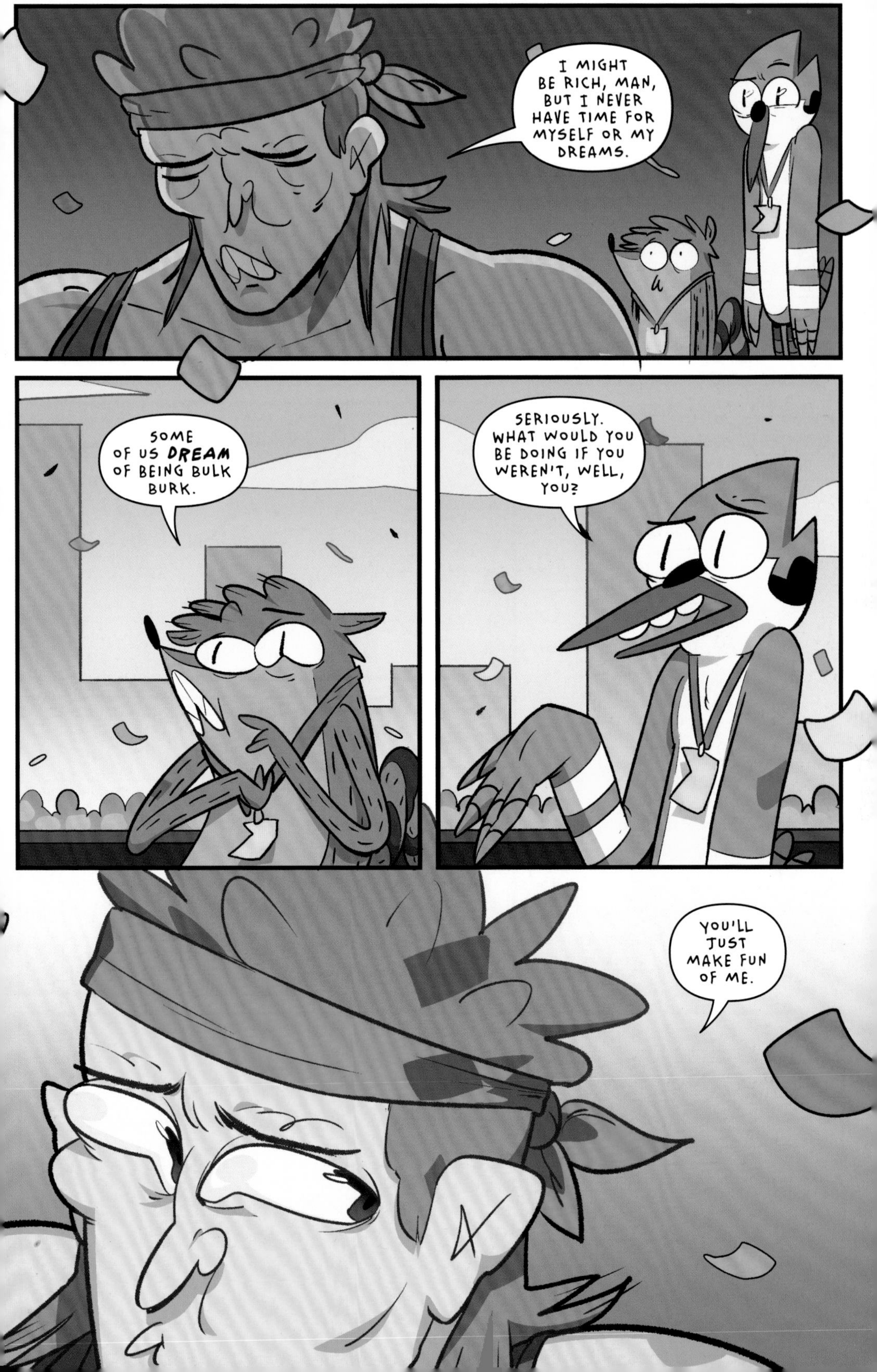
I MIGHT BE RICH, MAN, BUT I NEVER HAVE TIME FOR MYSELF OR MY DREAMS.
SOME OF US **DREAM** OF BEING BULK BURK.
SERIOUSLY. WHAT WOULD YOU BE DOING IF YOU WEREN'T, WELL, YOU?
YOU'LL JUST MAKE FUN OF ME.

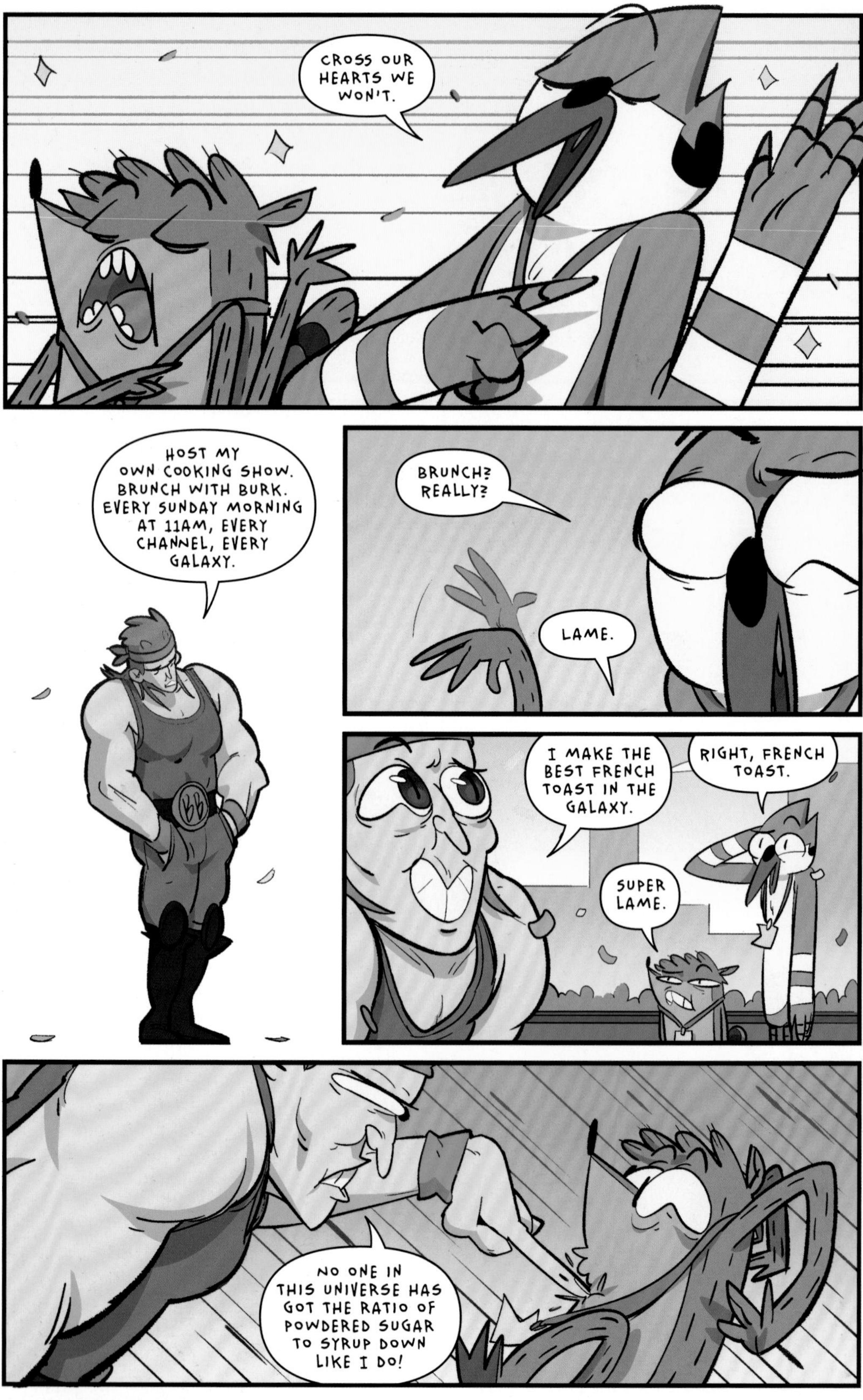
CROSS OUR HEARTS WE WON'T.
HOST MY OWN COOKING SHOW. BRUNCH WITH BURK. EVERY SUNDAY MORNING AT 11AM, EVERY CHANNEL, EVERY GALAXY.
BRUNCH? REALLY?
LAME.
I MAKE THE BEST FRENCH TOAST IN THE GALAXY.
RIGHT, FRENCH TOAST.
SUPER LAME.
NO ONE IN THIS UNIVERSE HAS GOT THE RATIO OF POWDERED SUGAR TO SYRUP DOWN LIKE I DO!

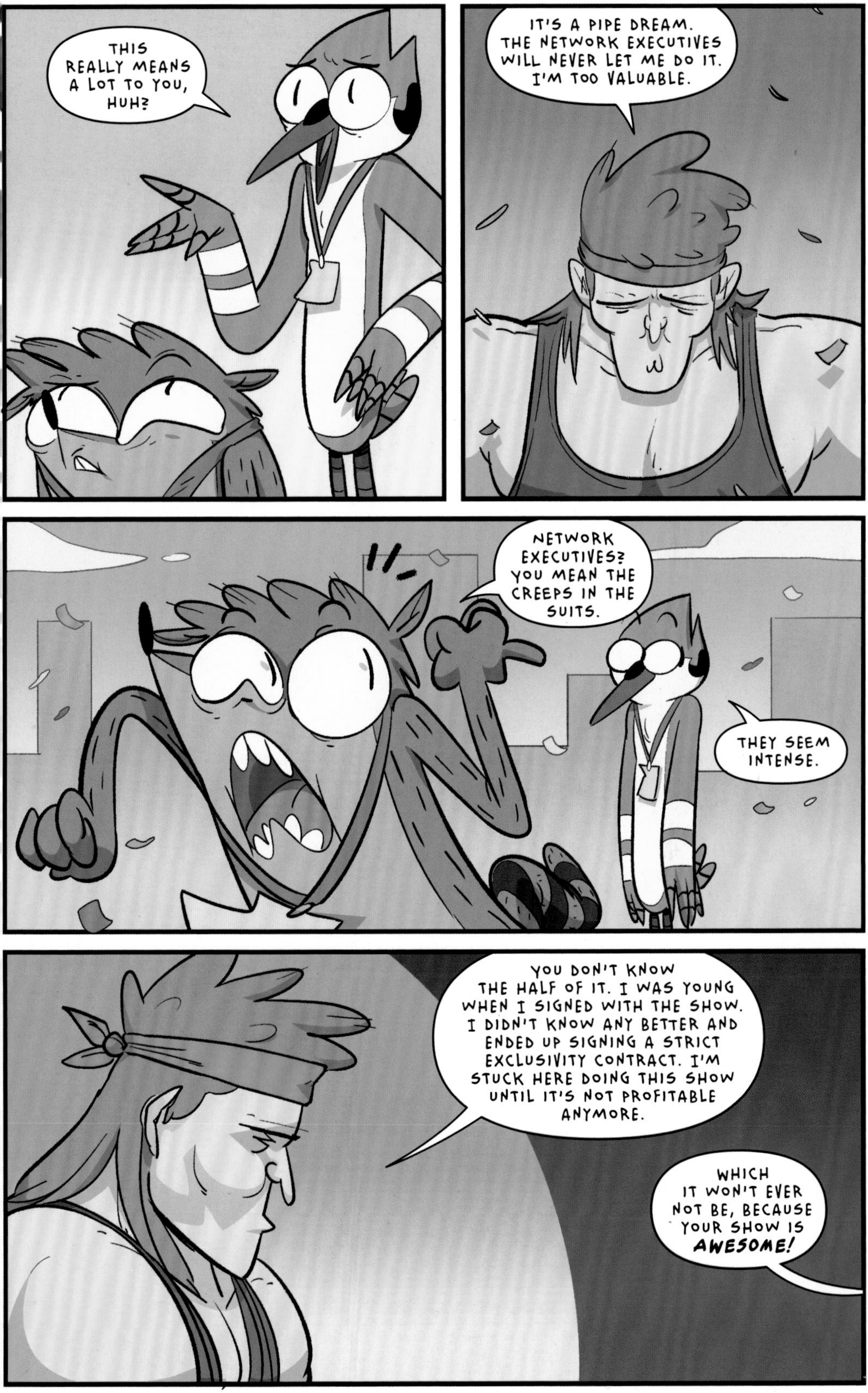
THIS REALLY MEANS A LOT TO YOU, HUH?
IT'S A PIPE DREAM. THE NETWORK EXECUTIVES WILL NEVER LET ME DO IT. I'M TOO VALUABLE.
NETWORK EXECUTIVES? YOU MEAN THE CREEPS IN THE SUITS.
THEY SEEM INTENSE.
YOU DON'T KNOW THE HALF OF IT. I WAS YOUNG WHEN I SIGNED WITH THE SHOW. I DIDN'T KNOW ANY BETTER AND ENDED UP SIGNING A STRICT EXCLUSIVITY CONTRACT. I'M STUCK HERE DOING THIS SHOW UNTIL IT'S NOT PROFITABLE ANYMORE.
WHICH IT WON'T EVER NOT BE, BECAUSE YOUR SHOW IS AWESOME!

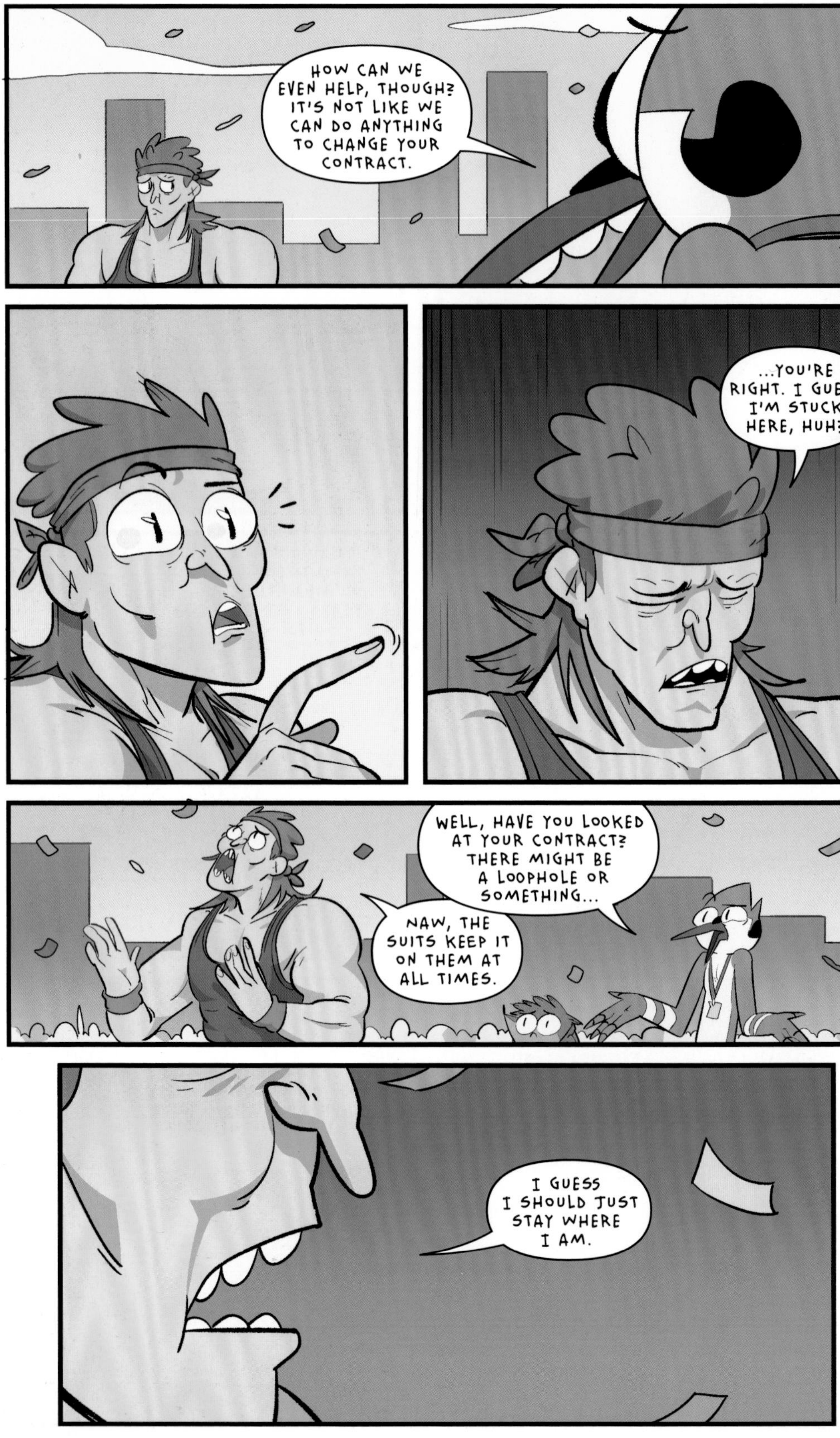
HOW CAN WE EVEN HELP, THOUGH? IT'S NOT LIKE WE CAN DO ANYTHING TO CHANGE YOUR CONTRACT.
...YOU'RE RIGHT. I GUESS I'M STUCK HERE, HUH?
WELL, HAVE YOU LOOKED AT YOUR CONTRACT? THERE MIGHT BE A LOOPHOLE OR SOMETHING...
NAW, THE SUITS KEEP IT ON THEM AT ALL TIMES.
I GUESS I SHOULD JUST STAY WHERE I AM.

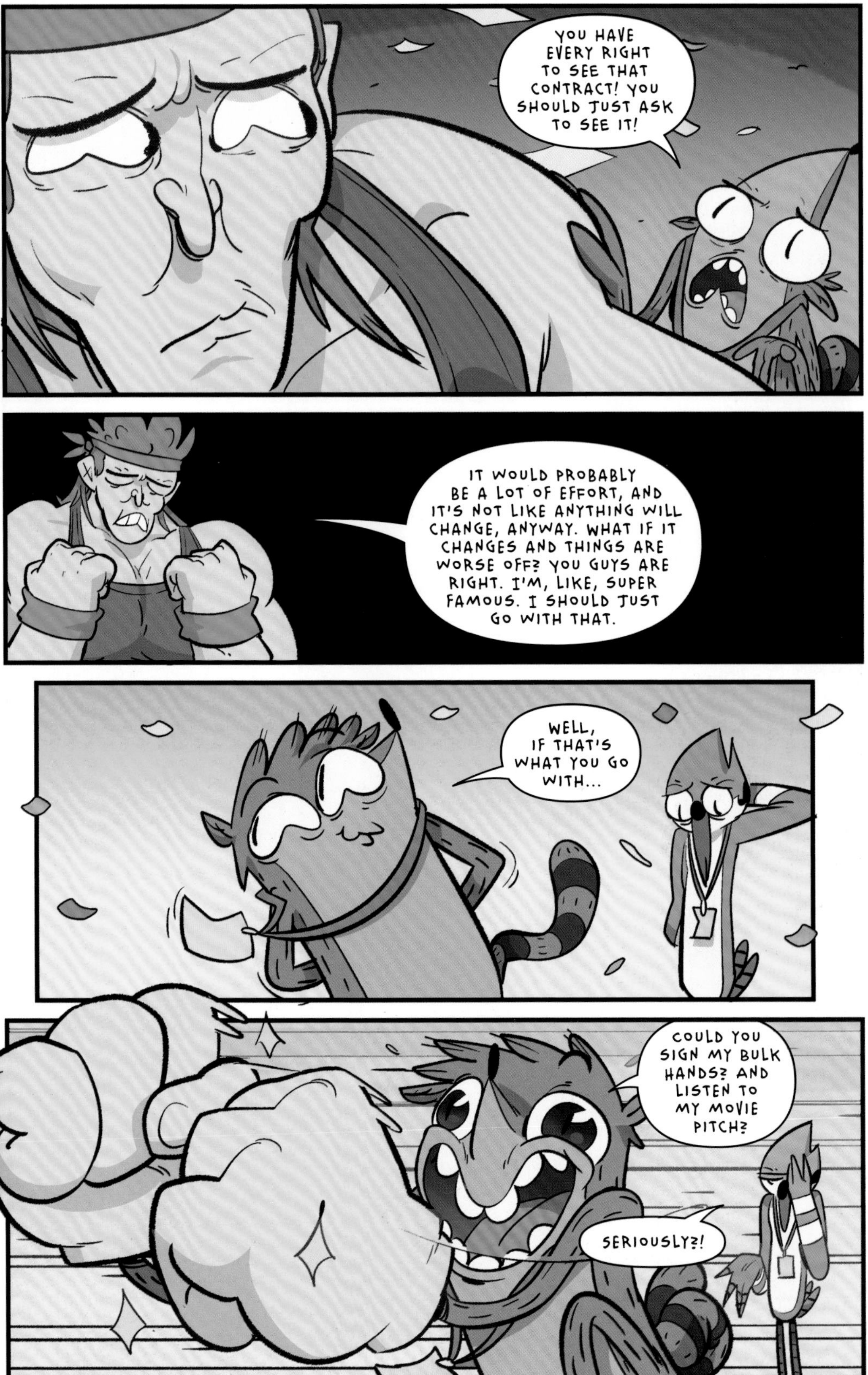
YOU HAVE EVERY RIGHT TO SEE THAT CONTRACT! YOU SHOULD JUST ASK TO SEE IT!
IT WOULD PROBABLY BE A LOT OF EFFORT, AND IT'S NOT LIKE ANYTHING WILL CHANGE, ANYWAY. WHAT IF IT CHANGES AND THINGS ARE WORSE OFF? YOU GUYS ARE RIGHT. I'M, LIKE, SUPER FAMOUS. I SHOULD JUST GO WITH THAT.
WELL, IF THAT'S WHAT YOU GO WITH...
COULD YOU SIGN MY BULK HANDS? AND LISTEN TO MY MOVIE PITCH?
SERIOUSLY?!

THERE YOU ARE. COME ON, YOU'VE GOT YOUR 2:30 PANEL COMING UP, AND WE'VE GOT TO TALK ABOUT YOUR LITTLE STUNT BACK THERE.

YEAH, YEAH.

I GUESS YOU'D BETTER GO.

THE CONTRACT CALLS.

SO, ABOUT MY MOVIE PITCH...

YOU TWO HAVE FUN.

AUTOGRAPHS ARE $40 PER ITEM AT THE AUTOGRAPH HALL.

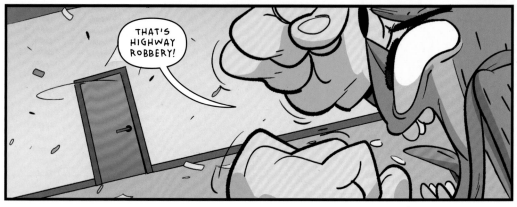

THAT'S HIGHWAY ROBBERY!

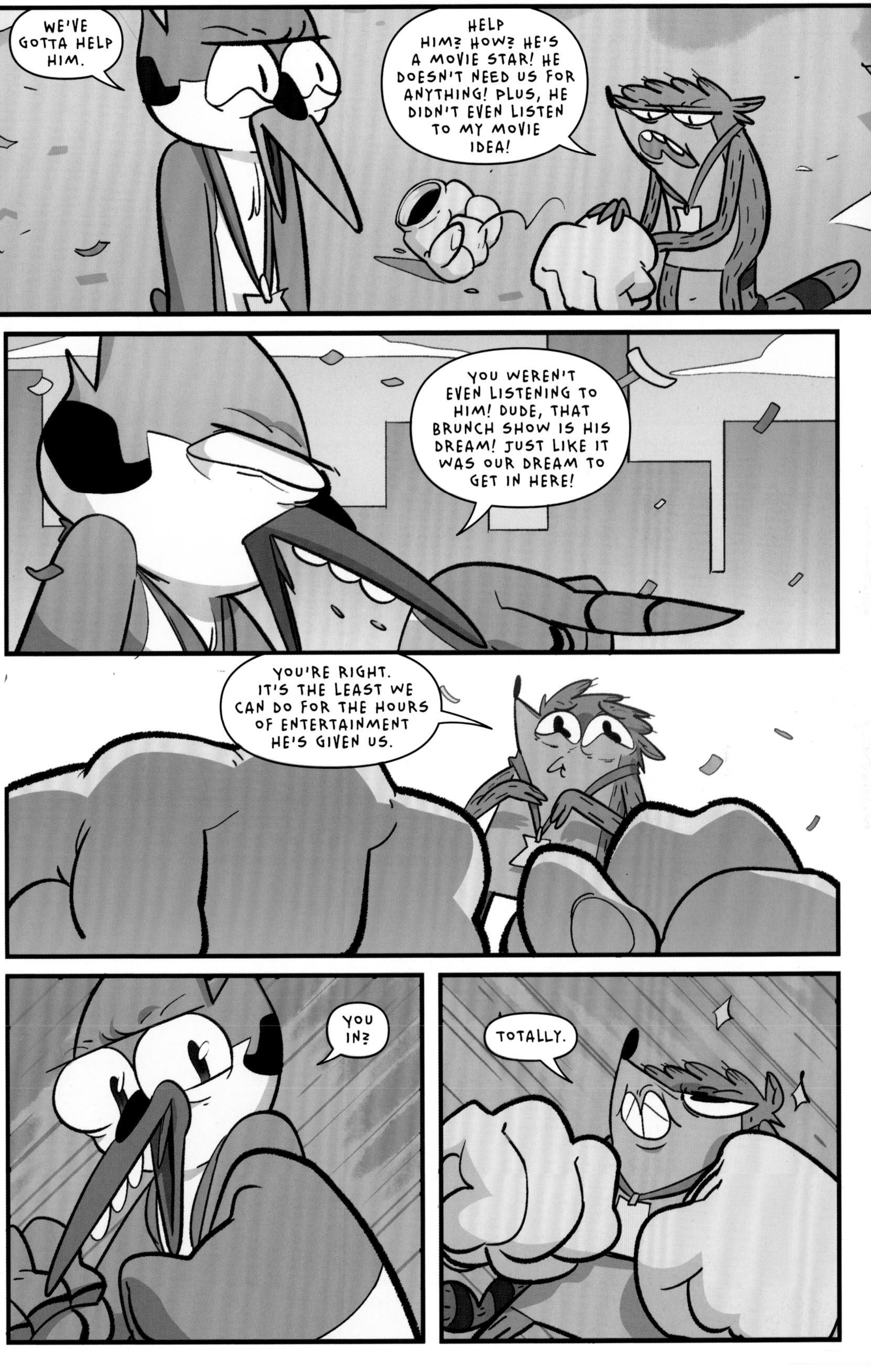
WE'VE GOTTA HELP HIM.
HELP HIM? HOW? HE'S A MOVIE STAR! HE DOESN'T NEED US FOR ANYTHING! PLUS, HE DIDN'T EVEN LISTEN TO MY MOVIE IDEA!
YOU WEREN'T EVEN LISTENING TO HIM! DUDE, THAT BRUNCH SHOW IS HIS DREAM! JUST LIKE IT WAS OUR DREAM TO GET IN HERE!
YOU'RE RIGHT. IT'S THE LEAST WE CAN DO FOR THE HOURS OF ENTERTAINMENT HE'S GIVEN US.
YOU IN?
TOTALLY.

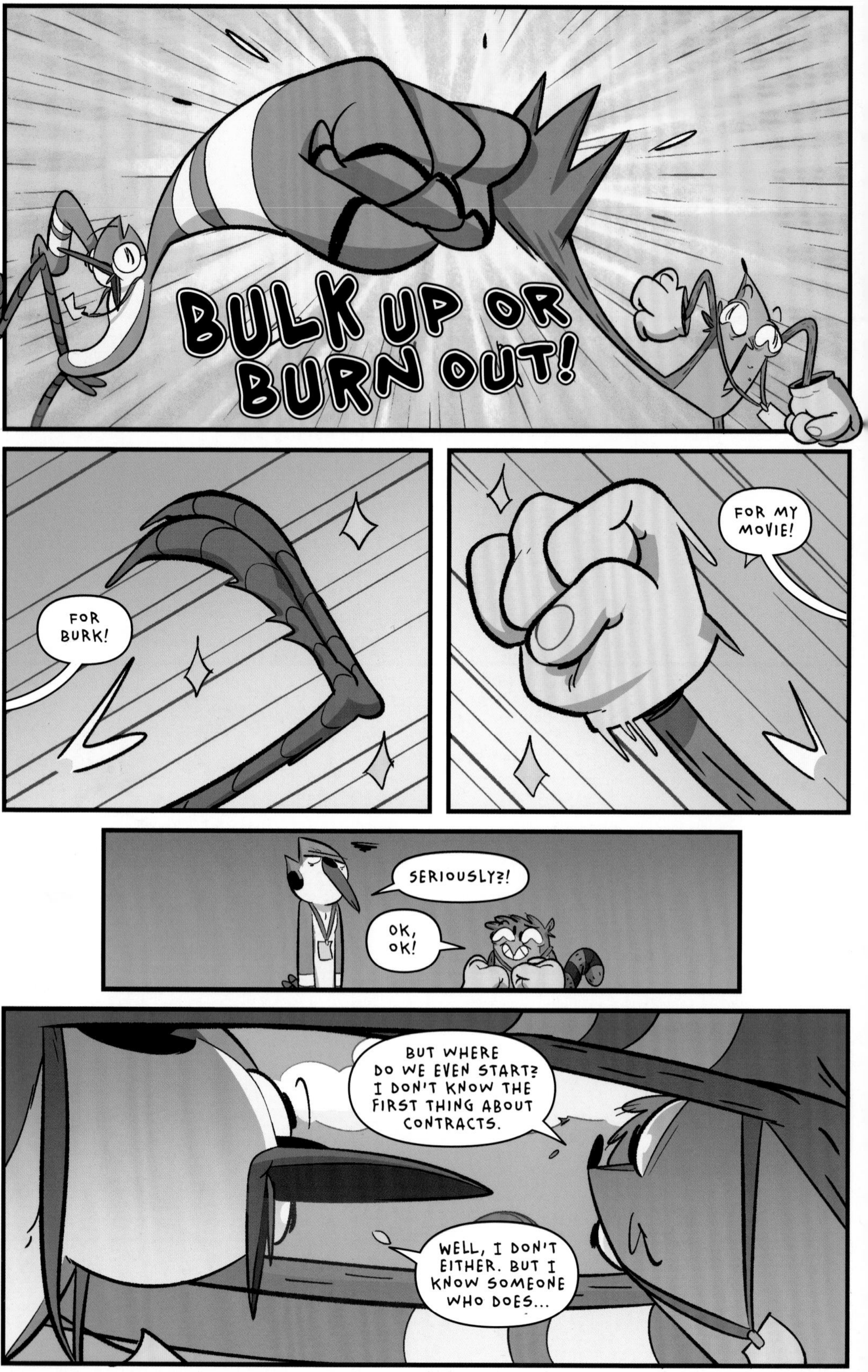
BULK UP OR BURN OUT!
FOR BURK!
FOR MY MOVIE!
SERIOUSLY?!
OK, OK!
BUT WHERE DO WE EVEN START? I DON'T KNOW THE FIRST THING ABOUT CONTRACTS.
WELL, I DON'T EITHER. BUT I KNOW SOMEONE WHO DOES...

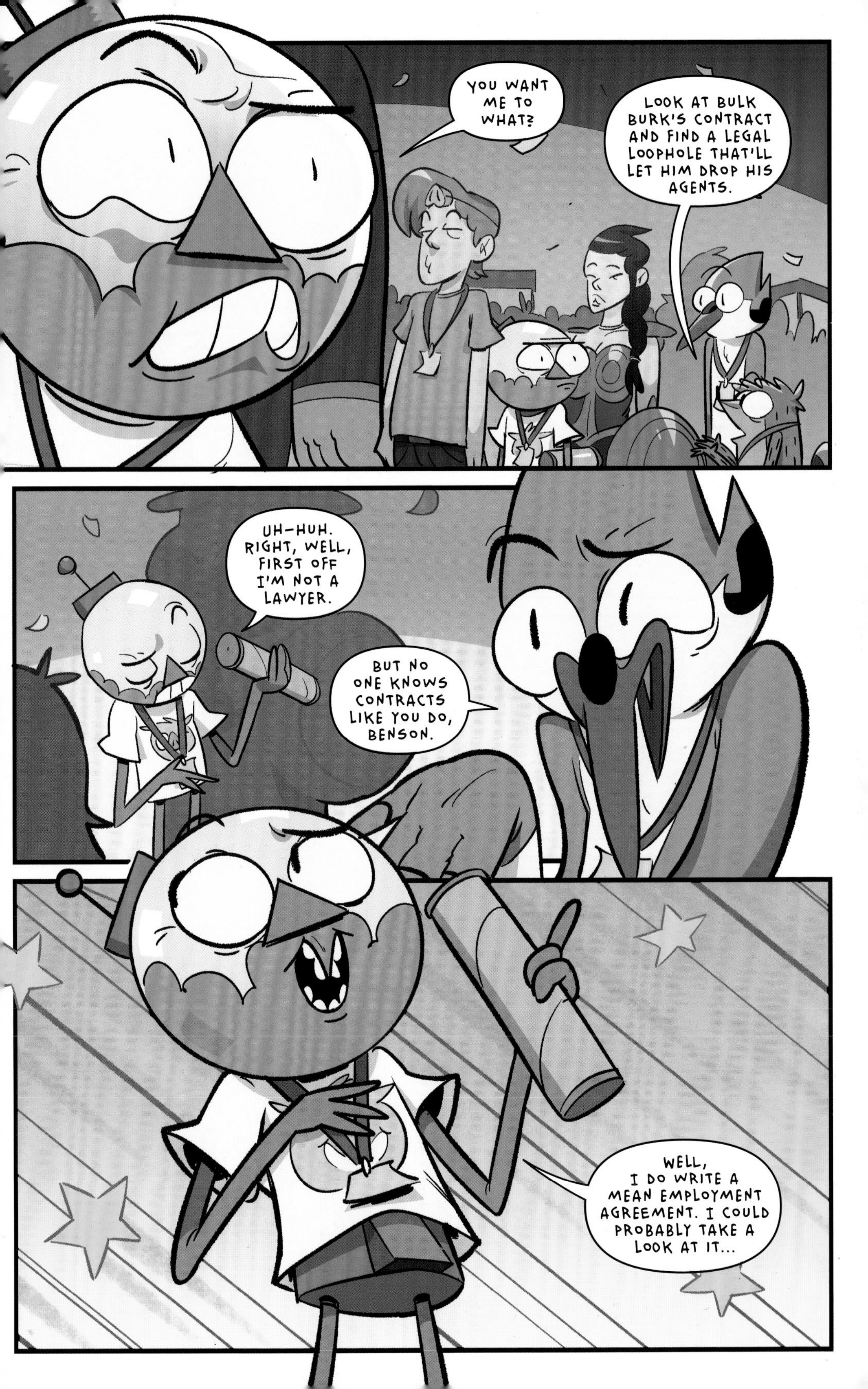
YOU WANT ME TO WHAT?
LOOK AT BULK BURK'S CONTRACT AND FIND A LEGAL LOOPHOLE THAT'LL LET HIM DROP HIS AGENTS.
UH-HUH. RIGHT, WELL, FIRST OFF I'M NOT A LAWYER.
BUT NO ONE KNOWS CONTRACTS LIKE YOU DO, BENSON.
WELL, I DO WRITE A MEAN EMPLOYMENT AGREEMENT. I COULD PROBABLY TAKE A LOOK AT IT...

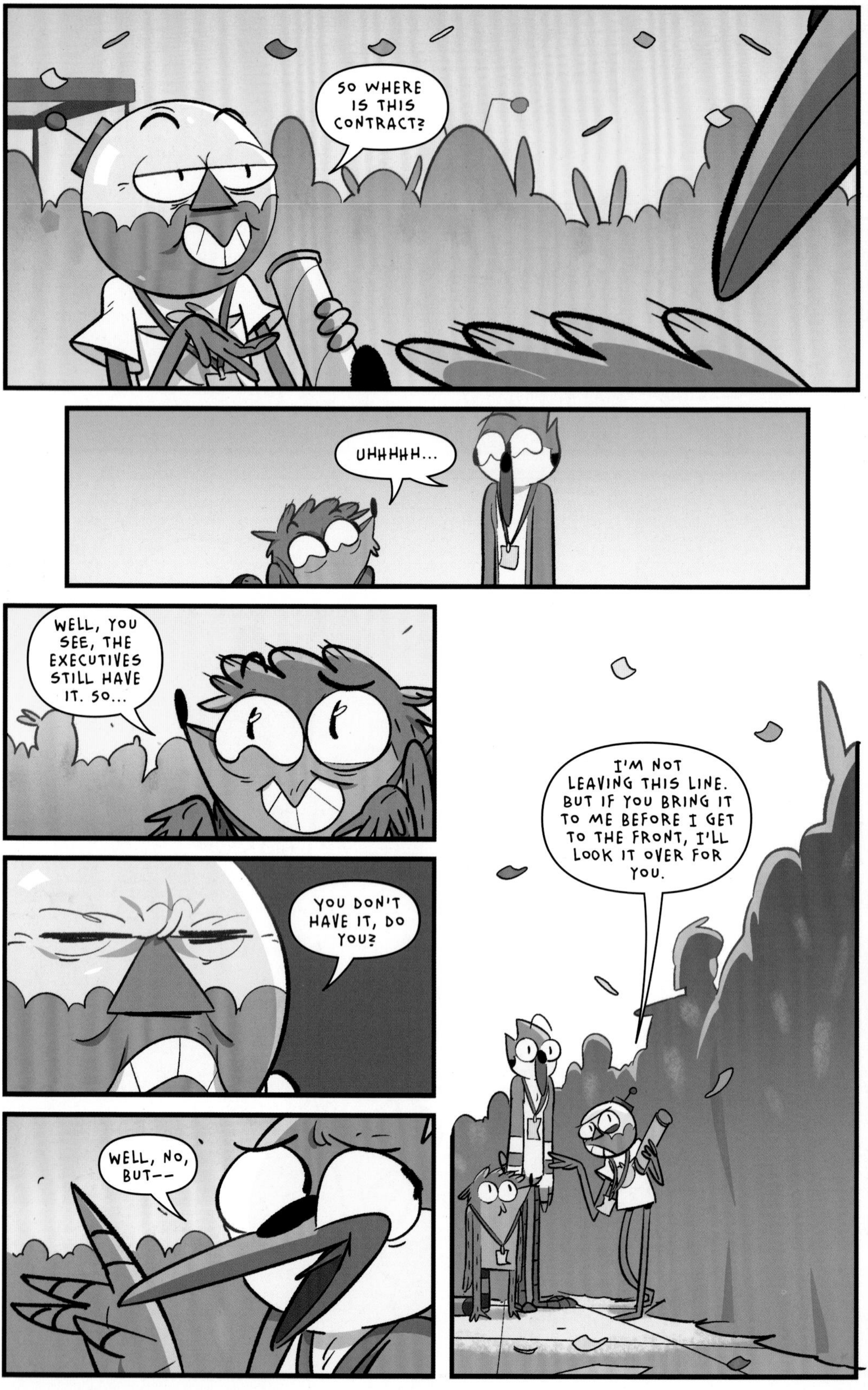
SO WHERE IS THIS CONTRACT?
UHHHHH...
WELL, YOU SEE, THE EXECUTIVES STILL HAVE IT. SO...
YOU DON'T HAVE IT, DO YOU?
WELL, NO, BUT--
I'M NOT LEAVING THIS LINE. BUT IF YOU BRING IT TO ME BEFORE I GET TO THE FRONT, I'LL LOOK IT OVER FOR YOU.

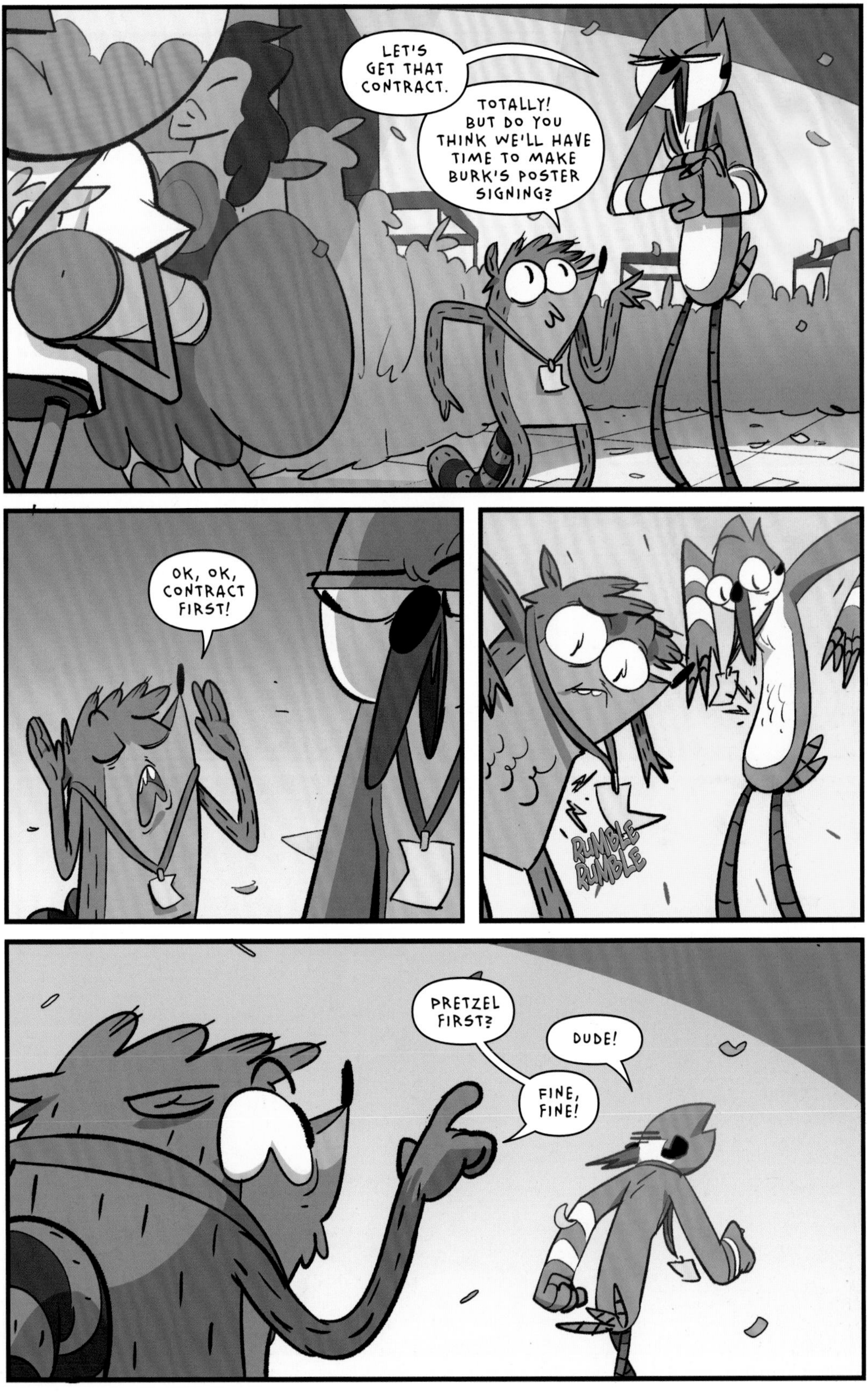
LET'S GET THAT CONTRACT.
TOTALLY! BUT DO YOU THINK WE'LL HAVE TIME TO MAKE BURK'S POSTER SIGNING?
OK, OK, CONTRACT FIRST!
RUMBLE RUMBLE
PRETZEL FIRST?
DUDE!
FINE, FINE!

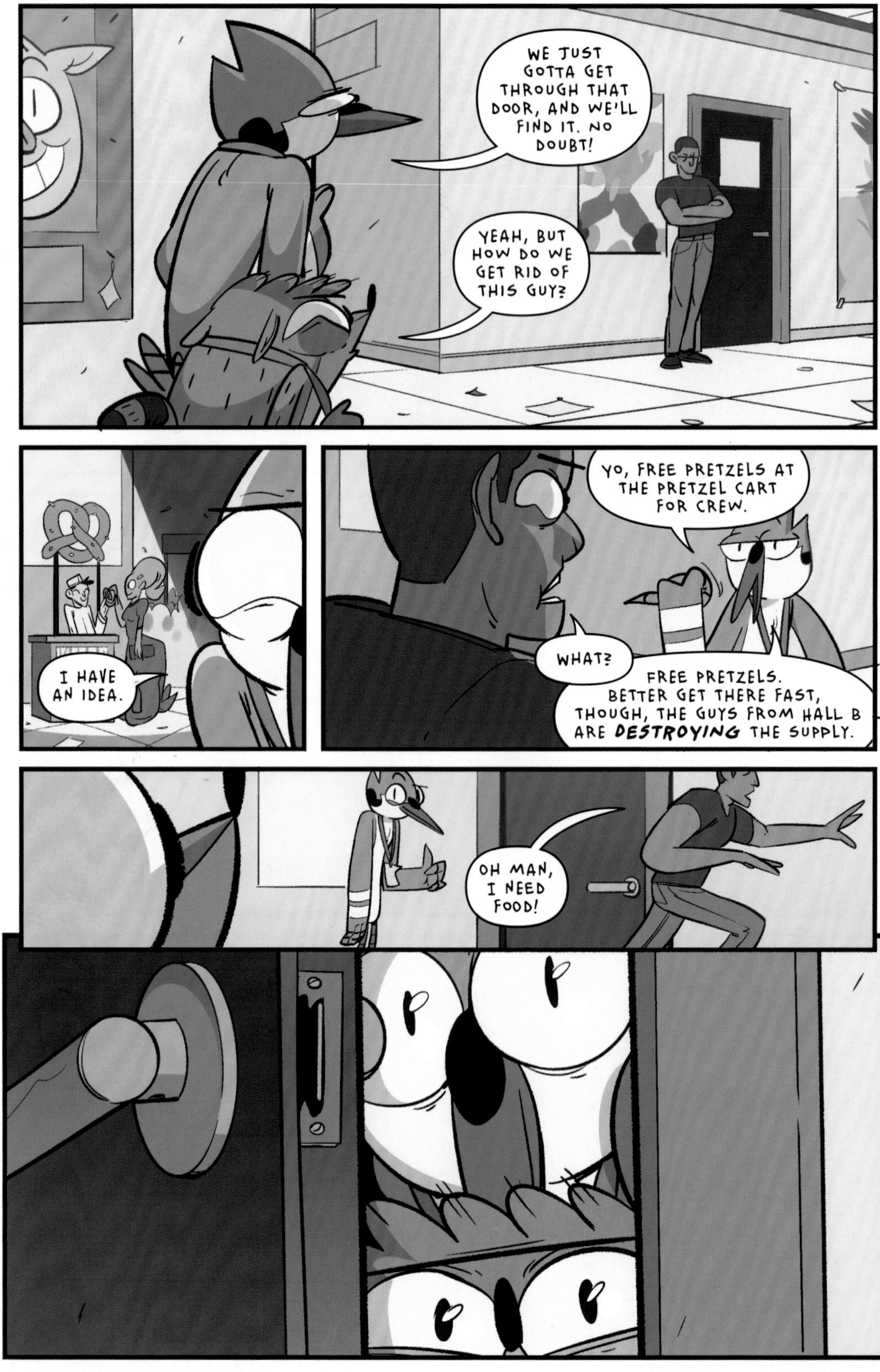
WE JUST GOTTA GET THROUGH THAT DOOR, AND WE'LL FIND IT. NO DOUBT!
YEAH, BUT HOW DO WE GET RID OF THIS GUY?
I HAVE AN IDEA.
YO, FREE PRETZELS AT THE PRETZEL CART FOR CREW.
WHAT?
FREE PRETZELS. BETTER GET THERE FAST, THOUGH, THE GUYS FROM HALL B ARE **DESTROYING** THE SUPPLY.
OH MAN, I NEED FOOD!

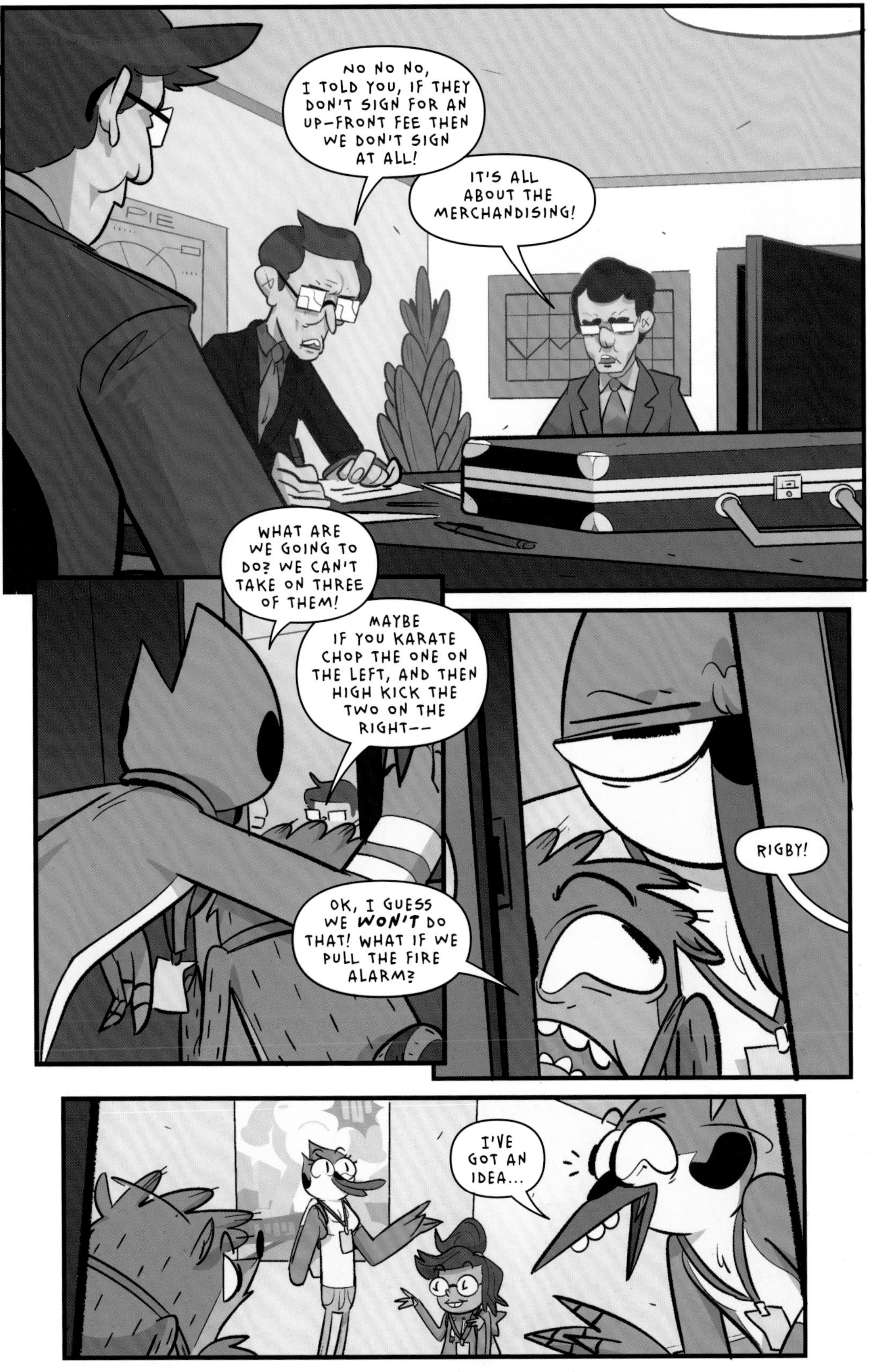
NO NO NO, I TOLD YOU, IF THEY DON'T SIGN FOR AN UP-FRONT FEE THEN WE DON'T SIGN AT ALL!
IT'S ALL ABOUT THE MERCHANDISING!
WHAT ARE WE GOING TO DO? WE CAN'T TAKE ON THREE OF THEM!
MAYBE IF YOU KARATE CHOP THE ONE ON THE LEFT, AND THEN HIGH KICK THE TWO ON THE RIGHT--
RIGBY!
OK, I GUESS WE WON'T DO THAT! WHAT IF WE PULL THE FIRE ALARM?
I'VE GOT AN IDEA...

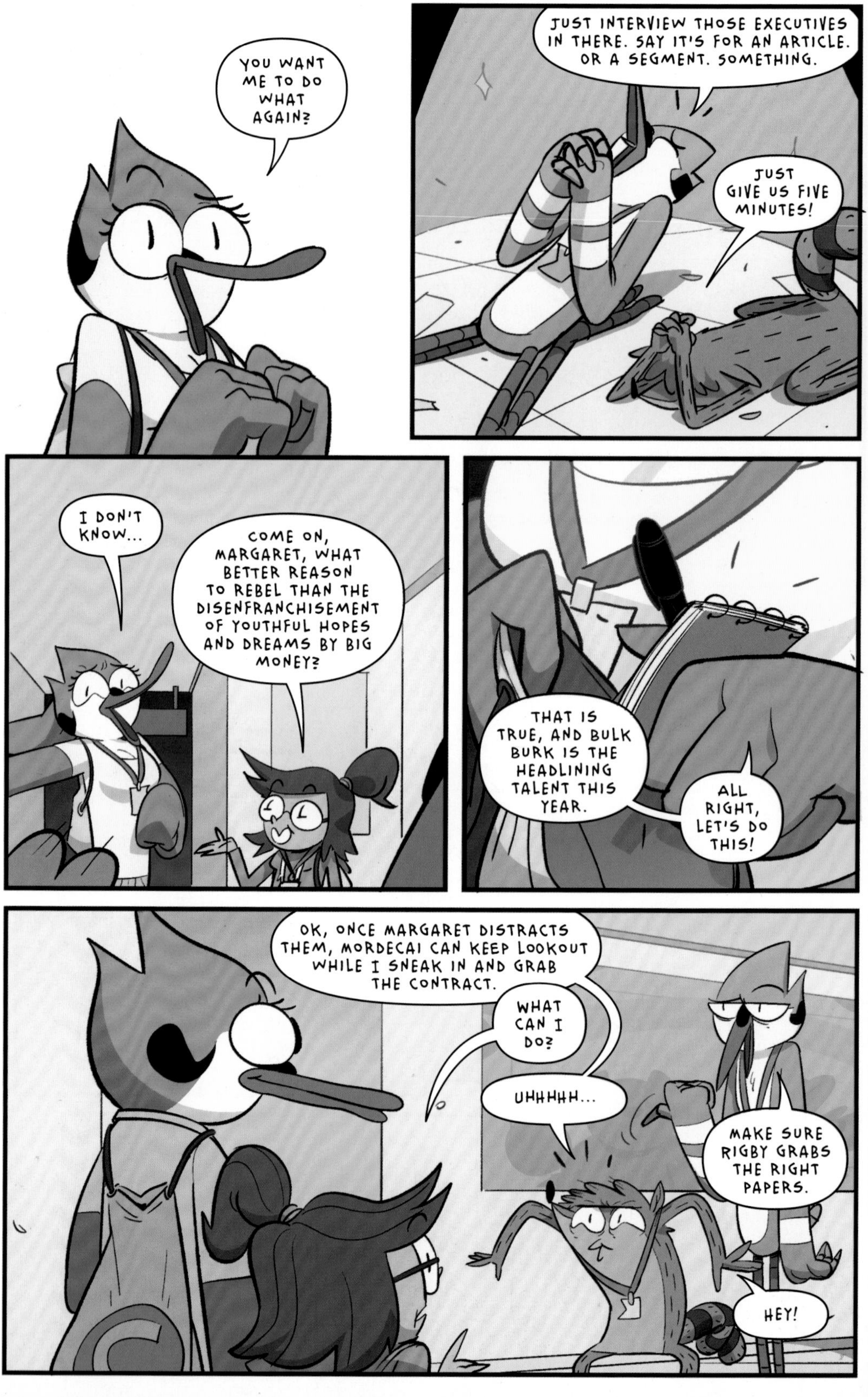
YOU WANT ME TO DO WHAT AGAIN?
JUST INTERVIEW THOSE EXECUTIVES IN THERE. SAY IT'S FOR AN ARTICLE. OR A SEGMENT. SOMETHING.
JUST GIVE US FIVE MINUTES!
I DON'T KNOW...
COME ON, MARGARET, WHAT BETTER REASON TO REBEL THAN THE DISENFRANCHISEMENT OF YOUTHFUL HOPES AND DREAMS BY BIG MONEY?
THAT IS TRUE, AND BULK BURK IS THE HEADLINING TALENT THIS YEAR.
ALL RIGHT, LET'S DO THIS!
OK, ONCE MARGARET DISTRACTS THEM, MORDECAI CAN KEEP LOOKOUT WHILE I SNEAK IN AND GRAB THE CONTRACT.
WHAT CAN I DO?
UHHHHH...
MAKE SURE RIGBY GRABS THE RIGHT PAPERS.
HEY!

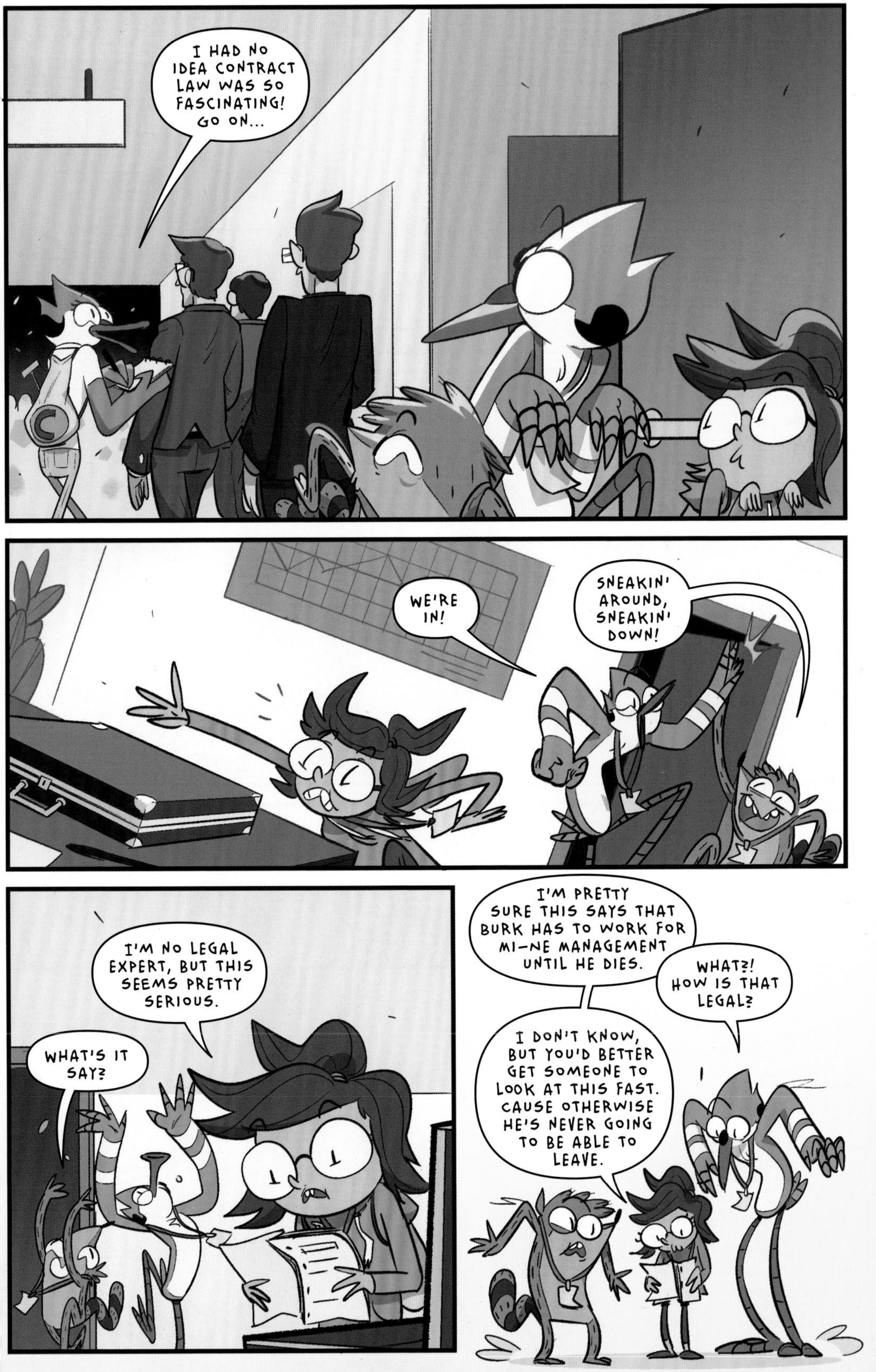
I HAD NO IDEA CONTRACT LAW WAS SO FASCINATING! GO ON...
WE'RE IN!
SNEAKIN' AROUND, SNEAKIN' DOWN!
I'M NO LEGAL EXPERT, BUT THIS SEEMS PRETTY SERIOUS.
WHAT'S IT SAY?
I'M PRETTY SURE THIS SAYS THAT BURK HAS TO WORK FOR MI-NE MANAGEMENT UNTIL HE DIES.
WHAT?! HOW IS THAT LEGAL?
I DON'T KNOW, BUT YOU'D BETTER GET SOMEONE TO LOOK AT THIS FAST. CAUSE OTHERWISE HE'S NEVER GOING TO BE ABLE TO LEAVE.

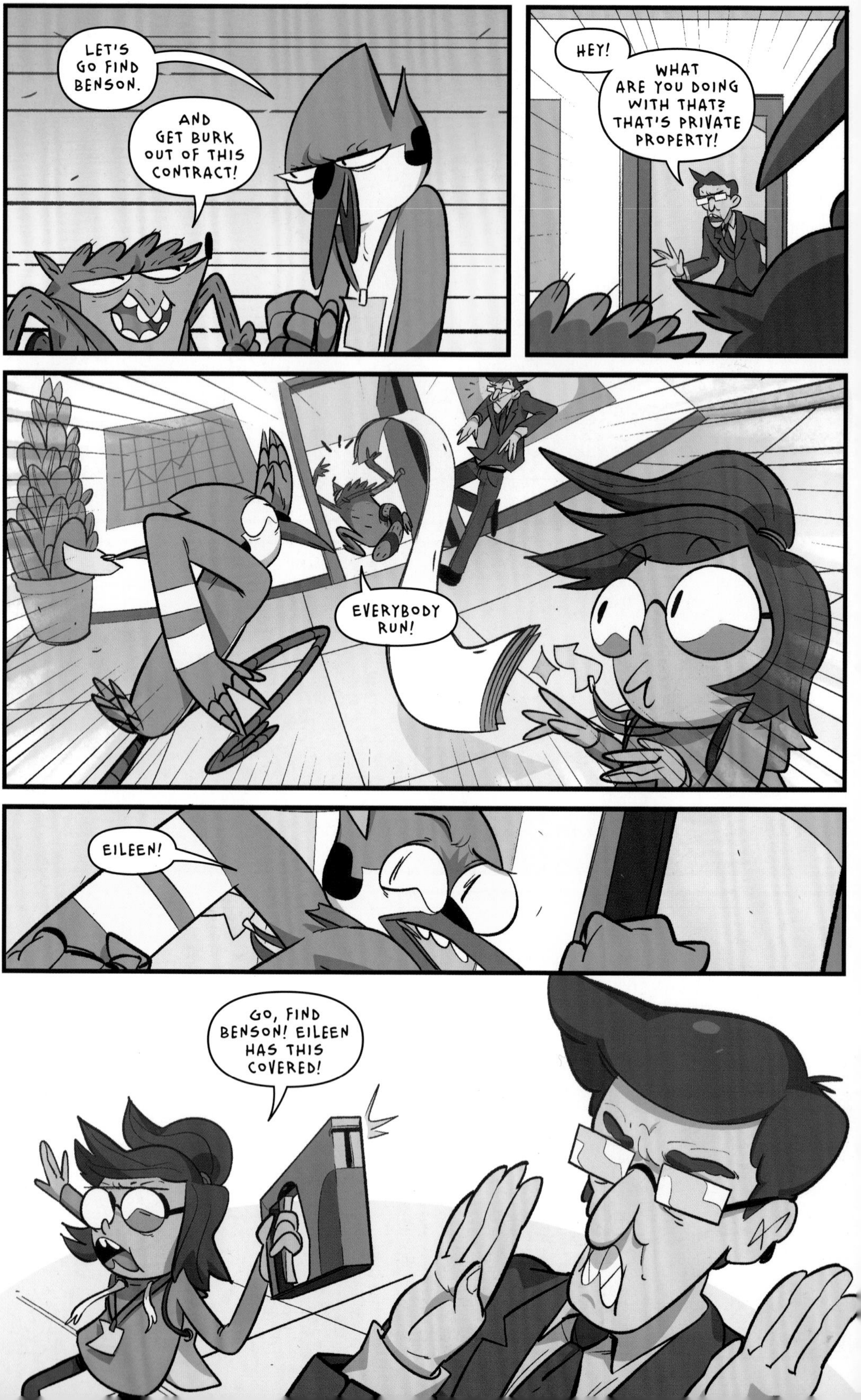
LET'S GO FIND BENSON.
AND GET BURK OUT OF THIS CONTRACT!
HEY!
WHAT ARE YOU DOING WITH THAT? THAT'S PRIVATE PROPERTY!
EVERYBODY RUN!
EILEEN!
GO, FIND BENSON! EILEEN HAS THIS COVERED!

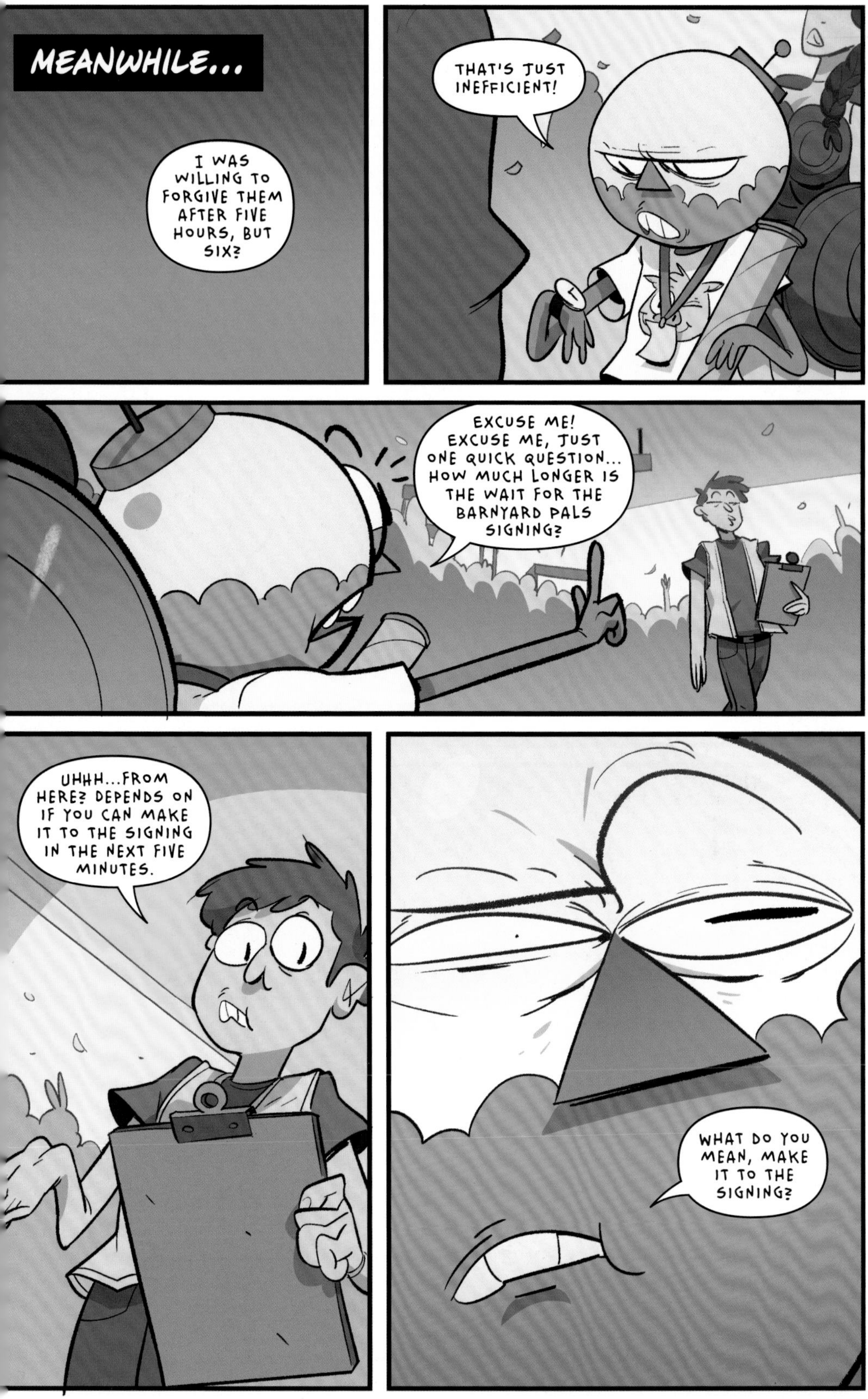
MEANWHILE...
I WAS WILLING TO FORGIVE THEM AFTER FIVE HOURS, BUT SIX?
THAT'S JUST INEFFICIENT!
EXCUSE ME! EXCUSE ME, JUST ONE QUICK QUESTION... HOW MUCH LONGER IS THE WAIT FOR THE BARNYARD PALS SIGNING?
UHHH...FROM HERE? DEPENDS ON IF YOU CAN MAKE IT TO THE SIGNING IN THE NEXT FIVE MINUTES.
WHAT DO YOU MEAN, MAKE IT TO THE SIGNING?

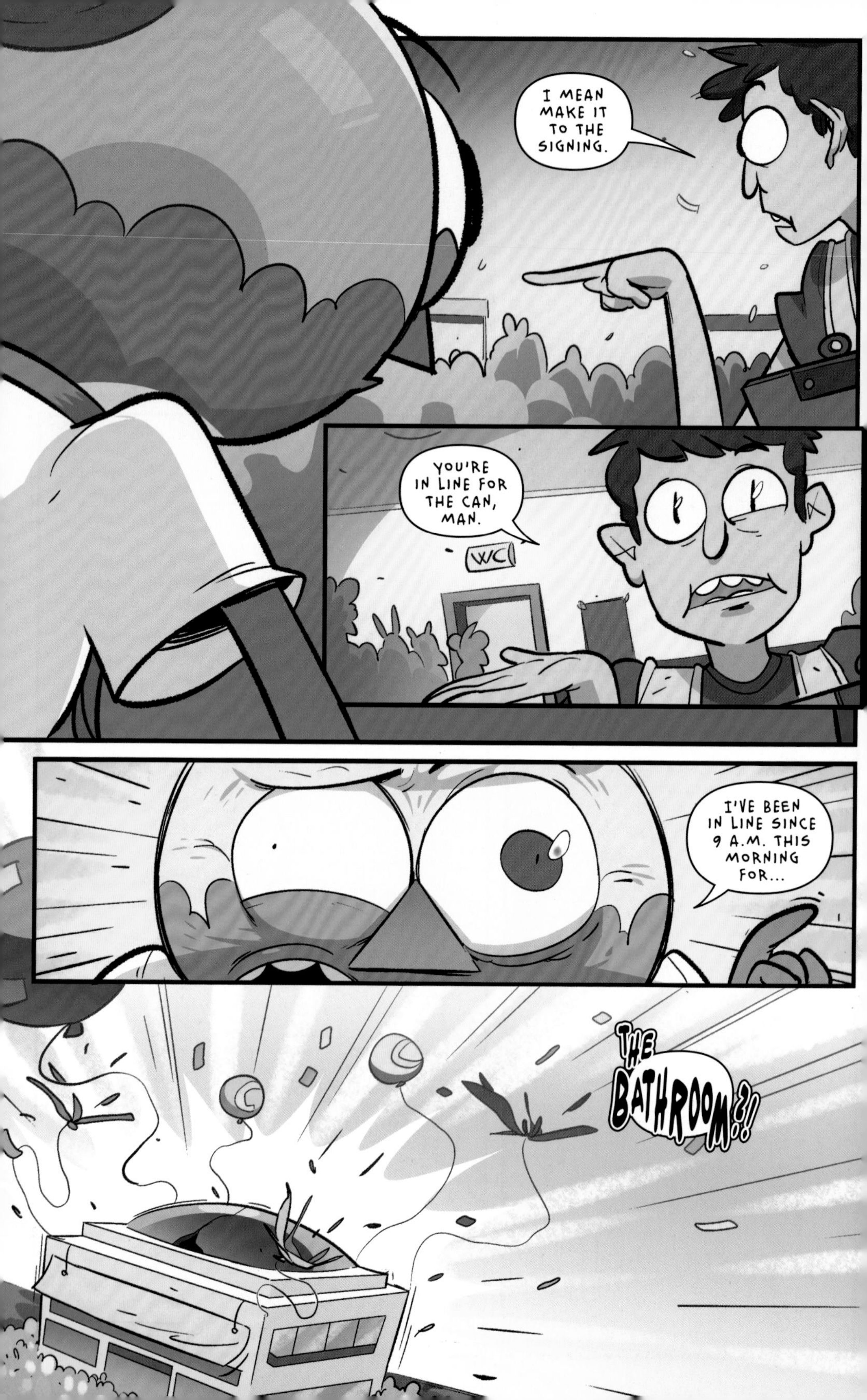
I MEAN MAKE IT TO THE SIGNING.
YOU'RE IN LINE FOR THE CAN, MAN.
W/C
I'VE BEEN IN LINE SINCE 9 A.M. THIS MORNING FOR...
THE BATHROOM?!

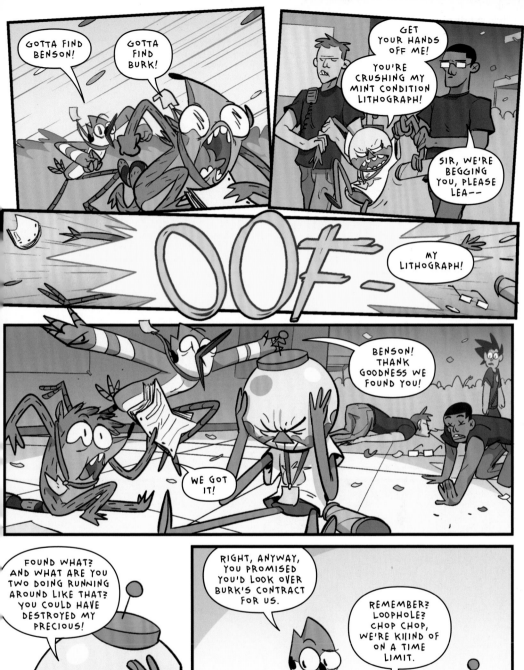

GOTTA FIND BENSON!

GOTTA FIND BURK!

GET YOUR HANDS OFF ME! YOU'RE CRUSHING MY MINT CONDITION LITHOGRAPH!

SIR, WE'RE BEGGING YOU, PLEASE LEA--

OOF

MY LITHOGRAPH!

BENSON! THANK GOODNESS WE FOUND YOU!

WE GOT IT!

FOUND WHAT? AND WHAT ARE YOU TWO DOING RUNNING AROUND LIKE THAT? YOU COULD HAVE DESTROYED MY PRECIOUS!

RIGHT, ANYWAY, YOU PROMISED YOU'D LOOK OVER BURK'S CONTRACT FOR US.

REMEMBER? LOOPHOLE? CHOP CHOP, WE'RE KIIND OF ON A TIME LIMIT.

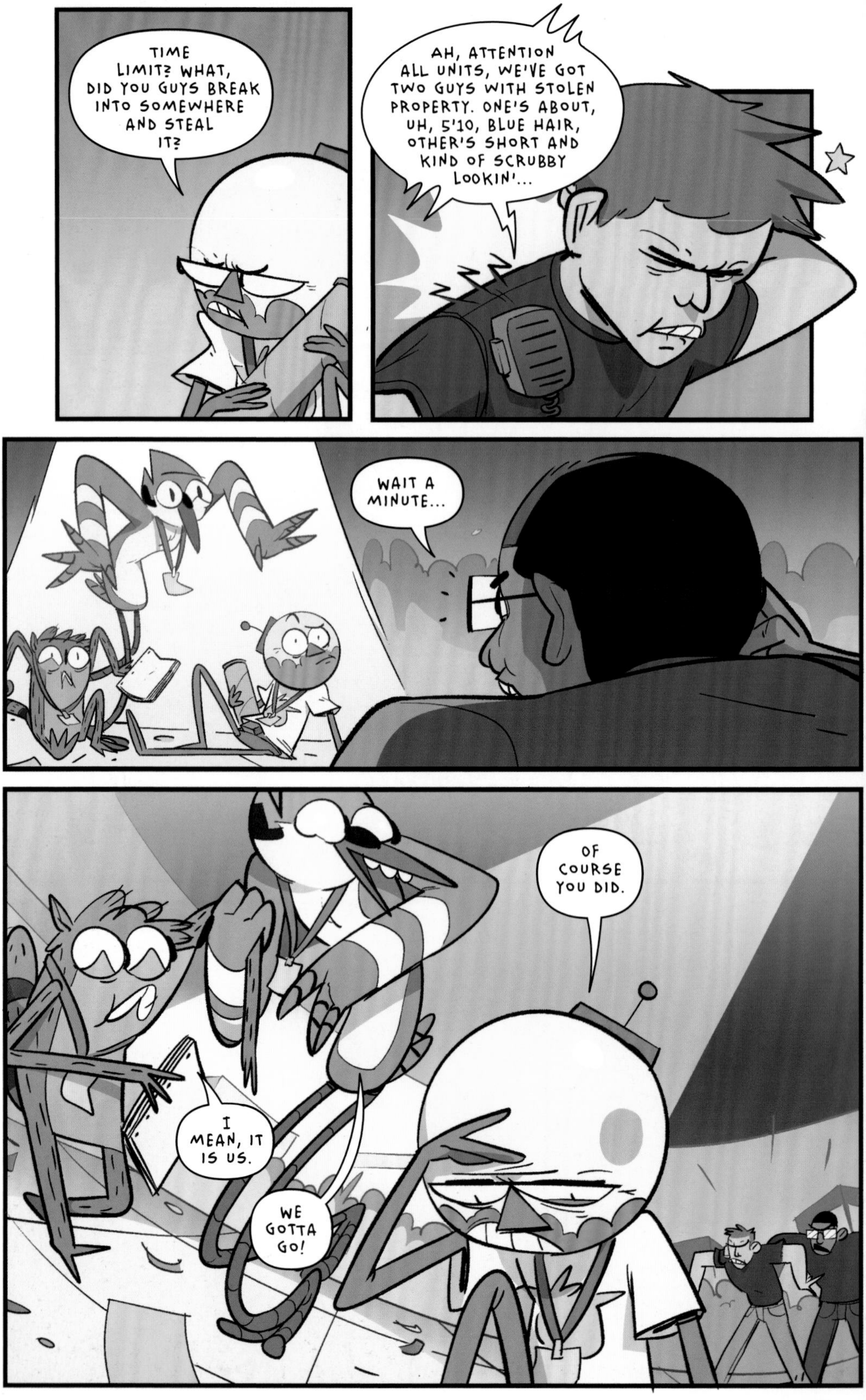
TIME LIMIT? WHAT, DID YOU GUYS BREAK INTO SOMEWHERE AND STEAL IT?
AH, ATTENTION ALL UNITS, WE'VE GOT TWO GUYS WITH STOLEN PROPERTY. ONE'S ABOUT, UH, 5'10, BLUE HAIR, OTHER'S SHORT AND KIND OF SCRUBBY LOOKIN'...
WAIT A MINUTE...
OF COURSE YOU DID.
I MEAN, IT IS US.
WE GOTTA GO!

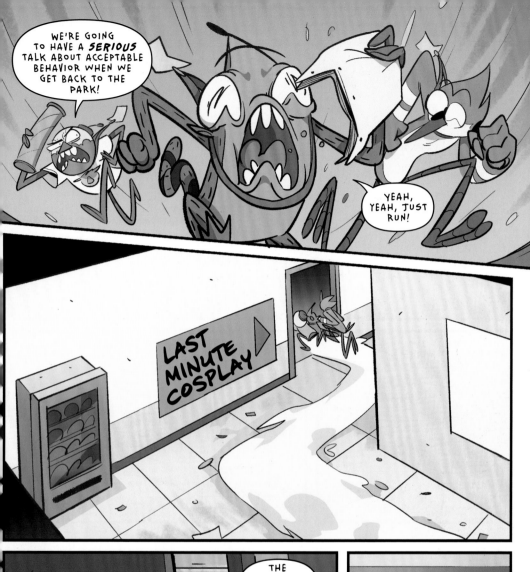

WE'RE GOING TO HAVE A *SERIOUS* TALK ABOUT ACCEPTABLE BEHAVIOR WHEN WE GET BACK TO THE PARK!

YEAH, YEAH, JUST RUN!

LAST MINUTE COSPLAY

THEY FELL FOR IT!

THE OLDEST TRICK IN THE BOOK!

SHHHH!

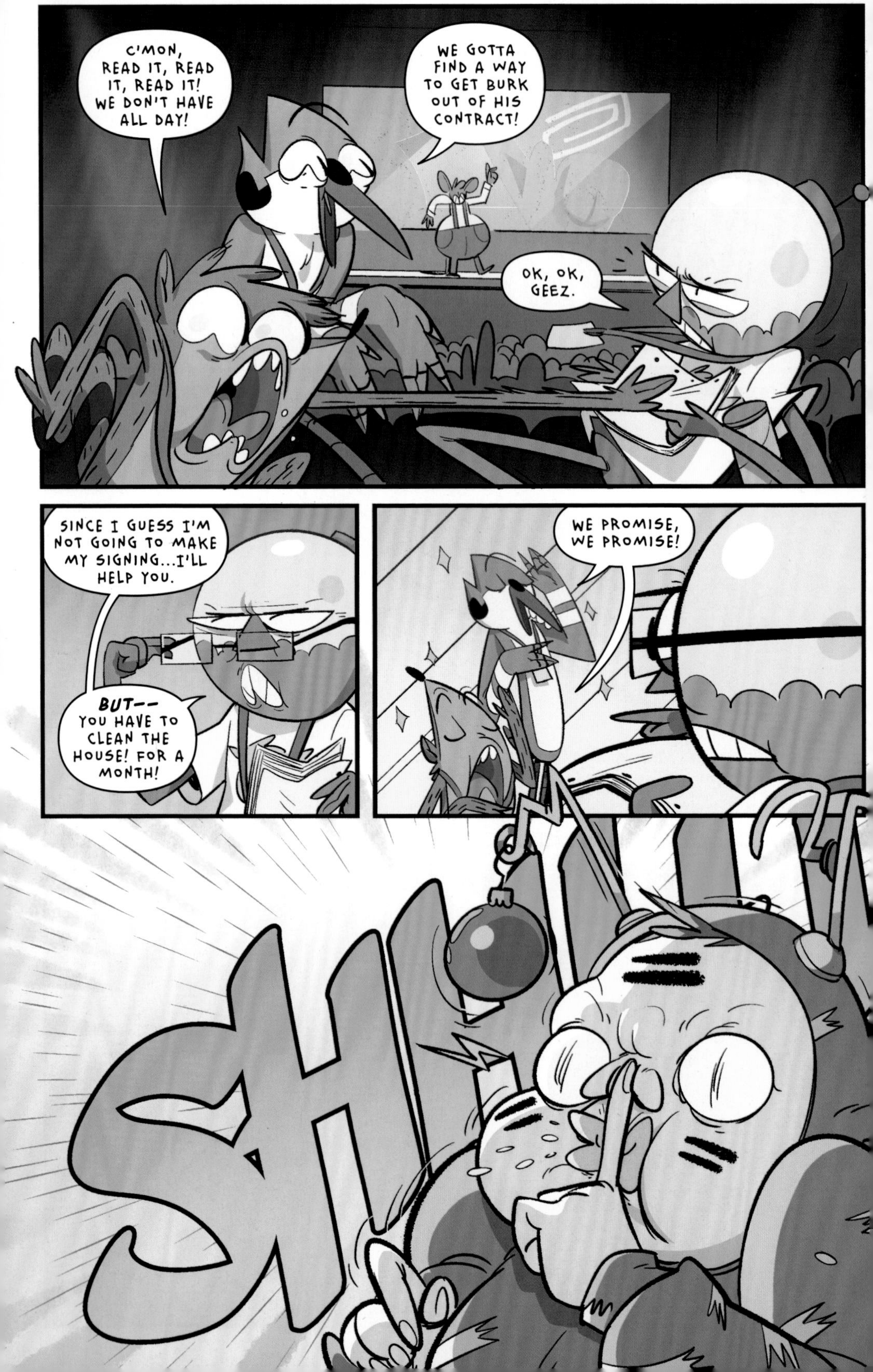

C'MON, READ IT, READ IT, READ IT! WE DON'T HAVE ALL DAY!
WE GOTTA FIND A WAY TO GET BURK OUT OF HIS CONTRACT!
OK, OK, GEEZ.
SINCE I GUESS I'M NOT GOING TO MAKE MY SIGNING...I'LL HELP YOU.
BUT-- YOU HAVE TO CLEAN THE HOUSE! FOR A MONTH!
WE PROMISE, WE PROMISE!
SH

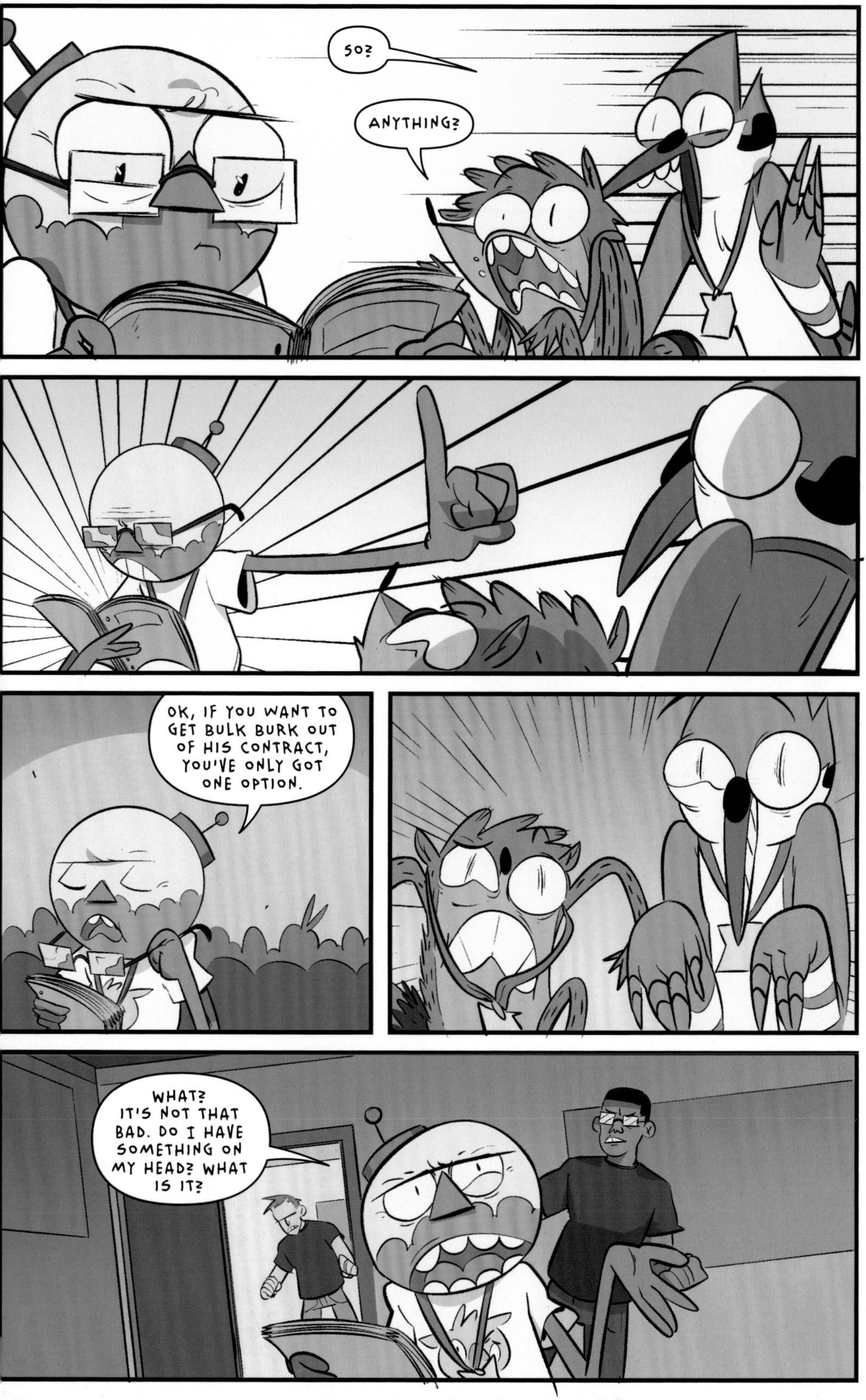
SO?
ANYTHING?
OK, IF YOU WANT TO GET BULK BURK OUT OF HIS CONTRACT, YOU'VE ONLY GOT ONE OPTION.
WHAT? IT'S NOT THAT BAD. DO I HAVE SOMETHING ON MY HEAD? WHAT IS IT?

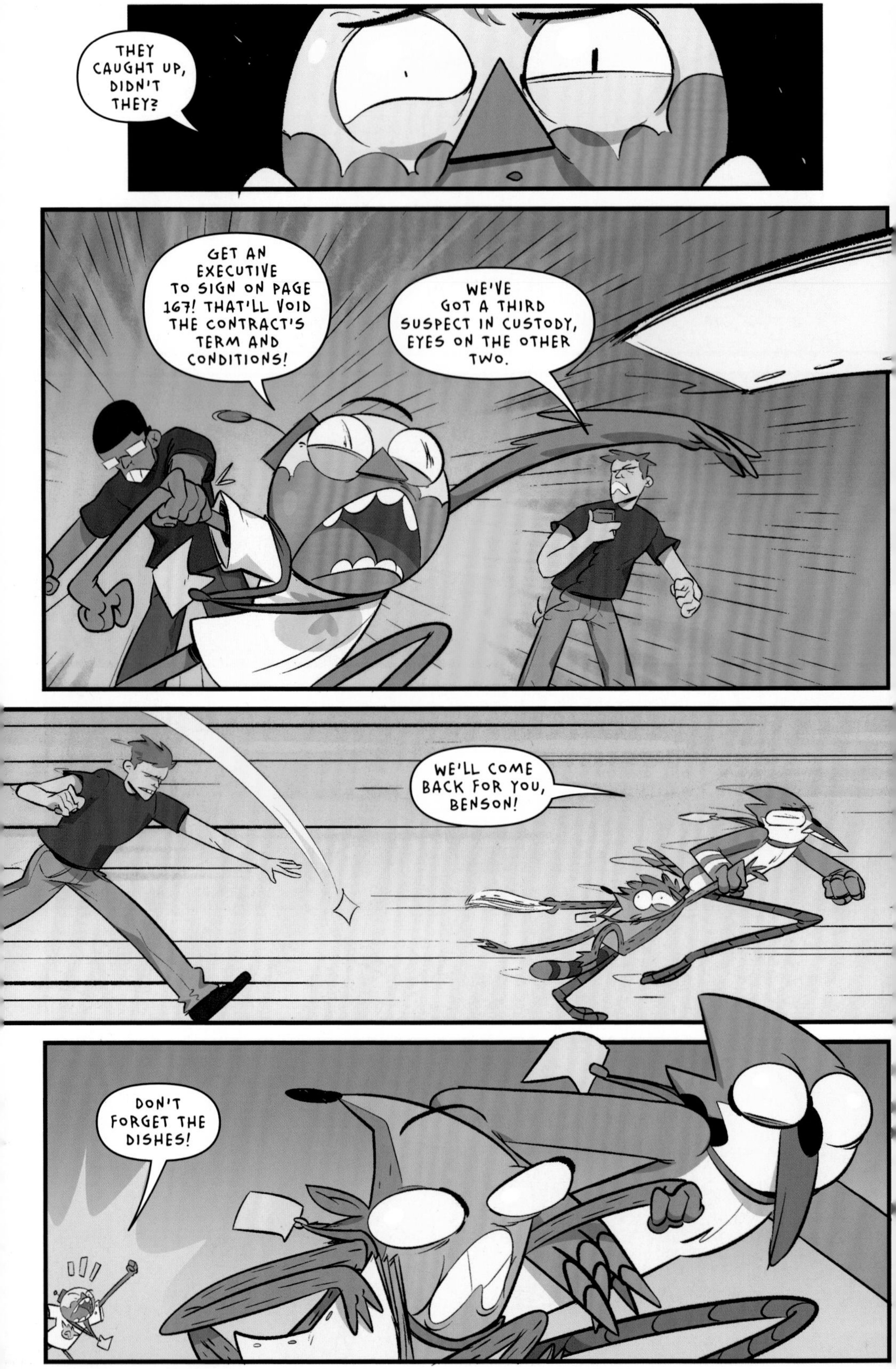
THEY CAUGHT UP, DIDN'T THEY?
GET AN EXECUTIVE TO SIGN ON PAGE 167! THAT'LL VOID THE CONTRACT'S TERM AND CONDITIONS!
WE'VE GOT A THIRD SUSPECT IN CUSTODY, EYES ON THE OTHER TWO.
WE'LL COME BACK FOR YOU, BENSON!
DON'T FORGET THE DISHES!

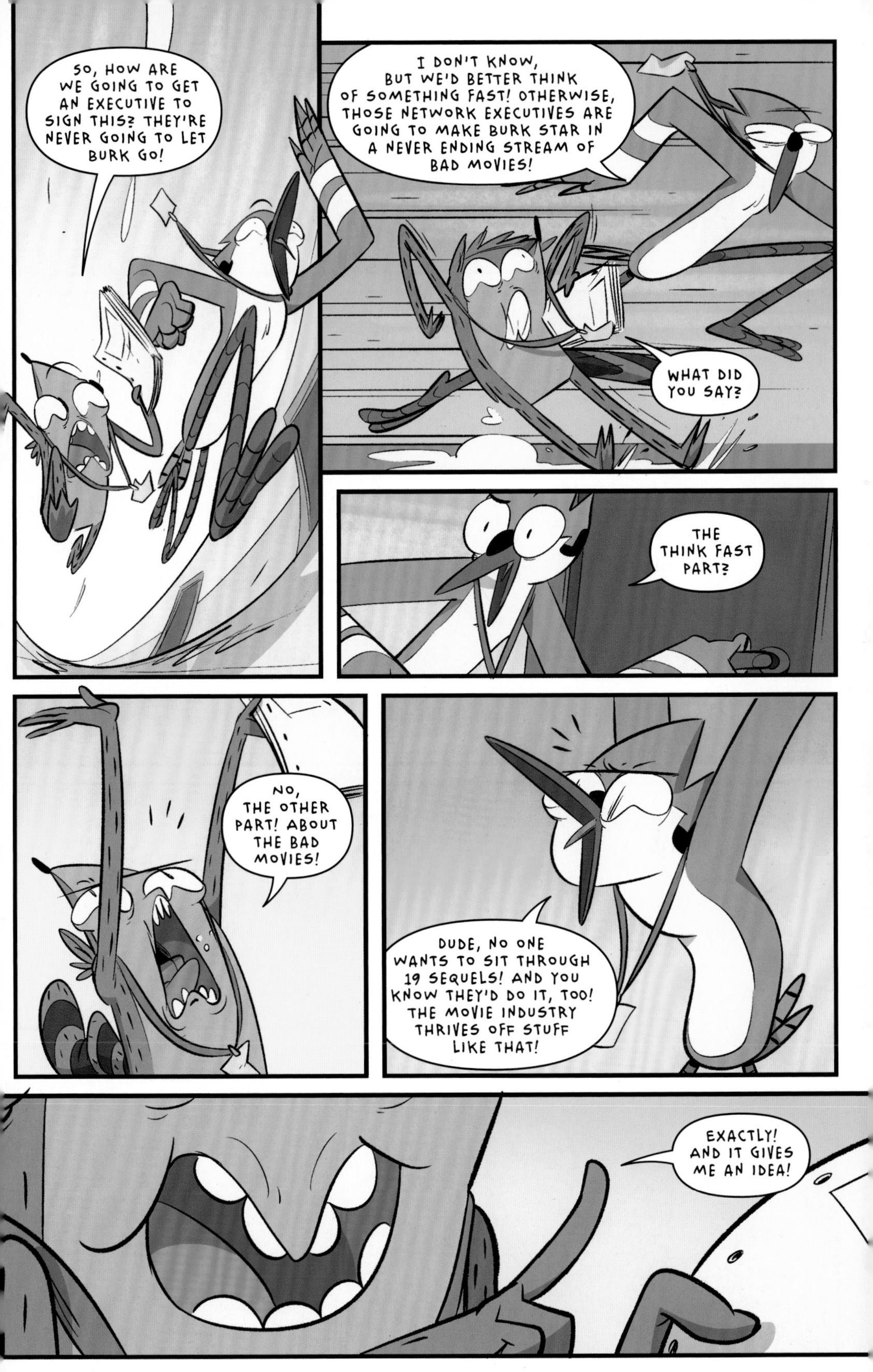
SO, HOW ARE WE GOING TO GET AN EXECUTIVE TO SIGN THIS? THEY'RE NEVER GOING TO LET BURK GO!
I DON'T KNOW, BUT WE'D BETTER THINK OF SOMETHING FAST! OTHERWISE, THOSE NETWORK EXECUTIVES ARE GOING TO MAKE BURK STAR IN A NEVER ENDING STREAM OF BAD MOVIES!
WHAT DID YOU SAY?
THE THINK FAST PART?
NO, THE OTHER PART! ABOUT THE BAD MOVIES!
DUDE, NO ONE WANTS TO SIT THROUGH 19 SEQUELS! AND YOU KNOW THEY'D DO IT, TOO! THE MOVIE INDUSTRY THRIVES OFF STUFF LIKE THAT!
EXACTLY! AND IT GIVES ME AN IDEA!

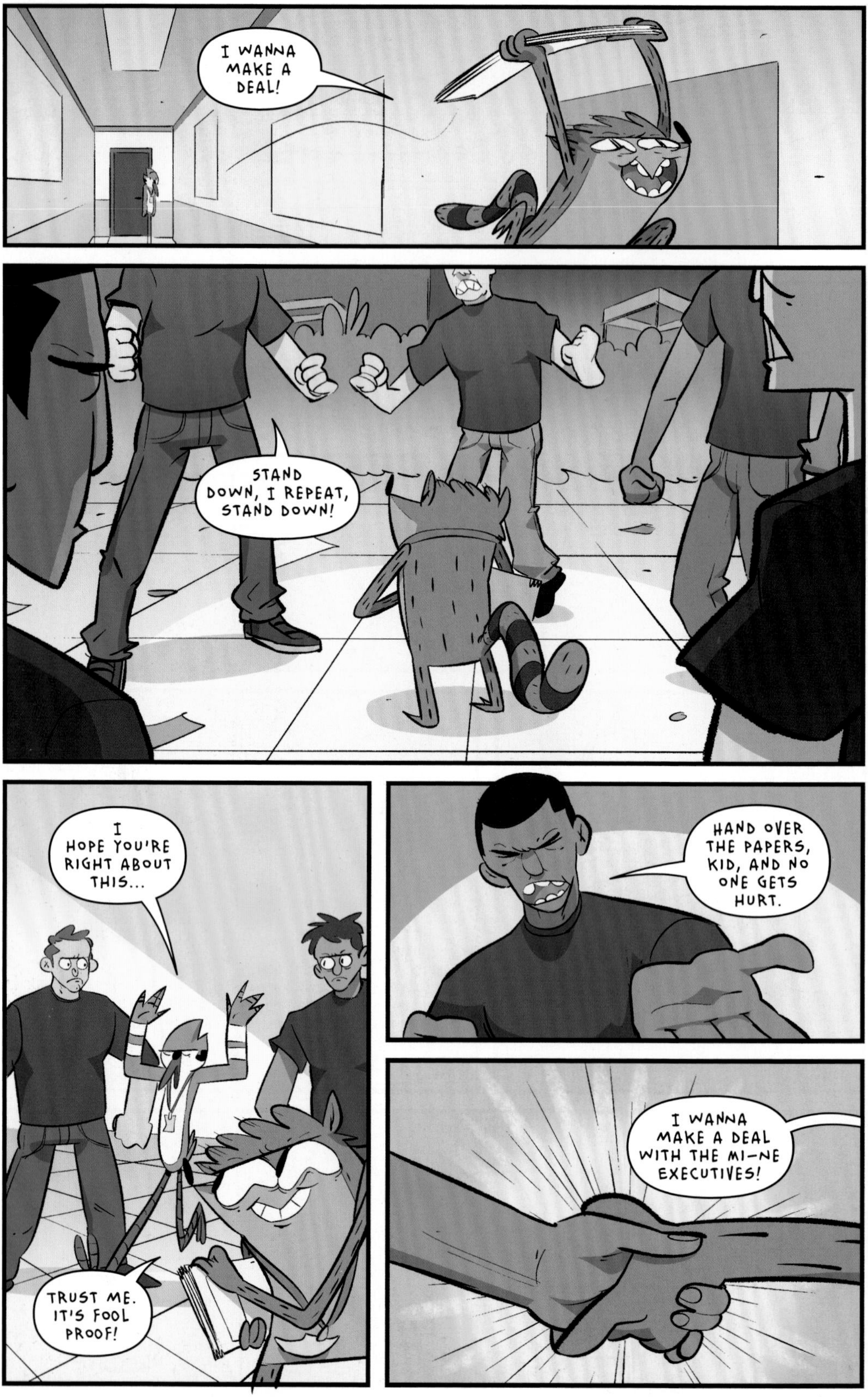

I WANNA MAKE A DEAL!
STAND DOWN, I REPEAT, STAND DOWN!
I HOPE YOU'RE RIGHT ABOUT THIS...
TRUST ME. IT'S FOOL PROOF!
HAND OVER THE PAPERS, KID, AND NO ONE GETS HURT.
I WANNA MAKE A DEAL WITH THE MI-NE EXECUTIVES!

THERE IT IS!

WHAT ARE YOU ALL WAITING FOR? GET IT!

THEY SAID THEY WANT TO MAKE A DEAL...

A DEAL YOU SAY? I'M INTRIGUED. WHAT DO YOU HAVE THAT WE COULD POSSIBLY WANT?

SOMETHING YOUR KIND THRIVE OFF OF. SOMETHING SO IRRESISTIBLE YOU WON'T BE ABLE TO DO ANYTHING *BUT* AGREE!

AND WHAT IS THIS ITEM SO TEMPTING WE'LL CAVE TO YOUR EVERY DEMAND?

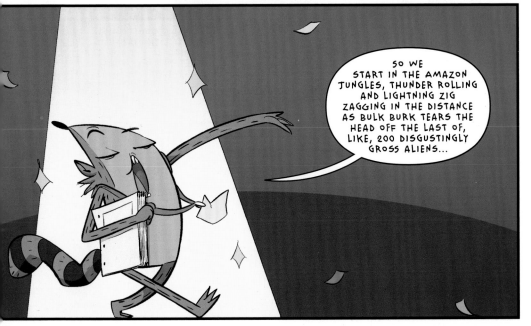

SO WE START IN THE AMAZON JUNGLES, THUNDER ROLLING AND LIGHTNING ZIG ZAGGING IN THE DISTANCE AS BULK BURK TEARS THE HEAD OFF THE LAST OF, LIKE, 200 DISGUSTINGLY GROSS ALIENS...

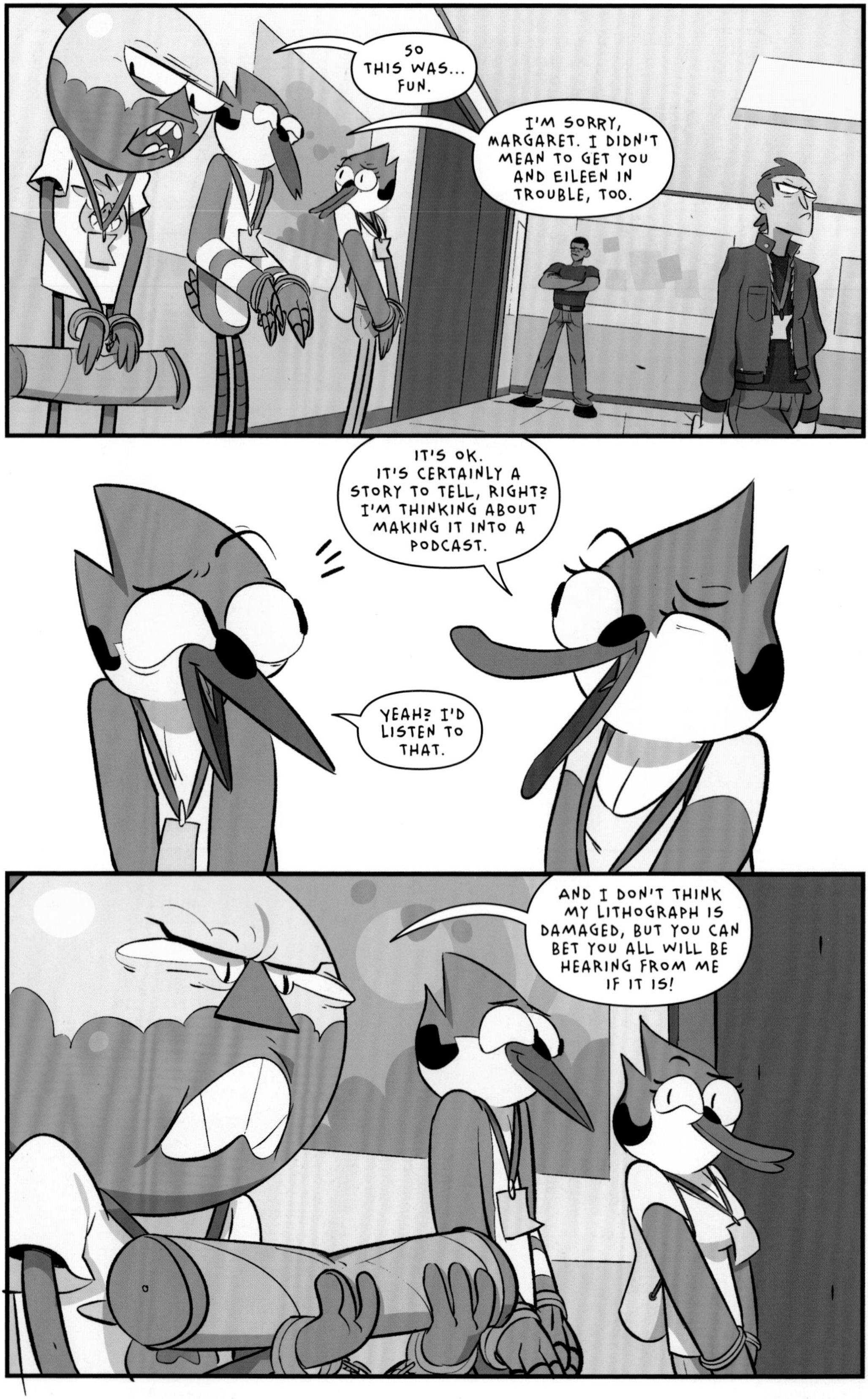
SO THIS WAS... FUN.
I'M SORRY, MARGARET. I DIDN'T MEAN TO GET YOU AND EILEEN IN TROUBLE, TOO.
IT'S OK. IT'S CERTAINLY A STORY TO TELL, RIGHT? I'M THINKING ABOUT MAKING IT INTO A PODCAST.
YEAH? I'D LISTEN TO THAT.
AND I DON'T THINK MY LITHOGRAPH IS DAMAGED, BUT YOU CAN BET YOU ALL WILL BE HEARING FROM ME IF IT IS!

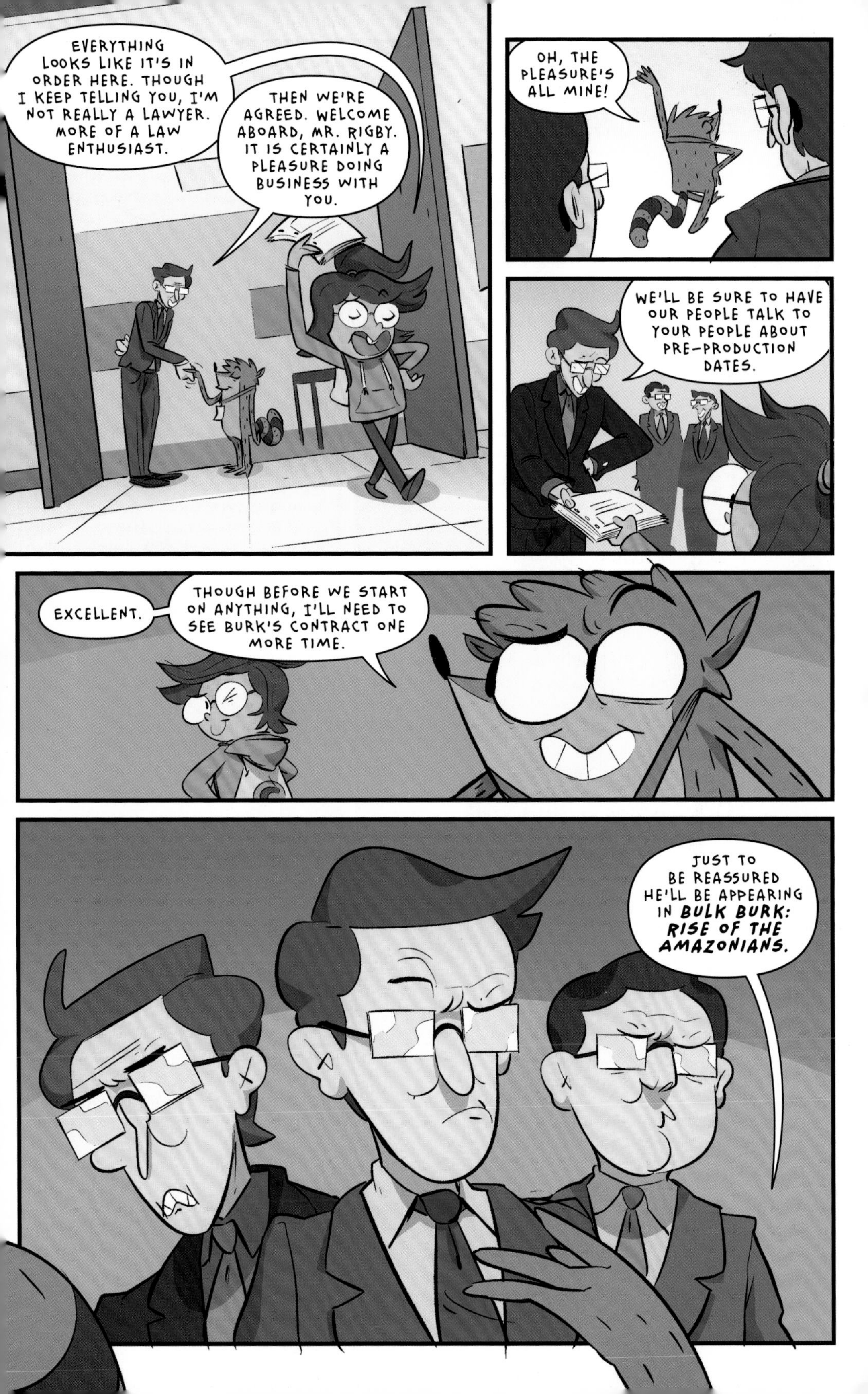
EVERYTHING LOOKS LIKE IT'S IN ORDER HERE. THOUGH I KEEP TELLING YOU, I'M NOT REALLY A LAWYER. MORE OF A LAW ENTHUSIAST.
THEN WE'RE AGREED. WELCOME ABOARD, MR. RIGBY. IT IS CERTAINLY A PLEASURE DOING BUSINESS WITH YOU.
OH, THE PLEASURE'S ALL MINE!
WE'LL BE SURE TO HAVE OUR PEOPLE TALK TO YOUR PEOPLE ABOUT PRE-PRODUCTION DATES.
EXCELLENT.
THOUGH BEFORE WE START ON ANYTHING, I'LL NEED TO SEE BURK'S CONTRACT ONE MORE TIME.
JUST TO BE REASSURED HE'LL BE APPEARING IN ***BULK BURK: RISE OF THE AMAZONIANS.***

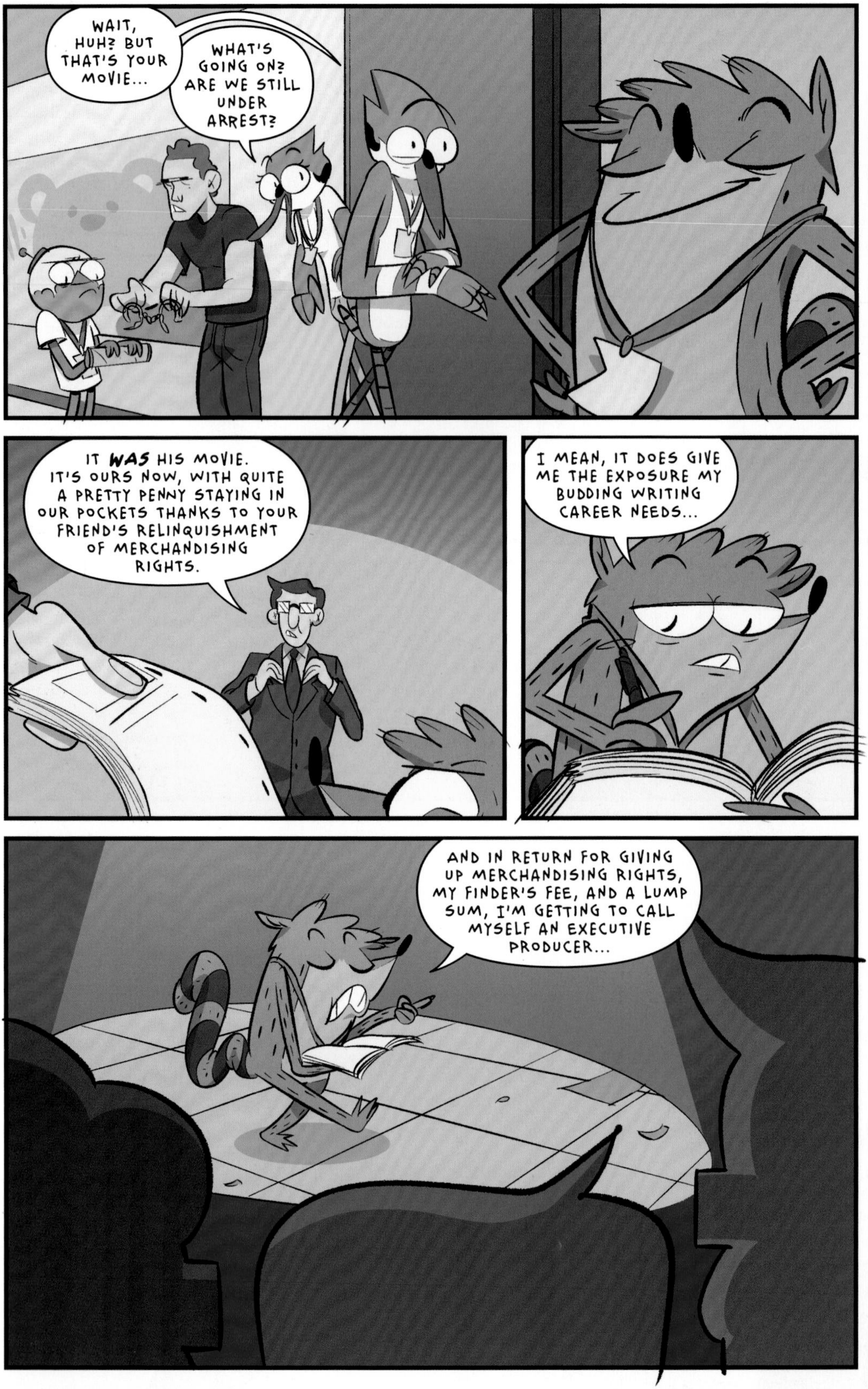
WAIT, HUH? BUT THAT'S YOUR MOVIE...
WHAT'S GOING ON? ARE WE STILL UNDER ARREST?
IT WAS HIS MOVIE. IT'S OURS NOW, WITH QUITE A PRETTY PENNY STAYING IN OUR POCKETS THANKS TO YOUR FRIEND'S RELINQUISHMENT OF MERCHANDISING RIGHTS.
I MEAN, IT DOES GIVE ME THE EXPOSURE MY BUDDING WRITING CAREER NEEDS...
AND IN RETURN FOR GIVING UP MERCHANDISING RIGHTS, MY FINDER'S FEE, AND A LUMP SUM, I'M GETTING TO CALL MYSELF AN EXECUTIVE PRODUCER...

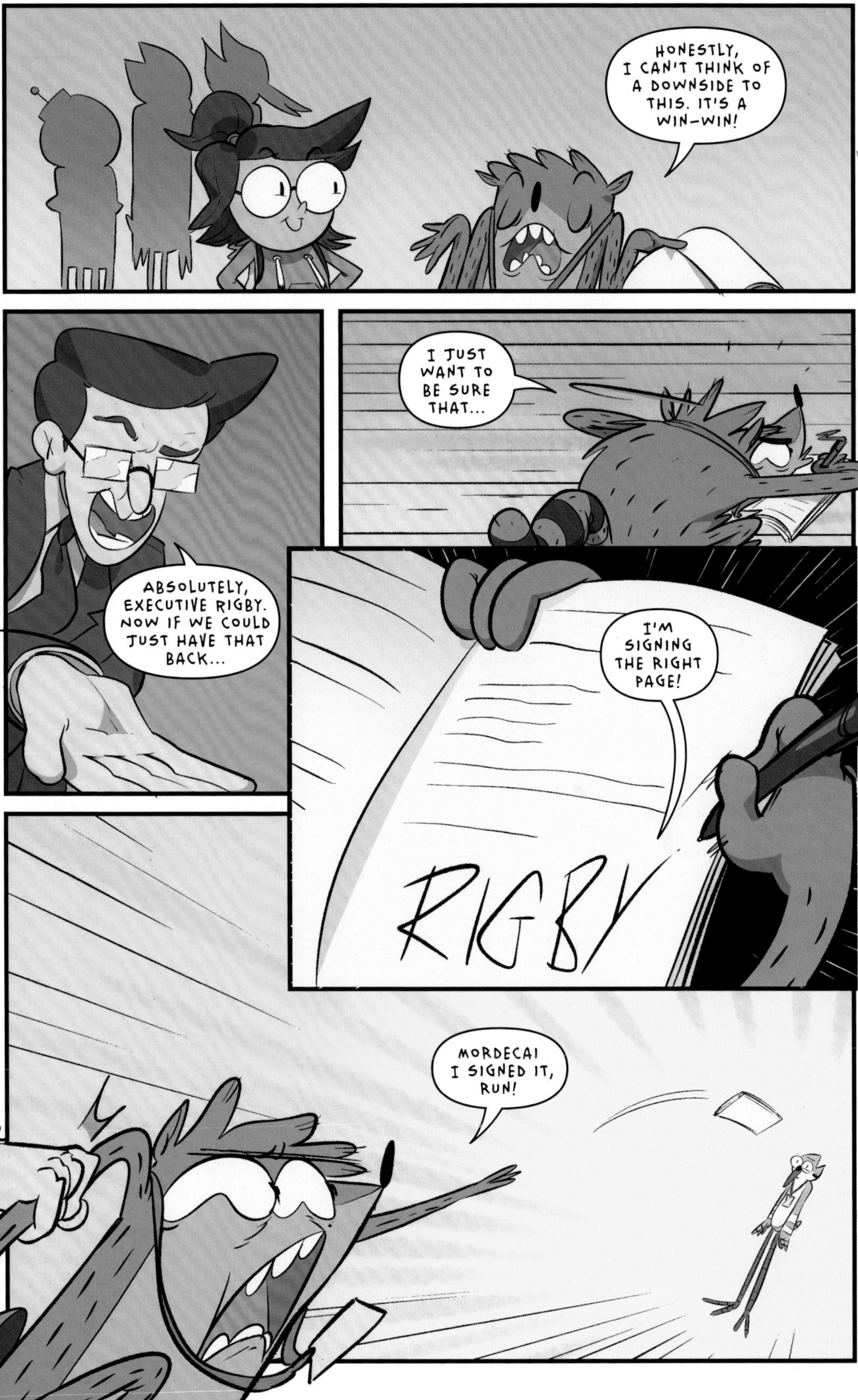
HONESTLY, I CAN'T THINK OF A DOWNSIDE TO THIS. IT'S A WIN-WIN!
ABSOLUTELY, EXECUTIVE RIGBY. NOW IF WE COULD JUST HAVE THAT BACK...
I JUST WANT TO BE SURE THAT...
I'M SIGNING THE RIGHT PAGE!
RIGBY
MORDECAI I SIGNED IT, RUN!

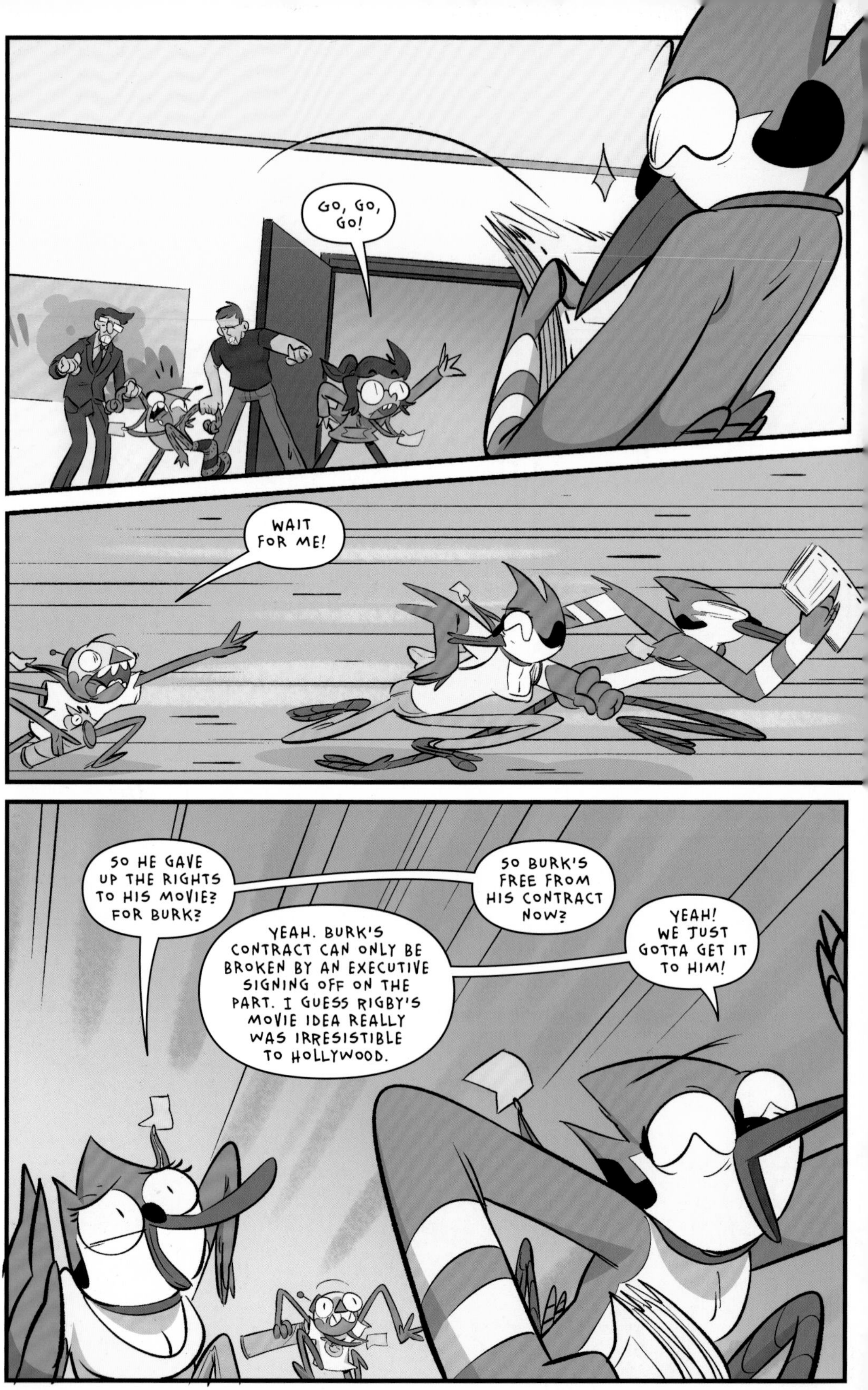
GO, GO, GO!
WAIT FOR ME!
SO HE GAVE UP THE RIGHTS TO HIS MOVIE? FOR BURK?
SO BURK'S FREE FROM HIS CONTRACT NOW?
YEAH. BURK'S CONTRACT CAN ONLY BE BROKEN BY AN EXECUTIVE SIGNING OFF ON THE PART. I GUESS RIGBY'S MOVIE IDEA REALLY WAS IRRESISTIBLE TO HOLLYWOOD.
YEAH! WE JUST GOTTA GET IT TO HIM!

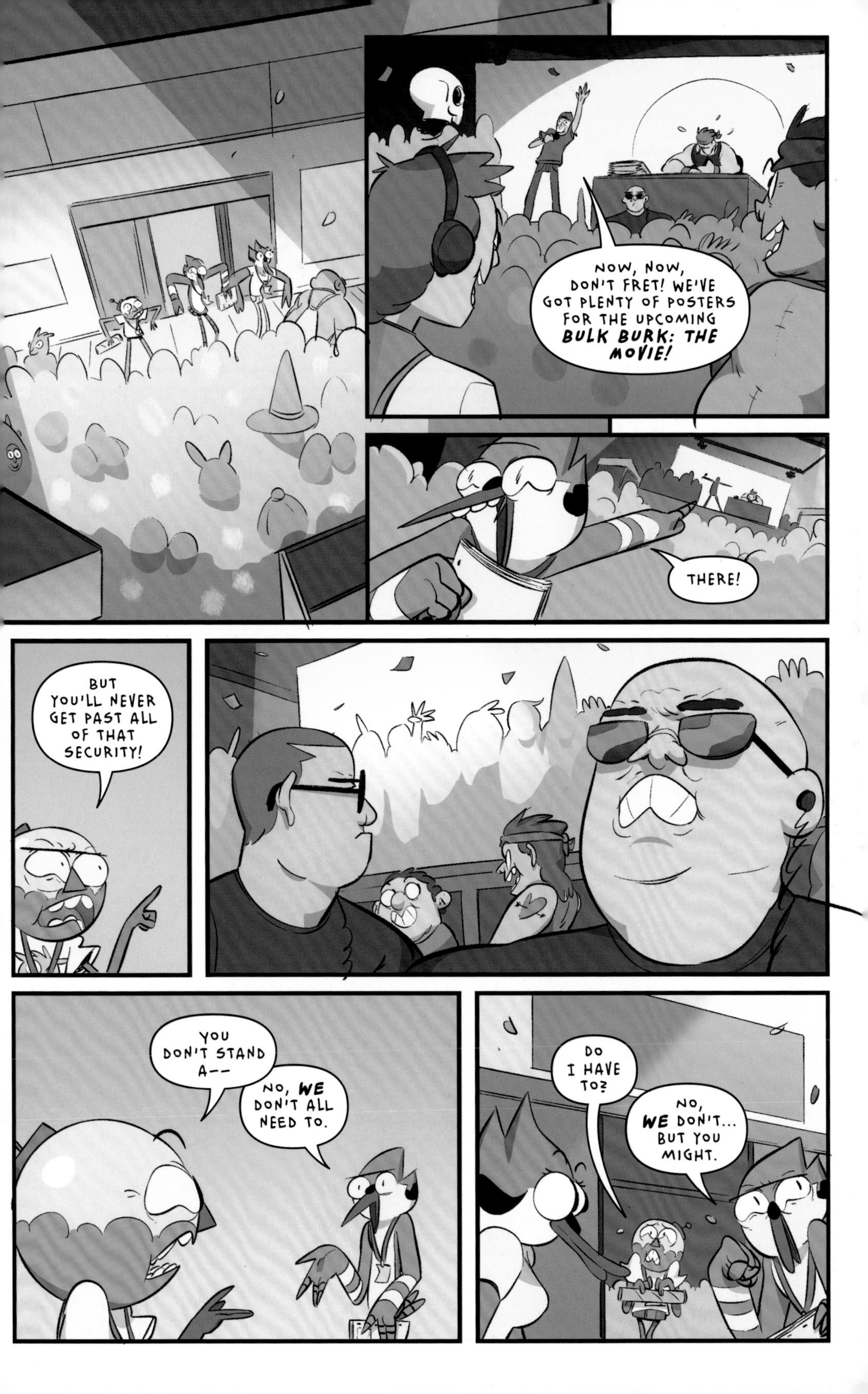
NOW, NOW, DON'T FRET! WE'VE GOT PLENTY OF POSTERS FOR THE UPCOMING BULK BURK: THE MOVIE!
THERE!
BUT YOU'LL NEVER GET PAST ALL OF THAT SECURITY!
YOU DON'T STAND A--
NO, WE DON'T ALL NEED TO.
DO I HAVE TO?
NO, WE DON'T... BUT YOU MIGHT.

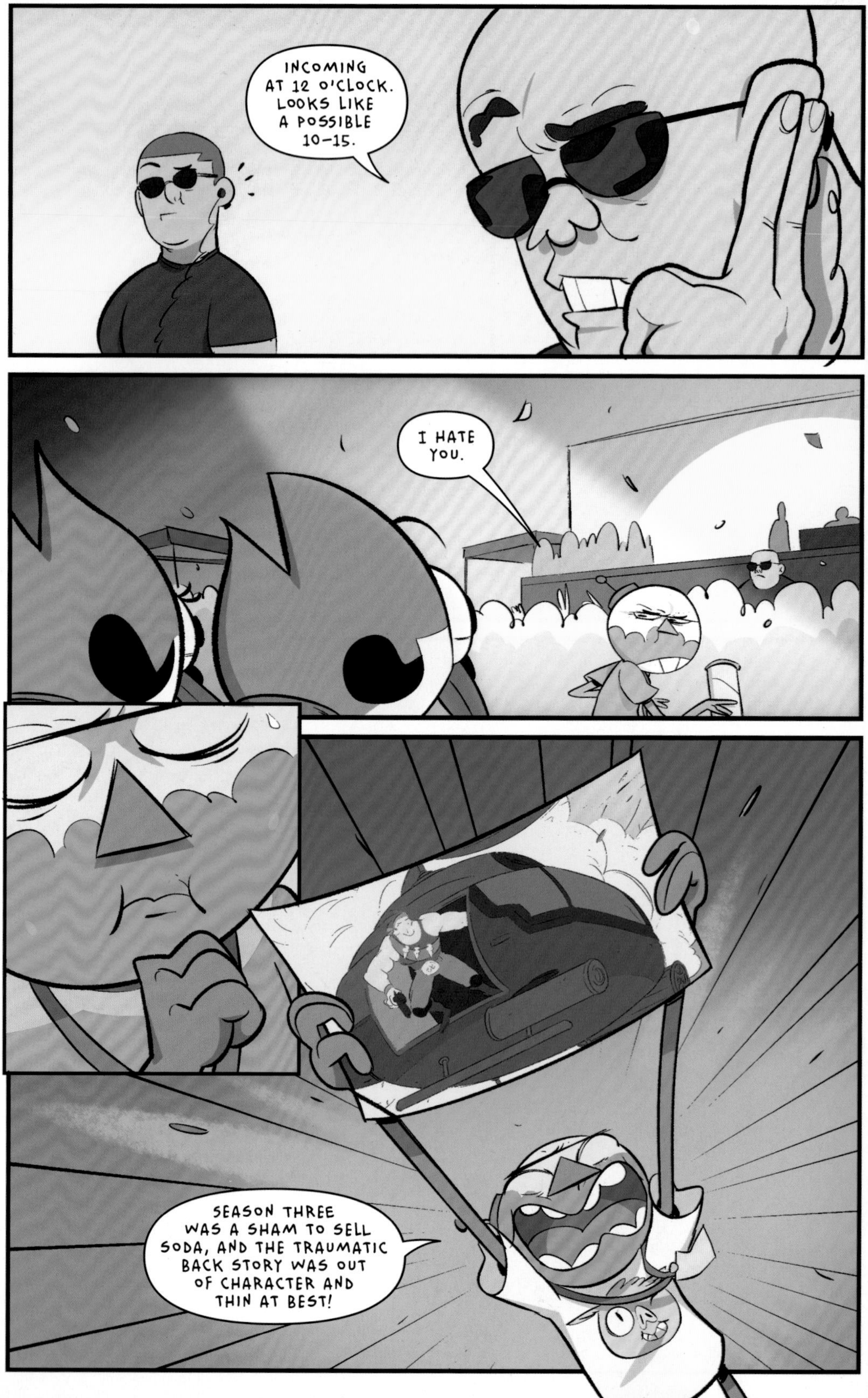
INCOMING AT 12 O'CLOCK. LOOKS LIKE A POSSIBLE 10-15.
I HATE YOU.
SEASON THREE WAS A SHAM TO SELL SODA, AND THE TRAUMATIC BACK STORY WAS OUT OF CHARACTER AND THIN AT BEST!

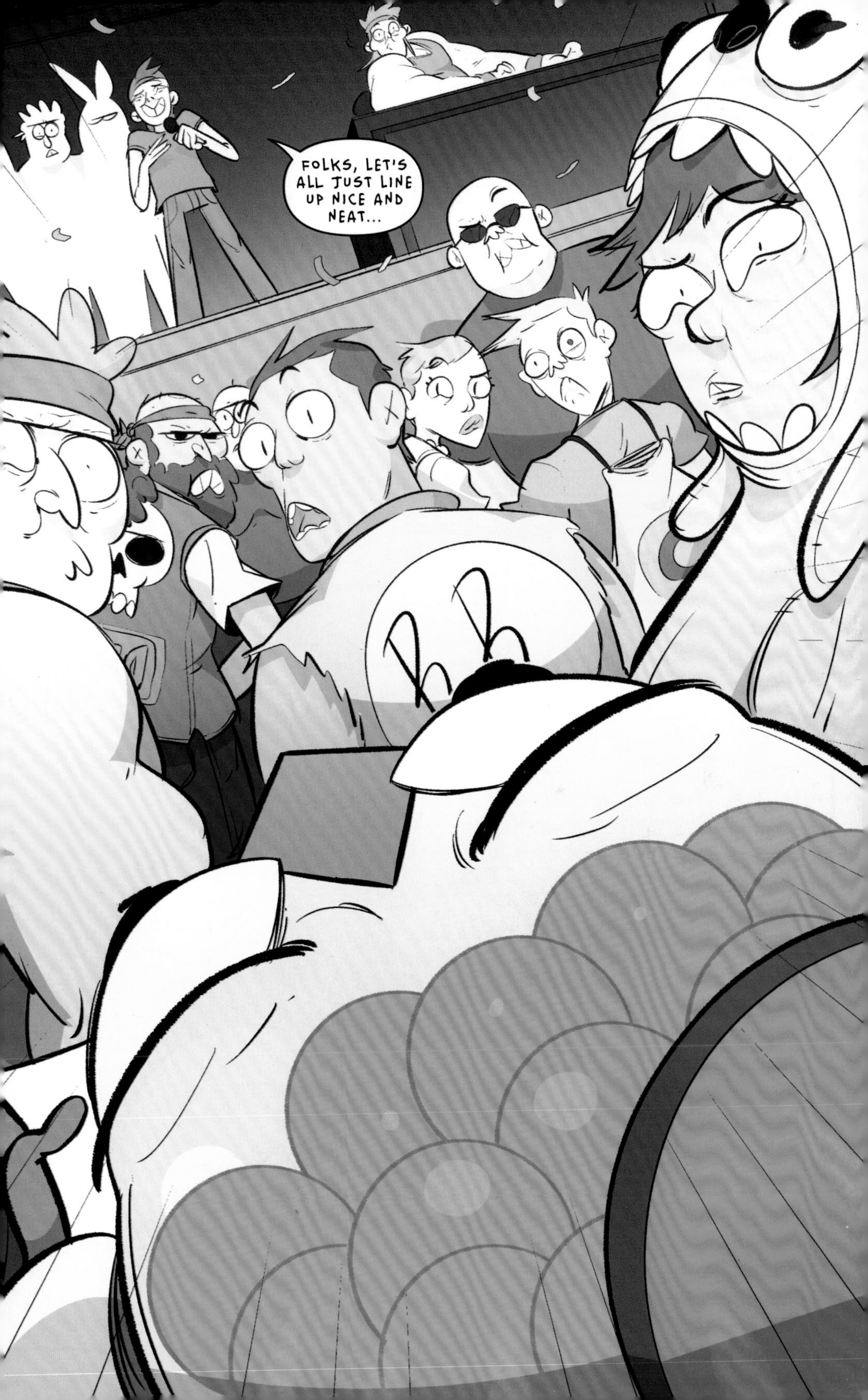
FOLKS, LET'S ALL JUST LINE UP NICE AND NEAT...

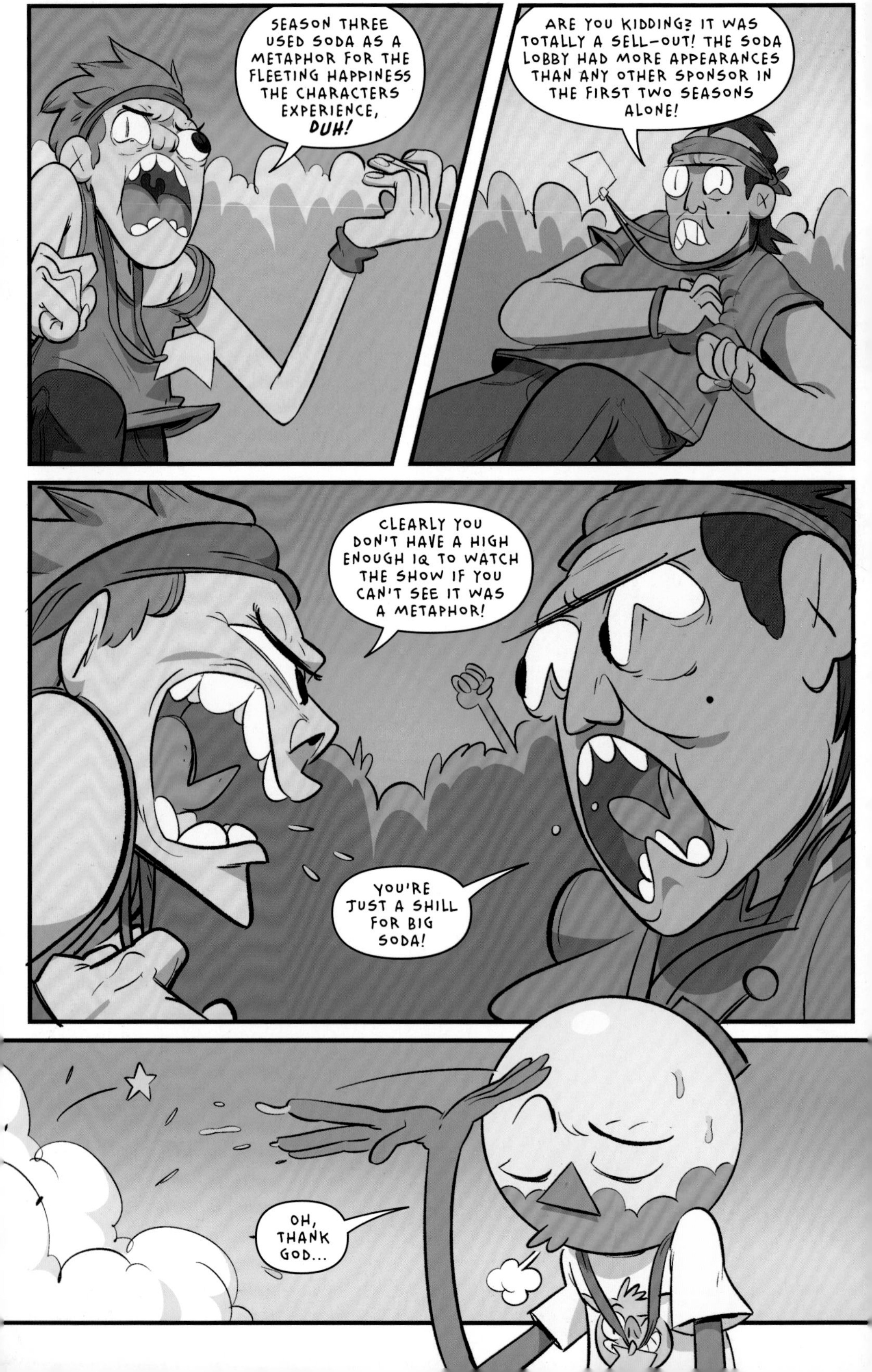
SEASON THREE USED SODA AS A METAPHOR FOR THE FLEETING HAPPINESS THE CHARACTERS EXPERIENCE, DUH!
ARE YOU KIDDING? IT WAS TOTALLY A SELL-OUT! THE SODA LOBBY HAD MORE APPEARANCES THAN ANY OTHER SPONSOR IN THE FIRST TWO SEASONS ALONE!
CLEARLY YOU DON'T HAVE A HIGH ENOUGH IQ TO WATCH THE SHOW IF YOU CAN'T SEE IT WAS A METAPHOR!
YOU'RE JUST A SHILL FOR BIG SODA!
OH, THANK GOD...

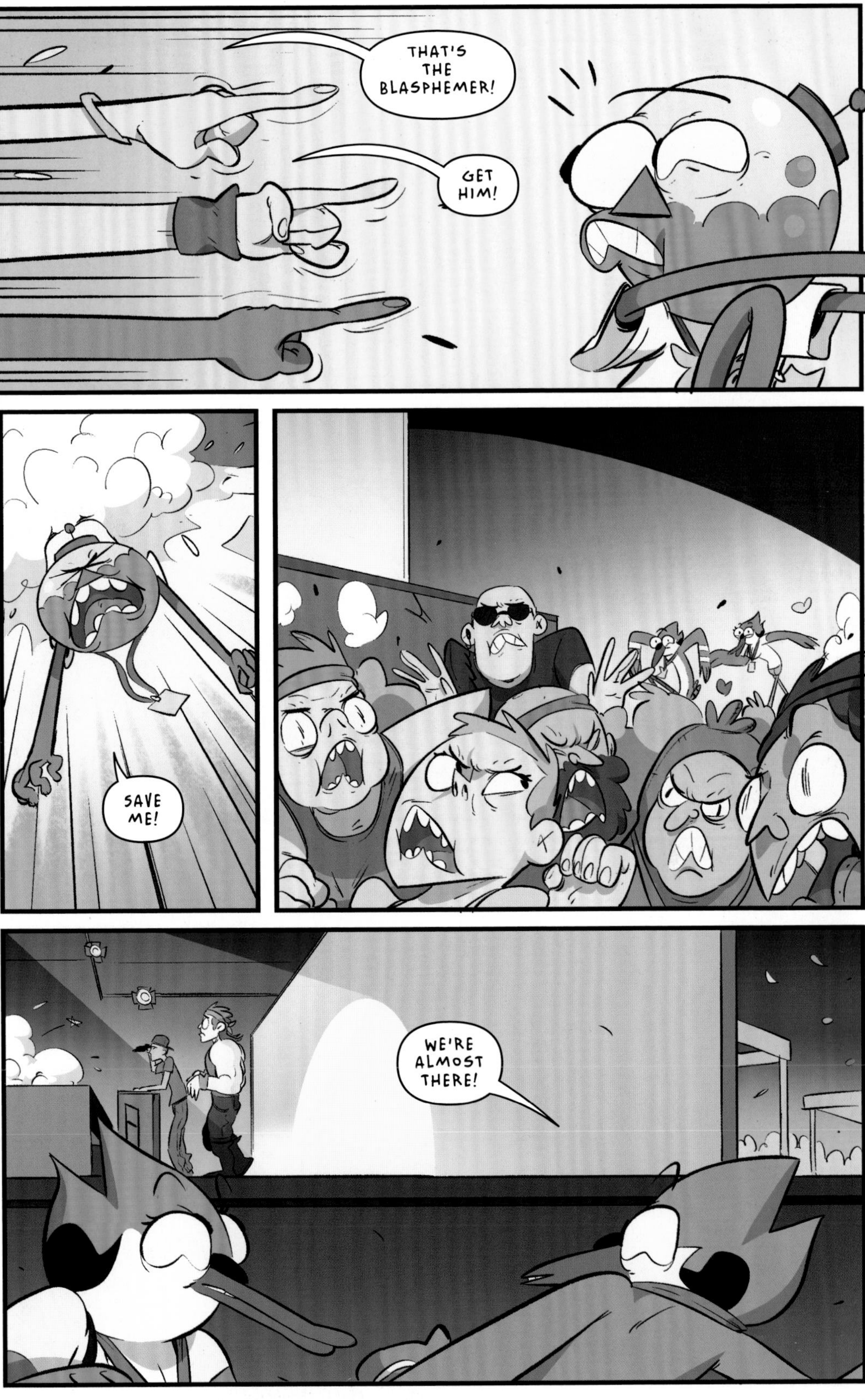
THAT'S THE BLASPHEMER!
GET HIM!
SAVE ME!
WE'RE ALMOST THERE!

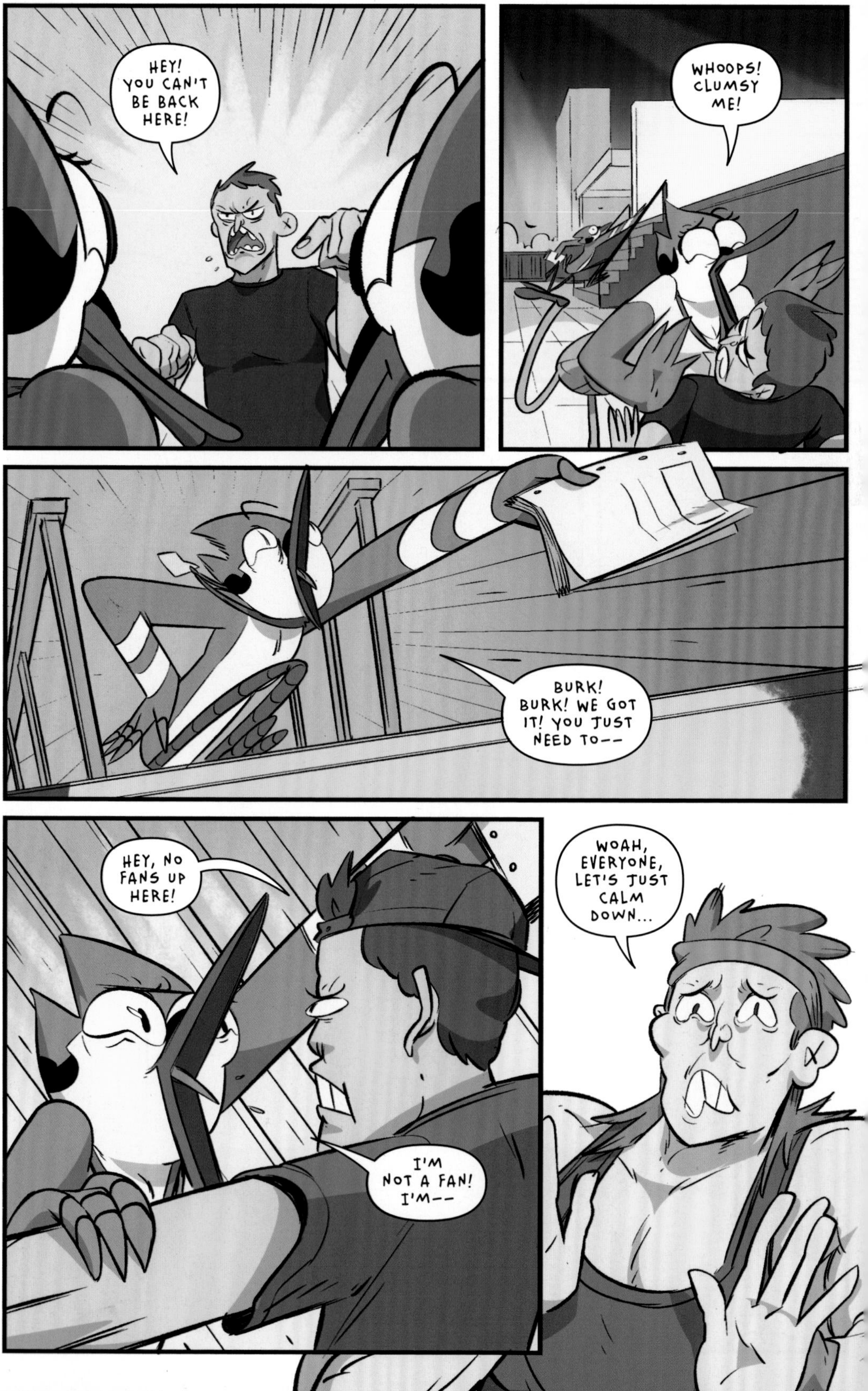
HEY! YOU CAN'T BE BACK HERE!
WHOOPS! CLUMSY ME!
BURK! BURK! WE GOT IT! YOU JUST NEED TO--
HEY, NO FANS UP HERE!
I'M NOT A FAN! I'M--
WOAH, EVERYONE, LET'S JUST CALM DOWN...

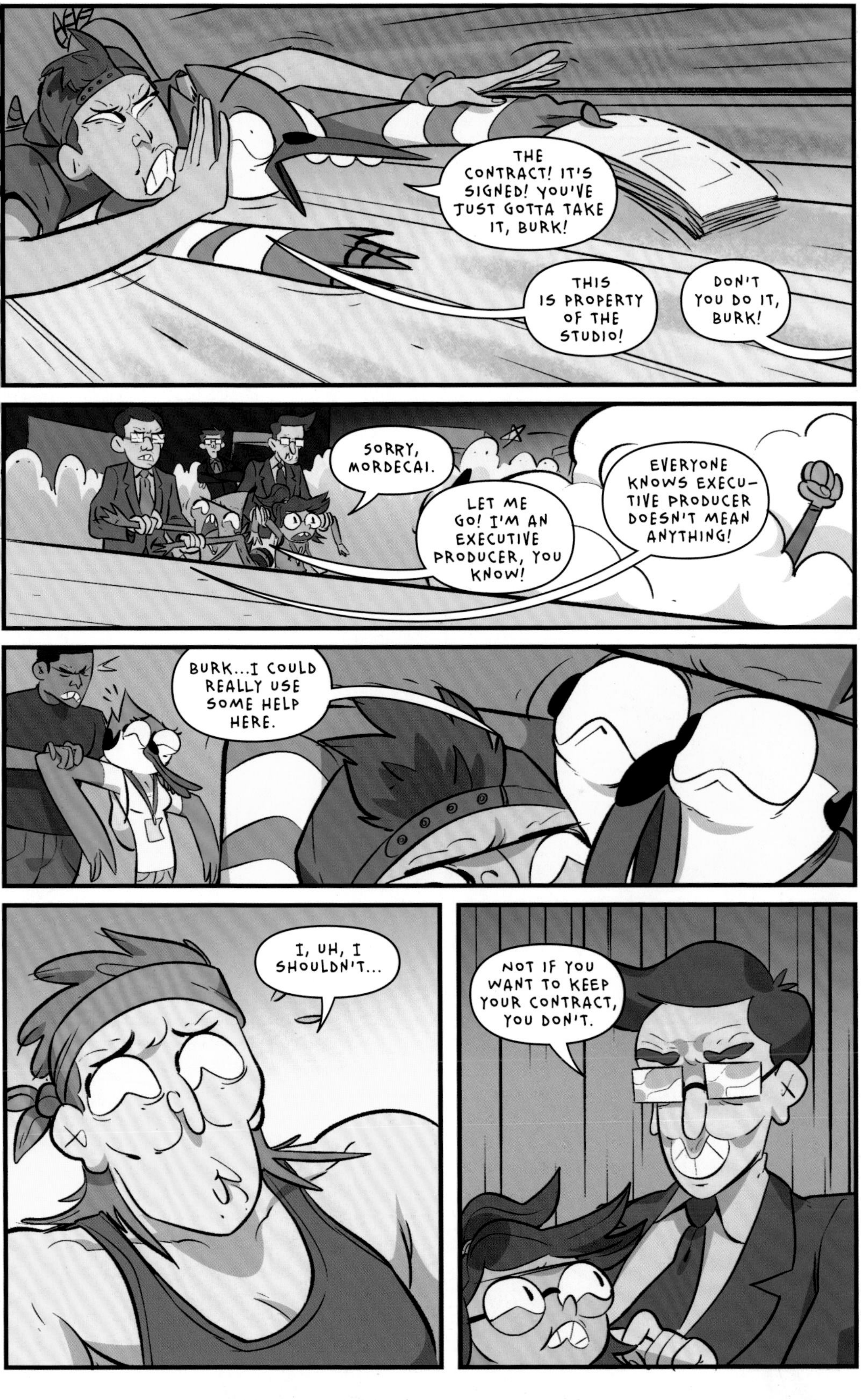
THE CONTRACT! IT'S SIGNED! YOU'VE JUST GOTTA TAKE IT, BURK!
THIS IS PROPERTY OF THE STUDIO!
DON'T YOU DO IT, BURK!
SORRY, MORDECAI.
LET ME GO! I'M AN EXECUTIVE PRODUCER, YOU KNOW!
EVERYONE KNOWS EXECU-TIVE PRODUCER DOESN'T MEAN ANYTHING!
BURK...I COULD REALLY USE SOME HELP HERE.
I, UH, I SHOULDN'T...
NOT IF YOU WANT TO KEEP YOUR CONTRACT, YOU DON'T.

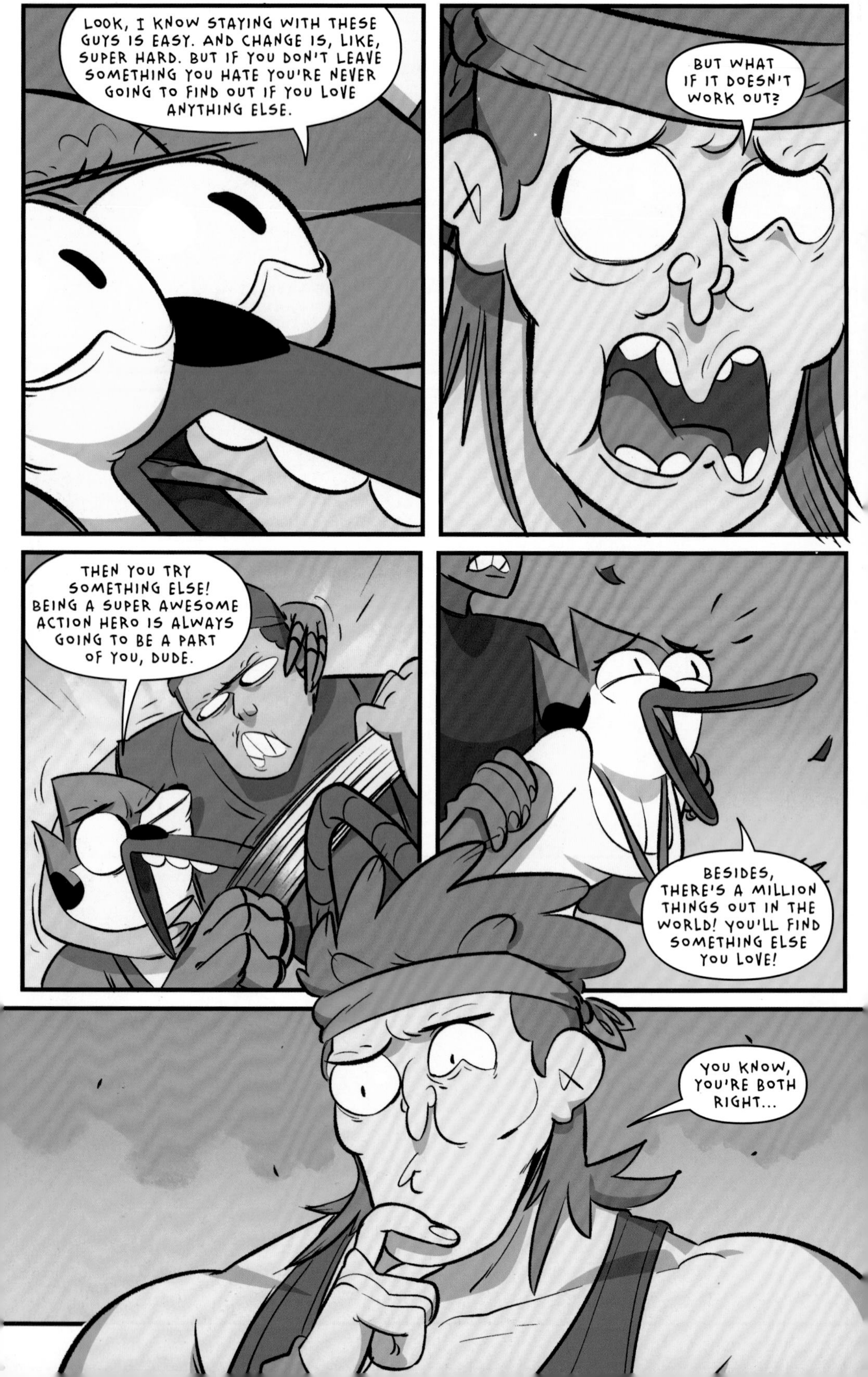
LOOK, I KNOW STAYING WITH THESE GUYS IS EASY. AND CHANGE IS, LIKE, SUPER HARD. BUT IF YOU DON'T LEAVE SOMETHING YOU HATE YOU'RE NEVER GOING TO FIND OUT IF YOU LOVE ANYTHING ELSE.
BUT WHAT IF IT DOESN'T WORK OUT?
THEN YOU TRY SOMETHING ELSE! BEING A SUPER AWESOME ACTION HERO IS ALWAYS GOING TO BE A PART OF YOU, DUDE.
BESIDES, THERE'S A MILLION THINGS OUT IN THE WORLD! YOU'LL FIND SOMETHING ELSE YOU LOVE!
YOU KNOW, YOU'RE BOTH RIGHT...

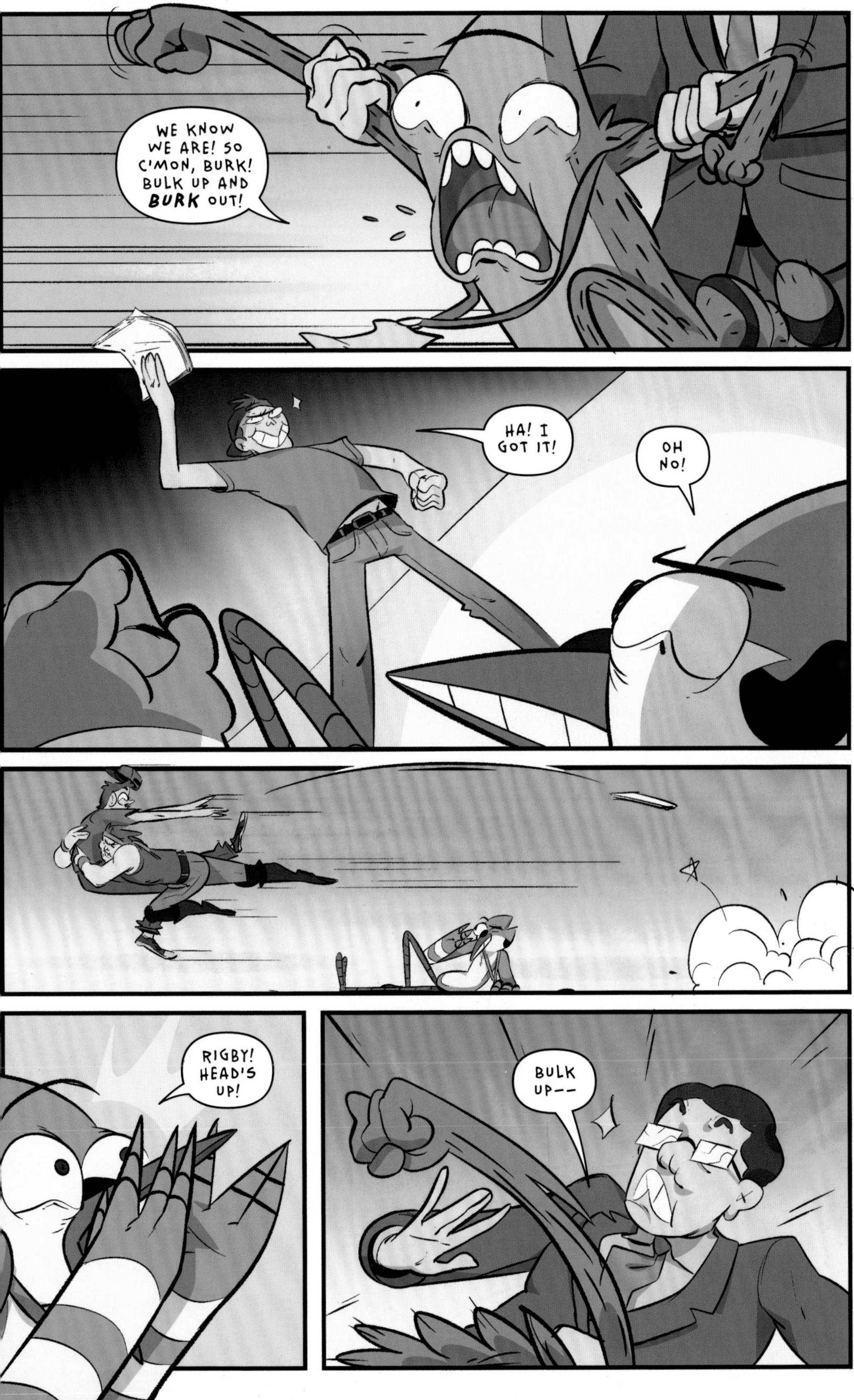
WE KNOW WE ARE! SO C'MON, BURK! BULK UP AND **BURK** OUT!
HA! I GOT IT!
OH NO!
RIGBY! HEAD'S UP!
BULK UP--

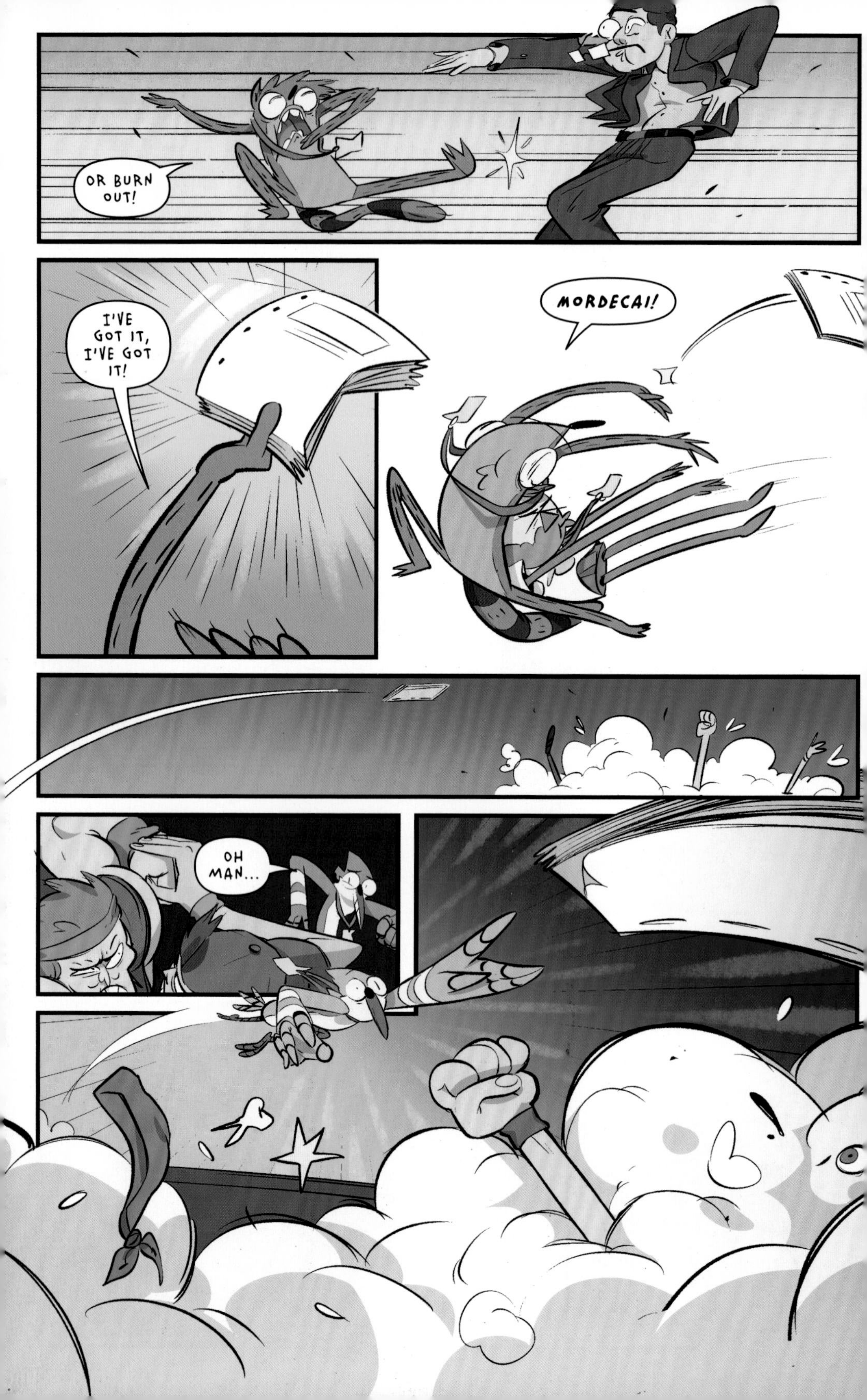
OR BURN OUT!
I'VE GOT IT, I'VE GOT IT!
MORDECAI!
OH MAN...

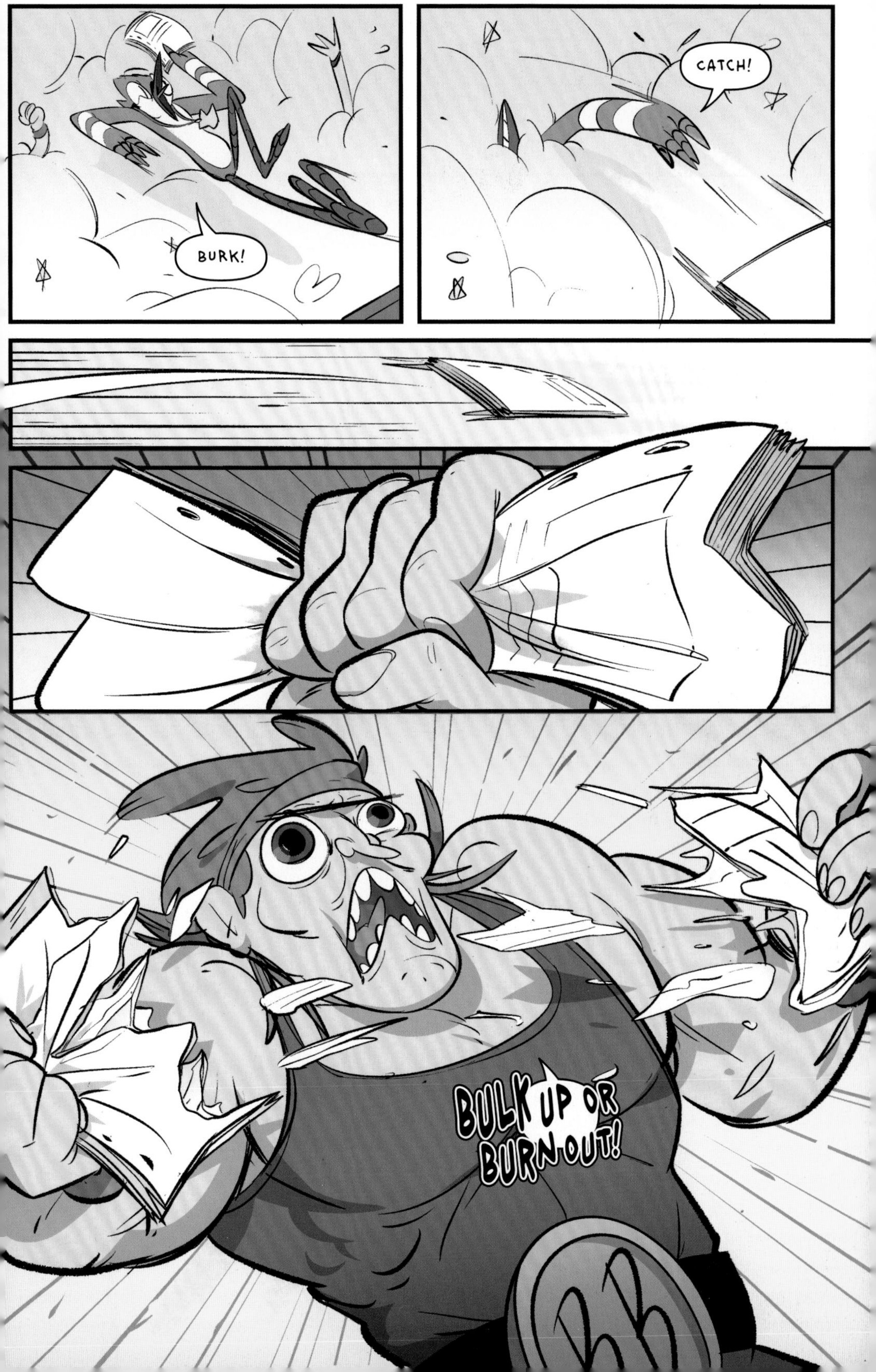
BURK!
CATCH!
BULK UP OR BURN OUT!

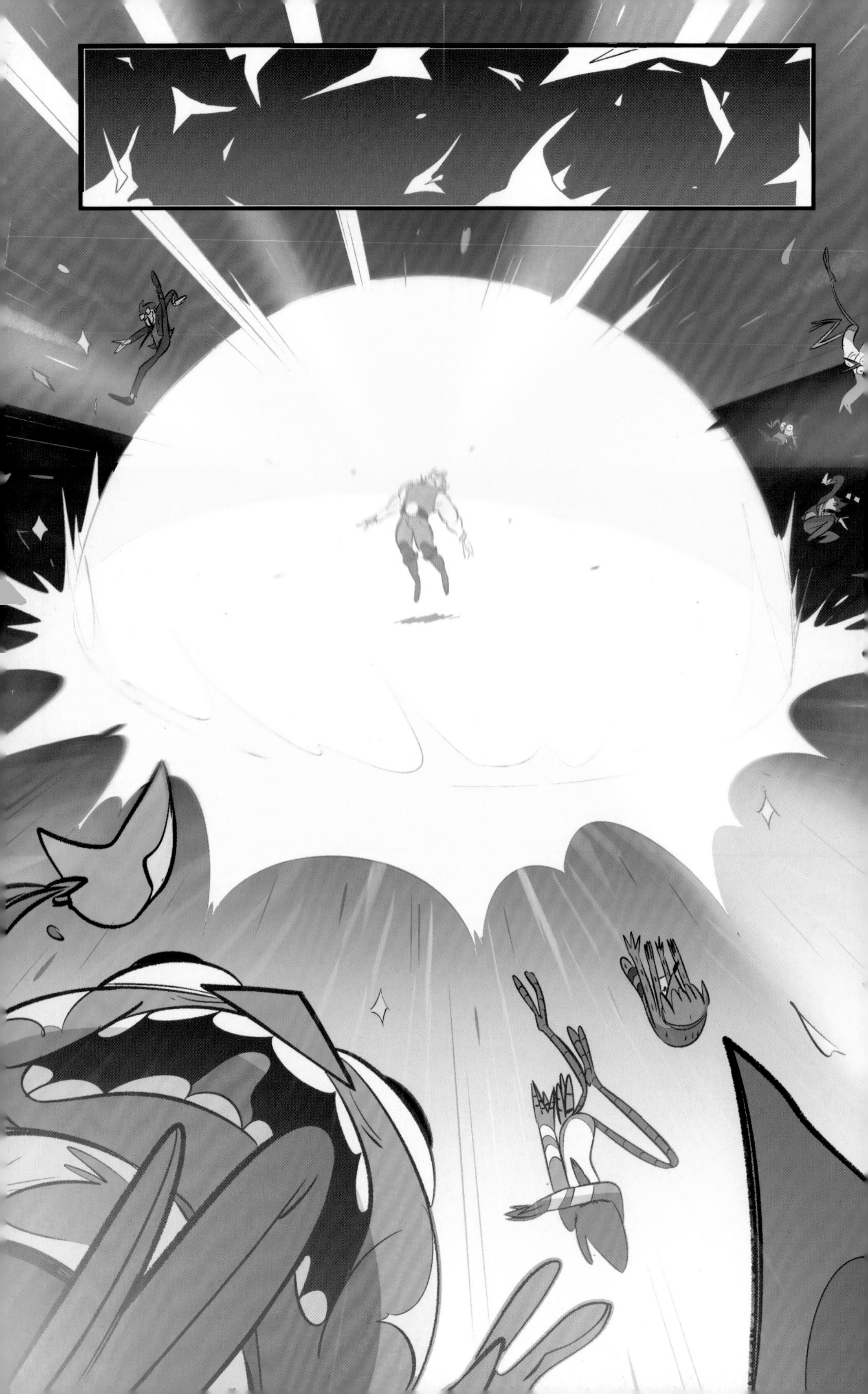

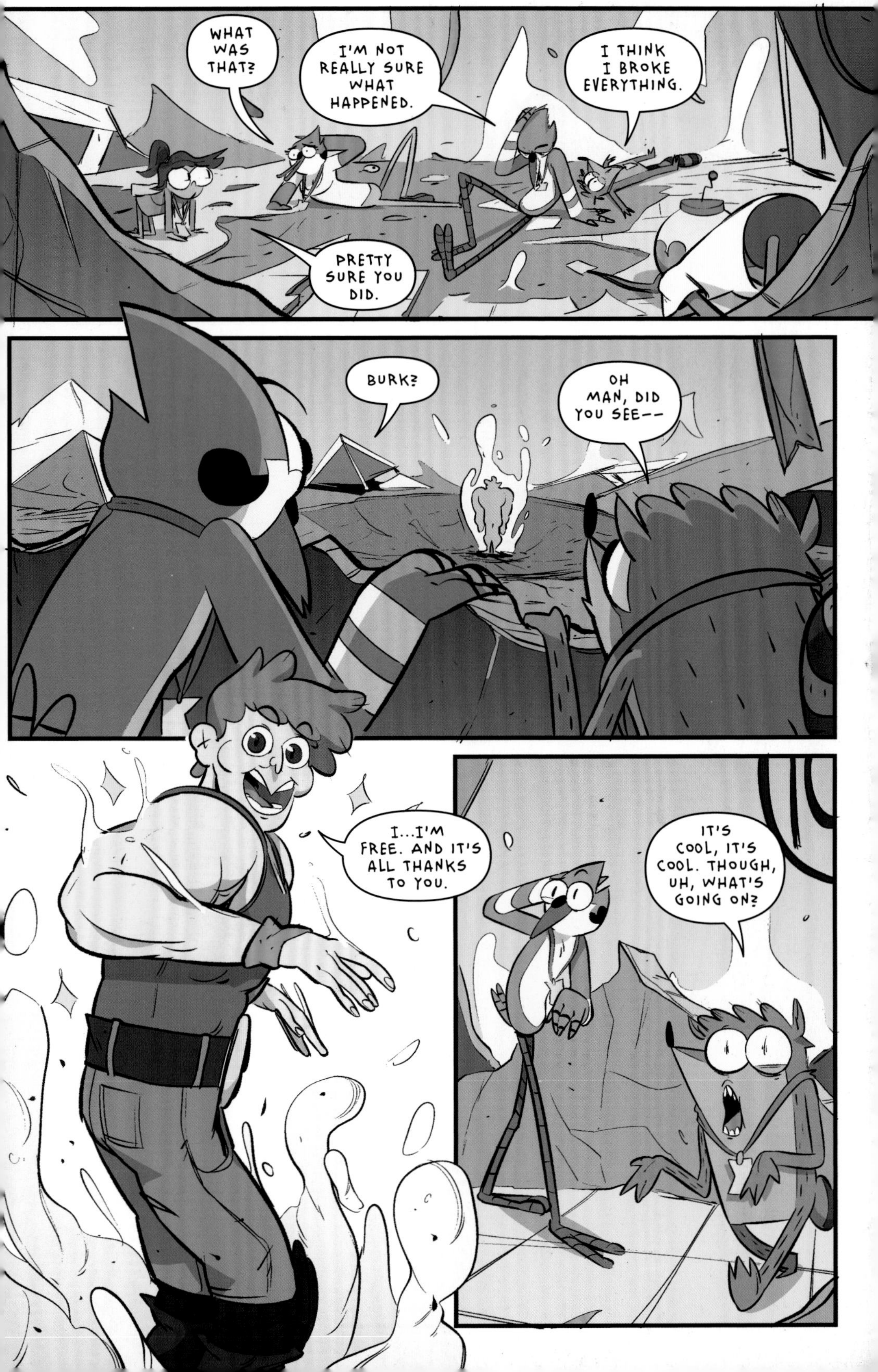
WHAT WAS THAT?
I'M NOT REALLY SURE WHAT HAPPENED.
I THINK I BROKE EVERYTHING.
PRETTY SURE YOU DID.
BURK?
OH MAN, DID YOU SEE--
I...I'M FREE. AND IT'S ALL THANKS TO YOU.
IT'S COOL, IT'S COOL. THOUGH, UH, WHAT'S GOING ON?

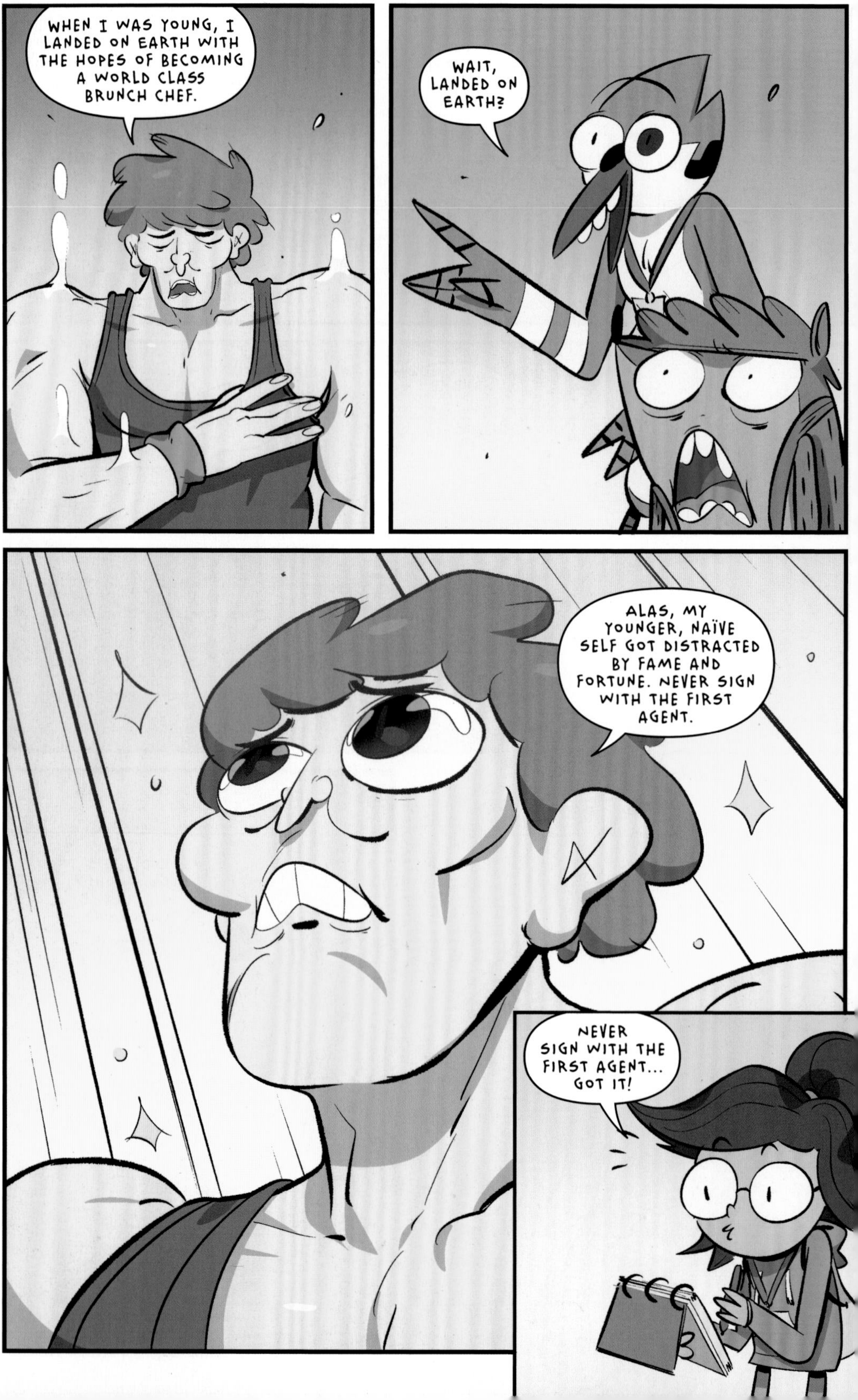
WHEN I WAS YOUNG, I LANDED ON EARTH WITH THE HOPES OF BECOMING A WORLD CLASS BRUNCH CHEF.
WAIT, LANDED ON EARTH?
ALAS, MY YOUNGER, NAÏVE SELF GOT DISTRACTED BY FAME AND FORTUNE. NEVER SIGN WITH THE FIRST AGENT.
NEVER SIGN WITH THE FIRST AGENT... GOT IT!

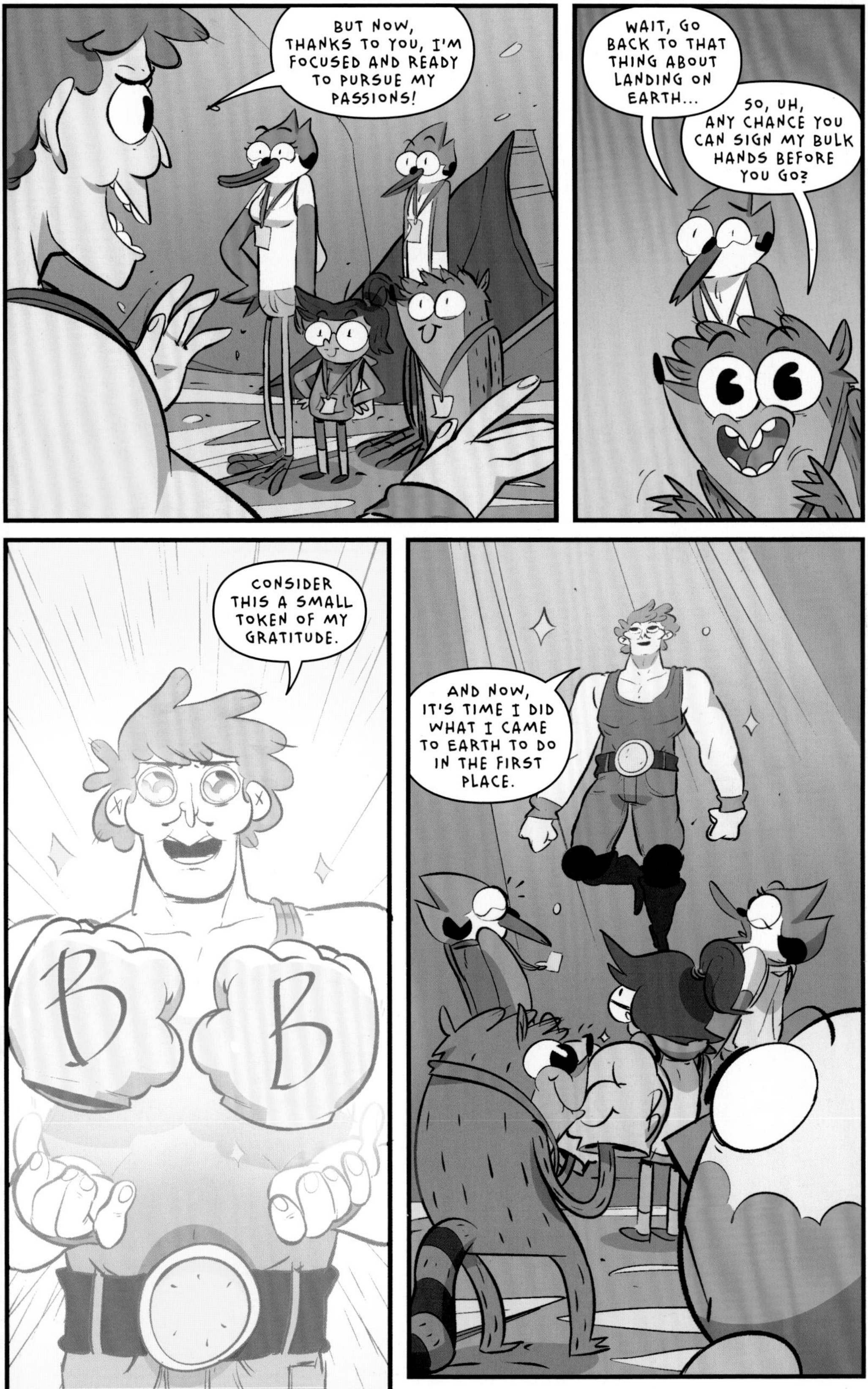
BUT NOW, THANKS TO YOU, I'M FOCUSED AND READY TO PURSUE MY PASSIONS!
WAIT, GO BACK TO THAT THING ABOUT LANDING ON EARTH...
SO, UH, ANY CHANCE YOU CAN SIGN MY BULK HANDS BEFORE YOU GO?
CONSIDER THIS A SMALL TOKEN OF MY GRATITUDE.
B
B
AND NOW, IT'S TIME I DID WHAT I CAME TO EARTH TO DO IN THE FIRST PLACE.

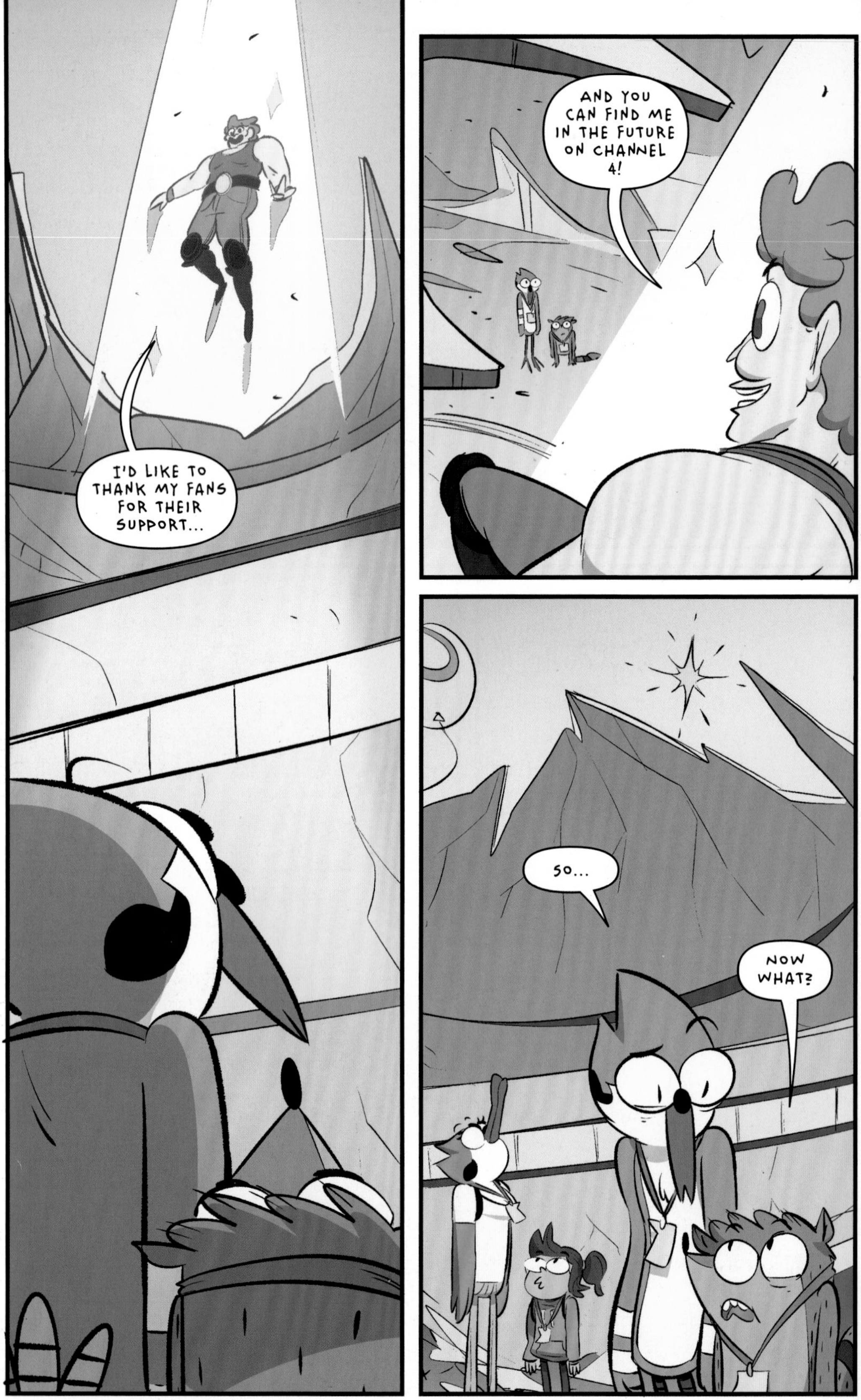
I'D LIKE TO THANK MY FANS FOR THEIR SUPPORT...
AND YOU CAN FIND ME IN THE FUTURE ON CHANNEL 4!
SO...
NOW WHAT?

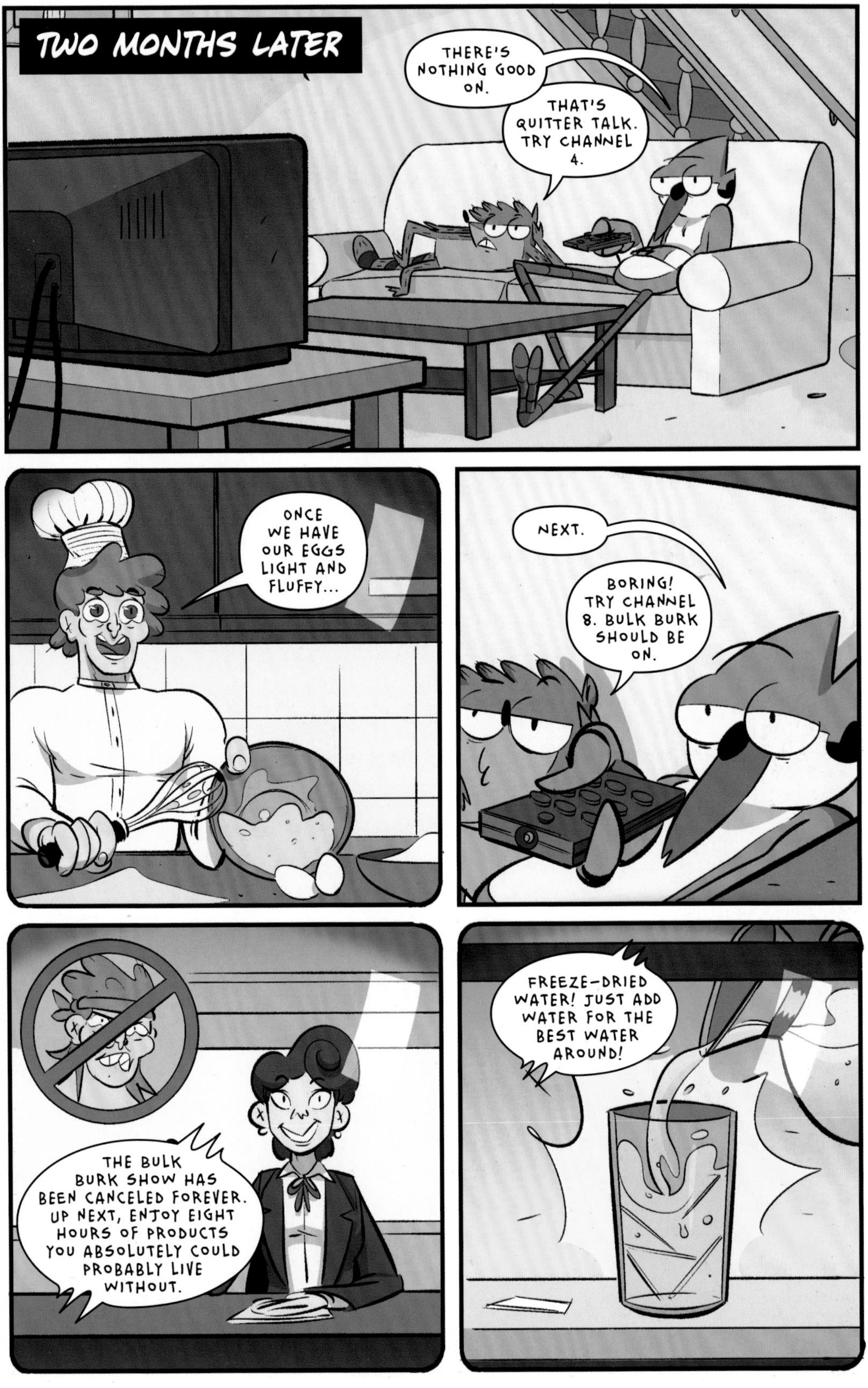
TWO MONTHS LATER
THERE'S NOTHING GOOD ON.
THAT'S QUITTER TALK. TRY CHANNEL 4.
ONCE WE HAVE OUR EGGS LIGHT AND FLUFFY...
NEXT.
BORING! TRY CHANNEL 8. BULK BURK SHOULD BE ON.
THE BULK BURK SHOW HAS BEEN CANCELED FOREVER. UP NEXT, ENJOY EIGHT HOURS OF PRODUCTS YOU ABSOLUTELY COULD PROBABLY LIVE WITHOUT.
FREEZE-DRIED WATER! JUST ADD WATER FOR THE BEST WATER AROUND!

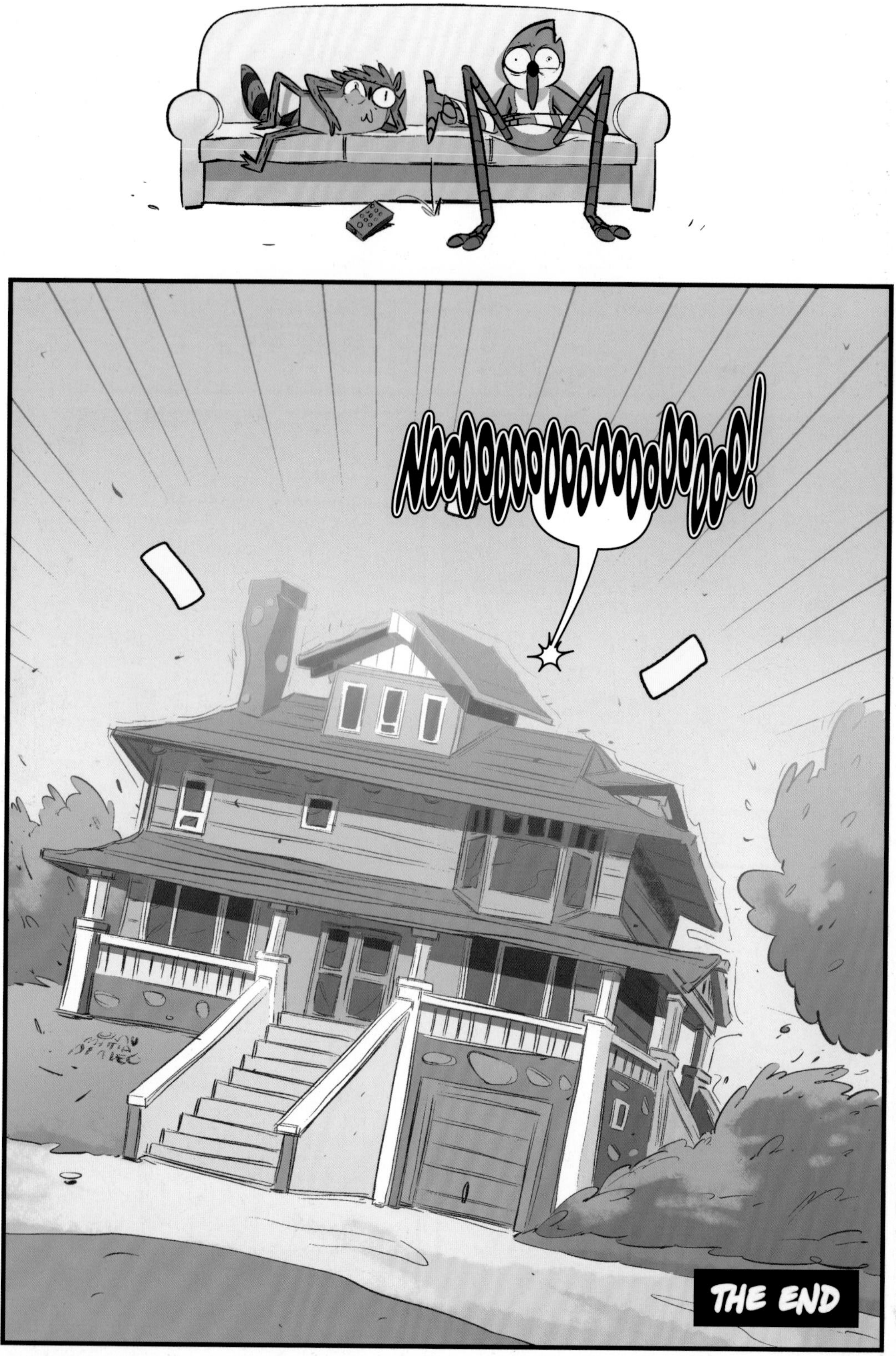
NOOOOOOOOOOOOOOOOOOO!
THE END